ILLUMINATION

ILLUMINATION

Bill,
Live your adventure!
Sheila M Sullivan

BOOK 2 OF THE F.O.K. SERIES

SHEILA M. SULLIVAN

This book was improved with the expert edits done by my editor, Kristen Tate. Kristen has more patience than anyone I know when dealing with my creative letter placement and horrid use of grammar. Somehow, she finds the story and helps it breath. You may contact Kristen through her website at www.thebluegarret.com. Christie Lee Duffy brought fresh eyes to the project and delivered another clean copy. Christie Lee may be contacted at www.EvenFlowEditing.com

All errors, issues, and things that cause the writing to be less than perfect are the mistake made by me, the author. I am somewhat hazy when it comes to the rules of grammar. There were some years when diagraming sentences was done. Those sentence maps did not help me improve my grammar. Thank the grammar gods that people like Kristen and Christie Lee exist. There will be mistakes in this book. I apologize. They are my mistakes, created from my brain and somehow, they slipped through the artful edits. If you feel the need you can correct them.

You can reach out to me through my website, www.sheilamsullivan.com.

Copyright © 2017 by Sheila M. Sullivan
All rights reserved.

ISBN 978-0-9989648-2-9

Book Layout and Cover Design by Phillip Gessert www.gesssertbooks.com

Author Photo by Robert Knapp at www.modernartphotgraph.com

Dedicated to My Love,
Janine-you inspire me always

CHAPTER ONE

FEDEX LETTERS

Frances, up early, could not identify exactly what was wrong, but she felt off and distracted. Over the past eight months, she had taken the steps to reclaim her life and feel comfortable in her loft. Her youngest sister and the baby of the Kavanagh clan, Theresa, had stayed with her past her initial promise of two weeks. She had basically moved from New York. Having her sister stay with her gave her some sense of security. Not to mention that Theresa's skills in full-scale set design came in handy as she helped Frances remodel the loft. The fresh paint and room dividers changed the space in such a way that Frances felt comfortable in her own home again. She still had dreams about Ethan standing in front of her building with the gun and what they had learned later were fake explosives strapped to his body. Frances knew that Detective Molly Woods had made sure her team had removed every last video camera and microphone that Ethan had hidden in her place and throughout the building. The face-lift did not erase the experience, but the passage of time was starting to blur the facts and the images. Still, the sinking feeling Frances had deep in her gut was lurking, ready to break out. She walked to the wall of windows and found her mood matched the darkness of the filtered early morning light. San Francisco had changed her heart in ways she had never anticipated.

The fog bouncing off the buildings and silently tumbling through streets made the morning soundless. The stealth shadow filtering through her mind was releasing an energy, but she felt it would not reveal the full message to her. The harder she tried to grasp it, the more it receded back into the darkness.

Theresa was still sleeping soundly behind the ornate room divider she had built for some privacy. Frances knew that Ethan was dead and no longer a threat; yet she still found herself startled by shadows and loud noises. Her conscious brain knew that the noises were not a threat from him, but her desire to survive sent her seeking cover and back to those moments in her loft when the gunfire broke out on the street. She shook her head and closed her eyes hard, attempting to forget the trauma of that night. Frances focused on those deep rhythmic breaths of her sister and quietly walked back to her own bed. Why was she so worried? She was not alone. Sleep was not going to come jump back in bed with her, and so Frances decided to try some meditation. Dana, her dearest friend and one of the first people she met when she moved to San Francisco, had told her that she was getting herself wound too tightly getting ready for her first full gallery show. Dana had a way of putting everything in practical perspective. When Frances had first introduced Dana to the Buena Vista Irish Coffee Club, there were some questions from the core group. Why had Frances brought a senior citizen out? Was she working on getting a Girl Scout merit badge? It did not take long for the group to see that Dana embodied the fact that seventy-plus was the new middle age—added to her life and experiences, she outranked them all in many aspects. They soon fell in love with Dana too, and she was a key member of the Buena Vista Irish Coffee Club.

With Dana's voice in Frances's mind guiding her toward meditation, she decided to give it a go. It was time to center and stop causing hurricanes in her brain. There were times to worry, and getting ready for this event was not one of them; it was time to focus and get it done.

She sat cross-legged on the center of her bed and shut her eyes. Frances's brain quickly kicked her eyes back open. A deep breath in through the nose—she shut her eyes hard, telling herself to be quiet and focus. Her lungs were bursting and, without any form or control, the air exited out with a loud exhale. Another deep inhale through the nose and her shoulders shot up to her ears. This was not working. She was tenser than when she had started. One more time, she told herself to relax and tried to picture a beach. This caused her mind to recall a recent news story about whales that had washed ashore, where people tried to save them. Frances's forehead furrowed, and she felt her heart ache.

"What are you doing?" Theresa asked. "You look like you're in pain. Are you constipated?"

Frances fell backwards into her soft pillows. This was confirmation that she was not finding the much-touted tranquil peace others gushed about finding through meditation. The fact that she jumped when Theresa had spoken told her she was still suffering. She had thought her world was starting to feel like it was right-side up again. The latest flinch told her she was mistaken.

"I wonder if I will ever feel comfortable again?" Frances asked.

"Sorry. I didn't mean to scare you. It hasn't even been a year. Didn't Molly suggest a group for you? It might help."

"I was attempting to meditate. Dana said I was too worried about my first show and to let the art flow."

"If that is what you look like attempting to relax, I would hate to see what you look like when you're stressed. You can't ignore that Ethan spied on you and killed multiple women. The guy was beyond creepy. I don't think this stress is about your upcoming gallery show."

"Okay, Dr. Theresa, I am not going back to that group. What those women experienced was so much worse. Ethan never physically hurt me."

"Are you forgetting what he did to you in the alley? He attacked you."

Frances took a deep breath in and rose from her bed. Theresa was right. She was scared, and she tried to avoid thinking about what happened as that led to the slippery slope of what might have happened.

"Why are mornings so difficult? I so wanted to be sleeping. Why are you up so early?" Frances asked.

"Things to do. I heard you trying to relax and your tranquil stress woke me up."

"No, it didn't. Want to fix breakfast?"

Frances didn't wait for an answer and rushed into the bathroom and shut the door. She realized that it was not necessary to rush for the bathroom now, as it had been when she was growing up. The bathroom became one of the most important rooms when you had eight kids sharing one bathroom and five of those kids were girls. Time and distance from those days put a smile on Frances's face as the warm water came out of the showerhead. It had been a long time since she was forced to take a cold shower because she was low on the birth order. Agatha, Edna, and Bernard always dominated the hot water in those formative years. When someone figured out that flushing the toilet in the guest bathroom directly below the kids' bathroom would force scalding hot water on the shower goer, it made life more entertaining. One morning, Bernard screamed so loud when Agatha had flushed the toilet three times on him that Mom Kavanagh locked everyone out of the guest bathroom. It meant you had to hold our morning pee a lot longer if you didn't get up before the shower schedule.

The warm water filtered through Frances's hair and onto her back. She could take a long luscious shower without the fear of losing hot water—one of the best things about having her own place. As the steam cloud got thicker in the bathroom, Frances let her mind go to the shadows she was trying to nail down. She reached for her soap. It was a nun-on-a-rope soap that Edna had given her last Christmas. *That was it.* Frances had not heard from anyone in her family for over a week. She had been so busy with getting the paintings properly varnished and a couple of them framed. Her mornings had been strangely quiet. No text messages, no phone calls, no emails from the Kavanagh clan. She had finally been granted her wish for silence in the morning, and now she was missing the usual cascade of messages.

Smells of bacon and coffee were penetrating the steam cloud in the bathroom. Frances turned off the water, standing still in the shower as the silence from the family started to sink into her mind. The shadow was fully exposed in the light, and it was strange. She quickly toweled herself off and threw on her robe.

"Theresa, have you talked to Mom?" Frances asked.

"Not recently."

"I love bacon." Frances picked up a slice and took a bite. "I think I figured out why I'm so out of whack. I haven't heard from anyone in the family. No one. Not Mom, Edna, or even Brice."

"Relax. You're busy and they are busy too. Yesterday when I came home, you didn't look up from what you were doing. You finally grunted. I took that to be a hello."

"Sorry. I hate doing the whole varnish thing. The painting isn't quite dry yet, and Nathan told me I had to get the varnish on it. Sometimes—"

"Here, try this…a friend at work made me a coffee like this the other day, and it was amazing," Theresa said.

Frances took the cup and looked at it with some concern.

"You were too young to know this game. Agatha and Edna were the masters of altering the flavor of Kool-Aid without changing the look of the drink. One time it had so much hot sauce in it, I was in pain. The worst was the baking soda lemonade. Have you talked with anyone from the family?"

"Baking soda lemonade? No. I'll have to ask about the baking soda and drink jokes though."

"They put a tablespoon of baking soda in my glass of lemonade at the family picnic. I think I was eleven when they did this, so you were still in diapers. I erupted a half-second after drinking it. Completely emptied out my stomach. I threw up all over the dessert table."

"That is so gross. They really did have the best jokes."

"No. No, they didn't because I was often on the receiving end of those jokes," Frances said. "This doesn't look like normal coffee. It is rather pale."

"I promise no baking soda. It has a tablespoon of coconut oil, a tablespoon of butter, and a few dashes of cinnamon, cardamom, and turmeric. Trust me, you are going to like it."

Frances eyed the coffee and decided it was worth the try. "If I lose my cookies, you are cleaning it up." The first sip was tentative, and she barely let the hot liquid penetrate past her lips. As the spices mingled with her tongue, she decided it was not a disguised drink and took as full a sip as the hot liquid would allow. She allowed her tongue to swim in the silky flavor of the coffee. "Okay, I think I have a new favorite drink. This is awesome."

"Better than an Irish coffee?" Theresa asked.

"Never. But a nice breakup of the normal morning Nespresso. It tastes so sophisticated and adult. Have you made one for the boys yet?"

"Nope. I am going to head to the shower. I don't want to be the laggard this morning."

Frances took her sophisticated cup of coffee to her closet to find the day's throwaway clothing. It never failed—when she cleaned up her paintings, she ruined a shirt. Paradoxically, it had something to do with an attempt to be neat. The vibration of a phone took Frances out of her closet. Theresa was in the shower. Frances went in hunt of the morning's intrusion from the outside. The offender was Theresa's phone. She had left it on the counter. By the time Frances got to it, she had missed the call. Frances started to turn away and back to choosing a shirt she wouldn't mind burning after work. A series of beeps announced a flurry of incoming texts.

Part of Frances felt a small twinge of guilt picking up Theresa's phone. It wasn't any of her business, but the last time Frances had heard that sort of message barrage was a Kavanagh family text meeting. She looked back at the closed door of the bathroom and listened a few more moments to the sound of the water in the shower. Theresa was still enjoying the abundance of hot water herself. Frances took the phone and read the text stream from Agatha. She was dictating the Kavanagh July Fourth celebration. They were going to the parade and then rounding out the celebration at Mom and Dad's.

Frances set Theresa's phone down and walked over to her own silent phone. Maybe she had mistakenly shut it off or forgot to charge it. She picked up her phone, fully charged and bereft of messages. She was not included in that very normal family discussion. Confusion crossed over Frances's face. The shower shut off. Frances hurried back to her closet and pulled on the first T-shirt within reach, adding cutoff jeans and a pair of slip-on shoes that were covered in various layers of paint. Her heart was pounding. Should she ask Theresa about it? What was the reason? Did they forget to include her on the texts? There was a fine line to tread, and Frances was balancing a thousand feet above the ground.

The buzzer from the front door caught her in the midst of conspiracy theories about Theresa and the family. Frances took a quick look at the camera and saw that it was a FedEx delivery person. This was crazy early to be getting something from FedEx. Maybe Theresa was getting something. Frances directed the driver to the elevator and her loft. She was waiting at the open door when the driver handed her an overnight envelope addressed to her.

Frances slowly shut the door, noting that the return address was that of a law office. Should she wait? Theresa would be coming out of the shower soon.

"Hey, Theresa, I received a special delivery FedEx envelope from a law firm in St. Louis," Frances called out.

"What?"

"Come out when you are done."

Frances walked to her sofa and sat down. She couldn't wait any longer and tore open the outside envelope, revealing a sealed white envelope inside.

"Now that is overkill."

"What's overkill?" Theresa asked. She was drying her hair, and the towel she had wrapped around herself was barely staying in place.

"I told you, I received a letter from a law office in St. Louis."

"I was in the shower. I didn't think they were serious?"

"Who was serious?" Frances asked.

"That is not what I meant to say. I am waking up and didn't hear you. What did you receive?"

"I received a letter from a law firm in St. Louis. I hope I am not being sued by an old business client, but it sounds like you know something I don't."

"There was a meeting, but I didn't think Agatha was serious. I only thought Mom and Dad were thinking about some changes."

Frances glanced at Theresa and knew she was going to say something else. It was not worth the effort at this point. It was not a past business client; Theresa confirmed this was family-centric. The weight that was pressing down on her right now made each movement that much harder. Frances opened the second envelope and pulled out a letter, a copy of a will, and a third letter-sized envelope.

Dear Frances Olar Kavanagh,

I am writing to you at the request of your parents and family. This letter is to instruct you to destroy any previous versions you may have of your parents' last will and testament and health care directives. They have redrafted their estate papers and wanted to be sure that this latest copy of their desires be preserved and understood by their children.

Should you have any questions, please do not hesitate to call our office. You are provided a copy of their new estate papers as a courtesy. You are not required to act in any capacity.

Enclosed is another letter for you from your parents, included per their request.

Sincerely,
Matthew Beilstein
Beilstein, Marker, and King LLP

"It looks like Mom and Dad have redone their will and some other stuff," Frances said.

"Yeah. What's that?" Theresa asked, pointing at the smaller envelope.

"A pizza. What does it look like? I haven't opened it yet. The attorney states he included it at the request of our parents."

"Who pissed in your cheerios this morning?" Theresa asked, grabbing the envelope off Frances's lap. "It looks like Mom's handwriting."

"I'm not the one having to keep track of stories." Frances took back the envelope, crumpling it in her hands. Her thoughts were running a mile a minute. The last time her parents had done their estate papers, she was included in the discussion. The whole family was included, even though Theresa was claiming she was not there. But she had been present as their parents walked through their wishes and asked each one of them if there were any objections. Frances had not said a word in those meetings. She knew that Bernard, Agatha, and Edna would be put in charge. Why had they updated everything? That family meeting was only four years ago. Dad had decided it was time to put things in writing after his close friend had died with nothing in place. It had scared him into action. No one likes talking about their own death.

To: Frances O. Kavanagh

From: The Kavanagh Family

It should come as no surprise to you that Mom, Dad, and the family have taken the steps needed to purge our family from your sins—with the guidance of the Bishop and Father

Riley, who suggested that you be excommunicated from the Catholic Church. The family has agreed to follow the way of the church and banish you from the family. As of the date of this letter, you are no longer a member of the Kavanagh family.

Do not contact anyone in the family. You have chosen your life of sin, and you are not going to influence any of our children to believe that what you do is morally sanctified. It is not.

Your lack of respect for what happens to Mom and Dad in the community over your poor life choices displays such a lack of caring that we are all ashamed to share our good name with you.

You made your choice. You forced us to this decision. When you die, you will not have a burial place in the family plot. All papers have been signed and notarized by the attorneys.

If you do not understand this letter or the packet sent by the attorneys, you can contact their office. You will have to pay for the time yourself. What you have done to our family can never be fixed.

The Kavanagh Family

"It is Bernard's handwriting. I recognize his writing," Frances said as tears filled her eyes. She looked up at the ceiling of her loft, wishing the sky would come down and swallow her up. Theresa had sat down on the furry blue chaise lounge and was reading through the will. Frances's hands were shaking slightly as she dropped the letter onto the couch next to her. Her mind was shattering memories of the family she thought she had into shards of glass. The words were written with such precision that one might have thought a computer script program had been used, but she recognized her brother Bernard's perfect penmanship. Her tears spilled out without any signs of stopping.

"Frances? What does this all mean?" Theresa asked.

Frances buried her face in her hands and did not stop Theresa from taking the letter. Through her fingers and blurred vision from her tears, she watched as her sister read the words. Theresa's back was to her, but Frances knew she was now crying too.

"Did you know about this?" Frances asked.

"No."

"Are you sure?"

"Frances. This is a mistake. Mom and Dad would never do this."

"You were reading the will. What did it say?" Frances asked.

"I don't know." Theresa looked down at her lap. "I never saw the other will. I wasn't part of that discussion. It looks like it still puts everything into the family trust."

"You knew about this; you were part of this one?" Frances stood, walked past her sister, and went to her piano. The piano that was so much a part of her life now felt distant—nothing more than a heavy piece of furniture. Would the family take the piano back? Was it really hers? She screamed out in pain and pounded the keys of her piano. Frances sobbed uncontrollably, unsure of what to do. In her heart, she knew that Theresa was not telling her the truth. Lost and alone, cast out Frances stood and turned toward her baby sister.

"Why did you lie to me?"

"Frances, what are you talking about? I haven't lied to you."

"You are still talking to them. Where are the estate papers?" Frances turned and walked to the furry blue chaise lounge and picked up the papers. She saw the names of the beneficiaries of the family trust had been changed. Hers had been removed, but Theresa's was still there. "Why are they still talking to you? You're the one who actually has a girlfriend."

"Frances."

Frances went to her closet and slammed the door. "I can't believe I just put myself in the closet. I am not going into hiding. This is my house. My life. No one will bully me away from who I know I am." She felt completely alone.

"Frances, please open the door. We need to talk. Please," Theresa said through her tears.

Frances decided she wanted to make Theresa hurt as much as she did and opened the door. "I am going to ask you one more time. Why did you lie to me?"

"Frances, I didn't know how to tell you that I am trying to be that bridge between you and the family. Mom and Dad love us."

"Looks like you fixed it. I'm out of the family and you're not."

"This wasn't supposed to happen."

"You did know about it then? I saw the text messages on your phone."

Frances walked over to the sofa and sat down. "I don't understand."

"I don't either. We can fix this. I know we can. I think this was Bernard who was behind all of this . . . You must believe me. I am here for you."

Frances didn't move when Theresa sat down next to her and hugged her. She felt the shadow of darkness peek around the corners of her memories, and she was convinced that Theresa knew more than she was saying.

"I need some space and time to think. I am going to go hike through the redwoods," Frances said as she rose from the couch and shoved her feet into her boots. She turned back to Theresa, who was crying on the couch. "Alone. You are not welcome." Frances walked out of the loft and quietly shut the door.

CHAPTER TWO
BUENA VISTA IRISH COFFEE CLUB

The past two days had stretched time—much like Frances realizing she had chosen the wrong day to shop at the grocery store. She always managed to shop on the days when only one checker was open and the crazy coupon hoarders had fifteen filled carts in front of her. With the banishment from her family, her world had lost its tether. She was free floating like a rogue balloon in the Macy's Thanksgiving Day Parade. She felt herself crashing into doors, chairs, and counters with more regularity. Frances was up early in order to take a walk out to Black Point and along the bay below Ghirardelli Square before meeting the rest of the gang for the latest gathering of the Buena Vista Irish Coffee Club. An Irish coffee was the perfect way to top off a good walk. She needed to decide if she was going to bring the topic of Theresa's betrayal to her crew at the table. Theresa was now firmly entrenched as one of the regulars of the BVICC.

Decided on her route, Frances quietly gathered her shoes and exited the loft without disturbing Theresa, who was snoring louder than a buzz saw this morning. They had said fewer than a handful of words to one another since the arrival of the letter and Frances's discovery of the family text meeting on Theresa's phone. Frances was on an island, and she needed her friends to throw the life preserver and pull her onto the lifeboat. As she walked toward her truck, she had to force herself to breath. Was her body shutting down on her? This was crazy. *Relax. You have Dana, Cheryl, Winter, and the boys. It isn't okay, but don't stop breathing over this.* Frances swallowed hard and climbed into her truck. "Snow White, we are in desperate need of our dwarfs and the good fairy godmother."

As Frances drove toward the best kept secret of free parking in the city, she thought about how the friendship foundation of the Buena Vista Irish Coffee Club was set in rebar and cement. Her heart beat with a strength drawing from Winter, Dana, Cheryl, and the boys. When she started this tradition (an excuse to enjoy Irish coffees), she had no clue that she would need these friends as much as her own flesh and blood.

An hour later, a rush of conversation and the aromas of aftershave and coffee met Frances as she slowly pushed her way through the crowd filling the Buena Vista. She knew better than to make eye contact with people waiting for a table and put her head down and dove through the crowd. It was hard going—the place was so packed, she knew she stepped on a few feet and not floor. Her cowboy boots could be deadly to other people's feet. Winter had texted, letting Frances know that she, Russell, and Simon had secured the last available table. One last push through the bodies of heavily dressed people and Frances was free of the crowd and smiling at the Irish coffee Russell was holding up for her.

"Perfect. I could use one of those. I did a power walk along the bay out to the edge of the jetty and back. Had I known the energy needed to get through the crowd, I might not have done such a long walk. Why are there so many people this early in the morning?" Frances asked.

"I think a whole new crowd feels the need to socialize in this place through their Snippet or Snap-choke or whatever people are using to annoy the crap out of others on their smartphones," Winter said.

"I want to point out that you are going to be a mother, not a grandmother. You make it sound like those young whippersnappers are causing you some consternation this morning. Thank god, you don't have a lawn because you'd be the one spraying the neighborhood kids with a hose if they even looked in your direction," Frances said and kissed Winter on the cheek.

"You incubate an alien in your womb and then you'll understand I'm not cranky. I'm changing, and it all has to do with these strong-ass hormones," Winter said.

"Where's Theresa this morning?" Russell asked.

"She's coming. I think she took the bus. Before she gets here, I need to talk to you all about something rather serious."

"Why didn't she ride with you?" Simon asked.

"I was getting to that, and I don't want to focus on this because we are here to celebrate—"

"Frances, come and help me!" a voice called through the crowd

"I hear Cheryl, but I don't see her," Frances said.

"She's over at the end of the bar," Simon said, pointing.

Frances stood and leaned over the table. "Okay, before I go rescue Cheryl, quick news flash. My parents kicked me out of the family trust. Bernard, our oldest brother, kicked me out of the family, and I need to find someplace to bury my own body."

"What? Body? Did you kill somebody?" Russell asked.

"Frances! Get over here," Cheryl called out again.

"You sit down and explain," Winter said.

Frances sat back down and tried to organize the most economical way to explain what was going on with her, Theresa, and the family. "The family has a plot and a small crypt in a cemetery in St. Louis. I am no longer welcome to be buried there when I die."

"That is morbid. Do families still…what century are we in? this is really strange." Winter made a face at her herbal tea. "I so want an Irish coffee—this is torture."

"How rich is your family?" Russell asked.

"Upper-middle, not much different than yours."

"Very. My family does not have a trust or a family crypt," Russell said.

"Attention, FOK, get your ass over here and help me," Cheryl yelled just as the crowd noise had magically died down. The result was Frances jumping up with a face as red as a boiled lobster.

"I'm on my way, Cheryl." Frances put her best crowd-diving face on and went to the voice.

Cheryl's laughter worked as a foghorn and guided Frances safely through the waves of tourists to the end of the bar. Frances had remembered Cheryl was picking up the cake for their little celebration of Winter's pregnancy. One couple stood between Frances and Cheryl. Frances took in their "If it smells like chocolate . . ." sweatshirts and knew they would provide little resistance. Dana was supposed to be here this morning, but the trip to the city from San Quentin Village was not one Dana took very often. Frances heard her father's voice broadcast through her brain replaying the mantra *what happens in the family is private and doesn't leave this house.*

"Wow, that is quite the pre-baby-shower cake," Frances said as she finally reached Cheryl at the end of the bar.

"Do you think it's in poor taste?" Cheryl asked, looking down at the cake decorated to resemble a pile of dirty diapers.

"Too late to do anything about it now. I think it's awesome. It is exactly what I needed. Not sure what Winter will think. She's in the I-have-an-alien-growing-in-my-body mood."

"Here, you can carry these over to the table," Cheryl said, holding out a bag of baby-themed plates and napkins to Frances. "Mary, our ever-faithful waitress, said they would bring the cake out when we want it."

Frances made the trek back to the table. She smiled, thinking about the cake. It was a work of art, but she wasn't sure whether the mommy-to-be would appreciate it. When Frances reached her chair, she noticed that Winter and Russell were locked in a rather serious discussion.

"That's all I'm asking for in return. You can understand where I'm coming from with this request," Russell said.

"What's the request?" Frances asked. Cheryl quickly joined her at the table, wrangling a bouquet of helium balloons shaped like Minions. Frances had failed to see Theresa behind the flock of balloons. Theresa quietly sat down next Russell.

"You are so cute and so worked up about this. Had I known that you were going to extract such a heavy price, I might have asked Frances to be my birthing coach," Winter said.

"Ouch. You know that I would love to be your coach . . . Wait, isn't Jason going to be your birthing coach?" Frances asked. "Where is Jason this morning? This party is for all three of you."

"Winter, you wouldn't deny a woman her last wish on this planet, would you?" Russell asked.

"Russell? Your mom is dying? I saw her last week. Oh my god—"

"Relax, Frances, Russell wants Winter to name her baby after him," Simon said.

"Everyone, hold up. Jason and I are going to name the baby. Nice story, Russell. I will be sure to scream the next time I see your mother. Does she know she's part of the walking dead?" Winter asked.

"Your mother is alive? I'm confused," Cheryl said.

Laughter engulfed the table as Russell was banished to go get the next round of Irish coffees for the table and one herbal tea for the pregnant lady. Frances was rather curious to know why Jason was not there with them this morning. How was Winter going to deal with the little blob of protein once it was on the outside of her womb, expressing its own little opinions?

"Hello, my adult toddlers," Dana said.

"Yeah! Dana, you made it." Winter slowly rose, holding her belly, to give Dana a hug.

"Now I know that Winter has been replaced by an alien. Since when has she ever said the words *yeah* and *Dana* in the same breath?" Simon said.

"Frances said it was a mandatory round table. In my whole long life, I have never attended a pre-baby shower. I was curious. The baby is clearly in the oven. I figured out that another baby shower is going to be thrown for her." Dana handed over a rather large gift bag stuffed with pink and blue tissue paper spilling out over the edges.

"Has she spilled the beans yet? Are you adding a brilliant little girl to the world or a deficient XY?" Dana asked.

"Hey, as a full grown XY, I take some offense to that," Russell said.

"Well, are you going to tell us? You are far enough along to know the gender of your baby, right?"

"Dana, Jason and I are going to wait on divulging that information. It is personal, and I resent anyone for asking."

"Please tell me. You're having a Muppet. I've always wanted a Muppet baby. They are so cute," Frances said.

"Seriously. Are any of you adults?" Winter asked. "I am not sharing the gender of the baby. I don't need to hear other people's horror stories on how girls are harder or boys require living in an uncivilized house until they are adults. From what I can tell, people are all too eager to pass judgment based on the gender of the baby. Not going to do it. Frances, Muppets don't have babies. They are puppets."

"Where's Molly?" Simon asked.

Winter grabbed Frances's shoulder to steady herself as she slowly lowered back into her chair.

"Slow motion is so cool. Winter, you are making me feel like I am in an action movie," Simon said as he slowly moved to match Winter's speed.

"Why would I know where Molly is?" Frances asked, feeling her face flush and trying to keep her mouth from smiling. She was really hoping to see Molly here and felt her heart ache a little, but she would not admit that to her crew. They reminded her of sharks, and she was glad they were too distracted by Winter to smell the drop of blood.

"When do we get to open presents? I want cake," Dana said. "I was promised cake."

"I want to open presents—I can't wait for you all to see what we got her," Russell said. He quickly clamped his hand over his mouth. "Shit."

"Russell, you said *her*...do you know?" Frances asked.

Frances focused on Russell, trying to determine if he did in fact know that Winter was having a girl. He was the one who had taken Winter to her last ultrasound appointment. Russell and Simon were both filling in more and more for Jason.

"Winter, let us help you find a name for your baby. A name is super important. Don't scar your baby for life with crazy initials—ask Frances," Theresa said, helping Winter out by redirecting the conversation.

"I'll appease the crowd, but I am not going to give into peer pressure. Russell, I'll put you down for Russell Jenkins. I suppose Jenkins could be a first name too."

"For a butler on my future downstairs staff," Dana said.

"I have a brilliant idea," Cheryl said. "This is taken from a friend at work. She and her family came from Ghana. They don't sweat this naming thing at all. When she went into labor, the female family members let everyone know when the baby was about to come into the world. The family gathered around her and everyone started shouting out names. When the baby's head was fully out of the birth canal, whatever name was said at that moment became the baby's name."

"Right, I can hear it all now. Frances will be in the delivery room shouting random words—*toaster, Muppet baby, shit, oh my god no one said anything about blood*—and then she'll faint. I do not want my child stuck with the name *vomit, shit,* or *she's fainted,*" Winter said.

"Cheryl, you are seriously on crack with that suggestion. Like I'm going to be anywhere close to the birthing room," Frances said. Thinking about the words that could be shouted made her laugh so hard she had to focus on not passing out from the lack of oxygen. The pain had started in her neck, and she grabbed the table, trying to calm herself down. It was no use—as she took a breath of air, she snorted so loudly the table next to them broke out in laughter. Tears streamed down Frances's face as she tried to get herself under control. Her abs hurt, her throat hurt, her neck hurt from the laughing. Simon and Russell fueled more laughter as they started shouting out words that might be said in the labor room.

"You know they don't use forceps anymore," Winter said.

"Holly Golightly. Only one of my favorite characters," Simon shouted.

"Not exactly true. You say that about any one of Audrey Hepburn's roles. I'm surprised you wouldn't be yelling out Audrey Hepburn," Russell said as he grabbed Simon's hand and kissed the back of it.

"Time to cut this table off. I can't hear myself barking my orders over your laughter," Mary said, delivering another round of Irish coffees and one herbal tea. "Y'all know that Winter will name her baby and might even surprise herself when they bring in the birth certificate. The fun part will be her explaining to the kid and everyone else how the baby came to be named *Fuck this hurts, I want drugs.*"

Everyone within earshot laughed over Mary's comment. Frances thought she was going to die right there, right now as her laughter completely shut off her air supply. She had gone full throttle into such a heavy laughter that her body convulsed with the pain of it all.

"Yup. Cut off. Brian, no more for the coffee club today." Mary passed her hand across her neck mimicking the international signal of slicing one's throat. "Now, all of you stop teasing our pregnant Winter. You know, I could have my kids name the baby for you. After my sixth child, I let the kids do it. We were out of ideas."

"You have seven children?" Russell asked.

"Indeed, I do. Sometimes my mister counts as number eight. Not Catholic, not Mormon, we were just incredibly horny, and I forgot to take my birth control pills consistently. Such a pain to remember," Mary said.

Frances and Simon pushed a chair out so Mary would join them.

"You must have cake with us," Frances said.

"I want to know what your kids named your baby," Russell said.

"My seventh and final child—got my tubes tied after her, and to make double sure, I made my mister get a vasectomy—anyway, lucky number seven is our little Lucia Mercedes Rock Paper Scissors Rain Smith." Mary stood and shook her head smiling all the way back to the kitchen.

"Where's she going?" Russell asked.

"She's going to get the cake," Theresa said. "Do you think she was serious? Her kids really named the new baby Rock Paper Scissors?"

"I know she is. I met Lucia. I think she's about seven now," Frances said. "My initials are cool compared to Rock Paper Scissors. That is a whole different issue. I suspect it was her brothers who came up with that fun."

"Winter, you do need to think about what the initials spell out. We don't want a repeat with another little FOK running around the earth," Cheryl said.

Frances realized that she really did not know Jason's last name and suspected that she was not the only one at the table in the dark. Frances looked at her watch and started to get antsy about getting back to preparing her canvases for her art opening. She was over this whole naming issue that appeared to have the rest of the table fully captivated. Frances sized up Winter and figured her kid was going to have a very normal, boring, Midwestern name. You can take the girl out of Edwardsville, Illinois, but you can't take the conservative naming practices of Edwardsville out of the girl.

"Frances, you're not going anywhere." Winter was so forceful in her command, silence overtook the table.

"Good god, woman. You've got the bossy mom voice down," Dana said. "Relax, I think Frances was making room for your cake."

"I was. You, my dear, are in an interesting naming world with your Keller last name," Frances said. "That is, if you are using your own name. Or are you going to give the baby Jason's last name?"

"The baby is going to have my last name. Jason agreed to take my last name when we get married."

"That's a twist. When was Jason castrated?" Russell asked.

"Who's castrated?" Jason asked as he came up and planted a kiss on Winter's cheek. "I can't believe you all are still here, but I came to get Winter. Remember, we are meeting with the baby proof people."

"Baby proof people? Are you having your baby proofed?" Theresa asked.

"What is baby proofing anyway? Wait—I know, you are having your house baby-proofed for the baby. You know, you don't have to do that until they are moving around on their own," Dana said.

"Hey, man, I think it's really cool you are taking Winter's last name when you get married," Theresa said.

"What's that?" Jason asked.

"It appears the bull might not even know he's been castrated," Simon said.

"We talked about this…you agreed that I wasn't going to change my name because of all the professional licensing and degrees," Winter said.

"Well, you don't have a career anymore, so it doesn't really matter, does it? You have got to stop telling people I'm taking your name," Jason said.

The table watched as Jason dropped Winter's hand and pushed his way through the standing room only crowd toward the door. Frances watched Winter's face fall as Jason kept walking toward the door. Part of her felt she needed to run after him, bring him back to Winter. Before she had another minute to think about retrieving Jason, Molly Woods, the latest member to join the Irish Coffee Club, showed up, towing Jason behind her. Frances tried to tone down her excitement of seeing Molly and focused her attention on Jason by jumping up to make room for him at the table.

"Look who was trying to make a break for it. Thanks for showing me where the gang is this morning," Molly said. "What gives? Why all the long faces? Isn't this a party?" Molly dropped a wrapped box in front of Winter.

"Pre-baby jitters. Now, Jason, the man-child, take a seat and you two open the gifts. I want to eat cake," Dana said.

Jason stood staring at the table. He didn't move. Molly wedged a chair between Russell and Theresa. Everyone waited to see what Jason was going to do. Simon stood up and gave him his chair next to Winter and pointed at Frances to sit. A collective sigh of relief traveled through the party as Jason took a seat and a drink from Simon's Irish coffee.

"Jesus H. Christ in the mountains, you knuckleheads need to figure this stuff out. You two are going through all the emotions of growing a little human. Now, you all stop teasing Jason. I think it would be tough for any man to walk into a conversation where people are laughing about castration. Most men tend to be sensitive about that topic. Jason, you need to stop acting like a rooster scratching the dirt backwards." Dana blew him a kiss across the table.

"I'm sorry. You're right—there is a lot going on in my head right now. Time to open presents. Forgive me, Winter," Jason said.

Frances handed Winter a beautifully wrapped box. Before Winter had complete control of the box, Theresa dove across the table to remove the card.

"What the heck? Theresa, give her back the card."

"Frances, you forgot to sign the card. Remember?" Theresa said pointedly.

"I can tell by Frances's face that's not true. What does the card say? Give it to me," Winter said.

"Dana's right, you do have the mom voice down. Damn, girl," Simon said.

Theresa slowly handed the card over to Winter. Frances sat back and shook her head as she remembered what she had written. It was too late. This would have been funnier had Jason not walked away pouting about being castrated.

"Read it out loud. We all need to hear how Frances put her foot in her mouth," Simon said.

Congratulations, Winter and Jason, on your forthcoming little blob of protein. If you haven't thought of a name yet, how about Isabella Marie Ann Keller? Hope you love the baby blanket. It's so soft I think they might have made it out of baby kittens.

Love,
F and T

"I don't understand what is wrong with that?" Dana asked.

"Apparently, Winter has told other people she is having a girl, so getting upset with me was not warranted," Simon said. "Not to mention making a baby blanket out of baby kittens...really, Frances?"

"Frances, only you," Winter said. The tears flowing down her face had everyone unsure of what to do next. "Frances, you are such a shit. I'm not going to name her with a name that spells out I.M.A. Keller."

"Great name for a cop though," Molly said.

"Better name for a doctor or a criminal. That would be bad ass," Cheryl said as she took another sip of her Irish coffee.

"Jason, you need to relax. Winter has crazy hormones as the little alien is growing inside her body. It is a weird experience. I'm the only one at this table who has gone through the process. Everyone needs to take some deep breaths. Winter, you get a pass right now. You can't help your emotions."

"Dana's right, you know. Sometimes pregnant women snap. Last year, one of the most interesting cases that came through the department was a pregnant woman who shot her husband in his jewels. He made the mistake of saying she looked like a hippo in a dress."

"Molly, maybe bringing up violence is not a good table topic right now," Cheryl said.

"Oh, I want to hear more about breeders gone crazed," Russell said. "I'll go get us another round."

Frances tried to get Russell's attention and shoot him the shut-up-now face. Thank god, Dana got everyone focused on the gifts. One by one, the gifts helped change the topic of conversation, and Jason and Winter were able to kiss and make up.

"That's a cake?" Winter asked, as Mary brought it to the table. "I think I'm going to puke."

"I knew I shouldn't have gone with the dirty diaper cake. It does look like poo," Cheryl said.

"It is awesome," Russell said. "I love chocolate."

"Careful. No one needs to know what you like," Simon said.

"We have our gift. Let me go get it." Russell was up and getting Mary's help to part the crowd.

"We hope you like it," Simon said.

"That is…way over the top…we can't—"

"Yes, you can. After all, when we push the baby around town, we want people to stop and stare because she is going to be beautiful and her uncles are so proud of her," Russell added. The rest of the table was speechless, looking at a baby pram that looked like it came straight from Buckingham palace. It was a deep navy blue with silver accents, large white spoked wheels, and a mother-of-pearl handle.

"Let's eat cake now that all the gifts are done," Dana said.

The cake was finally cut into and shared with Mary the waitress, who finally took a break and sat down with the crew. Simon and Russell delivered cake to the kitchen and bar staff. What had started out as a dicey morning turned into a great celebration. Frances caught herself watching Molly as she laughed with everyone. She fit in so effortlessly with the gang.

CHAPTER THREE
WHAT WERE THEY THINKING

T raffic was stopped on Van Ness. This was not an unusual occurrence at this time of the early evening. If the last fifteen minutes were an indicator, traffic was stopped. She checked her map on her phone and saw that she was only about seven blocks from Harris' Steakhouse. She looked out the rain-streaked window and wished she was instantly sitting inside the restaurant being treated to a wonderful steak dinner by Russell and Simon.

"Any idea what has the traffic stopped?" Frances asked her taxi driver.

"Nope."

"The phone shows red through the whole city. What do you think is going on?"

"No clue."

"Quite the talker," Frances said.

She caught the driver's glance in the rearview mirror and made a split-second decision.

"I'll pay you now. I'm going to walk the rest of the way." Frances hit the pay button on her phone and was out into the drizzle. At least it was mostly downhill. Frances pulled her fleece collar up on her jacket. Why had she not brought an umbrella? It felt good to be out walking.

25

She had been spending so much time in her loft that she forgot what air not adulterated with paint, varnish, and brush cleaner was like. She stopped looking at the people stuck in their little boxes on wheels in both directions on Van Ness. She lengthened her stride and was feeling quite good.

Frances spotted the telltale green awnings of Harris' restaurant on the corner of Van Ness and Pacific. Before entering, she took off her jacket and shook it out, letting the water drop. Her hair felt like it might be plastered to her head, but she attempted to plump it up with her fingers. She wiped her face and took a couple of deep breaths. It had taken her longer to walk the blocks than she anticipated. One more look at the parking lot that was Van Ness Avenue and Frances walked through the door into a very fancy steakhouse. Before she had a chance to get her bearings, Russell was there to swoop her up.

"Frances, you made it. We are in the piano lounge tonight."

"No reservations? Thank god, because I'm a little underdressed," Frances said.

She followed behind Russell, who was walking faster than usual. Frances slowed and dropped Russell's hand when she saw the green U-shaped booth was inhabited by Simon and a woman whom Frances did not know.

"Come on, Frances. Why'd you stop?" Russell asked.

"You said it was you and Simon taking me out to celebrate my upcoming gallery opening. Who's that?" Frances asked, pointing at the woman.

"Come over and find out. She's a good friend. Behave yourself." Russell walked over to the table.

Frances followed and now wished she had stopped to check out her hair in the women's restroom. This was not fair. She wanted to talk to them about what was going on with her family, Theresa, and life. Now she had to put up with small talk. Her face couldn't hide her disappointment. Screw it. This was a stranger and sometimes strangers handled drama better than close friends.

"Frances, so glad you made it," Simon said, standing up to give her hug. "Let me introduce you to our dear friend, Ryan Larsson."

Frances tilted her head. Had she heard the name correctly? In front of her sat a beautiful woman in a spaghetti strap dress. No man hands.

Her fingers were elegant with a French manicure. Not to mention the most amazing gold-blonde hair—the kind of hair that fairytales were written about. The last name, combined with the strong shoulders, blonde hair, and bright blue eyes, had Frances thinking this woman might be Swedish.

"Do you like Swedish fish?" Frances asked as she sat down opposite Ryan.

"I love them. They are a secret pleasure. I don't buy them though because I end up eating the whole package in a matter of minutes," Ryan said. "So, Frank, Simon was telling me that you have a gallery opening coming up. How exciting."

"Frank?" Frances asked.

"I get it," Simon said. "Frances's nickname with us is Franny. I tried to call her Fanny after Fanny Brice but, alas, she did not appreciate the association."

"Is your name really Ryan?" Frances asked.

"I get that all the time. Yes. It is a family story that I don't want to bore you all with right now."

"Russell and I thought it would be okay to include Ryan in your celebration. She's in town for one night. We didn't want to cancel."

"Simon, it's okay. I feel—"

"You look great. Relax. You've been working so hard that we never get to see you anymore. I figured we could bribe you with a steak."

"Great. Now I seem like I'm easily purchased with meat."

"This could get fun. Any type of meat, or are you specific?" Ryan asked.

"That is for me to know. Looks like I need to catch up. What are you drinking? It looks so adorable. Are those mini aging barrels?" Frances asked pointing at the drinks on the table.

"The uniform of the drink doesn't give it away?"

"Those look like baby martinis."

"Ryan and I are both drinking dirty martinis with Grey Goose. Extra dirty." Simon took a sip. "I think I order a martini here because of the presentation. Don't you love these little wooden barrels filled with ice? Plus, these martini glasses make my hand look so masculine. All martinis are best when chilled."

"I'm up for one of those," Frances said, waving down the waiter.

She took a moment when Ryan and Russell were talking to assess the situation. It really did appear that she was a good friend visiting. Ryan's laughter was easy and her conversation smart. The meat comment had Frances wondering what she was up to as this woman was beyond feminine and her make-up was impeccable. How does a person get their make-up to look so effortless and amazing? Frances picked up the knife of her place setting and tried to catch her reflection without being completely obvious. All she saw was her tomato-red face, crazy hair running a million different directions, and two black eyes. Great. The one time she actually put the effort into wearing mascara she chose one that bled in the rain.

"Now Frances, Russell and I have some words of advice over your family situation."

"Are they going to help me feel better?" Frances asked.

"Oh, Franny...nothing we say is going to take the pain away. No. You are battle scarred for life and it is...you are free to live your own life."

Frances bit her bottom lip. She wondered if they could see it quivering. The music filled in the silence at the table. Frances looked down at her lap, wanting to run, to scream, to cry...and the room started to spin.

"Frances? Frances, you need to keep breathing," Simon said.

She felt his arm around her shoulders and she leaned her head against his. "I feel so lost."

"Sweet girl, you will process all your feelings. Have you had a chance to sit down and talk with Theresa?" Russell asked.

"A little. She keeps telling me she had no clue this was coming. What I don't understand is why. She's the one with a girlfriend right now. Not that I consider Kelly good for her, but—"

"Frances, do you think there is something else going on here that has nothing to do with your sexuality?" Simon asked.

"Excuse me. I'm going to use the ladies room," Frances said and slid out of the green booth seat before she completely lost it.

Without waiting for anyone to acknowledge her statement, she walked off in the general direction she felt the bathroom should be located. She was so distraught that when she walked into the kitchen, it took her a moment before she realized she was not in the right place.

Frances quickly turned herself around and was met by a waiter. Her heart sank as she realized she would be walking by the table on her way to the restroom. Maybe she could pick up a tray of food and no one would notice. She would blend in and act like the help. Frances put her head down and walked back out into the piano lounge and tried to power walk past the table.

When she opened the door to the restroom, she wanted to scream. Ryan was standing at the mirror, gently moving a couple strands of her golden hair into a more perfect position. Frances shut her eyes and walked further into the room. She didn't see the other woman, who had finished washing her hands and walked directly into her.

"Hey."

"Oh my. I am so sorry. I didn't see you. Sorry," Frances said, and the tears spilled out.

The woman gave Frances a look that almost resembled fear and practically ran out of the restroom.

"Rough room," Ryan said. "Do you often walk into bathrooms with your eyes closed?"

Frances came over to the sink and wet her fingers. She knew it was an exercise in futility. Her hair was not going to be tamed with a couple drops of water. Her curls were creating more curls with the dampness, and she knew that they would collide into huge masses of curly red tangles. Ryan handed her a hand towel and pulled a brush out of her handbag.

"This might help." Ryan said. "I'm sorry about your family. Sounds like this is a new turn of events."

"Unless you have a blow dryer and some serious hair straightener, that brush might never come back."

"Nonsense. Let me give it a try. Do Russell and Simon do this to you a lot?"

"Do what?"

"Set you up? Then lob one heck of an emotional grenade? I swear they have the worst timing."

"Oh god. They did. I bought the line that you were a friend visiting," Frances said. "I'm so embarrassed."

"Don't be. The boys were not fair to you. I am visiting, and this is the only night I had available."

"What do you mean they were not fair to me?" Frances asked.

"Well, I am here in a dress that I would not normally wear to a meeting with friends. You are here in something I would much prefer wearing. These shoes are killing me."

Frances looked down and realized the woman was wearing three-inch red leather heels. They were amazing and her toes were manicured with a polish that matched her shoes. This woman was serious about getting dressed for a date. The whole time they were talking, she had been working on Frances's hair.

"You have beautiful hair," Ryan said.

The thoughts running through her head were shooting around so fast she had no time to completely understand them. What was she going to do? She was so hungry.

"I don't know what they told you—"

"It's okay. I'm not much into the dating market either. They mentioned they might have a friend coming, but it was tentative."

"Those sneaky rat bastards. You'd think they would've learned from the whole fiasco with the—"

"Oh. You're the one who ran out of the restaurant when you were kissed by your blind date. Now, was it the fact the blind date was with a woman or was it because she kissed you?"

"You know that story?"

Frances glanced at her reflection in the mirror and did notice that her hair had been slightly tamed. The contrast of her button-down Oxford shirt over her white T-shirt was quite the contrast to Ryan's form-fitting black dress. Frances tried to wipe away the mascara that now made it look like she had played four quarters of football. Her cheeks were practically black.

"Let's have a little fun with the boys. It might take your mind off your heavy news. When I was newly single after my first divorce, those two hired a stripper-gram and sent it to my office. They are improving. At least you are sensibly dressed." Ryan took the wet paper towel from Frances's hand and gently worked on removing the mascara. "They introduced us through love. Want to play with them a little?" Ryan asked.

"I'm game. But before we go out there, I need you to know that I am not dating anyone right now. There was some serious . . ."

"Frances, it's okay. I've made a new friend tonight and when I'm in town again we can go out and relax. I'm sorry I won't be here for the opening of your show. I make it a point not to date a woman who comes with family drama."

"What? Are there women without drama?"

"Too soon. Sorry. I was trying to make a joke. Cultural differences. I think the definition of drama is family."

"Where do you live?" Frances asked.

"Sydney, Australia."

"You can make anything sound sexy."

"My Australian accent can be a curse at times. I'll explain later."

The bathroom door opening, a woman entered and paused, clearly unsure whether she should stand behind them or walk between them. Frances thought about the strange bathroom etiquette. She stepped closer to Ryan to allow the woman enough space to walk around them to the bathroom stalls. Ryan encircled Frances with her arms and pulled her into her chest.

"I know you were wondering. I hope this hug settles it for you," Ryan whispered and lightly kissed Frances on the lips before leaving the bathroom.

When she let go, Frances felt a little light-headed. Was it her perfume? The softness of her lips was divinely silky. She smelled like a mix of jasmine and sandalwood. Feminine and masculine, with a balance that could very easily become intoxicating. How could the boys introduce her to a woman who lived in fucking Australia? Ryan was already taking a sip from her martini when Frances returned to the table.

"Glad you made it back. I was wondering if there was a traffic jam in the ladies' room," Simon said and laughed nervously.

"We were comparing lipstick shades," Ryan said.

"The ruse is up, boys. How could you set me up on a date with a woman who lives in Australia? Are you kidding me? That is in a different fucking hemisphere," Frances said. She downed her martini in two gulps.

"Now, Frances—"

"Talk to the hand because this head is not listening. Ryan served you both up in the ladies' room."

"Oh, sweetie, we wanted you two to meet. I've talked you both up to one another. Ryan, have you shared with Frances what you do?" Simon asked.

"Let me. I can't wait to see her face," Russell said and clapped his hands. "Ryan is a photographer."

"As in professional photographer?" Frances asked.

"A fucking great one. You know that framed photograph Theresa helped us hang in our loft?"

"You mean the ghost cloud and the horse? That is amazing. Oh my god, you're a serious photographer. You have your own galleries."

"Well, I don't know how serious I am, but I do enjoy it," Ryan said.

"Holy crap. Your work is being shown at SFMOMA."

"Should I be worried?" Ryan asked.

"Only for the safety of Russell and Simon, who did not exactly connect the dots for me. Yes, I do acknowledge that they have told me about you. They have bragged on your photos appearing in *National Geographic* and hanging in some pretty amazing places."

"Frances, take a breath—you sound like you might be hyperventilating," Simon said.

"You set me up to meet this woman and gave me no warning. I thought I was eating out with the boys and—"

Frances was silent as Ryan stood up and walked over to her side of the booth. It didn't take the boys more than a second to shift their seats to allow Frances to scoot.

Ryan sat down next to her and lifted the napkin out of Frances's lap. She slowly dipped the napkin in a water glass and then gently finished wiping the mascara away from under Frances's eyes. "I think you look better without the raccoon eyes. Let's order. Then we can talk about anything and everything."

CHAPTER FOUR

A CRY FOR LOVE

The ice had melted into the whiskey Frances had poured herself hours earlier. Crumpled wads of paper surrounded her chair and the overflowing wastebasket. Her hand was cramping from the number of attempts at writing her letter of truth—both her truth and the bridge she hoped it would build with her parents and family. Why did the truth hurt so much? The charge to be true to herself was costing more than she had ever anticipated. She wanted to run to her parents, to change their minds, to help them see that this was not a choice. Her possible love for another woman was not one made out of spite or intended to hurt them. It was part of her as much as her eye color or her heartbeat. Frances pulled the thought like she was pulling salt water taffy in her brain. Her sister, Theresa, was not out of the family, yet she was currently in a relationship with a woman.

Dinner earlier that night with the boys and Ryan had put her in a good mood once she got over two small but serious facts: first, she had been ambushed; and second, Ryan lived more than seven thousand miles away, in a different hemisphere. She did smell nice though. And she had a successful career as an artist. Frances raised her head off the table and looked around her loft. It was well after two in the morning.

She needed to get to bed. Theresa would be home from the theatre in about an hour.

She had started writing the letter that was sitting in front of her three hours ago. This one came out of several half-starts and feeble drafts. Her handwriting was getting worse with each word she wrote. It struck her that this letter could be seen as an artist's attempt to portray a worm traffic jam. Could she even read what she had written? No wonder people didn't handwrite anything anymore. There was no spell-check. Not to mention, it was almost impossible to read the black lines that represented her heart. Right now, it looked like her heart was full of worms.

Frances wanted her parents and her family to know how much she loved them. This was a different world than the one her parents grew up in, and it was not a sin against god for her to love. The tears started to fall again as Frances thought about the undercurrent of hate written into the letter that Bernard had sent from the family. Silence from the family was so loud that Frances covered her ears as she thought about the absence of conversation from all of them. Even Theresa was drifting further away. Frances looked at the calendar on her desk and saw that Theresa had penciled in the next visit from Kelly, her girlfriend. Maybe that would help. It had been a while since Theresa and Kelly had spent any time together. Frances could see how overwhelming the Kavanagh family—her family—could be to the rest of the world.

Frances's world was falling into so many pieces that she worried she would not be able to recover from the loss. The family excommunication had stopped her worrying about her gallery show. What could she do to get them to take her back? Would the letter help? She picked up the letter and tried to read her words.

Dear Mom and Dad,

The changes in my life were revealed to you in a most public way. I never intended for any of this to be broadcast so openly. There is no easy way to walk through this truth with you. The truth is inconvenient and it is painful. I never wanted to cause anyone pain by living my truth. You taught us all that family would always be there to support us, lift us up, and take care of us.

I believe in our family. I'm grateful for the strengths you instilled in us all as you raised us to be Kavanaghs. I love you. There have been many sleepless nights as I agonized over my own realizations of what I was discovering about myself. This is not a choice, nor is it a phase. My life is open to falling in love with a woman. There is no shame or guilt in this. The pain comes from the reaction of the family and the letter that was sent.

Even though this life—my life—does not meet your definition of a moral or Catholic life, I know that I am at peace with God. While I will not speak for Theresa, I will say that we are both the women that you raised. We are loving, compassionate, and intelligent. I love you all with all my heart and soul. Deep within my soul, I hold everyone in this family with love.

I appreciate that you need time to think through these realities. This life I live is not to disappoint you or cause you humiliation. This is who I am, and I accept myself.

Love, your daughter,
Frances Olar Kavanagh

CHAPTER FIVE
READY TO BE HUNG

"Take it as a good omen," Theresa said.

"What?" Frances asked. She looked out the truck window and thought about how easily Theresa had returned to the motions of life, almost as if nothing had happened. Frances turned to look at her sister behind the wheel driving toward the San Francisco Ferry Building. Hours of talking and crying had brought them to an understanding, one Frances was not quite sure she believed.

"The fact that the sun is out this morning. No fog. No rain. Blue skies and sunshine. You better get yourself out of this truck as soon as we get there. You don't want to lose Dana to the Bee Guy in the Ferry Building."

"Good point. Do you want a coffee?" Frances asked.

"Nope."

"Scone?"

"Get going." Theresa pulled the truck up to a loading zone at the front of the building. "The ferry is going to be docking and you're out here wasting valuable time."

Frances squinted up at the bright orb making her naked appearance in the sky, free of her normal gray shroud in the San Francisco skies. Maybe Theresa was right and the exposed sun would bring good luck.

Frances shook her head, thinking that she could not have evolved into an artist who was so egocentric as to believe the sun shining was at any way linked to her gallery opening. She quickly took her focus to the task at hand. She must get Dana a latte and scone to tame that part of Dana that hated coming into the City for any reason.

Dana's breakfast procured, Frances walked to the ferry terminal behind the building. She was so distracted by the uncannily smooth surface of the water in the bay that she walked into the ornate black iron railing protecting the public from the cold water below. Fortunately, the pier was empty at this early morning hour and no one saw her lack of grace. Thank god the railing was there or she would have been going for a swim. She kept staring at the woman looking back at her from the dark gray-green water mirror. The water woman was watching her. Frances was captivated by the ghostly gray skin and the tangle of curls that floated untamed just below the surface. While Frances was pulled into the siren's reflection upon the water, she failed to notice the gang of seagulls closing in around her.

The approaching ferry boat caused a wave across the surface of the water. The wave blended the water woman into the blotches of gray and green, taking her away. Frances turned her attention to the big boat pulling into the dock. She checked the coffee and scone. Would her simple attempts to appease Dana work? With everything going on in her emotional, fractured life, Dana was her solid ground, and she needed her level-headed friendship. The diesel engines for the ferry went into a low hum. This forced the birds to scatter briefly around her. Frances made the mistake of drawing them back with a rustling of the scone bag. She looked around and had visions of Alfred Hitchcock's movie *The Birds*. The flock of birds surrounding her caused a shiver down her spine as she stepped slowly toward the area where the commuters flowed off the ferries into the City. A few other people were waiting on the pier, but Frances was mostly alone with an obstacle course of seagulls tilting their heads back and forth, sizing her up.

Frances tucked the little white paper pastry bag into the pocket of her pea coat. Another person, who was actually eating a muffin, walked into the gang of birds, and Frances was freed. She had a rather strange fascination with watching people stuck in patterns. The commuters on this ferry were lined up and ready to bolt off as soon as the gates were lifted.

It started with a trickle of a few people. Young and surefooted, they raced off the ferry in front of the main rush of human commuters. This was followed by a strange lull and then another rush of people, all of them focused robots, faces cast downward as they rushed past Frances without any acknowledgement that another person was there. The dark block of people were dressed in hues of blue or black that were as ugly as a bruise on the skin. They appeared to run on an eerie autopilot.

Frances smiled as she saw a brilliant splash of orange bobbing in the crowd. Dana's face glowed against the looks of frozen determination passing by Frances. Dana was so careful coming down the steep incline of the gangplank that Frances found herself wanting to go help her. Dana's orange coat and red hat were all the brighter against the uniform of office workers. This contrast gave Frances an idea for a painting. She pulled her phone out and typed herself a note: *Painting idea—the morning commute. One person in bright color and everything else monochrome blues with a bleed of the color happening through a series of paintings.*

As Frances sidestepped a few of the robo-workers, she wished she had copied the idea of the guy who hid behind a couple of tree branches down at Fisherman's Wharf. He randomly jumped out from behind his branches, scaring the crap out of unsuspecting people, usually tourists. As the day wore on, he would draw a crowd watching the reaction of those poor souls who failed to notice the man behind the branches. What would happen if she put her hands up over her face and then jumped out, yelling? With this focused crowd on their way to their cages in the glass buildings that made up most of the financial district, she wouldn't even see a ripple in the flow of people.

Instead, she decided to create a game and hopped through the speed-walking commuters at an angle, traveling upstream against the flow. The challenge took her concentration as she spun, sidestepped, and wove through the crowd looking for the red hat and the orange jacket that screamed out the happiness of Dana Rainer.

Frances finally looked from the tail end of the commuter school of guppies and saw Dana. Their eyes met, and Frances held up the hot cup of coffee. She breathed a sigh of relief when Dana smiled, raised her phone, and snapped a picture of Frances on the dock.

"Good morning, Madame Artiste," Dana said, returning Frances's hug and taking the coffee. "I'll gladly take that. Did you know there is a no-talking section on the ferry? So many rules that aren't written anywhere. Jesus H. Christ, these people are miserable."

"Did you get into trouble?" Frances gave Dana another hug. "I was worried you might have decided to do something else instead. I have a scone from Mariposa Baking Company. I know you are doing the gluten-free thing now," Frances said, offering up the treat.

"I can't say no. You know I adore scones, and I haven't had one in ages…It smells scrumptious. Frances, you knucklehead. You didn't need to ply me with these treats."

"Dana, I want you to know how special you are to me. Before we go meet up with Theresa, who is waiting in a no-parking zone, I should tell you that we are talking again, although I still don't understand why I'm out of the family and she isn't."

"I love you, Frances, and don't you forget that. Your family will come around."

Frances and Dana walked to a bench that faced the bay and sat down. The sun felt good on Frances's face as she tried to keep her emotions in check. This was not going to be the time to go into what all of it meant. Frances really had not begun to scratch the surface. She figured she was in denial, but then it was her heart she was protecting.

"Don't blame your sister for their faults. She has her own journey with this family. Her own lessons to learn. On the surface, it would appear that you both should be in the same place due to your loving the smarter gender. Give yourself and Theresa some space. Today we are here to focus on you and your beautiful paintings." Dana took a bite of the scone. "I love vanilla orange scones—this is decadent."

"I am…what if no one shows up?" Frances couldn't keep the tears back.

"Take a deep breath. Try to keep yourself focused," Dana said. Frances gladly accepted Dana putting her arm around her shoulders. "Poppycock and horseshoes through a glass window. You already know that your crew is going to be there, and we are not chopped liver. As far as your family goes—they can wait. Tell me that you are going to fight for what you know is true to you, okay?" Dana put her hand under Frances's chin. "You are a beautiful, talented, loving young woman whom I love dearly."

"Dana, I don't know what to do."

"You don't have to know right now. Right now, you have a brilliant show to get ready for, and I'm here to help."

"One more thing, Dana. Theresa is still talking with the family."

"That's great. It means you can repair this—"

"I'm not making it clear. She told me that they basically banned her from the family too. But that wasn't the truth."

"Did she get a letter too?"

"No. I need to focus on tonight. We had probably better get going…I hope she doesn't have a parking ticket." Frances wiped her eyes. "Do I look okay?"

"Frances, you look beautiful. Although—"

"What? Although? How can you say those two words *beautiful* and *although* together?"

"What did you do to your hair?"

"Dana, your acute power of observation is truly exceptional. Felipe sent me to his hair stylist, who added some low lights to help bring out the red."

"Low lights? That's what they call taking out a black Sharpie marker and redacting your hair in chunks?"

"Thanks, Dana. I'm quickly thinking about wearing a turban tonight."

"Oh, Frances, you look beautiful—it isn't like you to do something like that. Maybe we can get Russell to help out. I'll call him."

Frances slipped her arm into Dana's and guided her through the growing crowds in the Ferry Building and out into the swarm of people, cars, buses, and the morning noise of San Francisco waking up for another day. She took a deep breath as she walked past the baker's group setting up their farmer's market booth for the day. Her nostrils were trying to persuade her brain to walk back and buy some freshly baked bread. Frances glanced over her shoulder, taking in the colors and the people of the farmer's market, and loved her home city. It was such an unusually beautiful sunny morning, and she was going to capture it all. She liked her increased senses as she was waking up to the reality that she, Frances Olar Kavanagh, was presenting her first full gallery show that night. Other parts of her life might be off the rails, but this painting life was spreading out before her with possibilities.

Theresa had maneuvered the truck to the line of other trucks unloading for the farmer's market. Frances was not surprised. Theresa had a way of getting exactly what she wanted without threat or force. Her talent for quiet manipulation might have come from being the last one born into a family of eight children. It was like Theresa had a Jedi mind.

"Frances, Dana, over here." Theresa was standing on the running board of the truck and waving her hands over her head.

"She is simply amazing," Frances said as Dana had shot her a concerned look.

The ride to the gallery took longer than Frances thought it would in the morning traffic, but she was glad to be quiet for a moment. Felipe was going to run through the list of the art collectors who he wanted her to focus upon when they arrived. Frances was learning the importance of being groomed to sell her paintings, her creations.

When she had first received the invitation to do a solo gallery show, Frances had shot it down. She felt Nathan, the gallery owner, and Felipe, the gallery manager and Nathan's partner, were trying to make her feel better after everything that went down with Ethan and Olivia. Frances knew Nathan felt responsible for serving her up to Olivia, who was the owner of the previous gallery he managed. He had failed to warn Frances that Olivia was married and preyed upon the naïve. The issues with Ethan were more difficult. Nathan had not protected her from him. Frances had pushed that connection out of her mind. But it lurked close to the surface.

The spectrum of emotions rising in her heart was causing her to wonder if she was having a heart attack. This was not what she should be focused on at this point. *Breath*! She screamed it in her head and then said aloud, "Focus on your fucking breath, Frances. You are *not* having a heart attack."

"Frances, you are not having a heart attack. I told you yoga would have helped you out here. How do you think I stay so easygoing?" Dana said reaching out and taking Frances's hand in hers.

"You know you are the only reason I am doing this."

"Nonsense. You own this Frances. This is your life."

Thankfully, Dana had convinced her to do the show, no matter Nathan's motives. It was time for her to put her work out into the world and release it. Frances watched Theresa and wondered if she had received any more messages from the family. What did she know that Frances didn't? Frances turned her focus to the city outside her truck window.

"Frances, I brought your black dress and the tuxedo dress that Nathan sent over. I didn't know which one you would want." Theresa was parking the car in front of the gallery.

"I vote for the tuxedo dress," Dana said.

"That would be my vote too. But Felipe wants me in a skin-tight black dress. It—"

"Take both...I need to move the truck." Theresa didn't wait for an answer and was out of the truck before Frances processed what her sister had said to her. She grabbed the two garment bags and handed one to Dana. Frances walked through the doors of the gallery and stopped. All the colors, the brush strokes, the images she had created were hanging in the gallery. Her chest caved in and she stuttered through a couple gulps of air. Her heart beat so fast she thought she was going to take flight like a humming bird. This was not real. Dana touched her arm and she fixated on Dana's hand. The room was spinning and Frances grabbed for Dana, dropping the garment bag as her world went from color to a bright white and then nothing.

"Frances! Come on, Frances, wake up." Felipe was gently tapping Frances's cheeks with the back of his hand.

Frances opened her eyes to the concerned looks of Felipe and Dana.

"She's okay. Come on, let's get you off the floor. Good thing Dana is so strong—she helped keep you from smashing your head against the concrete floor," Felipe said.

A wet paper towel was on her forehead. She took the paper towel and put it on the back of her neck.

"I fainted?"

"Brilliantly," Dana said. "Like a true artist here to witness the slaughter of her little lambs."

"Dana . . ." Frances took the hand up from Felipe, who easily got her back to her feet and guided her toward the back of the gallery and the office. As they walked, Frances peeked around the gallery at her giant six-by-eight-foot canvases. They were her little lambs, and she was letting them go. *Breathe, Frances.* "Baaa baaa."

"You are so overly dramatic. This is not a slaughterhouse, ladies, it is an art gallery. Nathan would die if he heard you call this a slaughterhouse," Felipe said.

"What if no one buys a painting?" Frances asked.

"Then you are in great company, my friend. Think about all the artists who never sold anything. You paint because that is what you must do. These are your unique creations for the world. Snap out of the drama. Leave that to us boys." Felipe helped Frances sit on the sofa in the office. "Dana, if you need anything, I am out in the gallery. Get me."

"Frances, you can take about a twenty-minute rest. Try to empty that monkey brain of yours and float. I'll be floating right next to you." Dana got down on the floor and put her legs up on the wall. "This is one of my favorite yoga poses. I don't need the wall, but I figured if you wanted to try it you could copy me. Get your butt as close to the wall as you can and let your system help regulate the heebie-jeebies."

"Now that is true science. I think I'll stay on the couch. I already did my floor dive for the day. Got that out of the way."

CHAPTER SIX

WOODS

Homicide Detective Molly Woods looked at the stack of evidence and notes creating the chaos on the top of her desk and sighed. She swiveled in her office chair to face the boxes filled with more items collected from Ethan's home, his grandmother's house, and the two storage units they had uncovered. The web of murder and money laundering that Ethan had participated in was growing larger by the week. The enormity of what they had uncovered since his death led the Personal Crimes Division to create a special section. Molly was promoted to lead detective on the Ethan Charna case, and any hopes of wrapping the case up quickly due to Ethan's death by SWAT eight months ago were gone.

Molly went back to the still photos created from one of the snuff films that Ethan had made. The painstaking process of identifying the victims, mostly women, in the film was a gruesome task. The FBI had offered their assistance when the link was made to Ethan's ex-girlfriend, Annette, who had disappeared without a trace. It also opened up the investigation beyond the Bay Area and the state of California.

"Todd, do you have any more information on Ethan's financial records?" Molly asked.

Detective Todd Gruggs had made it clear that he had not been happy to be assigned to work under Molly as he felt the command should have been his due to his having been on the force a year longer. Molly knew she was going to need his help and decided to confront him directly about his feeling that he had been jumped over for the promotion. She knew Todd was an avid runner and so challenged him to run the course from the Escape from Alcatraz Triathlon. She bet her promotion on the outcome of that race. He took the challenge.

Molly had disclosed that she had a top time in the triathlon. Todd had kept up with her until the very last section of the sand stairs, when he slipped and fell face first into the top step. Molly stopped and came back to help him. That was the end of any grumbling. A different type of respect was formed over those sand stairs. Molly further cemented their friendship when Todd's daughter was born, and Molly made sure he was covered to spend as much time as possible with his wife and new baby. She was careful, but he was a strong detective and smarter than the average inspector.

"You know what I find fascinating?" Todd answered.

"Are we talking the case or just in general?"

"This case. The guy was loaded. His grandmother had millions in the bank, and they lived like they were barely making it. The only thing the guy paid on time were those storage units and his rent."

"Have you been able to trace those other monthly charges to other storage units or rentals?"

"Got a couple of guys working through those numbers. One of the monthly deposits went into Emily Alexander's account."

"What was the amount?"

"It was thirty-five hundred dollars on the fifth of each month," Todd said.

"Did we ask her about that money?" Molly asked. "I better go over her interview again."

"We are bringing her back in to ask her about this and that box we found addressed to her but was never sent."

"Have you had a chance to catalogue the contents of the box yet?"

"I'll be on it soon. It was checked over for explosives and other agents, but it looks like it contains papers."

Molly watched Todd for a moment as he started to say something and then went back to typing on his computer. She looked back at the pictures on her desk, and a shiver went down her spine. The expression on the woman's face was haunting. Her last moments were captured on film, and they were horrifying. Molly closed her eyes and gathered her strength. She needed to call her uncle. He had worked as a lead detective for thirty years at the San Francisco Police Department. He had investigated and helped solve the worst serial murder case in the Bay Area during the height of the hippie era and the protests against the Vietnam War.

One of the harder adjustments for her and her team was the fact they now had a dedicated administrative assistant. Molly, not used to the extra help, found herself at a loss and continually saying the wrong thing to Lucy, their assistant. Lucy was a real breathing person who probably could do more than schedule her meetings and keep the printer paper tray full. Molly stood and realized that another night had been spent in her office trying to identify Ethan's victims. The captain had warned Molly when he assigned her this role that it was going to tax her beyond anything in her prior experience.

She stood and walked around the large room that had been turned into their command center. A corkboard had pictures of missing women and the dates they had first been reported missing. The FBI had provided the majority of the pictures. It was a long shot that they would match any to the victims in the films. Another column had Ethan's known travel dates. It was still unclear how Ethan had met his victims.

The money trail was starting to produce some leads. The assumption was that Ethan befriended the women in some way, although there were also three identified male victims. In those films Ethan donned a mask. They identified him by the tattoos on his hands and neck. What caused a person to dance with a devil? Did they trust someone like Ethan?

She was tired and wished she had gone home instead of coming back to the office after answering another call from a detective in the Personal Crime Unit supervising the collection of evidence at a rather disturbing murder and suspected suicide case. The link was not likely because Ethan was killed at the standoff with police. What made the detective call her was the very distinct display at the murder scene. Molly agreed it was odd, and pictures were taken. She would go through the pictures with her team and see if there was any reason to think the murder could be related. It really seemed unlikely. Molly yawned and stretched her arms, relieved that no one else was in the office at six thirty in the morning. She went out to refill her coffee.

The coffee tasted like someone brewed it with dirty socks. She took a sip and quickly dumped the cup down the drain of the water fountain in the hall. As she walked back into her office, she froze. On the edge of the large work table was a purple and gold balloon bouquet. The helium balloons danced in the blowing air from the vent directly above them. She walked over and picked up the small stuffed husky that had a note hanging from a collar.

Ms. Molly Woods, you are personally invited by the artist to her gallery show, Bleeding Paint, The Work of Frances Olar Kavanagh 7 p.m. tonight.

"Are you going to the Fuck gallery opening?" Lucy asked as she dropped another stack of photos onto Molly's desk. Molly jerked her head to the right because she had not seen Lucy come into the office. The motion caused her to wince, as pain shot down her back from the strange movement.

"You read my invitation? Why did you call it F—"

"Powers of keen deductive reasoning. Don't flatter yourself, Detective, it's written on the balloons. F-O-K. Sure looks like a play on the F-word to me."

"Those are her initials."

"Those are fucking awesome initials," Lucy said as she exited the room again.

"I had a friend whose initials were W.T.F. Now those are fucking awesome initials," Todd said throwing his jacket on the table.

"Language people. I seriously do not want HR coming down on me due to a misunderstanding."

"Molly, you know me. I'll say everything is fucking okay." Todd winked and took a seat at the table. The comment brought instant giggles to Lucy. Molly turned and realized that she needed to let go of the whole responsibility of worrying and get into the solving of the crimes at hand. Her mind went to Frances, and she realized she wanted to go there more often than she would admit to herself or anyone else.

The thought of going anywhere but her own bed caused Molly's head to hurt. Frances was making a valiant attempt to forge this friendship. Why did things have to be so complicated? This was a different type of danger for Molly, and she was not sure she wanted to pay the price. Frances had impacted Molly so unexpectedly. Molly smiled as she remembered Frances's infectious laugh after she pointed out that her name was very close to 'Hollywood.' Molly shut her eyes and thought about Frances playing her piano in her loft the night Ethan had shown up to confront Frances and possibly kill her. Molly rubbed her face and shook her head. It was important not to get romantically involved with a person connected to an on-going case. The more they uncovered, the scarier this Ethan Charna had become. It was not lost on Molly that Frances had thought she was friends with this man.

"Hey, Molly. Hey, Todd. I didn't expect to see you two here after being on that murder scene most of the night. That was some gruesome business." Officer Mark Walters took a seat next to the balloon bouquet and started to gently bat the different balloons around. "Captain said he wants to know if we have a copycat killer or something like that with this case and that other one. What's with the balloons? Is it your birthday?" Mark asked.

"My secretary deduced what they were in less than a second. What's your excuse, Officer?" Molly asked.

"I'm not a secretary. I'm an administrative assistant. I have a bachelor's degree in criminal justice and a master's in English," Lucy said as she loudly dropped another load of pictures on the table in the center of the room and quickly exited the office.

Molly raised her eyebrows and winked at Mark.

"Heck, I know you're a dyke, but man you are harsh. We haven't called them secretaries for years. Don't pull me into your harassment issues with Human Resources. Best get that report done—you only have about thirty minutes." Mark stood and walked out of the office.

"Great. There go my hopes of ever leaving the office to get some sleep," Molly said.

"Who said you can go home? We need to get through these photos, and those nerds finally got an accounting of what was on all those external hard drives found in the second storage unit," Todd said.

"Todd, you need to go home and sleep too. You look exhausted," Molly said.

"My mother-in-law is in town helping Leslie with the baby. That woman has a list a mile long for me to do. I might go find an empty office and take a nap."

"Too bad we aren't in Mayberry."

"What?" Todd asked.

"You know, you could go take a nap in the comfy cell. The only crime in that town was the drunk who would come and lock himself in a cell until he sobered up."

"You two can't go anywhere. I have some things you need to see. I completed that work you assigned me yesterday," Lucy said.

Molly walked over to Lucy's desk. "You know, if you keep over-performing, you are going to make the rest of us look like we're napping all the time."

"I am going to write some killer novels. Now, I used Google Maps to do an overlay of where the victims the FBI wants us to focus on were found, or at least where parts of them were found. Notice anything odd?" Lucy asked as she projected her map onto the screen that had been set up against the far wall.

Molly walked over to the computer and took over. She drew a blue line from each location, connecting the dots. She noticed that Todd had stood up and focused on the screen. The shape was distinct. It was a seven-point star. Molly stepped back from the computer and looked at the image blown up on the screen.

"Woods?"

"I know. That is not a coincidence. Where do the other two crime sites we were asked to view work on this map?"

"Give me a couple of minutes to get that information," Lucy said.

"Todd, those victims were dumped in specific spots in the City. Did the FBI agent say anything to you when he gave us those ones? They might already know this information."

"Nothing was said, other than they suspected these women died in similar ways based upon the autopsy reports showing similarities in injuries to wrists and ankles, and the fact they all had burns on their tongues."

"Got the info," said Lucy.

Molly looked back at the screen with the two most recent cases and felt her blood run cold.

"That's on purpose." Todd said.

"It isn't a coincidence, Todd. I don't know how, but the killer or killers know about this pattern," Molly said.

"I don't know how anyone born after 1975 would know about that shape. I thought it was a legend."

"What are you talking about, Todd? I only noticed the bodies were being placed at locations that had some historical significance to the City," Lucy said, walking toward the projection.

"Do you think your pal Aaron and his geek squad downstairs might be able to help us speed up the search on those archived photographs from those different murder scenes?" Todd asked.

"Aaron and his geek squad might have something up their sleeves. Or maybe we can tap into something the FBI might have access to because going through the amount of video Ethan shot over the course of a decade is slow business."

"Lucy, please get Aaron Choe up here as soon as he is able. God, I hope he's in this early."

"I still don't get what you two are seeing," Lucy said.

"You might if I finish the drawing." Molly then traced out what looked like a bear within a seven-point star. "It was the special badge that used to be given to detectives when they joined the ranks of having solved more than one hundred cases."

"Do they still do that? I've never seen one."

"I have. My uncle got one when they solved the serial murder case."

"That means this killer, if . . ." Todd sat down and placed his face in his hands.

Molly finished his thought. "We need to figure this out or we are going to have many more bodies. This killer is going to try to break some records. But why?"

CHAPTER SEVEN
BREAKING DOWN

"I heard you fainted." Theresa walked in and sat down next to Frances on the soft red sofa that was a pop of color in the all-white gallery office.

"I was walking a very thin line, and then Dana told me that my baby lambs were going to get slaughtered. That did it. I was out."

"Are you okay?" Theresa asked.

"No. But I need to be. Do you remember what Mom and Dad always said?"

"They said lots of things."

"I didn't want to believe the reality. When I passed out, I was standing on the porch at home. Grangran was there and she was telling me to run away. To leave the family."

"Frances, what are you talking about? We have a great family."

"Theresa, they have kicked me out of the family over the fact I might love women. And they do it hiding behind god. What the heck? You weren't banished. What do I not know? I am not ashamed."

"Calm down."

Frances closed her eyes and wished she could talk to the usually rational trio of her older siblings, Agatha, Edna, and Brice. The lines were getting thinner, and Frances was afraid she was going to fall into an abyss so deep she would never hit bottom. "Mom and Dad always told us that family blood meant we would always have people in this world who would fight for us."

"That is still the case," Theresa said. "I'm fighting for you. I am here."

Her head hurt and her stomach was punching down on her intestines, causing Frances to shift her position in search of relief. Theresa could get away with so much compared to what Frances could do in the family. This concept of family was exploding in her brain. The foundation was taken away with silence and a letter. When Gall was killed—hit by a car when Frances was still a child—Frances found comfort in the noise of her family. He was gone, but there was still an abundance of noise in the house. Had she mistaken that noise as love, when it was really her place being cut further from the family?

Frances pulled her phone out and studied the pictures she had snapped of the collage she had made on one wall in her loft. It was over fifty pictures covering four generations of the Kavanagh clan. Pictures of Grangran as a young woman, her parents, the herd of brothers and sisters, and then the nieces and nephews. Each photograph instantly connected Frances to the warmth of her family roots. She had believed these people made her stronger. How could she change now? These people were a part of her. She stopped scrolling when a picture of the Kavanagh clan appeared, showing them at their annual Fourth of July picnic. It had become part of the family tradition. Those who wanted to brave the crowd would go watch the St. Louis parade and then stumble their way back to the mothership and party late into the evening.

The next picture was taken in the beautiful fall foliage of St. Louis. The reds and golds in the leaves were muted backdrop to the red-haired Kavanagh clan. This was an old picture as the hair styles sported by her older sisters paid homage to the days of hairspray and Farrah Fawcett feathers. Frances touched the face of her brother, Gall. He had his arm around Frances. This would be the last posed family photo ever taken. No one said it was because Gall was killed. But that was the last time the family had gathered for a picture except for the weddings that happened. Gall had died at the hands of a drunk driver a few weeks after that picture had been taken. Frances let the tears start to fall.

"What are you doing?" Theresa asked. "You need to stop crying—you are going to make your eyes all puffy."

"I'm missing Gall and the noise of the family. It got me through so much, and now I'm sitting in silence."

"I told you. You have me," Theresa said.

"Do I?" Frances asked.

"Hey, you two. Come on out. Nathan has arrived with some lunch. I think it would be a good idea to get your blood sugar up, Ms. Artist," Dana said.

"Dana, we'll be right out. Could you give us a second?" Theresa said. "I am here to support you, Frances. I left Kelly and my studies at NYU to be here with you."

"You're the one who had to announce to Bernard, to the family, that we're gay. Before that, they didn't know."

"What are you talking about? CNN ran a story about you and Emily being in some strange love triangle with that snuff film creeper, Ethan." Theresa's eyes were tearing up.

"I'm nervous. I wish the family was here. I want them to know all of me. But that isn't going to happen. After getting the letter—"

"They will come around. I promise you that I am going to fight for you. This is a moment in time. Trust me," Theresa said.

"Ladies, there is some wonderful food out here getting cold." Felipe came into the office and took Theresa's hand and Frances's hand and pulled them up, guiding them out to the small feast set up on his glass desk in the gallery. Frances turned and gave Theresa a hug. She let herself feel the warmth of Theresa's cheek on hers and took a deep breath.

"Air! I need to tap out. You're squeezing all the air out of me," Theresa gasped.

"Sorry. You are keeping me grounded. There is so much we need to talk about and that I am trying to understand. Hey, Dana come and get in on this hug—you are my real anchor in this life." Frances opened up her arms to bring Dana into the hug.

"Frances, it is not my responsibility to give you peace in your life. Get yourself a rope and tie it around your waist. Put glue on the bottom of your shoes and stick yourself to your world," Dana said, putting her arms around Frances and edging Theresa out of the hug.

"Theresa, do you think Mom and Dad will call soon?"

"You mean Mom. Dad never calls." Theresa picked up a plate and helped herself to some of the Thai food that was laid out on the table. "I love green curry."

Frances turned to the table of food and let the intoxicating aromas of curry, satay, and peanut sauce take her mind away from the knowledge that her heart was processing. She was alone, and Theresa was not open with her about what was going on inside the family. Frances felt the walls of glass getting thicker. She could see Theresa but no longer was she able to reach out and touch her—to see if the image of Theresa was real or imagined.

"Nathan, you are so sweet to bring us lunch." Frances turned and smiled at Nathan. He was a different man than the one who had left so many months ago. His hair was gone, as were sixty or so pounds. When she first saw him at the gallery, she hadn't recognized her friend. She took her plate of food and went and sat next him. He didn't have any food but was drinking something out of a thermos.

"I am so proud of you, Frances. These paintings exceeded my expectations. When I sent out the special invitations with the brochure, I got more responses than I ever anticipated. This is going to be a sardine event tonight." Nathan placed a hand on each arm and looked directly into her eyes. "Frances, you look so scared. Push those fears aside. You will shine tonight."

"Sardine?" Frances asked.

"Turn of phrase, my dear. It means we are going to be at capacity crowd here tonight." Nathan said squeezing her shoulders.

"Only because of you and Felipe. I think I need to pinch myself."

"You're here. This is really happening. No one paints big like this, and that puts you into a whole different category. The courage you captured in these paintings . . ."

"Nathan, you are only saying that—"

"Shush. This is my business, and I am not going to show anything unless I know I…What's my first and only mantra?"

"This is not art, it's business," Frances said.

"Are you channeling that teacher from *Ferris Bueller?* Where is your excitement? This is a great business. You did the hard work, and now let Felipe and I help sell you. The artist who understands my mantra will never have to worry about buying supplies or eating. You will be rich. People want to know the artist because it makes them feel cultured, important—they live vicariously through your courage. Many only wish they could create. They are cowards. But cowards with money." Nathan squeezed Frances's hand and, leaning on a cane, walked toward the table with the brochures of her art.

Frances watched a group of people dressed in black setting up tables and placing flowers around the gallery. It was starting to transform into quite the elegant place, and her paintings popped in the embellishment of the added lights. This was going to happen. She checked her phone, hoping to see something from Molly. The invitation had been sent to her office. She opened her email and even scrolled through the ads and spam, but there was nothing from Molly.

Tonight her show was opening, and she really wanted Molly to be there. Was she placing too much expectation there? She was going to be on display tonight. How was she going to answer the questions about the paintings? What was she going to do with this world? The gallery was losing its echo as the softer materials were placed. Six white leather benches had been brought in to add some comfort for the guests. A black grand piano was positioned in the corner of the gallery. Frances walked over and sat down at the keyboard. This was all happening. Here she was, and the paintings were done.

She let her hands lift the cover to the keys. Frances's heart settled down as her fingers found the music in the keys. The music floated softly through the gallery. A few of the busy bee workers stopped to listen to Frances playing. She knew that a piano player had been hired for the evening. Frances wanted to hide in her music. Maybe she could play and not trip over her explanations of why something was painted this way or that. Frances felt Dana's hand gently rest on her shoulder. Frances continued to play.

"What's up?" Frances asked.

"Frances, you play so beautifully. Felipe wants to go over some of the people coming in tonight. Time to get to work, kid. I had no clue about the production behind an opening. Good thing you have Nathan and Felipe in charge because I would have hung the paintings and opened a bottle of wine and left it at that," Dana said.

"I'll be there in a minute. Do you think Molly will come tonight?" Frances asked.

"Did you invite her?"

"She got the same invitation you all did. She's the only one who has not responded at all."

"I can call her for you, if you'd like? What else are you not telling me?"

"Don't go there. We are just friends."

"And I own a bridge I can sell you." Dana walked back toward Felipe, shrugging her shoulders. "I tried. She'll be over in Frances time."

CHAPTER EIGHT
SHADOWS REVEALED

M olly clicked her pen as she stared at the printed version of the map Lucy had produced earlier. She recognized the dot-to-dot drawing connecting all the locations where the bodies were left so many years ago. What had her really confused was how these latest killings appeared to be copying the same pattern. Molly studied how the killer had recreated the police shield. The seven-point star had been a symbol for the SFPD since 1849. The bear was added to the special detectives' badge in 1941. Her uncle had worked that case and she knew he had more detail than what was found in the thin file in archives. Molly called her uncle and left a message. The new killer or killers had placed his victims in staged scenes in the same locations; her instincts were screaming that this action was not by coincidence.

"Molly, I can see the steam rising from your brain. Care to talk through what you're thinking?" Todd asked.

"We were given twenty-two women and two men that the FBI agents believe were victims of Ethan based on the comparison of the two confirmed snuff film victims and what we have learned from his very careful notes that we were able to link to those two films. What I am not getting is the connection of the eight people—seven women and one man—who were killed here in San Francisco. We can't possibly be the first people to see the badge in how they were placed around the City?"

"When I spoke with the agent assigned to help us, he said this was the first he had ever seen," answered Lucy.

"Lucy, you are a gem. We map plot all the time. Aaron said he thinks he might have a way to get us the results we want so we don't have to manually go through the process of physically matching the faces of our missing persons with the victims in the stills taken from Ethan's snuff films. I forgot to let everyone know. The Captain has given us Aaron and his band of brainy geeks to help us sift through the victim face matching on Ethan's case."

"Man, this is rough. If we do match the faces, then those cases are closed and any hope those missing persons' families had is gone."

"Lucy, I know this hard, but we need to get this information, and I do hope we can bring closure for some of these families." Molly walked over to her desk.

"It was hard because Ethan was so good at not lighting the faces of the victims. His use of masks, and even cellophane, really distorted the faces," Todd added.

"Hey boss, Twiddle Dumb and Twiddle Dumber are done interviewing Emily Alexander," Lucy said, looking up from her phone.

"Watch it. Don't let them hear you call them that—I do not want to deal with HR. Thanks. Would you mind calling the gallery and letting them know I won't make it tonight?" Molly said.

"Do you have some dry cleaning you'd like me to pick up? A kid to drop at a dentist appointment?"

"Funny. I'll be back in a few."

Molly left the mess of a puzzle and headed toward the questioning rooms. She hated that they put Emily in such a situation, but their offices were now off limits to anyone not investigating the murders. The items her team had uncovered would be difficult for anyone to deal with, and Molly figured that Emily had some questions about what they shared with her today.

"Hi," Molly said to Emily, walking into the small room. "Heard you wanted to see me. Can we get you anything? More coffee?"

"No thanks. Detective Woods, am I...do I need a lawyer? Would you tell me if I needed one? I don't understand why I was brought in here again. I answered all these questions right after Ethan was killed. What is going on here?"

Molly almost choked on her gum. She really needed to remember to take the gum out before walking into a questioning room. Emily was pale and had dark circles under her eyes. This was in stark contrast to the tan and very fit graduate student Molly first met the night Ethan had committed suicide by SWAT. Molly pulled a chair out from the small table and sat down, not exactly sure how she could reassure this young woman who looked so broken.

"Emily, you are not a suspect, and we…I appreciate all your help as we put together this rather difficult puzzle that Ethan has left behind. Your question tells me that my team has done something that has you on edge. Are you okay?"

"No. Since Ethan went off and killed himself, the picture that you all are creating of him is not the guy I knew. He was . . ."

Molly stood and went to the open door and instructed her detective to retrieve the two items they received into evidence earlier in the week.

"I can't imagine knowing what you are going through right now. I really appreciate you coming back in to answer our questions. I know I am asking you to trust me when I say you are not a suspect."

"I get you. You are playing the good cop. Your two buffoons threatened me with jail. With jail! I didn't do anything wrong. I was a fucking victim in this mess too."

Molly took a deep breath and tapped the table harder than she had planned with the back of her knuckles. She needed to control those guys. "I am sorry for the misunderstanding. I will talk with my officers. You are not going to jail. You are not a suspect in any way in the matters we are investigating."

"It wasn't the two grunting idiots in here. It was the officer who drove me to the station this morning. I haven't been able to go home since all of this happened. I know you guys searched my place and my computer lab. It sure feels like I am being looked at for something," Emily said. "School is on hold right now. Your *team*, as you call them, has put me through the cross-examination wringer. I feel like a criminal. All the videos that were shown to me were a violation of my own privacy as well as Frances's. This is all so maddening. As I said, I am not the criminal. I am a victim here too."

Molly stood when Todd came into the room carrying a banker's box and small clear plastic bag that held two keys. She noticed that Emily slouched in her chair as Todd came in and turned her face to the floor. Molly wanted to drop everything and put an arm around her. This once very vivacious and strong woman looked so small and scared. What had her officers done? Molly made a mental note to watch the video feed of the questioning.

"Emily, I want you to talk with only Todd or myself from this day forward. You will not need to deal with any other officer of this police department on this matter. Is that okay with you?"

"I would rather not have to deal with any of you," Emily said.

"Thanks, Todd. You can set those two items on the table. Before you leave, would you please get ahold of the officer who drove Emily here this morning. I want him in my office. He can stew for a while. Don't say a word to him."

"You do use psychological mind manipulation," Emily said.

"Only when deserved. Again, I'm sorry for the behavior of that guy. And I noticed that you had a physical reaction to Detective Gruggs coming into the room. He is one of the good guys. Emily, I promise you that I am going to take care of you from now on, and if there is anything I can do, let me know. The box has been x-rayed and reviewed to make sure it is safe to open. You can see that the label was addressed to you. Do you know what Ethan might have put in this box he mailed to you?"

"After everything that has gone down? I have no clue, and quite frankly, I don't want to open that box."

"Do I have your permission to open the box?"

"Oh my god—really? Yes. Open the fucking box."

Molly put on a pair of gloves and placed a clean sheet on the table and set the box on top of it. She was glad to see Todd had returned with the camera and had started taking pictures of her going through the process of opening this box. Her day was not going to end anytime soon, and she was running on fumes. Her anger was percolating over the way Emily had been handled.

The clock on the wall of the cramped room showed ten minutes after two when Molly worked the X-Acto knife quickly and cleanly through the packaging tape. There was no question that the keys in the plastic bag belonged to a safe deposit box. Maybe the box would give them the answer as to where that safe deposit box was located. There were so many holes in the story of what Ethan had been up to, and there were some voices on her team who did not believe Emily knew nothing about Ethan's serial killing.

Molly decided to honor the silence in the room and worked carefully. Her gloved hands made this a little more difficult. Molly usually left this to her forensic unit—a lot less issue with chain of custody when her crime team handled the evidence.

Molly held her breath as she lifted the top of the box to reveal a DVD in a case, a Moleskine notebook, several photographs, and a Zippo lighter. Before anything was touched, Molly recorded each item and let Todd take pictures of the box's contents. Underneath everything was a thick manila envelope. Seconds were turning into minutes, and those minutes were ticking louder in Molly's ears. The careful handling and recording of everything made this whole scene turn sideways.

"Do you really need me here?" Emily asked.

"Yes," Molly said as she noted that the envelope had notes written to Emily, along with four dates. The last date was the day that Ethan died in the street. "Emily, it is unusual because these items need to be examined, but would you like to look at any of these items?" Molly asked.

"I am actually nervous. I might not want to know what Ethan recorded here."

"Have you been here all day?"

"Arrived at 8:30 this morning. This is not what I call a fun day."

"How about I have some people go through these items and record what they are and then you can look at a summary. Let me get you out of here for some lunch." Molly stood and walked to the door.

"Am I having lunch with the enemy?"

"Ouch. This is coming to a close. I could make some suggestions if you would like to get some help with working through the feelings—"

"I didn't know. How can I deal with what those jerks showed me? They showed me scenes from…he killed those women…I didn't know them."

Molly took Emily into her arms as the tears fell. Detective Gruggs came up to her, but Molly used a quick wave of her hand to send him away. This was the part of police work that most people never saw—the aftermath and its impact on the innocent inner circle. Molly could not imagine that anyone could be harder on Emily than she was on herself for not picking up on Ethan's deadly art form.

"Emily, I think a walk outside would be a good thing. There's a place we can grab some really good nosh around the corner." Molly let go of Emily and handed her a Kleenex. Emily declined the Kleenex and wiped her face on the inside of her T-shirt. Molly felt there was something so childlike and innocent in that motion. "You could not have stopped him, Emily. There are no words that anyone can say that will reassure you. I want you to take care of yourself."

One thing Molly would never get used to was the flickering fluorescent lights in the questioning room. She waited a few moments before walking into the room. Molly tried not to add more stress to Emily as she sat down in front of the items that had come from the box. Todd had come into the room and sat as far away as the closet-sized room would allow.

"Emily, is there anything on the table that you recognize?" Molly asked.

Silence fell on the room, and Emily let out a hiccup that was followed by tears. "Can I pick up the pictures?"

"Yes."

"Do I need to put on gloves?"

"You're fine. Everything was checked by us while you were out getting some fresh air," Todd added as he placed a box of Kleenex within Emily's reach.

Molly watched as Emily picked up the top picture. It showed her and Ethan dressed in red flannel shirts and overalls. Emily's attempts to stop the tears caused her to sound like she was choking a cat.

"Emily, would you like me to close the door? You don't have to hold back your tears for us," Molly said.

"These tears…I am crying…" Emily ripped up the picture into four pieces before Molly could calm her down.

"Emily, you must stop. I promise you that should we be able to release these items to you, and then you can do whatever you want with them."

"What can you get from a picture of Ethan and me going to a Sadie Hawkins dance? We were in our senior year of high school. This has nothing to do with . . . He's dead. You killed him."

"Molly, let me take this one." Todd cleared his throat. "Emily, this is a difficult task. That anger you have inside over this lives in this case. Ethan is dead. The breaks we get come from the strangest places. That picture might contain something in the background."

Molly reached out and gently placed a hand on Emily's shoulder. She felt Emily lean toward her touch. "What Todd said is very true. There are reasons that I am not able to share with you right now. But everything we can learn about him and put into solving the unsolved missing persons and murders helps another family find closure."

"I understand. I am so tired and don't feel like anyone is looking out for me. Is it my choice if I continue to answer your questions?"

"Yes," Molly said and sat down across from Emily. She knew that they were close to losing her help. The captain was very clear that the information concerning the latest murders in the City were not to be public knowledge. Molly knew that she had to appeal to Emily's heart. It was selfish on her part because she knew that Emily's knowledge of Ethan's world was so controlled. "You are always free to go. Know that you have helped us sort things, and I want you to know that we, Todd and I, are here to help you any way we can."

"The damage has been done. I saw him gunned down by your army. Why?"

"Emily, he fired the first shot. We didn't know what threat he posed to Frances, to the officers and spectators. I know you have heard this explanation before."

Molly had spoken these words so many times they sounded hollow in her mouth. There was something missing about Ethan and why he chose the very public way he died. He had filled the trunk of his car with hundreds of copies of one snuff film. The two computers in his car contained most of the information concerning how he planned to film the murders. It was not an accident. Ethan wanted them to find this information. That became clearer as they realized Ethan tested his lies out on Emily. She was his unknowing filter.

"Inspector Woods, I want to know something," Emily said. "Did you give the order to the SWAT army to fire?"

"I was not the one who gave the order. However, I do take responsibility for all the actions the police took that day."

"This is a dangerous world, and I wondered who ultimately took responsibility for his death. Those men who pumped him full of bullets, or the woman who gave the order?"

Molly watched as Todd hid his fists under the table. He was ready to burst over Emily's tone and questions. "Emily, would you mind telling me more about what you remember when you and Ethan hung out? Did you ever notice anything about his home, his family?"

"I really do want to help. All I can say is what I already said. We spent most of the time over at my house. Or out being teenagers wandering through the main cemetery in town and pulling pranks on the majority of the jerks in our class. His house wasn't any fun because so many places were off limits and he shared a room with his younger brother. He really didn't have a family. You know, he didn't have any parents. His grandmother raised him. I don't know what else to tell you."

"Thanks." Molly shot a look toward Todd. This pain needed to close. "Emily, would you mind if we called it a day?"

"Do I have to come back?"

"No. You have helped us as much as you can. We will deliver these items to you when we are able."

"I do want a copy of the estate papers. Maybe I never have to go back to school."

"I'll be back with a copy for you." Molly picked up the papers and left. She needed time. Lucy had already made multiple copies when they had gone out to get a breather earlier in the day. Todd had started to correct Molly but quickly caught on to her stall. That shadow of darkness was stronger than ever in her mind. Was she wrong about Emily? She had been over her testimony. Behind her were the familiar heavy footsteps of Todd.

"Molly, what's up?" Todd asked.

"The first time she talked about hanging out with Ethan, she said they spent a lot of time listening to music in his bedroom. She never said he shared a room with his younger brother."

"How do you store all that information? Do you have a computer for a brain?"

"Trust me when I tell you this is both a power and a curse. What I'm trying to figure out about those inconsistencies is why?"

"Molly, this woman is so freaked out she moved out of her place and has not gone back to school. It has been months. Who walks away from a PhD program at Stanford?"

"Why is she so scared? Ethan is gone," Molly said. "I think she knows something more."

"Who is she protecting?" Todd asked.

"I don't know. Maybe herself? I think I will have Lucy read through her interview transcripts again. Would you mind walking a set of the estate papers back to her and let her know that we are always available. I need to go down and have a chat with Aaron about getting those photographs scanned into the database."

CHAPTER NINE

THERESA'S HOME

Theresa looked at her phone and saw that she had missed four calls in the last two hours. She looked for Frances in the gallery before going through her list. Theresa thought she had made it clear to the Kavanagh clan that the best way to talk with her was through email. She made sure to have them wipe her number out of any more family text meetings.

"Mind if I go out and enjoy some of the sun?" Theresa asked over her shoulder to Frances. Without waiting for an answer, she was out the glass doors of the gallery and crossing the street to find a spot in Union Square to find out what was so important.

Outside, alone in the center of the square, Theresa held her phone up to her ear, listening to the latest voicemail left by their mother. The square was filled with an interesting mix of people. Theresa walked toward the artwork on display. She found the statue of the Greek Goddess of Victory, Nike, to be a rather odd monument choice for the area. Was that how Nike shoe company came up with their name? Random thoughts raced through Theresa's brain as she sat down on a step facing Macy's on the square. She liked watching people, and the square was full of people today. It was a good sign for Frances.

Theresa looked around and pushed down any fears that Frances was going to come out and bust her for talking with the family. Theresa pushed her speed dial and waited through half a ring.

"About time. I called you over twenty minutes ago."

"Hi, Mom. I've been busy."

"I talked with Father Riley about getting you back into Notre Dame. He said that you are still eligible to return right where you left off. He said students take leaves of absence all the time."

"Did you find out if they would take my credits from NYU?"

"One step at a time, little bird. Your father and I are okay with paying the tuition and living expenses for you as long as you continue to stay in therapy."

"Thanks, Mom. I will. All of this was a distraction from my real calling in life. I know it was a mistake. I was thinking that I need a little more time to get myself together. The counselor agreed that my progress is good and wants me to keep seeing him for another couple of months. I think he's helped me, and I don't want to stop yet."

"Bernard? Bernard, pick up the phone. I think you have something to say to your sister." Theresa heard her mother's muffled voice. "Your baby sister, Theresa—she's on the phone. No, I don't know where you put your glasses. You don't need your reading glasses to talk on the phone. Pick up the phone. Honestly, I don't know what any of you would do without me."

"Hey, Theresa. Heard you are finally making some progress."

"Bernard, apologize to your sister."

"Got it, Mom. Yeah. Mom says you've been going to a counselor and are working on changing your ways. I am sorry that I got so mad at you at the anniversary celebration." Bernard hung up the phone.

"Guess he didn't want to hear any more from me," Theresa said.

"You know how your brother can be. Honestly, I don't know why he has his own house... Bernard, would you take the garbage out to the curb? Your father had to go out of town."

"Where'd Dad go? Thought you guys were going to Agatha's fundraiser tomorrow night."

"Some client of your fathers demanded he attend their shareholders' meeting. He's in Los Angeles for the next three days."

"Hey, Mom, thanks for helping me get back into Notre Dame. I've got to get some things done first. Love you."

"Love you, little bird."

Theresa hung up the phone and thought about the look on Frances's face this morning. For a moment, Frances looked like she could break her in two. It was a look she had never seen before. Theresa leaned back against the metal stair railing and thought about how she could approach Frances about leaving. Maybe it wouldn't be so bad, now that Frances knew she was still talking with the family. Why didn't she tell Frances the truth about talking with the family? Theresa knew she was really only focused on her own future. Frances had her education and degrees. It was her choice to leave all of that to pursue art. Theresa watched a couple stop to take a picture in front of the base of the Nike statue.

Theresa knew that she could never tell Frances that she had gone to their parents' anniversary party. Frances so easily accepted her story that she had gone back to New York to visit Kelly. She knew she didn't have to worry about Frances and Kelly talking, as they did not really care for one another.

The gallery was starting to become claustrophobic with all the prep for Frances's show. She was happy for Frances, but she was over the drama of it all and ready to get on with her own life. A smile crossed her face as she stood facing Macy's on Union Square. She had money to burn, and this could be the perfect time. She had a slush fund. Theresa had been pocketing the money her mother had been sending to see the counselor. She went to one session and knew it was bogus. If her mother wanted to believe that a person could be talked out of being gay, she wouldn't argue. Theresa had learned years ago to agree and then do what she wanted. Theresa had a couple thousand dollars in her bank account now. One thing she was good at was capitalizing on an opportunity.

CHAPTER TEN
A CHANCE FOR HOPE

Frances walked over to Nathan and gave him a gentle hug. He looked exhausted to her. His thin body barely filled in his dark, expensive suit. Felipe joined in on the hug fest. This was really happening. In a few minutes, the doors would open and there would be no do-overs. A couple of people were already standing outside, waiting for the VIP treatment that Nathan and Felipe spent time cultivating—the preview for the special buyers. Piano music filtered into the office.

"Do I pass?" Frances asked as she turned to face Dana.

"Pass? What do you mean? Are you asking if you pass as a woman? You look marvelous. I love the classic look of a tuxedo dress. If you are applying for a butler job, you need a more rigid back."

"Dana, I am worried about your fascination with *Downton Abbey*. You don't think I look like I'm a hostess?" Frances asked.

"Think about that very carefully. In fact, you are a hostess. You are selling your paintings." Dana gave Frances a big hug, being careful not to smudge any part of her.

"Has anyone seen Theresa?" Frances asked.

"I still think you should have left the low lights in your hair," Felipe said. "The last time I saw her, she was commenting on Russell putting that red back into your hair. I think she stepped out with Russell and

Simon for a few minutes." Felipe slipped his arm into Frances's. "Shall we go meet your future?"

"Yes."

Frances walked out into the gallery and had to remember to shut her jaw. Her heart beat faster and she felt her palms sweat. Great. Now she had that dead fish palm. Her hands were cold and wet. This was not good.

"Frances, what are you doing with your hands?" Felipe asked.

"They are sweating. I need something to wipe them on—I can't shake anyone's hand when mine are cold and slimy."

"Relax and take this handkerchief. You're going to do fine." Felipe went to go get her a drink.

As she stood in the center of the gallery floor, Frances noticed how the gallery was set to highlight each painting. They all looked brilliant as solo pieces, but then she turned in a full circle and saw the unity of her pieces. She was in awe over how the boys had thought of everything: the beautiful flowers; the waitstaff dressed in white waistcoats, holding silver trays filled with beautiful champagne flutes; the piano music directed at showing off her paintings. Her paintings looked brighter than she remembered. Had there been something in that chocolate chip cookie Theresa had insisted she eat? She was feeling a little more relaxed than she had thought she would. But her heart was fluttering.

She walked over to Nathan, who was standing next to a table that held a sign-in book along with a price list for the paintings. She tried not to gasp. Were they really thinking they could sell her paintings for those prices? It was more than a new car.

"Shall we?" Felipe asked and walked Frances over to the painting that anchored the show. It was a painting of the ocean. She had placed the horizon line an inch from the top of the canvas. In the deepness of the blues, she had streaked glimpses of pink, green, and purple that almost looked like neon lights in the water. The waves undulated with the iridescent paint. Frances tried to relax as the doors opened and Felipe and Nathan greeted each person by name. She noted which guests they hugged and which guests got only the handshake. She had so much to remember. Take the cues from the boys. As the gallery started to fill and Frances stood alone next to her ocean, she felt a calmness splash over her. This was her life. She felt strong and powerful as she watched the faces of the people who started to walk from painting to painting.

Frances turned to meet Felipe's smiling face as he brought up a young man and a woman who was sporting gloves. It almost looked like she was wearing a workout leotard. *Don't laugh, don't laugh* was playing through Frances's mind. *Stop staring at her outfit. These people have more money than most small banks. Felipe schooled you on them. Be sure to tell them they are the first collectors you have spoken with tonight.* Words were coming out of her mouth, and she had no clue if she was doing what was needed. Felipe seemed happy. He kept smiling.

"Do you mind if I ask you a question?" Frances turned to the young woman in the adult onesie. Frances ignored Felipe's look of concern.

"Ask away."

"How do you get in or out of your outfit? It appears as if there is no zipper. And did the jeweled gloves come with it, or did you find those first?"

"You are so cute. This is a one-and-only designed by Mako, a designer that we are supporting. I love it. And it is so darn comfortable. I don't feel like I'm wearing anything at all."

"It is unlike anything I've ever seen before. Seriously, though, how do you get into it?" Frances started to walk around the woman.

Frances ignored Felipe's extreme eyebrow raises. "I wondered if you were an ice dancer. Or possibly a performer with Cirque du Soleil."

"I wish, they have the best bodies. You're so sweet. Which is your most favorite painting? I must know all about it," onesie woman asked.

Frances didn't mind that Felipe moved them away quickly. She stifled a laugh and realized that the outfit was so form fitting that the woman was definitely full commando. *To be that tiny.* But really? Would she want to be that tiny? Frances liked her curves. She hoped no Cirque du Soleil performers overheard that conversation because compared to them, this woman was a stick figure. If the suit was brown and not bright electric blue she might be mistaken for one of those stick-bugs. Frances wanted to slap herself for such judgment.

"You look amazing," Winter said as she tackled Frances. "Sorry. I'm still getting used to my hefty middle weight."

"Thought about going out as a linebacker for the 49ers? Heard they are getting ready for open auditions."

"Funny. Seriously though, this is awesome. Your work looks real."

"Real? Winter…Never mind, let's get to some fun. Do you see the woman—"

"Did you hire her? Is she a performer?"

"Nope. She is wearing a Mako, and she and her husband are the richest fishes here, but Felipe rushed me away from them. Not sure why? Maybe it was something I said. I asked her how she gets into the outfit. There are no zippers. Maybe she isn't human. How does one use a bathroom?"

"You must stop. If you make me laugh too much, I might have this baby right here. I bet she steps through the neck hole. I don't know if I've ever seen a woman so thin."

Winter took hold of Frances and squared off in front of her. "Frances Olar Kavanagh, focus. Stop taking apart the überrich. They can't help the fact that money did not give them taste. Buck up, buttercup, and sell some shit."

"You are sounding like Dana."

Frances saw Nathan raise his hand, motioning for her to come over to him. Next to Nathan sat a very well-dressed man in a dark suit that had the slightest lavender pinstripe. Frances tried to place the man's face with a name in the prep materials that Felipe had drilled into her. Her brain's computer was coming up with nothing. Shoot. She trotted over to them, wanting to hide, when she realized she was responding like a golden retriever puppy. This was not becoming the artist. *Own this and let people see that you did create these pieces of art,* she told herself as she slowed her pace to avoid crashing through the wall.

"Thank you for coming over so quickly. Allow me to introduce you to the new owner of *Ocean Deep.*"

"Really?" Frances found herself gasping for air. *Ocean Deep* was one of her favorite pieces. She had debated for weeks about whether she was going to include it in the show. This painting clicked with her soul, and her heart hit a deep beat that echoed through her body at the thought of parting with it.

"Yes. I am actually not the owner. I am here representing the owner. He wanted me to tell you that the painting reminded him of a trip he had taken when he was learning how to sail."

"I...well..." Frances looked to Nathan for some help, but his attention was focused somewhere else. "Tell your..."

"Client. He's my client—"

"What the heck?" Nathan stood with the help of his cane.

Frances did not see what was going on behind her, but when she turned she felt the gallery walls close in, squeezing the air out of her lungs. She quickly reached out and put her hands on the table to steady her. Theresa and Russell were outside the glass doors of the gallery, arguing with the little guy wearing the headset. He was the gatekeeper for the evening. This portion of the evening was devoted to the "serious" art collectors. Or, as Nathan referred to them, the collectors easily persuaded to part with money in exchange for the chance to own an original piece of art. It is an emotion being sold, Nathan had told her—they must go beyond the physical painting. Most of the time, the buyers couldn't tell you one artist's work from another. As Frances realized that her paintings really were going to sell, she was beginning to understand the business Nathan was always talking about. But why did the first painting that sold be the one that she had not wanted to put out there at all?

"Are you all right?" the man who had bought her soul painting asked.

A tight blink of her eyes and deep breath allowed Frances the reset she needed for her brain to register. When a person is in a place they aren't supposed to be, the brain tricks you. The last time Frances thought she saw Dana in a crowded gallery show at the Legion of Honor she hugged a stranger who was not happy about it and called security. Frances shook her head because her eyes were telling her brain that her dad was standing outside with Theresa. As Frances inched closer toward the front of the gallery, her brain confirmed it. Patrick Kavanagh, her father, was standing outside, arguing with the doorkeeper.

It was too late for Frances to retreat into the gallery. Her eyes met her fathers' and she was six years old again and quite possibly in trouble, judging by the expression on her father's face. She ran to the doorway and squeezed past Nathan to throw her arms around her father.

The little girl instinct to fall into his arms was overwhelming. When her dad wrapped his arms around her, she fell into the comfort found in the smell of his Old Spice aftershave and prickly cheek covered in red whisker stubble. A knot formed in Frances's gut as her brain kicked in and reminded her about being banished from the family. What about the letter? What the heck was going on, and why was he standing here?

"Did something happen?" Frances asked, both her hands now holding her dads'.

"I came to…maybe we should go somewhere and talk."

"Dad? I can't go anywhere. This is my show. These people are here to see me."

"Frances, I traveled out here to see you." Patrick looked from Frances to Nathan and then to Theresa.

"Let's go in and have a drink to celebrate this most amazing surprise," Nathan said. "Why don't you all have a drink and a few minutes to chat in my office."

Frances guided her father into the center of the gallery and stopped. Her brain was screaming unintelligible words. Had she gone into complete deconstructive thoughts? A sharp pain struck the center of her chest, causing Frances to fall forward slightly.

"Do you need to sit down?" Theresa asked. "You are as white as a sheet."

"I'm fine." Frances turned to their father. "Why are you here?" Frances asked.

"I'm your father. I don't need a reason."

"Is there something you want? Something you feel you need from me?"

"Frances, stop being a jerk," Theresa said.

Nathan took Theresa by the hand. "Theresa, why don't you and Russell help me over at the dessert table. We can get a couple plates together, and you all can go into the office." Frances noticed he appeared to be leaning on Theresa to keep himself upright.

Felipe, alerted to the situation by the doorkeeper, walked up. "Mr. Kavanagh, what a pleasure it is to meet you. Your daughter Frances has created quite some amazing works."

"This is not work. This is a hobby." Patrick looked down at his hands.

Frances walked toward the back of the gallery. She wanted to lock that little girl who ran and hugged her dad deep inside. She did not need her father's approval or pride. It was clear that he was not going to recognize the work she had created. He wasn't here for her. There was something else going on that Frances couldn't put her finger on. She watched her sister, now laughing with Russell, take a plate of fancy mini fruit tarts, chocolate-covered strawberries, and chocolate truffles to the office. Had Theresa known he was going to show up here? Frances looked around at the crowd in the gallery. They appeared to be oblivious to the torture she was currently undergoing. She had been waiting longer than she knew for this moment, and in one phrase, her father reduced her work to something less than what a kid hangs on a fridge. It was not lost on her that he so quickly glanced at her work and reduced it to a hobby.

"Frances, I want to talk with you."

"Okay, Dad. I get that, but I am busy."

"Frances, Felipe and I have this for now." Nathan hugged Frances and whispered into her ear, "Go to the office and pull yourself together. Your tears are messing with your makeup. You set the time limit. You are in control here."

Frances left Nathan's embrace and walked back to the office. She knew her father was behind her. His footfalls had always been heavy. They used to tease Frances and say she inherited his concrete feet because when she ran around the house as a kid, her bare feet stomping made the house shake.

Entering the office, Frances reached for a napkin from the desk and tried to dab her eyes. "You have five minutes, Dad. Then I need to get back to my show."

"Frances, how can you put a time limit on Dad? He traveled out here from St. Louis," Theresa said.

"Why? Why are you here, Dad? I got the letter and understand being cut out of the family money. I am thinking about changing my name. I'm an artist now—maybe I'll go by my initials."

"I thought you would be happy to see me?"

"Really? Are you—"

"Frances, this is Dad. Show him respect."

"What about respecting me? My work? This isn't a hobby, Dad. This is my career. You can look away and act all disappointed. That worked when I was a child. Now...now respect is given when it is earned. You cast me off."

"No, I didn't. You will always be my daughter, and I will always love you."

"Dad, you...the letter. I'm not allowed to be buried with you in the family plot. Not that I want to be buried. I am leaning toward cremation myself. Or maybe doing that green burial thing."

"Frances, you are wandering," Theresa said.

"Dad, you never called me. Do you know what I've been through? No. Your silence broadcast exactly how much you cared. I am no longer part of the family."

"If that were true, Dad wouldn't be here. You can't have it both ways." Theresa started to pace around the office.

"Would you both please sit down. This is not easy." Patrick sat down on the couch and put his face in his hands.

Frances walked over to the desk and sat on the edge. She wasn't quite sure what to do. Part of her watched Theresa to see if she could pick up any cues or other surprises that the Kavanagh clan might unleash on her today. Theresa refused to meet Frances's gaze. The silence was growing louder as the three of them searched for something to calm the energy. Muffled music floated into the office, mixing with the sounds of laughter and conversations. This was her time, and she was not going back to whatever her family thought she needed to be.

"I'm sorry about that fucking letter. Your brother thought we needed to send it."

"But why? I am the same person. I grew up learning from you and Mom. If you didn't agree with the letter, why was it sent?"

"You are not the same person. You are not the girl I raised."

"No, Dad. I guess I'm not. I'm a grown woman now, and I am making my own choices."

Theresa jumped in. "Dad, you know that Frances and I did not choose to be this way. This is not a choice."

"Frances, you were married to a man. What happened? Is it this city? Mom said you stopped going to church."

"When was the last time you went to church, Dad?"

"Sunday."

"Really? You never went to church with us when we were little and marched off like little soldiers." Frances walked over to the door of the office. "Time's up. I need to get back out to the floor."

"Frances, will you please sit down? I'm not done talking to you."

"You don't understand. This is not your time. You were not invited. You could have picked up the phone at any time. You decided to show up at my gallery opening and say in the center of the gallery that this is just a hobby."

"This is a hobby. You had an excellent job. How do you think you could do what you want to be doing now? Was it painting? No. You made that money because I taught you everything you know. I gave you your clients. The reason you can do any of this is because of me. I am the reason you are alive."

"Dad," Theresa said as she reached out to take his hand.

"Dad's on a roll. Here I thought all those hundred-hour-plus work-weeks fixing clients' fucked-up problems were . . . well, gee, I guess I should thank you for my paychecks. It wasn't because I was problem-solving and losing my soul as ruthless white jerks squeezed more work out of fewer and fewer employees. I was called the axe lady. Where were you when I got death threats from employees I helped those companies lay off? I called you on more than one occasion, but you never took any of those calls."

"Do you hear yourself? You are hysterical. You waited until we land-ed the largest account we ever had, and then you left. No notice. Noth-ing. You are so ungrateful. No one else would have given you the role I did."

"This is about that national account? You told me you were going to hire me some help. I worked through six months of no sleep and constant stress, trying to meet the demands of what you promised that client. You way underbid that deal and...Dad, why are you here real-ly? The letter wasn't enough for you? You needed to come and attempt to humiliate me? To tell me that my paintings that are selling for over twenty thousand dollars are...You know what, Dad...I—"

"Frances, be very careful about what you say next."

"Why? It isn't like you can do anything else to me. I got it—I won't be at the same worm buffet when I die. You can all go rot together in the family crypt."

Frances turned the handle on the door and was ready to walk out, when Patrick stood and caused her to duck as he slammed the door shut.

"I'm not going to hit you. When have I ever hit you?"

"You don't remember? What is wrong with you?" Frances's tears ran down her face. She looked through her blurry, swollen eyes toward Theresa. She saw that Theresa remembered. Frances went and sat next to Theresa on the couch. "You came home one night drunk. This was shortly after Gall had died. I had lied to Mom about breaking all of Agatha's Barbie dolls. You called me down to the kitchen and asked me if I had lied. When I told you that I had and what I had done, you told me to pack my things—that there was no room for liars in the family. Then Bernard told you that I stole a candy bar from the Quik Stop. You closed your fist and hauled off and hit me so hard I fell against the counter and hit my head."

"I never did that, I never hit any of you kids. My disappointment in you was enough to keep you in line."

"No. No, Dad. I was there. We all saw it," Theresa said.

"Theresa, you decide to speak up now?" Frances was ready to scream.

"If I did that, Frances…I'm…I would never do that, and I think…that was a long time ago…I came to give you your job back."

Frances wiped her nose with her hand and searched the room for a Kleenex. Her head was pounding as her heart was shattering into pieces. She wanted to stand and run out of the room, but her legs were jelly. Did her dad just offer her job back? None of this was making any sense. *Get ahold of yourself, Frances.* Why wasn't Theresa saying anything? This was crazy. "You know, you sound absolutely crazy, Dad. My job? You are going to give me my job back?"

"There are so many things happening that you haven't been privileged to since you took your sabbatical away from the real world. I know I didn't praise you enough. I'm sorry."

"Now you're sorry? This really is…what is it? What are you not telling me? Theresa, do you know?"

"I think you should realize that Dad is here and he is offering you a place in the family company again."

"Thanks for connecting the dots for me, little sister. I am such a creative, I had no chance of doing the linear progression."

"Not nice. I've busted my butt for you, getting your paintings prepared and helping get this place set up."

Frances reached over and took Theresa's hand in hers. She was right. Her anger wasn't properly focused. The music had stopped out in the gallery. "Dad, what project are you needing help with that you would cause you to offer me my job after I've been written out of the family? What did you overpromise?"

"There is a company that is closing outside of St. Louis. You were the one who handled their acquisition. There were some very careful filings made. I need you because you would know how to close out those books."

"Continue to hide the real set of books? Dad. One of the reasons I left was the discovery of those ghost accounts. They were funneling millions of dollars out of the company. Stop. I am not having this conversation. I am not going to prison for you—"

"Sit down. Please sit down. I know there is a lot going on and I am sorry. I allowed some of this to get way out of control." Patrick covered his mouth with his hand. "I don't expect anything. I am here asking for your help. You hurt your mother…but she and I still love you."

"Strange way of showing it."

"Things will quiet down. The family is focused on the annual Fourth of July picnic and the weather is looking like it might actually be decent. I think you and Theresa should plan on coming."

"Do you think that the rest of the family will be welcoming? They all agreed with the letter. I have had no calls, no emails, and no texts from anyone in the family. The quiet is deafening. It gets the point across."

"I'll deal with the family." Patrick stood and walked to the door. "I'm going to go back to my hotel. I hope to see you in St. Louis."

The hesitation was enough to have Frances jump up and reach out to her dad. "I love you, Dad. I don't understand all of this, but I do love you."

"I love you too." Patrick stood away from Frances, avoiding her hug, and walked out the door.

Frances watched their father as he walked out of the crowded gallery. He never looked at any of the paintings. Frances gulped in the air, choking. It was a direct refusal of her and what she was doing. Frances couldn't see Nathan or Felipe through the crowd of people. She felt herself being pulled backwards by the collar of her dress.

"What the—"

"Frances, I need to help you fix your eyes. You can't go out there looking like a raccoon did your makeup. The smoky eye look is so out."

Frances saw that Theresa's face was red and her nose was running. This was not the night Frances had dreamed about. With her luck, she would walk out and run into Molly.

"Theresa, please be honest with me. Did you know that Dad—"

"No. I didn't know he was going to show up here. I talked to Mom earlier, and she thinks he is in Los Angeles dealing with a client."

"You talked with Mom?"

"Look. We need to talk. We will. Right now, you need to get out there and mingle."

Frances looked at herself in the small handheld mirror that Russell had brought into the office. "You can put lipstick on a pig, but it's still a pig."

"You are not a pig. You do look like you have been crying, but tell people it is over your art."

"The only thing I know right now is that I am alive."

CHAPTER ELEVEN
ACROSS A WORLD OF TIME

Cannery Row was quiet at 6:30 a.m. as Joshua Mills pushed his hard bristle broom across the sidewalk with short, quick strokes. He liked the quiet of the street at this time of the morning and watching the reflection of the rising sun in the windows of the Monterey Bay Aquarium across the way. A couple more pushes and he smiled with satisfaction over the neatness of his small claim to this world. The aquarium was mostly a blessing. Joshua took out a hard leather case and removed the last of his hand-rolled cigarettes. This habit was one he kept telling himself he needed to quit. "I'll quit tomorrow," he said aloud to no one. His first long draw on the smoke tickled his tongue and caused him to cough slightly. "Just a matter of time, old man...You better quit this disgusting habit."

"Talking to yourself again?"

"Hey, Alice. You're up early."

"I'm headed out in the boat to collect water samples. The grunt interns called in sick today. Wimps. I get to suck it up and play intern, recording the numbers Mel calls out while freezing in a fucking Zodiac. God, I did my time...why me?"

"You want some Dramamine with your coffee today?" Joshua asked.

"I need an espresso IV, stat. Mel's voice is so low and monotone that I'm predicting I'll be asleep in seconds. I'll have to tie myself to the boat for my own safety. During the last meeting he led, I would say half my fellow employees were asleep within five minutes."

"Exaggerate much?" Joshua handed over a giant cup bearing his stamp, an otter on its back drinking a cup of coffee, in gold ink. "Here you go—a quad Americano with a splash of half and half."

A couple more regulars had lined up behind Alice, signaling that the morning rush was upon him and the next hour would be a blur of frothing milk, pressing espresso, and listening to the local gossip. Joshua handled it all with an elegance that rivaled a dancer. His movements were quick and fluid as he produced his art.

"Hey, is there a Starbucks around here?" a tall man filling the doorway of Joshua's shop asked.

"Usual, Rick?" Joshua said, reaching over the counter to take his regular customer's mug. The running joke about asking for a Starbucks had ignited an unofficial contest with his regulars. A running tally was kept, and at the end of the week, the winner of the Starbucks pool received a free drink of their choice. "Your Starbucks does not count toward the pool. What are you down for this week?"

"Twenty-two. How am I doing?"

"Well, I don't think you are in the running—we went over thirty-six yesterday afternoon."

"How do you not throw things at these people? You are so nice."

"They usually buy something and then they become repeat customers. Not all of them. I can't help it if they ruined their coffee taste buds on chain coffee. Some people can't handle change." Joshua went back to work handling the next order.

He had started roasting his own coffee when he couldn't find the roasted blends he liked. The roasting allowed him to pump out a rich aroma to combat the strong salt brine smell coming from the bay. Sometimes the distinct smell of fish filled the street. It made Joshua wonder if the ghosts of fish could haunt Cannery Row with their smell. He did have a few customers who worked with the creatures at the aquarium. They seemed to always have a unique bouquet of rich ocean smells about them. His small barista job was a safe haven for his olfactory senses.

"Hey Joshua, don't mention you saw me this morning when my better half comes to get her chai latte today. The doc told her my blood pressure was reaching danger levels. I tried to explain to him and to her it had nothing to do with my diet and everything to do with having two teenagers each testing me in special ways. I need to sue that guy for violating my privacy. There is no more butter, bacon, or red meat in the house. The dog placed an ad on Craigslist looking for a carnivore family to adopt him."

"Rick, don't be making me an accomplice to a caffeine junkie." Joshua laughed and excused himself to go retrieve some more coffee beans.

"I have a feeling you might be joining the dog. Don't look now, but here comes your better half."

Joshua went into his back room to escape the coming verbal storm. He was not going to get into the middle of that one. Life was definitely fun on Cannery Row. When he felt enough minutes had passed to keep him out of the fray for aiding and abetting in a caffeine junkie's fix, Joshua came out to greet the next customer in line. What he was not prepared for was the woman standing three customers deep. The sight of her red hair and beautiful green eyes hit him square in the chest.

"What the hell?" Joshua said and recovered his muscle movement, hoisting himself over the counter with the swift ease of a gymnast. His heart was beating so hard and so fast he hoped his chest wall would contain it. He embraced Frances and held her tightly—he never wanted to let her go. This was bigger than winning the lottery for him. There were so many nights when he thought about how a reunion might happen. This was not one of the scenarios.

"Hi. I think I know you. Wait." Frances shook her head, looking at him with doubt in her eyes and then a dawning recognition. "Yeah. Um, this is my sister, Theresa," she said, taking a step back from him.

Joshua couldn't take his eyes off her. He knew he had opened a door into the past. He had not calculated that Frances would walk through the door so quickly. Words escaped him, and he pulled Frances into a second hug. The murmurs of his customers started to get louder. "I've got some coffee to serve. Hang on…don't go anywhere…I can't believe this. You can call me Joshua." Joshua was back over on the other side of the counter handling the next order in record speed.

"Well, you have some explaining to do," Theresa said.

"What?"

"You conned me into riding over here to deliver a painting. You said nothing of meeting up with an old flame?"

" Jen . . . I mean Joshua . . . is not . . . it isn't like that. We met in college."

"Why am I not remembering this Joshua person? With a reception like that, you'd think I would have heard about him," Theresa said.

"You were young and into your own life. I think your memory is going," Frances said.

"He must sell a lot of coffee and get great tips to pay for the painting he bought."

"For a girl who claims material items and money are not central to her life, you seem to focus on it quite a bit. Joshua comes from a different kind of family. My guess is he has been able to utilize his trust monies. Not to mention that he is selling a cup of brown liquid with some sugar flavoring for six bucks a cup—one heck of a mark-up."

"Yeah. There's something here you aren't telling me. A silver-spoon baby, who buys one of your most expensive paintings and happens to live less than two hours away from San Francisco, give or take traffic, gives you a hug that to me suggests you two know each other really well. And yet I've never heard you mention his name."

"Okay, Detective Kavanagh, I think you need to stop hanging out so much with Molly Woods. Only friends. That's it. Nothing to share here."

When they reached the front of the line, Joshua asked, "What can I get you two? Or do you trust me to come up with a special for you? Welcome to Find Your Porpoise Fine Coffee and Teas."

"Are you serious? That is the name of this place? He's lucky he has a trust fund."

"Theresa, don't be rude. Sorry, Joshua. It is . . . well, I'm in a little bit of shock."

"Shh . . . no one around here knows that my baby shoes were twenty-four karat gold. I'm making your drinks. Wow, I still can't believe you are standing here. This is one heck of a roller coaster morning."

"All arms are to remain inside the car during the ride," Frances added.

Joshua smiled. She had not forgotten their inside joke after all these years. He had to take a couple of deep breaths. As he was steaming the milk for the specialty coffees he was creating for Frances and her equally beautiful sister, he glanced out to the street and noticed a white truck with a huge crate in the bed. "Would that be the painting purchased from Frances O. Kavanagh's gallery show?"

"What powers of observation you have. Yes."

"Do artists always deliver their own work?" Joshua noticed his hand was shaking as he poured the homemade caramel syrup into the cup. He turned his back to hide the fact he was visibly shaking. To add more distraction, he hit the power button on his sound system. The voice of Nadia Reid filled the small shop with beauty and clarity as she sang about coming home to you. "I didn't have that cued up."

"What? What are you talking about?" Frances asked.

"The singer. I love her work. I got turned on to her by a friend who spent time in New Zealand studying plankton. She's singing about coming home to people she loves…or at least that is how I hear the song."

"You make coffee and interpret music. Is there anything you don't do?" Theresa asked.

"Windows. I don't wash windows. Try this." Joshua set two steaming cups of art in front of Frances and Theresa. In the milk froth of Frances's, he had made a silhouette of a sea horse, and in Theresa's, he had poured a shape that looked very much like the turd emoji.

"Is it safe to drink? You left a pile of shit in my milk."

"Theresa."

"Well, he did. Look at it. You get a sea horse, and I get a pile of poop."

"Safe to drink. You are having a hazelnut caramel coffee and, Frances, I made you a dark chocolate and cherry mocha." Joshua motioned them over to a small side counter. He helped Frances up onto the bar stool by easily lifting her. "I've got to take care of the next few orders. This way, we can talk while I work."

"No, Frances, you don't know him well at all. I almost feel like I need to tell you to go get a hotel room," Theresa said and slowly took a tentative sip of the coffee. "Okay, this is actually freakin' good."

"Glad you like it. My relief will be here in about fifteen minutes. Can you hang out? Want a pastry or muffin?"

"I'm good," Theresa said. "I don't know what you'd give me."

"Thanks, Joshua. We'll stay out of your way. Theresa, why are you being such a—"

"Don't say the b-word."

"You are acting so rudely that you are pushing me further down the alphabet, and I am thinking a c-word."

"Ouch. I'm serious. What's the story on this guy? Is he married?"

"I don't know."

"When you say trust fund, are we talking top one percent?"

"Theresa, I really don't know, but his family did have several very successful lumber mills and manufacturing plants."

"Top one percent. I wondered what a person like that looked like. He's got a very unusual handsome beauty about him."

Joshua stole glances at the two Kavanagh sisters when he had a chance. His heart had not slowed down. There was something else going on, and he wasn't quite sure what to think. There were two beautiful women. One a crush from college, and now that crush brings her younger sister, a woman with fire. He had received a call from his accountant, telling him that he should invest in a new artist being shown by a friend of his. When Joshua had learned the artist was Frances, he had said no. It took him two days to return his accountant's call.

He went to the gallery website and looked at a preview of the paintings. Opening night, he had arrived and stood outside. Joshua saw the painting *Ocean Deep* and fell in love. He called his accountant, who was inside the gallery, and instructed him to purchase that painting but not give his last name to the artist. They put the painting under the name of the new restaurant he was opening at the other end of the street. He paused between pouring coffees to wipe his sweating hands on the white but well-stained apron he had tied around his waist. A glance at the clock showed that his worker bees would be arriving, so he could go work on his restaurant. It was clear that Frances had figured out who had purchased her painting. She was here, with the painting, and had walked through the door. What did he do now?

Joshua stopped and looked at Frances. Their eyes met, and he noticed she did not flinch, did not turn away. Instead, she smiled. Her eyes were so green and bright this morning. Her red curls were trained into a beautiful cascade around her freckled face. Frances had a timeless beauty that still made Joshua's heart dance in chaotic rhythms. It was hard to realize the dream was now sitting in his place, sipping a coffee. This reality was crazy. It was magic. What was he going to do about it now? Andra Day's song "The Only Way Out" filled his shop. Joshua looked to the world out the door. He was no longer in the cage he was in when Frances and he first met. Fast forward, and he had opened the door to Frances again, proud of what he had done for himself. It was the only way for him to live a moment longer on this earth. He had to trust that Frances, the woman who painted the painting that captured him from the sidewalk, would understand and not question or expect a detailed explanation of every gory detail. The smile she had on her face, the relaxed way she sat in his shop. Frances was displaying a beautiful forgiveness, and Joshua needed to let go and let it play out.

CHAPTER TWELVE
CONTROLLED DISASTER

Molly pulled her car up to the gated garage entry and typed in the code Lucy had written in giant numbers on the top of the folder.

"Do you think she is trying to tell me something?" Molly laughed and handed the folder to Todd, who was riding shotgun this time around.

"I can't believe this part of the case is almost done. I expected the money laundering to take us more than a year to wade through," Todd said.

"We have Winter to thank for a huge chunk of the evidence that led us to the money."

"It kept her out of prison. I have to tip my hat to her. She owned her criminal responsibilities." Todd failed to notice the concrete pillar and slammed the passenger door into it. "Sorry. I'm sure that's going...yup there's white paint on the concrete now."

"No worries. It isn't my car. Did you see what Mark did to his cruiser last week?"

"Heard about it. I also heard that he was getting a desk job. That was his fourth cruiser to be totaled in six months."

"Why are we here again?"

"We are here to go over her interviews about how well she knew Ethan. The DA also asked us to have Winter sign these papers."

"Are you dating that prosecutor?"

"Not discussing my dating life with you." Molly smiled at Todd as they waited for the elevator.

"You hear about my marriage all the time. Throw me a bone. Lucy said something about you possibly dating a local painter?"

"What part of 'not discussing my dating life' did you not understand? Was it the word *not*? I don't ask you questions about your family. You talk and I am trapped."

"Lucky I like you."

Molly knocked on Winter's door and looked down at the transcript from Winter's interviews. She had been over and over these, but a couple of things were still giving her pause. No sounds came from the condo, and so Molly knocked again. "Lucy said she was here and waiting for us."

"Maybe she's in the bathroom. When my wife was pregnant, I think she peed every twenty minutes. Those babies were brutal on her bladder."

"TMI," Molly said and knocked again, this time a little louder.

"You needed to say my name after each knock—I'm hooked on *The Big Bang Theory*," Winter said as she opened the door. "I was stuck on the couch."

"Are you saying I'm robotic, like Sheldon?" Molly asked.

Molly followed Winter into the living room and noticed the couch. "I think I'd have trouble standing up from that even without being pregnant. That is one sleek, low rider of a couch."

"Would either of you care for any coffee? Water?"

"Nope. I'm fine."

"Me too," Todd said as he started to pick up random shoes and socks scattered around the chair he sat in.

"I was trying to get some shoes and socks on, but with this hard belly, my feet have been missing. I can't reach them. Once I drop a shoe or sock, it is lost to me."

"That is why slip on shoes work so well," Todd said. "Learned from my wife. She had similar issues. We replaced our couch too."

Molly watched Winter as she sat on her sofa and gently rubbed her pregnant belly, tears trickling down her face. The floor, from the bedroom to her media room, was littered with the lifeless carcasses of socks and shoes. They lay where they fell. A television news anchor was smiling on the television as he bantered unconvincingly with his co-anchor. Molly took the controller and pressed the mute button. She sat down on the couch and handed the packet of papers from the prosecutor to Winter.

"I had a dream that I was holding my daughter. We were outside, in a park, and I was laughing," Winter said, taking the papers. "Please don't think of me as a bad person."

"Winter…we are not here judging you. Because of you, we were able to take this whole ring down," Molly said.

"My attorney told me to sign the papers and then all of this would be over. No jail. That was the deal maker. I have no clue what I'm going to do now. My suspended law license…well, I won't be practicing law in this life again."

Molly glanced at Todd. This was not going to be as easy as she had thought.

Todd stood and walked over to hand the papers to a teary, pregnant woman. "Winter, we will make sure these papers are hand delivered. You didn't back down from rather powerful men. That takes courage."

Winter flipped through the papers, signing in a few places. "Now that's done. I sealed my fate when I set up those offshore shell companies. What can I help you with? I'm afraid my memory is rather suspect with all these hormones."

"We have a couple questions about your interactions with Ethan. I know there was a lot going on—"

"Are you guys working on those horrid serial killings happening now?"

Molly shot Todd a quick look. She had not talked to anyone about what she was working on except her uncle. The crew at the Buena Vista had tried to get her to talk, but she was good at dodging questions and changing the subject.

"Winter, we are always working on cases," Todd said. "Do you remember telling us that you had a crush on Ethan and were upset over the fact that he liked Frances?"

"I said that? Really? Like I said, my memory...I don't think I've ever been jealous of Frances. But I did find Ethan attractive. He was a tall, skinny Johnny Depp. There was some strange stuff going on between him, Emily, and Frances."

"Yes. We are aware of that triangle. Do you remember when you first saw Ethan standing in the street with the gun?"

"That I remember. I don't think I could ever erase seeing him holding that gun."

"Did you see anyone else on the street?" Molly asked.

"No. I don't think there was anyone else on the street. I only saw him. It all happened so fast."

Molly handed Winter a still shot taken from the security camera on the building. "Do you remember seeing this guy standing by Ethan's car?"

They watched as Winter studied the black-and-white photo. "I don't. My focus was completely on Ethan and that gun." Winter's hands were shaking.

"We have a better picture of that person. Do you know who this is?"

"He kind of looks like Ethan. Same nose—kind of makes me think of that cartoon character . . . you know...Sleepy Hollow—"

"Ichabod Crane?"

"Yeah. That lanky tall body and giant nose. I feel like I know this guy, but I don't."

"Well, you are close. That is Ethan's younger brother, Gabriel."

"He had a younger brother?"

"That answers our question. You didn't know he had a younger brother?"

"No. Why was he there?" Winter asked.

"That is what we are working on finding out. There was so much to go through in attempting to identify all of Ethan's victims, and this came to light about a week ago. Thanks for your help."

"I don't think I was much help. But that is so strange. Did Frances or Cheryl see him?"

"No. The only one who knew he was Ethan's brother was Emily."

"That makes sense. She grew up with him."

"We will get those signed papers back to the prosecutor. You have your copy. We need to go. Is there anything else we can do for you?"

"That's it?" Winter asked.

Molly struggled to stand up from the low designer sofa and dropped her folder of loose papers and photos. "This is a new kind of core workout. Todd, you can stop snickering."

"Would you mind collecting those socks as long as you're picking up? The socks are clean," Winter said through her own giggles.

Molly set her mess of papers on the coffee table as she collected the lost socks and shoes that documented Winter's failed attempts to get them onto her hidden feet.

"Why is Frances's teacup in this picture? It is the most unusual teacup I've ever used. I'm sure that is her teacup." Winter picked up a photo that was a close-up of a teacup filled with a dark red, almost black liquid and a disturbing-looking white hand holding it.

"Frances's teacup?" Molly asked, walking back over to Winter and deciding not to sit again.

"Like I said, I would never forget it. I'm sure that's her teacup. One doesn't forget a teacup and saucer that depicts the *Tale of Genji* with gold highlights."

"*Tale of Genji*? What other random pieces of information do you have?" Todd asked.

"I studied Japanese political economics in college. I was forced to take literature classes, and so I took a Jap Lit course. The class I thought I would hate turned out to be my favorite. Might have had something to do with the professor. He was hot."

"You know, where I come from, *Jap* means Jewish American Princess."

"Todd, where are you from again?"

"Jersey. The West Coast has taken the edge off my accent, but a week back with the family and I'm back to full-throttle Jersey boy."

"Back to the cup. Are you sure this is Frances's cup? Do you remember where you saw this?" Molly was wracking her brain for any details from the inventory made in Frances's loft during the investigation. She pulled out her phone to send a message to Lucy.

Please pull the inventory sheet and pictures taken of Frances Kavanagh's loft the night of the incident and keep this quiet.

"She was using it at that funky fire trap of a studio before she got her loft. I remember hanging out with her and she made me a Long Island Iced Tea, hold the ice and any form of water. That girl can make a strong drink."

"That counts as a form of tea? I'm still surprised you would remember the cup," Molly said.

"It had such an elegant feeling. The artwork was so detailed. When I looked at the cup and the saucer, it reminded me of *emaki-mono*—Japanese scroll art, maybe the first form of Japanese anime. It was the green background and the depiction of a scene inside a house. The roof is taken off, and you are like a god peeking into the daily life of the people. That was what was on the cup. I had never seen anything like it on a dish before. Made it much more interesting than just a cup."

"Did you ask Frances about the cup?"

"I'm sorry. I don't think I remember it coming up. At the time, we were probably talking about her ex-husband, Richard the dickhead."

"Winter, you have quite the explanation. You don't think you asked her where she got the cup? I am…the last time you saw that cup was at her painting studio?"

"Let me see the picture again." Winter studied the picture. "Wait…I don't think this is her cup. The colors aren't right, but this is definitely the same style, and those are scenes from the story. Help me up." Winter put her hands out, and Todd easily helped Winter out of the couch. "Excuse my waddle—life is not the same with the extra forty pounds around my stomach."

Molly finished getting the file back together and felt her phone vibrate.

The info is locked in your left top drawer. Anything else?

Molly thought about it and added, *Find an expert in Japanese porcelain and The Tale of Genji.*

Lucy shot back, *Cryptic and exciting—I am feeling like you have a break in the wall.*

Thank god, Lucy was not into using emojis, Molly thought, watching as Winter rummaged through her bookshelf. "I had no clue you had a whole second row behind the pretty books."

"Books are an addiction, and the architect came up with the idea for deep shelves as space was an issue. If I had a loft, it would look like a library. My storage space is filled with book boxes. I can't get rid of them."

"Can I help you look for something?" Molly asked.

"Nope. I'm close because I am in my college textbook section. Here it is." Winter walked over with a dog-eared paperback. "This is my copy of the first Japanese comic book."

Molly flipped through the color pages depicting *The Tale of Genji* scroll and saw the resemblance in the images. She walked over to the photograph and felt a tingle jump through her body as they now had a break. What it meant was confusing. "Can I borrow this book?"

"Sure. I won't need it for an hour."

Molly looked up and tilted her head.

"I'm kidding. I was being sarcastic."

"Thanks. I promise to get this back to you when we are done. Listen, I know you are close friends with Frances. Would you mind not mentioning the teacup to anyone? That photo was not supposed to be in that folder, and it is part of another case."

"I figured it had something to do with the serial murders. Your secret is safe with me. I feel it's a little odd because you are part of the crew that busted me...but I do owe you because without your strong testimony, I would most likely be having this baby in prison."

"That credit is undeserved. It was the FBI that really strong-armed the federal prosecutors. I'll see you at the BV?"

"Unless the baby decides to come, I'll be there."

Molly and Todd were silent on the elevator ride back to the car. Her mind was going a thousand different directions, and she was trying to slow it down. This was so complicated, and it was important not to jump to conclusions. A new fear reared up in her mind. What if the killer had...no, it was too random. There had to be many sets of those dishes based on the scroll.

"Starbucks for your thoughts," Todd said as they got into the car.

"Sorry."

"It might mean that those dishes were mass produced, and it is a shopping coincidence and nothing more," Todd added.

"We first noticed those strange plates in the pictures from those Beach Blanket murders, and now the teacups are showing up in the last two murder scenes. Lucy is an excellent researcher, and she had not come up with anything even close to those cups. She's gone through some of the best experts on china, and we get a connection by accident? A connection that has my blood running cold."

"Care to elaborate? I think we need to go back through the documented photos of all the murder scenes in the recent weeks. We might have missed the clues," Todd added. "I was serious about the Starbucks. My treat."

"I have a better idea. Let's stop at Andytown Coffee Roasters and then swing by my Uncle Henry's. I need to pick up a file."

"Never been . . ."

"You are in for a real treat. You have to try the Snowy Plover—they combine espresso and Pellegrino with brown sugar and whipped cream."

"I'm seeing a particular taste profile."

"True. It is similar to an Irish coffee, hold the whisky. We are on duty."

"Tell me more about Uncle Henry. We are out of the office. Spill the beans," Todd said.

"My uncle is starting to open up about what happened when they solved the case of the serial killer who left his victims on beach blankets. The similarities of some of what I was sharing with him over what we are finding caused him to . . . I don't know how to explain it. I thought he was having flashbacks or something. Then he leveled with me and said he had to talk to me but wasn't sure he could."

"Now if that doesn't make one curious."

"Tell me about it. I wonder what this identification of the china from Winter will jog in Uncle Henry's mind."

"Okay. You get to pick the coffee every time. This is my new addiction. Let's go shake down Uncle Henry for some advice," Todd said.

"Now let me do the talking. We don't want to spook my uncle."

CHAPTER THIRTEEN

JOSHUA'S OTTER PLACE

F rances stood on the sidewalk across from the Monterey Bay Aquarium and watched a bus release a herd of tourists into the front doors. This would not be the time to visit. Another large bus was idling behind that one, and the diesel fumes were quickly replacing any breathable air. Frances turned back to see Joshua talking to a young woman who was now working behind the counter. Theresa followed Joshua out onto the sidewalk. Frances couldn't stop studying his face. The light blonde peach fuzz stubble on his chin took her gaze down to his well chiseled chest, highlighted by the tight black T-shirt he was wearing. His biceps and forearms rippled, making his tattoos appear animated.

"You know, it's not nice to stare. Didn't your mother ever teach you that one?" Joshua asked.

Frances turned away, walked over to the bed of her truck, and looked at the giant wooden crate they had tied down with more ropes than were needed. There were so many questions running through her mind. When did he take the steps to…? She saw the rugged beauty in Joshua's form and wondered why she was feeling like she was mourning her friend. There he was, smiling and strong, right in front of her.

Was it that easy? Could they fall back into the friendship they had in college?

"I'm still in shock—don't take my calm exterior to mean I am hunky dory with everything. You might have been the inventor of ghosting, you know?" Frances walked over and punched Joshua lightly in his stomach. "Shit. That is rock hard."

"I work out. I can't apologize. It was a different world and a different time. I was so different."

"That's an understatement." Frances crossed her arms, looking at the crate. "This thing is a beast. It took three guys to get it into the truck. Do you have any help available?"

"Possibly. Drive it down the street to the corner. I'm putting this into my new restaurant, Joshua's Otter Place."

Theresa said, "I'm seeing a theme. Maybe you might want to spend some money with a marketing and branding firm to come up with a name that doesn't scream—"

"Theresa, no thoughts on his horrid naming scheme." Frances climbed into her truck and turned the key in the ignition. She watched as Joshua and Theresa walked down the street. What was wrong with her sister? Theresa had a snarky side, but this was getting downright rude. Did she sense that Joshua was new to this world? How long had he been here?

"Pull up right here, Frances," Joshua said, directing her to double-park on the side street next to his restaurant. Butcher paper covered the windows, blocking any views of the interior.

The streets were getting busy with tourists, and Frances decided to direct her sister to sit in the driver's seat. If anyone came up, that girl could sweet talk her way through it. It also gave Frances a chance to be alone with Joshua. "Stay in the truck. Don't move."

"I understand. I'm turning the radio to a station that plays something other than elevator music," Theresa said.

Frances turned and followed Joshua through the open corner door into Joshua's Otter Place. The smell of fresh paint and shellac filled the air. A couple of workers could be heard in the kitchen area of the building. A giant carved redwood bar captured her gaze. Jellyfish, sharks, otters, dolphins, and a huge whale swam through the base of the bar.

The carvings were amazing. Frances walked over and gently reached out to trace the detail of the bar.

"Quite the piece of art...it was part of this place when I bought the building. Took some serious elbow grease to restore it. Someone had painted it black and white."

"Crazy."

"Are you going to ask?"

"Do you want me to ask? I really don't know what to do. This is a first for me," Frances said.

"Thanks for sticking Theresa in the truck. I—"

"Why did you buy my painting?"

"Interesting. Not the question I thought you were going to ask."

"We need to get the painting in here so we aren't blocking the road." Frances walked toward the door. "Maybe if I wasn't so shocked. Does anyone around here know what you were?"

"Frances, don't do this. I bought the painting because I fell in love with it and I knew...I never stopped—"

"Joshua, don't say it. There is so much...you disappeared. You didn't even leave a note. No phone calls. You buy my most expensive painting and think that erases everything." Frances flushed hot, and fists balled in her pockets. Her anger tasted good, and she was having a hard time understanding that anger. Joshua expected too much from her. "Can we take care of the painting?"

Frances watched as Joshua gave some instructions to the workers who were putting in the finishing touches on his huge and very shiny kitchen. She wiped her hands on her jeans, shaking them out while thinking about the last time they she had seen him. His shoulders were so broad, his jawline so pronounced and strong. His eyes were the same and they sparkled. Stop it, Frances told herself. This is not going to happen.

"They will take it out of the crate outside. Don't worry. I told them to talk to the girl in the truck. Theresa will watch them. Now come and sit down."

"Where are you going to hang the painting?"

"Isn't it obvious? Over that fireplace." Joshua pointed to the wall behind him.

"It will…honestly, I didn't want to sell that painting, and it was the first one to sell. I thought this old man bought it. When I saw you standing behind the counter of the address that was given . . ."

"You freaked out? I'm surprised you recognized me."

"Joshua…I was in love with you when you were…you were my first true crush, and I hated myself for it. I never told anyone. What happened?"

"Frances, I was always Joshua. When we met in college, I was trying to play a role that everyone told me I had to play, but I knew it wasn't right."

"When did you know?"

"That is a loaded question because I still am working on this. Life is a journey."

Frances reached out for his hand. There was a gentleness about his strong hands. She turned them over and studied his palms. They were rough and calloused but still held an elegance that she recognized. Frances touched his forearm and then placed a hand on his chest. When Joshua covered her hand with his, she felt his heart beating underneath his flat chest. "Did it hurt? The transition?"

"Surgery was physically painful but emotionally freeing…how much time do we have?"

"I don't know. I'm not the same person you met in college."

"Nor am I."

"Where's the painting going?" Theresa asked. "Am I interrupting something? Frances are you going straight on me?"

"Jesus H. Christ in the mountains, will you drop the attitude? Who pissed in your Cheerios this morning?" Frances removed her hands from Joshua.

"Good morning, Dana. Frances pissed in my cereal this morning. I'm coming close to having to deal with Aunt Flo, and it's fierce. On the nice sister side, the painting is free and it looks amazing in the sunlight. I had no clue you put so many colors into it."

"That's why I fell in love with it. That gallery owner knew how to light the painting," Joshua said.

"You were at the opening?" Frances asked.

"I stayed outside. I had my accountant do the business side of the work. The guy running the door finally chased me away."

"You could've come in."

"I wasn't quite ready. And I didn't want to…it was your night, Frances."

"Some night. My dad crashed the party."

"What? I figured the whole Kavanagh mafia would be there. I remember when they dropped you off for your freshman year. That was a circus."

"Not going to go into the drama. Let's get this painting up."

Frances walked out to view her painting in the sunlight. A couple of people had stopped on the sidewalk to look at the giant painting that four men were now holding in the middle of the street. Frances knew she was going to lose the battle, and the tears started to fall. This painting was more a part of her than she wanted to share. Joshua placed a hand on her shoulder, and she covered his hand with hers and snuggled into his side. "I'm glad she's here with you."

"Are you bothered by my change?"

"I'm mourning and confused. *Bothered* isn't…I'm a little in shock because I see you and it feels so right. All of this feels so amazing. I am truly happy for you." Frances turned to Joshua and kissed him on his cheek. "Let's go see how she looks holding watch over your dining room."

CHAPTER FOURTEEN

WARRIOR DAUGHTER

F rances stood in front of the giant white canvas with a strange anger pulsing through her veins. It had been more than a week since she watched her father walk out of the gallery and not look back. The whole surreal experience sent her back to reading the letter over and over. There was something she was missing. She had read through the whole will and focused on the absence of her name in the estate papers. The dog was to be left a gift of twenty thousand. The dog was hated by her parents. It was a pug mix that Bernard had picked up and decided he didn't want, so he gave it to their parents. Theresa was still in the line of succession of inheritance. Frances tried to understand the difference, but now she was exploding with confusion and anger. What was the difference? Theresa was in a relationship with a woman. Frances was single and not flaunting anything.

Why was she always at odds with her family? Frances pulled out a couple tubes of paint, squeezing the colors onto her clean glass mixing plate. She dipped her brush into a small dish of mineral spirits and worked the wet bristles into mixing the gray with indigo blue. Frances wanted to thin the paint enough to remove the brush strokes. A flat watery finish was a match for her emotions.

Her brush loaded with the thinned dark paint took on the power of her anger. She stood to the left of the canvas and placed her brush three quarters of the way up and pulled the brush across the canvas in a quick jagged horizontal line. The thinned paint dripped down the canvas, each teardrop of muddied blue paint in a race with the next one to reach the bottom. The painter's tarp stretched under the canvas collected the drops, forming reflective pools. Frances quickly took the canvas off the easel and laid it on the floor. With gravity no longer working to pull the paint, she let the paint pool on various spots under the jagged line.

Frances ran over to her shelf of gathered materials and pulled out a box that contained some broken pieces of glassware, smashed wine bottles, and china. These were leftovers from her divorce. The sharp edges taunted her. She glanced over her shoulder at the exposed canvas. The image of the family texts on Theresa's phone cut into her, and Frances carried the dangerous box to her painting. She knelt down next to the painting and caressed the smooth white canvas with the tips of her fingers. She pulled out some matte molding agent that she had used with a different project and painted several lines in a chaotic unplanned design on the canvas. In one motion, she stood and grabbed the box with the remnants of broken pieces that represented her heart and shook it over the painting like she was seeding a new lawn. The sharp angles of the blue and green glass and china made the painting turn from flat smoothness to a possible weapon.

Frances stepped back and gasped. In the mix of broken pieces was the tea cup and saucer that Ethan had given her when she first moved into the artist studio near his. She had forgotten about that cup and the story that had come with it. It had broken during her move into the loft, and she had hidden it from Ethan. Frances ran to her bathroom, where she lost her lunch.

She decided to let this process sit for a while and grabbed a jacket as she walked out the door. She left the building without a destination in mind. Frances walked toward the bus stop and kept walking. Her breath was fast and shallow as she played back in her mind the conversation in which Theresa told her she was going to fix the family. But Ethan was walking with her. He was chasing her down the road. Why had she kept that stupid teacup? What did Theresa gain in lying to

Frances? Her thoughts were mixed up and crazy. Frances stopped and took a deep breath. A strength that Frances had not recognized before was fueling her, and she could not completely identify it. Her artwork was actually selling. Could that explain the surge in confidence? It had been too long since she had done anything close to spontaneous and fun. She pulled out her phone and acted in a moment of pure power as she hit Molly's name on her phone.

"What a surprise," Molly said when she answered her phone. "I was thinking about you. There is something I need to follow up on, and I was wondering if you were available?"

"Sure. You know the life of an artist…we have those flexible schedules unless the muse is with us. But I was calling to see if that offer to do paintball was still open?"

"Always. But I thought you were against guns of any kind. You know paintball uses a weapon?"

"I know. Cheryl and Theresa had said they wanted to come when we went. What's your schedule look like?"

"If I looked at my schedule, we would be going in 2075 and using walkers, canes, and oxygen. However, maybe I could squeeze in some official police work and then take the rest of the day for mental sanity."

"I'm game. Speak for yourself over the walker business. Where was the place you said was fun?"

"Fun is relative. It is east, out toward Livermore. Hang on a second."

Frances stopped walking and leaned against a building as she waited. The people and car traffic was increasing, and Frances realized that she had walked farther and longer than she had planned. She might Lyft it back to her loft.

"What about tomorrow?" Molly asked.

"Perfect."

"It's a work day for most normal people, but I need a break. Do you think Cheryl can take the time?"

"I'll ply her with the thought of fresh air. She's still having stinky office issues."

"Frances, are you okay?"

"Never been better. Should we go together? Or do you want to meet there?"

"If we use your truck we can all go in one car. Pick me up. Do you think Winter would want to join us?" Molly asked.

"Right…a pregnant woman…nope. I'll look for your email with your address and get the troops ready."

Frances turned and thought about walking back to her loft and then got a craving for Jay's Philly Cheesesteak and ordered herself up a Lyft. It was time to enjoy this city, and tomorrow she could get out some of her anger without being arrested for it.

CHAPTER FIFTEEN
DIFFICULT CONVERSATIONS PAIR WELL WITH CAKE

"How is the latest star of the fine arts world doing?" Simon asked as he hugged Frances.

"Stressed and processing."

"Traffic was rough...Russell said he might be delayed due to the cracks in the floor he must avoid between our door and yours."

"Funny. I want to laugh but that shtick is getting old." Frances walked to her Cookie Monster chaise lounge and sat down, pulling the blanket arms around herself. She watched Theresa in the kitchen pour some hot water in the tea kettle. What Frances tried to figure out as she watched Theresa was how much her little sister was sharing with the family about what was going down. Did she share with them that Frances had continued to date women? Was she even telling them the truth? Frances knew Theresa was lying to her.

"Simon, can I pour you a cup of tea?" Theresa asked.

"I think I'm okay right now. What's new with you?"

"Not much. Did Frances tell you about making a paintball date with Molly?"

"What? No! Who goes on a date to shoot at people with paint? I've heard of people going to painting parties where you paint one another and then roll around on a white sheet or something like that…makes for interesting times."

"Sounds messy. I like to stay clothed around paint. You know, most paint is toxic," Frances said.

"Is that why so many painters go crazy?"

"Could be…many used to keep their paint brushes wet and pliant by holding the bristle part in their mouth. I think they might have gotten high off of the minerals in the paint."

"Frances, I didn't know you were Google. Most strange set of knowledge," Simon said.

"Not strange. It might explain why Frances is—"

"Watch yourself, little sister." Frances rolled her eyes as Theresa's words registered in her brain. She felt like she was going to explode. Part of her wished she had Russell and Simon completely to herself. They kept putting off the celebration of her selling her show out. Now she wanted to chat about everything and nothing—Joshua, paintball, her newfound confidence, and the growing canyon between her and Theresa. She knew that both Simon and Russell had counseled many gay people through the rough transition of being cast out of all they had known previously.

"Hi, all," Russell said as he came in carrying a beautifully wrapped gold package.

"Is that what I think it is?" Frances pushed herself up and walked over to the kitchen shelf and pulled down four plates.

"Only your favorite. I went to Emporio Rulli. Glad this all worked out as I was working with a group up in Larkspur. I need to do more work for them because this place is addictive and only two doors down from their office. I finished off two mini fruit tarts on the drive home."

"Russell, you spoil me," Frances said and kissed him on the cheek.

"Sweet woman, don't think this is all about you." Russell winked. "But I do know how to get you to smile when all else fails—feed you a Primavera from Rulli's."

"What's that?" Theresa asked.

"It is only the most amazing dessert in the area. It is a chewy pistachio mascarpone cream cake topped with the sweetest fresh raspberries. I don't know how they came up with it, but each bite is like eating pure happiness."

Simon said, "Pure happiness? Come down from those heights of fancy to the real world. There is no chocolate in that dessert, so I will agree to disagree with you. The most decadent dessert is the hot fudge sundae."

"You are all wrong. The best dessert is a slice of true New York cheesecake from Junior's after the best Broadway play you've ever seen," Theresa said as she took her tea over to the sofa.

"Not going to get into it. This is the one, and you'll soon join me in the cult after your first bite," Russell said as he unwrapped the gold foil, exposing the Primavera. Powdered sugar topped each one of the raspberries with a cap of pure white. "I saw Frances's smile. How big shall I cut your piece, Franny?"

Frances held her hands up to form a wedge of about two inches at its widest point. She watched as Russell complied and carved out the first triangle piece from the round cake. Frances accepted it with careful grace so as not to knock any of the powdered sugar hats off the raspberries. She carefully pulled the prongs of her fork along the soft side of her piece and tickled her tongue with the taste. "It is better than ever."

"Well, our sweet sisters, we are here celebrating the conquering of the art scene with Franny. More importantly, how can Russell and I help you with the family drama? Have you heard from your dad after he sucker punched you at your gallery show?"

"I haven't heard from him. I don't know about Theresa."

"If you two haven't noticed…Frances is treating me like a traitor. I am not a traitor—I am more like an ambassador between her and the family."

"I don't know…you seem to have kept yourself placed pretty well in the family, and I am on the outside looking in without any sign of that changing. What do you expect me to think?" Frances took another large bite of the pistachio cloud heaven. Frances felt her anger flash through her brain as she knew that Theresa was speaking for herself. "The silence is the hardest thing for me right now. I went from a constant stream of communication to nothing. It is unreal. Although I might be getting used to it."

"I've heard people say that treating the banishment like a death helped them move through it," Russell said through a mouthful of cake.

"But that would mean the death of more people than I care to count."

"Frances, I'm sorry. You misunderstood."

"Russell, let me tackle this one. What Russell meant to say is that you are no longer the Frances your family members identify as who they believed you to be. In essence, you have killed that person to them. We will focus on you, Frances, as Theresa is in a different situation, and I suspect I might know why. But we will get back to that."

"I feel more alive than ever," Frances said.

"True. I got that feeling too when I came out of the closet. No more lying to yourself and that whole nine yards. What I'm trying to say is you treat it not as the death of your family members but of the old Frances, the girl who was in the closet, so to speak."

"My own death?"

"It isn't as morbid as it sounds. Think of it as more of a rising out of the darkness. Those people who truly love you will not be burned by your bright new spectrum of light and illumination. They will help you keep the energy that is fueling this light of yours. Those who fear your new light may try to put it out, but what usually happens is they go find their need for darkness somewhere else."

"You make it sound so simple," Theresa said and spit the bite of pistachio cake into a napkin. "I am not liking this cake. It has a strange flavor. Frances, why do you feel the need to be out of the closet?"

"I can't believe you are asking that question. You're the one who outed me."

"Not really. The situation with Ethan and Emily and the national news outed you."

"Theresa, you might need to take some responsibility for being the one who broke the news directly to the family," Simon said. "The other thing we need to work on are your taste buds…this cake is far from strange."

"Don't bother, Simon. She is a gooey butter cake, Jell-O-eating, Midwestern girl," Frances said, reaching over to capture the piece of rejected cake. "What if our parents never speak to me again? I don't know how... Theresa, are you back in the closet?"

"I'm not stupid, Frances. You already have your life plotted out and planned. Mom and Dad love us, and is it so hard for you to hide parts of yourself? You grew up doing it. Why be so out now? Apologize and tell them it was a mistake. They'll take you back."

Frances set down the plate and then her fork. She stood, folded her arms, and took a couple of deep breaths. "So did you tell Kelly that you are no longer gay?"

"No, I'm back in the closet. It doesn't mean I'm straight. It means I don't bring it up around the family."

"Russell and I have both seen families come to an understanding as everyone processes the changes. This is not easy for them either. Theresa is not the first person we've known who has measured the pain of being in the closet versus the loss of family. It is a choice that each person has to make."

"But Simon, I am... Theresa, you manipulate the situation to get whatever is best for you. Don't you think your lies... How can my family justify this? How do you live with yourself?"

"You know, if we could explain why people react in such hurtful ways, we would be multi-trillionaires. There are no answers. This uncharted water for you and Theresa requires you to decide how much pain you are willing to suffer to mend the gap," Russell said. "I am not going to judge either one of you. Know that I love you. For me, I live a better life being who I am and finding that some strangers treat me better than my own family."

Frances finished off her piece of cake and did feel better. Sugar was an emotional numbing drug for her and one that was still legal. Her heart was breaking into a million pieces, and she was glad to have the kindness of Simon and Russell with her. This conversation felt futile to her, but it also gave her some ideas. She had been so focused on the outer relationships and the lives of her parents and siblings that she completely ignored herself.

"I really don't know what to do."

"That's the thing, they don't either. Frances, you are hurting, Theresa is hurting, and every member of your family is—"

"I don't think Bernard is hurting," Theresa said.

The conversation felt like it was on a circular track that was spiraling down. What Frances wanted was a linear guide that warned her about what to expect. Instead, she was staring at the unknown and starting to quantify the loss.

"Frances, don't forget you have us. While Russell and I know that we could never replace your Kavanagh clan—nor would we want to—we love you more than I think you fully understand."

"Simon, I hear your words and feel the love, but it is different."

"Because we aren't going to dump you should you decide to go straight again." Russell laughed at his own joke.

"How long have you been waiting to say that?" Frances asked.

"My brilliance springs forth—I do not identify with lying in wait to spring a good line."

Simon and Russell stood and held out their arms. "Come in for a group hug," Simon said. Frances and Theresa joined the boys and hugged it out.

"You know what we could do. We could tell them about—"

"No." Simon cut Russell off.

"It totally helped Ronnette."

"Russell, I don't think…it was the symbolism, and you agreed she totally turned into a much better person after the whole experience."

"Tell us. What did she do?" Theresa asked. "Anyone want a warmer on their tea?"

"Maybe for this story we should open a bottle of wine."

"Simon, it's only 10:30 in the morning."

"Champagne or Bloody Marys then—this story needs something," Russell said.

"Now I'm truly intrigued," Frances said.

"Our friend Ronnette was similar to you two. She was raised in an Orthodox family so strict that she had to keep her wrists and her ankles covered. We're talking long-sleeve shirts, long skirts, and no fashion," Russell said.

"Move on—these are all background details."

"Simon, let me tell the story. You promised in session not to interrupt me."

"Are you two still seeing that therapist who wanted you to stop having sex for two months?"

"The same. As I was saying, Ronnette came to the party late in her life—"

"How late?" Frances asked.

"Again, a detail not needed."

"Not true. It proves you can be reborn at any age."

"Bored." Theresa groaned.

"Theresa, careful—this might help you. Now, I want no more interruptions—none." Russell pointed his finger at Simon and Theresa. "Ronnette was kicked out of her family, disowned, all communication cut off when she brought home her lesbian lover."

"I haven't even contemplated bringing a woman home to meet the family," Frances said.

"Russell would be the first to admit that Ronnette had some physical challenges that made her a little more difficult to sell in an arranged marriage. But she is a beautiful person."

"Long story...getting longer. Ronnette went through the birthing process again and was born into her new family."

"I'm totally confused," Theresa said.

"She found this place in hippyland up in Northern California that recreated going through the birth canal. The theory behind it is that you are starting your life as a brand-new baby."

"Strange. Russell, that is so strange... So did she, like, crawl out of a giant vagina?" Frances asked.

"She did."

"Gross."

"Not a real one, Theresa. A metaphorical one. She shaved her head and all her body hair off except her eyebrows to be like a newborn baby. Then she got into a warm tub of water. When she was ready, she went down a water slide, and we all caught her."

"What do you mean you all caught her?" Frances asked. "Was she naked?"

"She was, and she cut her own umbilical cord."

Frances stood up and shook her body out. The whole thing made her feel really strange. "This is too bizarre for me to wrap my head around."

Theresa was trying to stifle her laughter.

"What'd she use for the umbilical cord?"

"Black licorice rope. She cut it using her own teeth. We were standing on this really soft patch of grass, and there were towels laid out."

"The whole thing really was beautiful. The six of us who are her chosen family were all part of her birth. We honored her with a new name."

"Is this true? Russell are you giving us a line of crap?"

"I have the video." Russell pulled out his phone and started to play the video.

Frances watched with her mouth hanging open. Russell's description failed to mention the wall of cushions she had to push herself through at the bottom of the water slide. "What is that gooey stuff?"

"Red Jell-O," Simon said.

"Another dessert ruined," Frances said.

"Frances, our Aunt Janice ruined Jell-O years ago. Not forgetting the fact it's made from horses' hooves."

"That looked like quite the birth. You should've had the World Record people there because that is the tallest and largest baby I've think I've ever seen."

"All we are trying to share with you two is that the world has changed, and you can find your family."

"Did she keep her new name?"

"Yes. We are the ones who named her Ronnette."

"Oh. What was her other name?"

"Moriah."

"From Moriah to Ronnette? Please tell me you did not diaper and breastfeed her?"

"No. We ate cake, and she blew out a new life birth candle."

"For a moment, I thought you were going to say you ate placenta soup."

"Frances, that is really over the top," Russell said, sitting back on the sofa and crossing his legs.

"I'm over the top? I just watched a naked adult woman cut her umbilical cord with her teeth and scream. Theresa, want to go be birthed again?"

"If you've got a spare fifteen thousand, you can—"

"Moriah Ronnette paid fifteen thousand dollars to go down a gooey water slide and be renamed?"

"Frances, it was an intensive week-long therapy session. The birth was the jubilant end of her breaking free from all those emotional chains of her previous life."

"You know, I think I might see how I do on the paintball field before I think about being an adult baby."

CHAPTER SIXTEEN
PAINT THERAPY

"Whose bright idea was it to skip work to do this?" Cheryl asked, ducking behind a wooden barricade next to Frances as paintballs exploded around them. Each *thump, thump, thump* against the barricade made both Frances and Cheryl flinch.

"I thought I could get rid of some of my anger. I had no clue it was so serious."

"Frances, are you sure you weren't trying to show a very specific someone that you could be fun, spontaneous, and stupid? Next time you ask me to play hooky from work, it had better be for a spa day or a tennis match."

Frances carefully peeked around the edge of the barrier and came back to leaning against it. The sun was starting to beat down on them, and Frances found herself rethinking the judgement on therapy that resulted in an adult birth. She was drunk with strength. The dust, combined with her sweat, made her safety goggles almost impossible to see through. The bandanna covering her nose and mouth caused her to suck air with exaggerated gasps. Had it been a mistake not to take the full-face mask and look like a hybrid of Darth Vader and a motocross racer? When they first arrived at the park east of Livermore this morning, the air was cool and it all looked so inviting. It felt like someone turned up the thermostat as soon as she entered the paintball course.

"How can grass be so dusty?" Frances asked as she watched Cheryl get to her feet and peek over the top of the barricade.

"Is it me? Or is there a huge gender gap going on here?"

"What are you talking about? I was focused on the fact that there were so many people here."

"You didn't notice that out of the twenty or so people here, only three of us have boobs? Not to mention, I think the three of us are the only ones with the ability to legally order a beer or rent a car without a parent signature. Shouldn't these kids be in school?"

Frances turned to peek around the edge. "Crap. Those blue bastards are sneaking up on us. We need to move or we are going to get pummeled."

Cheryl ran first toward a giant concrete pipe. Frances heard her scream as she was hit in the rear with multiple colors of paint. Frances scrambled behind a hay bale in time to see Cheryl crab-walking toward another hiding spot. Frances couldn't stop laughing as Cheryl finally stood up and dropped her gun. Frances felt her heart rate continue to climb as she tried to figure out exactly what she thought she was doing. Detective Woods had organized their team and ordered her little commandos around, sending out Cheryl and Molly as decoys. It had worked. Once Cheryl got those toddlers to fire on her, they were quickly taken out by Molly and those who had played before.

"Frances, I want you to know those paintballs hurt. I know my body is going to be bruised for years after this. You're buying my Irish coffee this weekend. Theresa, you traitor, I see your bright orange paint color on my ass," Cheryl said as she exited the playing field.

"Three minutes. You made it three minutes, Cheryl," Frances yelled. She saw Molly motioning to her to get ready to run. It was her turn to take the heat. Since she had caused this crazy day, she figured she needed to do it. Originally, she had wanted to splatter Theresa with paint. But the paintball gun was a lot scarier than she anticipated. Why she had thought it would look like a Nerf gun was lost on her. Her heart was breaking over the fracture with her family, but it didn't warrant her shooting her sister with a paintball.

She got to her feet and crouched low behind the hay bales she was using for protection. Frances adjusted her bandanna and saw her goal. She was going to run toward a huge wooden spindle about twenty yards from the center of the field. It was a lofty goal for her to make. She looked to her left and caught the thumbs-up from Molly, who was poised to run and shoot as soon as Frances went for it. Frances tucked her chin to her chest and screamed as she fired her paintball gun wildly, yelling, "Say hello to my little friends!" as she ran.

When she was five feet away, Frances dove for the patch of green grass behind the spindle and was shocked when she realized that she had made it without being shot. How was that possible? She had heard the blasts of paint exploding around her, but she didn't seem to have taken a direct hit. Frances looked over her purple sweats to see she was dusty but not marked with any paint. "Holy buy a lottery ticket! What are the odds not one of those balls of paint hit me? ... really?"

No ref came to remove her, so she was still an active member of the red team. She had lost sight of Molly and the rest of her team. When she turned, she saw that she was only fifteen feet from the prize of this game, the blue flag flapping in the breeze. Frances stood up when she heard Theresa scream as she was taken out by a volley of paintballs. Frances shook her head and tried to remember the rules of the game. Why did the kid explaining the game keep referring to it as speedball? She wanted to know if they had a slowball division. That had resulted in a laugh and in her being the last one chosen to the team. The play clock showed they had only twelve minutes left of the forty-five minutes total to capture the flag and get it back to their home base.

She didn't think about it anymore and zigzagged through an obstacle course of hay bales, a wooden barricade, and the shell of a VW Beetle. When she arrived at the base of the tower, she realized she would have to climb to retrieve the flag. Frances dragged a hay bale over to climb on to get to the flag. She was shocked that no one was paying attention to her. It appeared she had been forgotten. Everyone else seemed to be pinned down as they exchanged paintball fire. She captured the flag and tucked it under her purple sweatshirt. Back on the ground, she was shocked that no one noticed the walking purple billboard for the University of Washington in the land of Cal and Stanford geeks.

"Hustle it, lady." A guy wearing a red armband came running up behind Frances.

She followed him and dove behind a wooden bunker as the paintballs covered the face of the bunker.

"That was close." Frances checked her gun and was shocked to see she was down to a quarter of what she had started with and had no memory of shooting that much.

"Give me the flag. I can run faster."

"True, but no one noticed me getting the flag."

"You were lucky. They noticed you now."

"No, they were shooting at you, not me. I was caught in the cross fire."

"Were you hit?"

"Nope."

"I think they think you are out of play. Strange. This is brilliant. Act like you are out. Leave your gun with me and walk back to our base. Don't step out of play, and then we win."

"Seriously? Okay. You don't think they'll notice I don't have any neon paint?"

"You are wearing purple with white letters, hard to tell. Don't take off your goggles though. Next time you might want to wear something a little less...soccer mom."

"You are lucky I already set my gun down." Frances got up and started walking with her face focused on the exit and took a strange route, like she was trying to make her way out of the field. She tried to make her body language convey she was out. She was fifteen feet from the red base, and the yelling and shooting continued around her. How could no one notice the blue flag was gone? She slowed her walk. Five more steps and then she was inside the red team's base and she raised the other team's flag. Her heart walloped the front of her chest as she felt the paintball hit the center of her back.

"Tooooo late!" Frances yelled as she hit the deck. Before she knew what had happened, she was being hoisted into the air by two large red team members. She caught a glimpse of Molly, who had taken her face mask off and was high fiving the rest of the team.

"Way to go, Kavanagh," Molly yelled.

"That was fun. I can't wait to take a shower," Frances said.

"What do you mean? That was just the first game, and we won. It was the fastest time ever," Molly said. "Come on, let's go regroup. We have a thirty-minute break."

"No judgment," Cheryl said as she took a long sip from her beer. "You talk to me about getting hit a hundred times in the ass with the hardest paint ever made and then you can question self-medication by beer at 8:30 in the morning."

"Hey, that was a blast. Can I sit with the red team winners?" Theresa asked.

"Sure. Want a beer?" Cheryl asked.

"I need some water."

"Beer has water in it."

"Cheryl, stop trying to get someone to drink with you. It's okay, we aren't going to do an intervention."

Frances stood up when Theresa sat down next to her. She couldn't bring herself to shoot her sister on the field of play, but she also was not wanting to be next to her at the moment. Frances, to hide her current dislike of Theresa, walked to the cooler that Molly had brought to grab a water and a bandanna. Frances was trying to locate her own place in the world, and she turned to watch Theresa, who was laughing and talking with members of the red team.

"A penny for your thoughts." Molly came and stood next to Frances, grabbing a protein shake for herself.

"Is it that obvious?"

"No. But for someone who basically won the game for us, you seem … well, rather quiet."

Frances looked over her shoulder at Theresa, and her heart broke a little more. "There is some family stuff going on that I am at a loss to understand."

"Want to take a walk and check out the gear that guy has for sale? I am looking for a new gun. We can take care of the official police business too."

Frances started walking toward the mobile paintball gun store, which was housed in a black pick-up truck. She didn't know how much she would share with Molly. This was outside her comfort zone. Her sister was lying to her.

"Molly, I really don't know that much about you."

"You haven't asked. To be fair, we really have not had that much time to be normal without a crowd. Before we go on—and I do want to continue this conversation—I need to show you a picture." Molly took out her phone and brought up a photo of the teacup from the murder scene. "Have you seen this before?"

Frances took the phone and enlarged the picture to focus on the teacup. "I had one similar. Ethan gave it to me when I commented on it. What is this?"

"It is a photo from a murder scene. Do you still have the cup?"

"Sort of—it is on a painting now."

"Interesting. Do you still have that painting?"

"I'm working on it now. It's in my loft."

"Why did Ethan give you the cup?"

"I was over chatting with him in his studio when he was working on a piece for an early gallery show. He made me some tea, and I had never seen anything like the teacup he served it in. It was so beautiful and delicate. I think I thought it made the tea taste amazing. The world was so new to me after my divorce. The next day, the cup and saucer were in my studio space with a note."

"Did he say where the cup came from?"

"Something about his grandparents being gifted the set from a Japanese family they kept out of the internment camps in California during World War II. Other than that, I really don't remember. I was surprised I still had it. It broke in the move, and I had hidden it in a box of art materials. Odds and ends that I thought could make an interesting painting or something. Why would a teacup similar to mine be in a murder scene? Ethan is dead. Do you think there's a connection?"

"Don't know. I would appreciate it if you kept this talk private. The work on the serial murders is being tightly controlled."

"Do you have any hard leads?"

"Who's the cop here? We have some very concrete puzzle pieces, but no, we are not down to naming possible suspects. Thanks for answering the questions. Now, what else is going on? You and Theresa appear to be less than friendly."

"In a nutshell, my family has banished me and not Theresa for the sin of loving women."

"Holy shit," Molly said.

"Now that's funny—I don't think I've ever heard you swear before. On the heavier side of my mood, I don't know if I'll ever be part of my family again." Frances tried to laugh as they arrived at the truck. Two boys from the first game were talking about the pros and cons of a particular gun. "Do you want to get into that conversation?"

"Nope. This was a cover. What's going on between you and Theresa is heavy. Are you sure you want to go play? We could call it a day and go hang out if you'd rather?"

"I'm okay. I . . . what I don't understand is that she has lied to our parents and said she's straight. I don't know where to start."

"Take a deep breath and begin."

"The short of it is that Theresa lied to me about being cut off from the family. I saw her phone with a family text conversation the morning I received a letter with a copy of our parents' latest will. I have been cast out. Cut out of the will."

"That's rough. I don't truly understand what you are going through because I lost my parents at a young age. My aunt and uncle raised me."

"I'm sorry. I...life is difficult when it comes to family. In my case, they installed the buttons and knew how to push them. I used to think I had disconnected the buttons, and now I find I want to have them pushed again."

"Odd. Really? You want manipulation and what almost sounds like torture? Why?"

"Why do you think? I'm a product of an Irish Catholic family. It gives me a reason to justify my particular attraction to expensive whiskey."

"Frances, I know you have a strange family. With all the shit you went through with Ethan, they weren't there for you. Theresa did come out, and she did support you."

"She's the one who voiced it to them. Made it real to them that I'm a lesbian," Frances said and looked at the boys to see if they had heard their conversation as Molly continued to pick up different items. "I don't even know which way to turn right now."

"I think you do. I also think you are struggling through this and having to face some other family issues. Theresa might have told them she's back in the closet, but they have got to know she's not being honest."

"Hey guys, they are getting ready for the next round," a kid with a red arm band yelled toward Molly and Frances.

"To be continued…and next time maybe with a couple of drinks," Frances said.

Molly took Frances into her arms and gave her a strong hug. "Yes. You have my number."

CHAPTER SEVENTEEN
BY THE AUTHORITY OF THE BUENA VISTA IRISH COFFEE CLUB

"Theresa, if you are searching for signs of god, why aren't you on a pilgrimage or something?" Simon asked as he shoveled a forkful of scrambled eggs into his mouth.

"I'm not even thirty yet. No need to have a quarter-life crisis. I was thinking about going back to church."

"You're not going to find any answers about your closet life at church. If you ask me, it will depress you more," Russell said.

"Winter, do you think you are going to raise your daughter in any particular faith?" Theresa asked.

"I might. I haven't really thought about that part of it yet. Right now, I'm focused on knowing where the closest bathroom is located as the baby is sitting directly on my bladder. And I'm wondering why no one mentioned the heartburn starts in utero? I thought I wouldn't deal with heartburn until the teenage years. The kid isn't even born yet and my heart is on fire."

"Can you take Tums?" Simon asked.

"I can see it now, that is a slippery slope. First Tums and then heroine. I had better not start. I only eat really bland foods now." Winter said.

Frances sat back and watched the bantering over religion with some weariness. The paintball experience had taken more out of her than she appreciated. This Saturday felt different all the way around. Mary, their usual waitress and unofficial member of the club, was not working. When Frances arrived and Molly wasn't there, her heart sank. The hug Molly had given her in the parking lot of the paintball course felt amazing. Frances shifted in her seat as she played with the fruit on her plate.

"Frances, you are buying all my Irish coffees this morning."

"Absolutely. You guys should've seen Cheryl's sacrifice on the paintball field yesterday. She took one in the rear for team—"

"More like a hundred, and it hurt."

"Oh…sounds like something I might like."

"Trust me, Russell—no. No, this was not sexual in any way, shape, or form. Being shot in the ass is not sexy."

"Well, some of us work on weekdays and were not invited." Simon took a sip from his Irish coffee.

"I wasn't invited either, so we can have our own club."

"Winter? There is no way they would let you out into the paintball field."

The crowd noise in the Buena Vista was getting loud enough to stop normal conversation at the table. Frances looked the crowd over, searching for Molly.

"Why do you look so anxious this morning?" Cheryl leaned over to Frances and asked.

"Not anxious. Just thinking…I can't really hear what the other side of the table is talking about."

"They are giving Winter a hard time over eating donuts."

"Hey all," Molly said, suddenly appearing next to Frances and taking an empty seat.

"Didn't think you were coming this morning," Frances said, trying to keep control of her own excitement over seeing Molly. Could anyone else detect her heart flutter?

"Work delayed me. But after yesterday's fun, I figured I needed to come and defend myself with the crowd."

"Molly, is it true you have your own special Batman costume for paintball?" Russell asked.

"Who described my black fatigues as a Batman costume?"

"Literary license—you looked so cool," Theresa said.

"Why not Batgirl?" Molly asked.

"Or Wonder Woman?" Russell added.

"Too many clothes for Wonder Woman, although I bet you could pull that off," Winter added.

Frances's face flushed several shades redder with Winter's comment, and she tried to rescue herself by dropping her napkin on the floor. When she bent over to pick it up, she smacked her head against the table and practically knocked herself out. She was seeing stars. It wasn't the way she wanted to get the conversation to change, but she felt Molly's hands helping her sit up and she instantly melted into her grasp.

"Way to go, Grace," Theresa laughed.

"Are you okay?" Cheryl and Molly asked at the same time.

"Nothing an Irish coffee couldn't fix."

"Well, please don't knock yourself out—I actually am here on some official police work too. Sorry I forgot to give this to you yesterday," Molly said and handed Frances a small sealed envelope. "There were a couple other advances made in Ethan's case."

"What's this?" Frances asked. The rest of the table was silent and focused on the envelope.

"It's a note from Emily."

"Do you know what it says? I haven't spoken to her since the night Ethan was killed in front of my loft."

"Frances, you don't need to open it here. I don't know what it says. I can tell you that Emily has learned quite a bit, and she expressed to me how sorry she was about how she acted. She's a victim in this too."

"That little bitch could have apologized to Frances a while ago," Winter said. "Throw that thing out—you don't owe her anything."

"I don't agree with Winter. You need to read it. You can read it to all of us—you don't need to go through this alone," Russell said.

"Sorry again. I guess my timing of handing you the letter was not—"

"Molly, it's okay. This way everyone gets the information at the same time." Frances ripped open the envelope and took out the folded piece of paper. It took her a moment to focus on the handwriting.

"Would you like me to read it to the table?" Simon asked.

Frances handed the letter over to Simon and stifled a giggle as Simon adjusted the distance of the letter from his eyes several times. "Do you want me to hold it over here so you can read it?" Frances asked.

"I've got it. Okay. Everyone ready?"

Hi Frances,

The first words that keep coming to my mind are I am so sorry. I am so sorry I did not discover the monster that Ethan was before he hurt anyone. I am having a hard time living with myself, the more I find out about what Ethan has done. Please know that I understand if you never want to see me again. I am asking that we meet. There are some things that I have learned that I think would help us both move past this horror. Molly has my new phone number. I have not been able to go back to my home or my computer lab since all of this happened.

Please know I am sorry, and I was so wrong about so much.

Emily

"Wow. That is…what's she talking about, Molly?" Cheryl asked.

"There is so much we are learning—work has been all-consuming."

"No wonder you are looking like you are doing a character study for the living dead," Russell said.

"Not nice, Russell. Maybe it's a good thing you don't date women. Telling them they look so tired that they resemble a zombie is beyond rude," Winter said.

"He's not wrong though. Molly, you are looking rather rough," Theresa said.

"With friends like these, I might need to find a therapist."

The table went quiet and they all looked from Frances to Molly and then back to Frances. Simon handed the note back to Frances. Frances took the note and asked Molly to put Emily's phone number on the paper. The world was falling down a rabbit hole again, and Frances felt herself losing her grip. Someone in the bar started singing "Whiskey, You're the Devil" in the background.

"Do you think you're going to call her then?" Molly asked.

"I do."

"Molly, what do you think about Emily?" Cheryl asked.

"I'm not sure I understand the question. Emily is a good person who was cast into a role by a manipulative, smart, evil person who really did a number on her."

"Frances, why don't you ask your shrink what to do?" Theresa said.

"I didn't know you were seeing a therapist," Russell said and turned to look at Simon.

"I don't think any of us did," Winter said.

"Thanks, Theresa. I was keeping this—"

"Okay, everyone, I think I've derailed the breakfast club enough this morning. Next round of Irish coffees is on me," Molly said. "This place is packed—I think it's time for that silverware game that I don't completely understand."

"It's not complicated. If you see a person that you would like to spoon, you pick up a spoon and point it in that person's direction. A second spoon gives you the point. If a fork or knife is raised, the rest of the table gets involved. A second knife cuts the person out of the gene pool and a fork is a possibility. Ties are broken with the salt and pepper. Let's play, and then you'll catch on," Simon said. He picked up a spoon and pointed it toward a man who could have been Sean Connery's double from the classic movie *Darbie O'Gill and the Little People*.

Frances mouthed the words *thank you* to Molly. She could not stop watching Molly as she threw herself into the game. The way her eyes sparkled when she laughed caused Frances's heart to soar. This could be a possibility. Frances took another sip from her Irish coffee and picked up her spoon, ready to cast it toward Molly, but pointed it in the direction of a Great Dane standing next to a bench across the street.

CHAPTER EIGHTEEN
CAN'T FIND THE CITY LIGHTS

Molly Woods unlocked the front door to her house and found the dark silence heavy. She stood silent and listened to her voicemail. Several days had passed since she had allowed herself some fun on the paintball field. She was exhausted. For the past week, she had been coming home well past midnight. She needed to at least leave a lamp on in her front hall. Tonight was not a night she wanted to be alone. The fact checking of items in the pictures from what Ethan had left Emily was proving more unsettling and arduous than she had expected. Aaron helped with some of the work. His computer identifier program only went far enough to identify that there were objects in the frame. Sometimes they got lucky and could lighten that area of the frame. No matches to the china service had been made yet. She pulled off her scarf and jacket, hanging them on the door handle to her front door.

"Hi, Siri, please play Heather Peace *Thin Line* album." Molly leaned against the wall in her front hall as she realized she used polite language to activate music into her house. How far would this go? Was it a sign of desperation that she had resorted to talking to her phone instead of pushing a button? Here she was, home again, and her conversation consisted of one-sided commands to a telephone.

Molly clicked on the light in the front hall and thought she caught the distinct smell of cherry pipe tobacco. A memory of sitting on the living room floor listening to her uncle run through the latest investigations he was working on came into her mind. Auntie had brought the pipe smoking to an end. She gave Uncle the option—the pipe or her. He wisely let the pipe go. Molly walked down the hall and listened to the music. The empty sounds of the house settled into the coolness of the night, and the creaks of the floor as she walked into the kitchen sounded over the notes of Heather Peace singing about running out of time. Molly took a breath and held it in for a count of ten before exhaling. It was too late to eat dinner.

This schedule was breaking her down, and she knew it was not something she could continue. She opened her fridge and stood in the light, staring at the food desert in front of her. A half carton of eggs and a plate of leftover something were the rather unappetizing options. Unless she felt like eating mustard or butter, it was rough going. She eyed the plate with the leftovers. Was it meat? Was it cake? Could it be meat-cake? She dared to raise the plastic wrap and sniffed cautiously. Molly wrinkled her nose and deposited what had morphed into meat-cake into the kitchen garbage can. "That's thoroughly disgusting."

Her stomach rumbled, almost in objection to her brain throwing away something that might have been edible. She opened her cupboard and carefully checked the loaf of Dave's Killer Bread that was on the first shelf. Another smell test, and she decided it was safe to toast. Tea and toast would help her get enough in her tummy to try to sleep.

She looked around the kitchen and was happy with how the remodel had turned out. It was a shame, she thought to herself. The concept of *having* a chef's kitchen and *using* one were very different in her world. She had been out walking in the neighborhood with her ex when she spotted the for-sale sign on this house. It was a long purchase road as her relationship ended before the closing. Molly wasn't sure she could swing the mortgage and the remodel on her single income. The bank had doubts too. Her aunt and uncle had stepped in with an additional down payment check that made her life a lot easier. How was she ever going to repay them? The toaster dinged, and Molly buttered the toast and spread it with her aunt's homemade marmalade.

A cough from her front sitting room caused Molly to drop her knife and pull out her gun, which was still holstered to her side. The only light in the front room was coming from the kitchen. Someone was in her house, and she had failed to notice. The door had been locked when she returned home. Molly reached for her mobile and silently sent a text to Todd and Lucy. *Need patrol car to my home immediately. Intruder.*

She carefully crept to the left side of the open door that led from the kitchen into the dining room and into the front sitting room. A second cough led Molly to focus on the area of the sofa. She made it to the edge of the dining room but could not see on the other side of the couch. Her gun out in front of her, she held a flashlight in her supporting hand up against her gun. Had the person heard her come in? What the heck was going on? The last person to break into her house was a homeless guy who took a shower and ate most of her food. He left a note explaining he would never be able to repay the owner of the house but thought it was the best shower in the city.

"Don't move! SFPD!" Molly said as she jumped to a spot where she could see the whole of the sitting room.

"Fuck's sake, Molly." Her uncle coughed uncontrollably. "Put your gun away before you have to explain to your aunt why she's a widow."

"What the hell? You scared the—how long have you been here?" Molly asked, putting her gun back in her holster and turning on the lights in the room.

"I thought we could go grab a bite to eat, but you didn't come home. I guess I fell asleep."

"Does Auntie know you're here? Is everything okay between you two? Are you sure you were here to see me, or was it just to smoke a bowl?"

"Honestly, the smoke was enjoyable. You make me sound like an addict. In answer to your question, your aunt and I are fine. I got your message and I came over to help you work through some of your case. Next time I'll wait outside."

"Sorry. This case has me on edge."

Todd and two uniformed officers burst through the front door.

"What the heck?" Uncle said.

"Todd, it's okay. My uncle came over and fell asleep."

"You sure?" Todd asked, looking from Uncle Henry to Molly.

"Thanks for getting here so quickly. Why are you here? I asked you to send a squad car, not show up yourself."

"Unfortunately, I was heading in from another crime scene. I had told them not to bother you. I need to know why you don't lock your front door. Are you crazy?"

Molly turned to the uniformed officers. "Thanks, we're fine here, guys. Todd will meet you outside." Turning back to Todd, she asked, "Todd, you've met my uncle?" She was going to ignore the front door issue because she did not want to admit she had forgotten.

"Briefly. Pleasure to see you again. This is an interesting situation."

Molly walked toward the kitchen. She agreed this was strange, but her emotions and mind were reaching a breaking point. "Todd, you want to stay and fill us in on what happened tonight? I'm making a cup of tea, would anyone else like one?"

"You got anything stronger than tea in this place?"

"I taught her well." Uncle reached for the bottle of scotch on the coffee table and handed it over to Todd.

"I'll get you a glass," Molly added as she realized she could use a stiff drink herself. "Ice?"

"Nope. I take this one straight—err, sorry Molly—no ice."

"Todd, relax, I am not a member of the feminist language lesbians league—you can use the *straight* word in my house." Molly handed him a glass and had him pour her a couple fingers' width of the amber liquor.

"Is that a thing? Language lesbians?" her uncle asked.

Molly smiled and turned to Todd. She briefly thought about her bed upstairs and sleep but pushed it out of her mind. That was a shadow life, when she used to come home and act like a regular person.

"So, what was found tonight?" Molly asked.

Molly watched as Todd drank the scotch down in one gulp. She handed him the bottle and watched as he poured himself a second drink. His eyes looked dark, and his five o'clock shadow had sprouted into a beard. The work was taxing them both, she thought, leaning back and studying the amber liquid in her glass. Scotch on an empty stomach.

"It was bad, Molly. A couple of teenage kids literally stumbled into the murder scene. I don't think we'll have to worry about them tagging any buildings in the near future. Those kids were freaked."

"Where was this?" Molly asked.

"The scene was set up on the east side of that carousel by the children's museum downtown."

"What do you mean 'set up'?" Uncle asked.

"Exactly that—unlike the Ethan Charna case we're working, this killer wanted . . ." Todd sat back and covered his eyes.

"Todd?"

"Molly, you'll see the pictures, but this…I've never seen anything like this before. There were two victims, and they were set up like they were having a very normal and fun picnic."

"That is really creepy. I'm not sure which has me more disturbed…the idea that someone actually put their victims into a scene or the fact the places are so public and no one is noticing this activity?"

"That's just the thing. When you first walk up, it looks like these two people were having a nice little bit of food and wine. They were dead, and the initial medical examiner felt those two people had been killed somewhere else and brought to that location. She couldn't immediately tell how they had been murdered. They looked like wax figures. I had to ask if they were human. The liquid in their glasses looked like something out of a horror film. I'm pretty sure it was blood."

Silence fell over them as what Todd had shared hung in the air. Molly looked around the house as the heater kicked on and caused a low rumbling from the basement. The horror of what was happening in the city was now inside her home. This house had stolen her heart when she was out walking. The home with the intricate scalloped shingles and the original stained-glass windows represented a safe haven from the city. Molly wanted to escape the reality of what Todd was talking about let the memories of when she and her ex had first moved into the house. It felt so warm and happy. It took them months to gently restore the natural red-gold luster to the wood accents throughout the house. A previous owner had decided to stain it all black. Her uncle had told her it was a lost cause, but Molly found the answer through a restoration group that helped bring back the old properties.

"Molly, there was a package in the picnic basket. It was addressed to the Chief."

"Shit. You all have someone that is going to continue killing. I don't miss this shit at all," Uncle said.

"Todd, you look like I feel."

"You know that map that Lucy put together? Do you have your computer?" Todd asked.

"I left it at the office. I don't think it would work into the design," Molly said.

"A point on the police shield?" Uncle asked.

"Yes. And the possibility that the bear on your special shield is going to appear in this grizzly connect-the-dot game?" Molly took a sip from her glass.

"Molly, I need to speak to you privately."

"Whatever you need to say, you can trust Todd. We are working these cases together."

"What I am going to tell you—"

Molly's phone rang. Looking down, she saw it was Lucy calling.

"Lucy, sorry. Todd's here and everything is fine." She listened for a moment, turning to look at her uncle and then Todd, and then said, "Got it. Todd and I will be there as soon as we can."

"Todd, the Captain wants us at the command center now. Uncle, do you want to come with us?"

"No, but I have to tell you something first. Molly, we didn't find the serial killer. The case was never solved. We got lucky."

"What do you mean you got lucky? You and your whole department received accolades for solving that case, and you got the bear shield."

"The guy we arrested was a bad guy, but he wasn't the serial killer. The killings stopped, and we figured that the killer had stopped or left the area."

Molly sat down. Conversations with her uncle over the years rolled through her mind. No wonder he never talked about the case or the specifics.

"I will never forget the murder scenes. We called them the Beach Blanket Murders because the bodies were placed on huge beach towels. They were so staged. It was rare to find anything out of place. Not sure how they got the bodies to the beach towels. The bodies were almost completely embalmed."

"What do you mean almost completely embalmed?" Molly asked.

"The medical examiner told us that the bodies were embalmed, but as the killings continued, it was as if they were running out of time and he or they did not finish the process. That was how we were able to start to figure out how long the person had been dead. To a point. It was clear the killer or killers were mocking the police department."

"That was over twenty-five years ago. There is no way that the person who killed the two tonight was involved in that case," Todd said.

"I need you two to promise me that you'll warn me before you release this information."

"Uncle Henry, I am not going to say anything." Molly turned toward Todd.

"You have nothing to worry about," Todd said. "Molly, we have so much to figure out. Let's go." Todd rose and walked toward the door. "I'll drive."

"Uncle, call Auntie and let her know you are staying here tonight. Your file boxes are in the basement. Would you mind going through them? I'll be back as soon as I can." Molly followed Todd out and made sure to the lock the door.

CHAPTER NINETEEN
GIRL TALK

S imon let Winston out the door and knew his diabolical plan would work. Winston did exactly as Simon predicted—he ran straight to Frances's door, barking the whole way. Russell came up behind Simon and gave him a love tap on the butt.

"Brilliant does not describe you. Do you think she'll take the bait?" Russell kissed Simon, holding him in a strong embrace. Both were waiting to hear Frances rescue the barking Winston.

"You don't think Winston will choose to stay with her and never come home, do you?" Simon asked.

"Hello, Winston? What's that? Simon and Russell are bringing over food and champagne for a much-needed girls' night?"

"You see through us." Simon walked up to Frances with Russell in tow, bearing a bottle of chilled champagne and a bag of goodies from Draeger's Market. "I told Russell if he was going to drag me down to Menlo Park, we had to have a shopping feast at Draeger's."

"Good work!" Frances threw open her door, stepping aside to let her three beautiful boys inside.

Winston ran straight for the couch and whined until Frances sat down next to him.

"Winston, honestly. Frances does not need a facial right now," Simon said.

"I don't mind. Sadly, it's the most action I've seen in a while."

"Oh my, the far-right Christians were right. Once a straight goes gay, it's straight downhill into bestiality," Russell said, popping the cork of the champagne.

"No politics tonight. I'm relieved you love Winston; otherwise, this would all be really awkward." Simon came over and sat down next to Frances on the couch with a platter of cheeses, nuts, and fruit.

"A knife?"

"Only if you are planning on killing one of us," Russell answered as he sat down in the chair closest to the brie on the generous plate of goodies.

"How goes the processing of the FOK'd drama?"

"I guess *strange* is the word I'd use? Did you make my initials into a—"

"I did! It's brilliant, right? I used it the other day when another friend had something horrid happen. I told him he was truly FOK'd." Russell laughed harder than Frances felt was necessary.

"What's new with Molly? I am thinking of a childhood rhyme right now . . ."

"Slow down there, Simon. This storyteller needs some food before I start down that rabbit hole. It has been much too long since we've had girl talk. Just the four of us." Frances gave Winston a big kiss on the top of his head. The giant dog snuggled into Frances, almost pushing her off the couch.

"Speaking of girls, where's the good witch?"

"You know, if I was more with-it, I might be insulted. Theresa is out with her theatre group buddies. They have been working until three and four in the morning trying to get the sets right for the upcoming show. Regional theatre is rough."

"I'm not sad. I miss us," Russell said.

Simon sat back and watched Frances attempt to eat without losing her bite to Winston and his thieving dog tongue. He wondered if he should be concerned that Winston had licked off most of the paint that had been had been spattered on Frances's face. "Do you think the paint Winston licks off your face is harming him?"

"Have you seen what your dog eats at the park? There were times I was truly scared that I would have some explaining to do over what he chomped down. Winston is better than a garbage disposal."

"Now back to the *strange* comment. You can't answer a question with a word like that and think your usual tactic of double-speak about our baby will make us forget." Simon took another hunk of cheese and some grapes as he settled his sights on Frances. He settled back, ready for the story.

"There were a couple of surprises. One was the fact that Molly gave me a full body hug at paintball. The other I can't really talk about, but it is really weird. A teacup similar to the one Ethan had given me was in one of the recent serial killer murder scenes."

"Remind us not to tell you any secrets," Simon said. "We applied no pressure, and you folded like a house of cards."

"This is all fine, but more boring background. We are not your mother's quilting group. I want to know about how Joshua fits into all of this flirting with Molly. Was this your first love? Was there an unwanted pregnancy that you are both now regretting?"

"Simon, you need to stop watching Netflix. No...well, no to the pregnancy, anyway, because that's not biologically possible."

"Because you didn't have sex?" Russell asked.

Simon jumped in. "Because Joshua was a woman. Our little redhead already shared with us when she lost her virginity."

"Simon, you have a memory like an elephant."

"A very skinny and beautifully sculpted elephant."

Frances almost choked as Russell squealed, registering what Frances had shared with him.

"You little hussy. You had lesbian sex in college."

"No. I wanted to, but I ran from it. I might have gotten as far as second base. You two are not making this easy. I really thought I had done something wrong in college. She was my closest friend."

"Of course you did something wrong, Frances, as the world and everything that happens in this world is directly related to and traced back to your actions."

"Russell, did you take your bitch pills today? Your edge is so sharp I might need to get my suit of chainmail to keep the cuts to a minimum." Frances took a sip of wine.

"Oh, Franny, relax and drink more wine. You know I love you. No hurt feelings. I'll be quiet and listen."

"Now I know you're gay. What straight man listens to a woman? Dana claims it is biologically impossible."

"Cheers to that. Now that I think about it—"

"Back to our currently scheduled programming. Did I mention that Theresa was a royal bitch to Joshua? Maybe she's spending too much time with you, Russell?

"What do you mean?" Simon asked.

"Theresa was so critical of Joshua and started asking really rude questions about his family and money. I don't know. It was strange."

"You are better than watching reality TV."

"Thanks, Russell."

"Theresa is harmless and she does love you. Look at all the handy things she's done for you here in the loft, like the canvas drying rack. Simply brilliant. Not to mention she's keeping you chaste," Simon said.

"What are you talking about?"

"When you returned from Hawaii, you had at least two very eligible candidates to start dating, but you muffed it."

"Or she didn't muff anything," Russell added, laughing so hard he snorted champagne through his nose. "Truly—had you muffed it, we all might be enjoying wine with Molly or Samantha right now instead of double dating with our dog."

"Simon, Russell, let me stop you both right there. I'm not dating anyone. Sorry, Winston." Frances gave the dog another kiss on top of his head. "That means no women, no men, and no Irish wolfhounds." Winston raised his head to look at Frances. "Winston, we are friends. I promise I'll always take you to the beach and the park. Understood?" Winston licked her face and went back to resting his head in her lap.

"Understood. Franny is going to start collecting cats and bags. Back to this mysterious old friend slash stranger who has a buyer purchase the most expensive painting in the whole show."

"I had no clue what to expect. I did not have a chance to really process what was happening. When we pulled up to the address, it was a small little coffee closet on Cannery Row. Smaller than our elevator."

"I thought you were told the painting was purchased for a restaurant."

"Turns out Joshua is opening a restaurant a few doors down from his coffee closet."

"At least he didn't buy it to destroy it like you destroyed his heart," Simon said.

"Would someone really do that? Buy a painting and destroy it?" Frances asked.

"If I could and it was an ex-lover, I could do something that twisted," Russell said.

The three sat in silence. Simon watched as Frances contemplated the fate of her paintings. He knew she was having a hard time selling her art, letting them all go out into the world. "I think we need some more to drink. The champagne is down to a drop. What shall we have? Red? White? Something harder?"

"Red," Frances said. "I've got a couple wines from Argentina. Let's try one of those."

"I'm on it—you continue," Russell said.

"Full stop. You can't put the non-muff diving all in my court. I invited Molly to the gallery opening, and she was a no-show."

"You know she's in charge of some special unit now. Did you call and talk to her?"

"No."

"I think you two need to get together and have lunch or something. She is an amazing woman, single, and we all have noticed you noticing her too."

"Not going to happen. She told me she doesn't date victims of cases she is investigating."

"Ouch," Russell said.

"Winter is not fond of her either."

"Winter is in a completely different universe now. That was Winter's subconscious rescuing her from a life of further crime," Simon said as he stood to help Russell bring over another round of food and drink.

"Do you think she'll become a real person now?"

"Not nice, Russell. Back to the painting. Theresa and Joshua hung it in his restaurant, and the two of them had some sparks flying."

"Now this is getting very interesting. Theresa's in a relationship and declared herself a gold-star lesbian."

"Are you going to see Joshua again?"

"I don't know. He invited us back to the restaurant when it opens. Theresa has always wanted to go to the aquarium."

"You didn't go while you were there?"

"No. Winter was having a meltdown because Russell skipped out on her doctor appointment. She was so desperate, she called Cheryl."

"Meow. Those two felines in the same room together without Frances? Reminds me I need to call that woman. You know Jason is pretty much gone for good," Russell said.

"Those two are always hot and cold. Winter getting pregnant is like dumping gasoline on the fire instead of water."

"Simon, who's being the bitch now? We must be happy for the newest member of our little family," Russell said. "What movie are we watching tonight?"

"That's a conversation speed bump. Guess we are done talking." Simon stood and moved further away from Russell.

"*Howard's End*?"

"Okay. That's a choice, Russell," Simon said.

"What is with you two tonight? Don't answer. I love that film—it's like watching a moving painting it is so beautiful," Frances said, pulling a blanket from the back of her couch over her shoulders. The sky outside had grown dark, and they all settled into their seats as Russell started the DVD.

CHAPTER TWENTY

MUSIC IN THE GARDENS

There were happenings at Golden Gate Park that drove home to Frances why she loved this city. Flower piano was one of the more unique and beautiful expressions at the Botanical Gardens. Someone got the rather amazing idea to decorate pianos and place them around the gardens for anyone to play. Frances wondered how someone ever came up with the idea to combine piano music and the blooming flowers. She had heard about this program through a friend who took her grandson, a budding piano player, to play the pianos in the gardens. When Frances walked on the wide path that led into the Great Meadow, she knew she had chosen correctly. It was a beautiful day to be living in San Francisco. A young girl was playing a beautiful piano piece as Frances slowly strolled, keeping her eyes alert for Emily. It had been quite a while since she had last seen her.

The music calmed Frances as she focused on the beauty around her. Her heart was nervous about seeing Emily. Frances enjoyed the time she had with her, but Ethan had placed a dark cloud over the whole encounter. He had secretly videotaped them having sex. Frances shivered and thought about how angry Emily was with her right before Ethan was shot and killed. The three o'clock meeting time had arrived, and Frances stopped and looked for Emily. An image of Ethan lying in a puddle of his own blood flashed, in color, through her mind. It was so vivid, Frances bit her lip, tasting the saltiness of her own blood. She dug around in her messenger bag, looking for a Kleenex. Maybe Theresa was right and she should not have come to this meeting alone or at all.

"Hi, Frances."

Frances spun around without moving the upper half of her body and almost tripped over her own feet.

"Hey, Emily."

Emily put out her hand in an automatic reaction to someone who appeared to be falling over. Frances caught herself and stood facing Emily. She didn't know if she should hug her or shake her hand. "Do you want a hug?"

"That'd be nice."

Frances took a step toward Emily, and the two women hugged as if they were meeting for the first time. Frances caught the slightest smell of jasmine as she pulled away from the awkward hug. *Keep an open mind, Frances, and do not close yourself down*, she thought. *You're a different person standing here, and so is Emily. Give her the space to be the person she is without putting your judgement on her.*

"Penny for your thoughts." Emily smiled slightly. "I was so nervous. Maybe because I need to tell you in person how this was all so...I didn't know . . ."

"Emily." Frances stopped and gave her a real hug this time. She stepped back from her, feeling a little awkward over the hug. She noticed the dark circles under Emily's eyes and her pale skin. "Are you okay?"

"I don't know if I'll ever be okay. This is what I look like without my daily run in the sun. To be honest, it was hard for me to come out and meet you here. And you?"

"Complicated question. I don't have an answer at this moment."

Emily instinctively brushed Frances's hair back behind her ear and stared into Frances's blue eyes. The sun had caught the edges of Emily's blonde hair, showing Frances the quiet beauty that had originally caught her attention when they first met. "Emily, you are so light, so opposite of who Ethan was . . ."

"Can we go find a place to sit? I am so tired. I haven't been sleeping well."

"Sure." Frances started to walk toward a bench that was on the edge of the Great Meadow. The flowers, the trees, and the sun were the perfect place for them to explore, with softness, the horror they had survived. "Emily, you need to know that I hate that Ethan is how we met and that he manipulated us both, but I don't want him to ruin the us that we had when we believed we were alone."

They sat down, and Frances took Emily's hands in hers. They were so cold, and Frances wanted to warm them.

"I never wanted to hurt you, Frances. You were so different from anyone else I had ever been with before."

"Because I'm older?"

"Not by much, so watch it. No. You were so new to this world, and you treated me…how to explain this?" Emily paused and placed a hand on Frances's arm. "You made me feel a new level of special each time you touched me. Even now. Your hands are so warm. I feel you."

Frances sat back and looked into the distance. She knew that they both needed to heal, and the journey would be stronger together. "Emily, Ethan was a very calculating and damaged person. That's what I tell myself because I don't think a normal person could do the things he did."

"I had known him since high school. I think about times when I had these strange feelings. I ignored them. Why did I? I trusted him. I loved him more than my own family. I put him on a pedestal. To think I believed I was as smart as him."

"Stop. This line of thinking is only going to lead you to a tortured hell. It isn't your job to have stopped him."

"I feel so helpless. He watched us have sex. He manipulated me to hate you. I was falling in love with you. The crazy thing is, one of the detectives shared some of his journal entries where he talked about me being smart. He knew if he could continue to fool me, then no one would catch him."

Frances squeezed Emily's hands and allowed her tears to fall.

"Ethan left a box with some items in it. He has left me a sizeable amount of money. Did Molly talk to you about what was in the box?"

"Molly is a friend, but we keep her work separate from the friendship. Although recently she asked me about a teacup that he had given me. It was like one that had been in a murder scene. Now that I think about it, I didn't ask her how she knew I had a cup like that."

"Was it really finely painted and delicate?" Emily asked.

"Yes."

"His grandmother had that set in the house. It was beautiful. One of kind, based on some Chinese story or something. Anyway, I had never seen a service for forty people before. The family seemed quite proud of it."

"It was a Japanese story." Frances sat back and tried to keep breathing.

"They sold it. One day, I had gone over to hang with Ethan, and his grandmother was crying at the kitchen table. It was such an odd day. Ethan was so…now that I think about it, he was cruel. He was teasing her over selling the china."

"Are you sure? He gave me a teacup and saucer when we had studios next to one another. This isn't making any sense."

"I'm sorry, Frances, I'm not following?"

"Are you okay? You are really pale."

"This is a scary world, and I don't know if I'll ever be…are we okay? I know we will never be lovers again, but are we friends?"

"Emily, I wish I could say yes because I know that's what you want to hear. I don't know. I'm here. Like you, there are things about our relationship so entwined with Ethan…Can you accept moving forward and letting our relationship be free enough to develop as it will?"

"Yes." Emily breathed a sigh of relief. "Thanks for being honest with me."

"Emily? Look at yourself. Look at me. We might not be in the same league, but you are in my heart, and that happened outside of Ethan. I am holding on to that as we find our way."

"You are so silly. There are no leagues. There are people, and then there are women. Trust me, Frances. You are all woman, with some serious mojo. One of the most endearing things about you is the fact you have no clue how fucking sensual you are."

"While I'd much prefer to keep talking about how amazing I am, I have to ask—you said that Ethan committed suicide and the answer was in what he left you."

"Ethan was getting ready to…"

"He was going to kill me. I felt that was what they weren't saying when Molly and her partner were going over the case with me."

Tears continued to flow from Frances's eyes as she knew she did not really understand how close to death she had come. Had Molly known and tried to protect her by not bringing up Ethan's journal?

"Emily, we could sit here and rehash moments and conversations we had with Ethan, but I don't think that's a good idea. Can we try to let that go? What are your plans going forward?"

"Frances, he had plotted out a fantasy where he killed us both. I don't know if I can ever let this go. It is in my head. When I close my eyes and try to sleep, I hear his laughter. I hear his voice. I see you and I can't reach you."

"Emily, it is over. We are okay. We are alive."

"There are so many things. I haven't been able to return to my house or my computer lab. I keep looking over my shoulder. Did you know that Ethan was rolling in money? All those stories about not having enough money to buy art supplies or make his electric bill. They were all lies. I loaned him so much money. Money I didn't have to lend."

"Get angry. He lied to you. He wanted to kill you. To kill me. No, I didn't know he was rich. Did the police tell you that?"

"No, he did. He put together a will and left some serious money."

"Are you going to take it? You don't have to take it. But if you do, you must not feel any guilt about that money."

"What if it all came from his killing?"

"I don't know the law, but if the money was from that, I don't think you'll be able to collect. I don't know—you need to talk with a lawyer."

"You're right. Thanks for meeting with me. My feelings for you are real. I'm going to get out of here for a while. I bought a car with some of my grant money. I know that I'll have to probably pay that back. But I needed something that was mine. I'm going to get in my car and drive."

"Do you know where you're going?"

"Nope. I am keeping the destination open. I have some friends from college that live in Portland, so I am going to start there."

"Keep my number in your phone. I am here."

"As a survivor?"

"As a woman who cares for you. I predict that if we are gentle with one another, a friendship will grow." Frances hugged Emily and held her tight. She didn't let go until Emily loosened her own hold on her. The two women stood, and Frances watched as Emily walked away, across the green grass of the Great Meadow, the sun on her back. The world around Frances came alive as a young man played a ragtime tune on an upright piano that sported painted dahlias. Part of her soul wanted to chase after Emily, but she needed to go on her own journey. Frances knew that the two of them had danced to the end of the current song.

CHAPTER TWENTY-ONE
SLOW, FAST, GONE

Frances did not mind the slowing traffic as she approached the Golden Gate Bridge. The traffic coming into the City was surprisingly light, leading her to wonder if she had mixed up her days. With the pace of a slug, the traffic moved forward. Gray clouds moved across the hills of Sausalito at lightning speed. Frances looked left to the steel gray of the Pacific Ocean and took the moment to recharge. It had been less than an hour, and she was already feeling the energy vampire that Winter had become. Cheryl tried to take up some of the slack, but for the last ten minutes she focused entirely on her phone, claiming work was pinging her.

"Each time I cross this bridge, I think about how amazing it is to live here," Frances said aloud but more to herself than the crowd in the car.

"Okay, I need to say that if you are going to be fucking Pollyanna, drop me off at the first airport stop and I'll take that home. Can't beat the twenty bucks to the airport, and then I can hop on BART," Winter said.

Frances glanced at Cheryl, who was in the passenger seat. Was Cheryl going to side with Winter and call her out on being overly sappy? For the moment, it appeared that Cheryl was completely lost to her data world as she quickly typed into her smartphone.

"Care to chat about why you are auditioning for the party-killer role?" Frances asked, glancing at Winter through the rearview mirror.

"Frances, were you really serious about airbags and seatbelts being lethal to pregnant women, or were you trying to come up with a reason you didn't want me riding shotgun? This whole fucking world sucks."

"Winter, you're the one who told me about the horror of the airbags. Now keep your seatbelt off your baby incubator. Care to tell me what's really going on? We probably have thirty minutes at the rate we're going before we pick up the birthday girl."

"You mean the birthday hag."

"Winter, you will be lucky to collect as many birthdays as Dana. Start talking, lady—we don't spend the time we used to spend together, and I want to know what is going on with you." Frances attempted to change Winter with another eye-catching glance in her rearview mirror. She smiled at her friend, who looked like she was on the verge of either bursting into tears or turning into the kind of giant monster that stomps through Tokyo.

"Do you think Dana will be surprised in a good way or a bad way?" Cheryl asked, without looking up from her cell phone screen.

"Welcome to the world…not talking about that…Dana is the one who suggested this trip for her birthday. Yeah, I think she's looking forward to dragging us all through a weekend of Italian cooking classes and roughing it at that Irish winery, Fitzpatrick's Barn-and-Breakfast. Sounds odd to me—the words *Irish* and *winery* together. It is apparently in what they call California's 'other wine region,'" Frances said. "I thought all of California was a wine region. Relax, take it from me, the Irish throw good parties, and I have the most amazing kitchen store to take you to. This is a must. The Big Little Kitchen Store is only thirty minutes from where we are staying."

"Great. Jason has left me, I can't drink because of screwing up the—what the heck is Irish wine anyway? Potato wine?"

"The Irish wine I am aware of is Guinness. Now, back to that other information thrown out so casually. 'Jason left me'? What happened this time?" Frances was focused on the traffic in front of her and gripped her steering wheel a little tighter. Maybe they should have left Winter behind. Dana was clear that she wanted to share the weekend with everyone, but this could be ugly. A sober, sad, and pregnant Winter was an unknown entity.

Traffic started to move when they cleared the tunnel and were on the downhill side that led into Sausalito. The hills were covered in soft green grasses, giving the scenery a pastel quality in the early morning sunlight. It was always fun to break through the clouds into the sun. Dana called this the best little banana belt, and she was right. Frances kept glancing at Winter, waiting for the explosion.

"You know, what I don't understand is how he can decide to leave and there is no penalty for him. His body is not being hijacked by an alien."

"Winter, what happened?" Frances asked.

"He was home when my team was getting me ready for my grand jury testimony."

"I'm not following you because that happened a couple months ago. Jason was at the pre-baby-shower party. How could that cause Jason to leave?"

"Frances," Winter glanced at Cheryl, "he confronted me over it. He had been stewing about it and listening to his friends who all watched the news reports. I finally told him the truth. I felt if I was going to marry this guy, I needed to be completely honest. I told him that I knew what my clients were doing and I helped them do it. With the money. I found the legal avenues to channel their money."

"Yeah. That is why your firm was shut down. You're the one who broke the case wide open."

"Jason completely flipped out. He wouldn't let me explain. In front of everyone, he wigged out and told me I should be in jail and said he wouldn't support anyone who worked for the devil. He said that I had a criminal mind, and there was no way he could ever be with a criminal."

"What?" Cheryl asked. "Aren't all lawyers criminals? Shakespeare had it right with the joke to 'kill all the lawyers.'"

"Not helping, Cheryl." Frances reached out and tapped Winter with the tips of her fingers. Sometimes a big truck was not helpful when a friend needed reassurance.

"Cheryl, why does everyone make fun of lawyers?" Winter's tears fell at such a fast rate, Frances was worried she would soak her shirt so much it would be an R-rated situation.

Frances took the Corte Madera exit so she could pull over in the mall parking lot. This conversation was not what Dana needed to walk into for her birthday fun trip. Frances's mind was racing as she tried to come up with something to pacify Winter. She wanted to ask her so many questions but was afraid of the answers. What Winter had shared before made it appear that she had no clue what was happening. That she was innocent. Theresa kept pointing out that Winter's energy was unlike anyone else she knew. Frances brought the truck to a stop, jumped out, climbed into the back seat, and took Winter's hand in hers.

"Winter, you are dealing with your choices. You might have figured out how to funnel the money, and you have a brilliant mind. I think I am not going to ask you any more about what you did or did not know. I firmly believe you brought in Molly to help you get out of what you knew was wrong. Jason needs time to process what he heard. Had you lied to him?"

"Not directly."

"Winter, one thing I am learning is that truth, no matter how horrible, is required. Even if it means the end of the relationship. The truth is messy. You need to know that you are honest with yourself. Take this weekend to leave all this in the City. Breathe. Let go. Call Jason when you return." Frances put her arm around Winter and tried to give her a hug.

"Does this count as getting to second base in the backseat of a truck?" Winter asked.

"Nope. We were not kissing."

"Frances, what's going on in that rusty hamster wheel you call a brain? I can hear it going squeak, squeak, squeak," Winter said.

"Not funny. My hamster is off drinking some Irish wine at the moment. Not only do I have you to worry about over the disappearing Jason, I was thinking about Theresa and Kelly. Last night, we picked Kelly up at the airport, and the woman was…well . . . I'm going to say I think she's unable to support Theresa through all this crap going on with the family. Can we go pick up Dana?"

"Yeah. I promise I'll pull myself into controlled Winter. Cheryl—"

"I didn't hear a thing," Cheryl said and continued to type away with her thumbs on her phone.

Frances was back in the driver's seat and had them pulling into the traffic flow on North 101 on their way to capture Dana. "You know, I am still processing the whole confusion over Theresa and being written out of the will and basically being told I am no longer part of the family, only to have my dad crash my gallery opening. It is a surreal world."

"Frances, I don't know anyone from a normal family. At least you have a family. I have no clue where my brother is or even if he is alive. My dad died years ago, not that it wasn't expected. You drink that much and, at some point, the liver is going to quit," Winter said.

"What about your mom? She's got to be excited about having a granddaughter," Cheryl said.

"Let's say that if she could remember that she had a daughter, she would be thrilled. My mom hasn't recognized me in over a year. I stopped going to the nursing home. I pay the bill every month and hope they are taking care of her."

"Winter, I'm sorry. I had no idea," Frances said, taking a right off Sir Frances Drake and onto Main Street.

"No big deal. Now you know why I've been hanging on to you guys harder than I should be."

"You do have us and the boys. You are not going to believe all the prep Russell and Simon are doing. They are so excited about this little one arriving, you'd think they were the fathers. Put your smiles on, ladies. We are here. Let's go get the birthday girl."

"Winter, I know I'm not your favorite, but I want you to know that I'm here too." Cheryl reached over the front seat and tapped the top of Winter's hand.

Before Frances had hopped out of the truck, Lulu was barking out her greeting and wagging her tail. Frances waved at Dana, who was standing in her open doorway. Dana's yellow house—trimmed in white and surrounded by a lush garden of flowers, trees, and an amazing honeysuckle hedge—looked like a painting of a quaint English country home.

"Morning, birthday girl," Frances called from across the street.

CHAPTER TWENTY-ONE

"Happy birthday, Dana!" Winter and Cheryl sang out together.

"Jesus H. Christ in the mountains. I'm way past girl age. You knuckleheads are announcing my business to the whole world. Now come get my suitcase." Dana gave Lulu a huge bone to chew on and placed her back in the house. "I hate leaving her; however, I think she gets to eat steak when Frank gets home. Dana's away so the mice will play and eat steak."

"I bet Doris Day is the one behind the whole eat-beef thing," Cheryl said.

"You could be right. I had not thought about that. I had two eggs for breakfast this morning."

"I'm not going to discuss the philosophical irony of living in a house with a live chicken and eating eggs and chicken meat," Frances said as she delivered Dana's suitcase and Igloo cooler to the truck.

"What's the cooler for, Dana?" Winter asked.

"Snacks. You can't have a road trip without salami and cheese." Dana heaved herself up into the back seat of the truck with Winter.

"I miss living here," Frances said, getting into her truck.

"Do you remember the first day you moved into the house next door?"

"I do. I don't think Cheryl and Winter care to be bored with that story."

"Sure, we do. We have at least a three-hour drive, completely dependent on traffic patterns, between here and Sacramento. All the little IT mice are in mass exodus to Lake Tahoe, and we have to take Highway 50," Cheryl said as she continued to type on her phone.

"Story it is then. Frances gets to the house and her side door was slightly ajar. Totally freaked her out. She had seen the sheriff deputies standing at the east gate of the prison. You know, the big house guards, less than fifty feet from her front yard. She starts walking down to them, and the neighbor on the other side intercepts her. Two things here: Frances had no clue that was San Quentin Prison, and she did not know those men never leave their post. Her new eighty-year-old neighbor said she would walk through the house for Frances. Frances let her do it."

"Well, if you tell the story like that, it makes me sound like I have no problem sacrificing an old lady and I'm a coward."

"No. You are all nuts for living next to California's death row. Frances, you didn't grow up here, so you are somewhat off the hook," Winter said.

"Does your chicken notice when you aren't around?" Cheryl asked.

"I think she eats steak too. I know she's building a nest in the sink window box as we speak."

"Dana, that is so gross." Frances merged the truck into traffic on the Richmond Bridge, and they were on their way. "Everyone, make sure you are buckled up, and Winter, keep that belt off your baby incubator."

"Road trip is officially started, and I am unplugging," Cheryl said, shutting off her work phone.

"I can't believe it. While I would have preferred doing a tour of Italy, this is close."

"Dana, staying in a barn-and-breakfast in Somerset, California is approximately six thousand one hundred and sixty-five miles away from Rome. I'm going have to squint pretty hard and drink something heavier than Sprite to believe I'm in Italy."

"Winter, you need to take a chill pill," Cheryl said, turning around to face her. "This is going to be awesome. I was researching this chef, and he is probably going to make better food than we could get in Italy. He's the real deal."

"Right. You keep telling yourself that and let me know when Santa Claus arrives."

Frances cracked open her window and let the scent of morning come into the truck. She was trying to let herself relax into the weekend. The heavy weight she carried concerning her family could be put on a shelf and left in the City, along with the strange possible connection with a teacup and Ethan. Theresa would figure her own way through, and Frances hoped they would continue to be in each other's lives. This trip with her friends was going to help her smile. Dana looked peaceful and happy, watching the world pass by on their way to good food, unknown wine, and an Irish bed-and-breakfast.

CHAPTER TWENTY-TWO
PROSPECTING ALIVE IN PLACERVILLE

Samantha Iverson stood on the very edge of a huge orange-tinted concrete patio, watching the chipmunks race around the hillside that led up to a small ridge. She closed her eyes to the warmth of the sun and pulled in a deep breath of air perfumed heavily by the pine forest. This was exactly what she needed after months of nonstop traveling and entrapment inside glass boxes listening to excuses and blame. She loved her job, but her latest client was challenging her desire to work.

She reached into her pocket and smiled over her stupid habit of checking her phone. This was her time. These four days were going to be unplugged from the world and spent enjoying time with her friend Sherri. The perks of spending time with Sherri meant being wonderfully spoiled with amazing food. Sherri's husband, Giovanni, was one of the most incredible chefs. Just thinking about his magic in the kitchen brought rumbles from her stomach.

"Good morning," Sherri said, handing Samantha a champagne flute filled with orange juice and sparkling wine.

"I'm so glad you called and invited me up this weekend." Samantha took a long sip from the morning cocktail.

"Come sit." Sherri patted the overstuffed cushion next to her on the patio couch. "Put your feet up and relax. You are no longer on the clock, and it is time for us to catch up."

"This place is amazing. I know you were expressing some reservations as the complications from building were starting to sound close to disastrous. But this…I don't think I've slept that soundly in years."

"It is finally starting to feel like home now that we are moved in and the business is getting well established. I'm going to have to run in about two hours. I told Gio I would help with the prep for his first cooking class."

"Now who's on the clock? I think I'll be fine. I can take Anteros and Fortuna out for a walk in the woods."

"Good luck with those two—they have mellowed in their mid-life dog years. You might have better luck curling up with them on the couch here and taking an afternoon nap."

Samantha leaned her head back into the soft burgundy cushion and enjoyed the tickle of the sparkling orange juice on her tongue. Maybe a nap was exactly what was in order. "When are you and Giovanni headed off to Italy?"

"You must join us on one of our trips. This next one is a gourmet food adventure through the hill towns of Northern Italy."

"Sounds wonderful but—"

"No excuses. You always have a place. I'll email the dates. I want to hear about you."

"Do you and Gio ever miss having the restaurant?"

"Nope. The headaches are all gone over dealing with…what's the word? I seem to be forgetting words more often."

"Could it be age?" Samantha asked, smiling. "What's the plan for the weekend?"

"You start pointing the age finger at me and what does that mean about you?"

"Am I going to be solo this whole weekend with you and Giovanni off teaching people his culinary secrets?"

"Don't pout. I am helping him set up his first class. It was moved at the last minute to the house. The kitchen at the winery is having issues with their oven. He thought about changing the menu, but he has such beautiful food planned that he decided to move it here. Personally, I think this is a nicer setting anyway. More room."

"Do I get to be the official food sampler?"

"You already know the answer. Think of it like having an entire downstairs staff preparing your lunch today."

"Sherri, have you offered Sam any breakfast this morning?" Giovanni asked through the open glass doors.

"What's on the menu this morning?" Sherri responded. "I knew he would be out to make us breakfast. I hope you are ready for a feast. I know it might be a stretch for you, given your Diet Coke and Snickers lifestyle."

"Hey, I only ate like that when we were in grad school together. I eat other things now."

"Nutter Butters slathered in Nutella."

"No, I eat my Nutella unadulterated, with a spoon."

"Enough of this idle chitchat—I need to live vicariously through you. Spill the beans on your love life."

"What does that mean?" Giovanni yelled over the sound of a blender.

"Love you, honey. Samantha lives in the metropolitan world. I am nosey and nothing more." Sherri winked at Sam. "Now out with it. Are you dating anyone, or is it a woman in every port?"

"You'll have to ply me with more of this sparkling OJ."

"How about fresh bread from the oven, Italian eggs, a light watermelon salad dressed in a honey vinaigrette, and an Italian espresso?" Giovanni placed a beautiful tray filled with small plates of food in front of Samantha and Sherri on the oversized foot rest.

"Yes. I'll talk now." Samantha filled her plate with a baked egg smothered in a beautiful tomato sauce swimming in garlic and herbs.

"Honestly, I've been so focused on work, I've not done any dating. Really. No time."

"Why are you smiling? You know you have the worst tells. I can read you like an open picture book."

"Well, I did try an online dating site. There were a couple of dates out of it, but that was months ago."

"Oh my god, were they scary? Were they guys? Or worse, were they kids? I heard about this story where these kids were catfishing 'old' people to get money."

"Brilliant evil little minds playing on someone's desire to love."

"Off topic. Tell me about the dates."

"I was actually sort of catfished."

"No! Are you okay?"

"Hard to say. I was actually quite taken by the woman. Her friends had set up her account and put a real picture of her on the dating site. Maybe she was the one catfished? Not sure."

"Now I'm confused. What do you mean?"

"Her friends didn't tell her they set up a date until right before the date, and then I gathered from her look of utter horror that she had no clue she was being set up with a woman."

"Was it a practical joke? How rude. I'd like to give those people a piece of my mind. People are so sick."

"I responded to the email because the writer had responded to my very obscure *Hitchhiker's Guide to the Galaxy* reference. It made me laugh. After some back and forth, a date was set up." Samantha started to snort and ended up getting some sparkling OJ up her nose. "The pain!"

The laughter continued and brought Giovanni out to refill their glasses and let his wife off the hook for helping. His kitchen prep had shown up, so all was good. Samantha tried to get herself out of pain and drank down a glass of water.

"That blasted book. I remember you quoting from that and Monty Python movies incessantly."

"Long story, even longer—she asked me if I was a professional."

"Professional what? A hooker? Like her friends would have set her up with a lesbian call girl?" Sherri was now laughing so hard she couldn't speak. "What were you wearing? If I know you—and I do—you were in a suit."

"I was. I responded by standing up and kissing her on her lips across the table."

"How forward."

"She kissed back. In the first moment of that kiss, she kissed back, and I felt something."

"Is she pretty?"

"Pretty? I would say she has a very elegant beauty. Her hazel eyes and red curly hair reminded me of this painting I saw of the Lady of Shalott. The crazy thing is, I had noticed her before. It wasn't until I saw her in person that I realized I had seen her at this place we escape from the office for coffee and lunch quite regularly."

"Did you see her again?"

"Well, she ran out of the restaurant after the kiss. No explanation. She ran like she was being chased by a pack of wolves."

"Or a horny lesbian."

"Not nice. I control myself."

"You attacked her."

"She set up the date."

"No, her friends set up the date."

"Think about her for a moment. You walk in, dressed to the nines as you always are, and confidence exuding from every part of you...Heck, I think I would have run too, although I still think her friends are evil."

"Whose friend are you? I will say her pictures online did not do her justice."

"Oh...you liked her."

"I admit, there was some interest."

"Where is this woman? Have you seen her again?"

"I saw her again, like I said, at this small coffee and bakery around the corner from my office a couple days later. She was dressed in purple sweats and clearly did not think she would run into anyone she knew."

"Hold it right there. Just because you overdress for every situation does not mean someone else dressing comfortably is a slob."

"Not what I said."

"Continue."

"She saw me and almost choked to death on a cinnamon roll."

"She sounds like a real winner. Sam, we need to find you a real woman. One who knows she's into women. You do not need to be the training dyke for a woman who is trying to figure out if she is or isn't into women."

"I'm not dating her. I walked away."

"But you can't stop thinking about her. I watched your body language. You think that kiss—"

"Stop getting inside my head." Sam laughed and gently punched Sherri in the arm. "I need to focus on work and not date anyone right now. This rollout of the new brick-and-mortar stores for this tech giant is driving me crazy.

"Why didn't you get her number?"

"Well, there was something else that happened that gave me more than enough reason to walk away."

"So mysterious and serious all of sudden."

"Do you remember that bizarre serial killer who was shot and killed by police in San Francisco?"

"Vaguely—I try not to focus on the news."

"This guy who killed women in sex films had fixated on this woman, Frances, and showed up at her loft with bombs or something like that. I really don't know the details because I have not talked with her. Crazy."

"Stay away from crazy. I know you believe you had found your soulmate when you met Eliza."

"I did. I miss her every day."

"I do too. You two were our favorite couple. I was wondering if you were staying away from Giovanni and me because it still hurts too much."

Samantha scooted closer to Sherri on the couch and wrapped her arms around her. "I love you and Gio so much. I would never stay away without telling you. I'm sorry. No, I think one of the reasons I slept so well last night came from being with people that she and I love so much."

"I hate to break up this little love fest," Giovanni said, "but some of our students have arrived early. What do I do with them?"

"Put them to work. I guess this is the one issue when not trying to sell wine. I should have called and postponed the arrival. It's only ten in the morning. My god." Sherri stood.

Through the open door that gave a full view of the giant kitchen and great room, Samantha saw Dana. Her heart skipped a beat. There, standing next to Dana, was Frances. Samantha stood and bolted along the side of the house to the patio door that led to her room. What the hell? Was this the universe playing a really peculiar joke on her? Samantha flopped onto the bed and screamed into the pillow. A scream of fear and excitement. Was this a sign?

"Not so smooth, ex-lax," Sherri said, standing in the open door of the guest room. Samantha sat up on the bed and looked down the hallway to the entrance. "If you're going to sneak around, you might want to shut the bedroom door. It appears the universe has shined down on me."

"She saw me?"

"She did. I find this whole thing rather cosmic."

"Sherri, this is not going to make for a relaxing weekend."

"Nonsense. I'm going to shut the door. You get yourself together and then join us for lunch. This should be most entertaining."

"Where is she now?"

"Her friends are trying to keep her from making like a jackrabbit and running from the wolf. I think they are playing keep-away with her car keys."

"She drives a truck."

"Oh, how stereotypical. Does she have a U-Haul trailer attached?"

Samantha groaned and pulled the pillow over her face as she flopped backwards onto the bed.

CHAPTER TWENTY-THREE

VULTURES, GUINNESS, AND CRAZY

F rances, Winter, and Cheryl were waiting out on the main deck at Fitzpatrick's Winery Barn-and-Breakfast. The main house was set about halfway up a hillside. Someone had cleared a level area that fit the large main house, a barn, and something that looked like a cinder block castle. The whole place was surrounded by rows and rows of grape vines. If one didn't know any better, this looked very similar to Napa. Upscale wineries were moving into the area. They had passed several very modern buildings boasting tasting rooms for their award-winning wines.

"What do you think those birds are doing?" Cheryl asked, pointing to the sky.

"Those are vultures. If they are circling like that, I would say they are checking out something dead," Dana said as she took a sip of wine.

"How come they are circling faster? Oh, they are ugly. Look, they are getting closer to—"

"Hellpppp! What the hell?" screamed an unseen man. That was followed by several high-pitched shrieks.

"What the heck do you think is going on?" Cheryl stood and walked to the edge of the porch she was sitting on with Dana.

"Guess whatever the birds were interested in was not dead." Dana took another sip of wine.

They watched as a bird shot straight up into the sky and then swooped back down to rest on the edge of the odd castle building. The other four landed on the gray walls, peering inside. Through a curved door in the side of the castle came a woman and man running and waving towels over their heads. The commotion brought several people out of the tasting room and bar that fed directly out to the deck where they had all assembled. Frances watched with amused fascination, relieved she was not the center of attention for once.

"Shoot. Looks like the vultures thought our sunbathers were food again," Marcie Fitzpatrick said and spat something over the railing.

"What?" Frances asked and tried not stare at the bulge in the woman's lower lip. She suspected that chewing tobacco was lodged in there. She watched as the strong woman with long white hair braided down her back walked back into the bar and grabbed a double-barrel rifle from over the door. She grabbed a box of shotgun shells that someone had placed on the bar for her. Frances, Cheryl, Dana, and Winter went and sat on a bench and watched as Marcie walked past the screaming couple to the center of the pea-gravel parking lot and loaded her shotgun. She raised the shotgun in the direction of the vultures and fired. The first crack made everyone duck. Frances noticed the birds didn't move. The screaming couple were now reduced to tears while they held each other in a crumpled heap on the porch.

"Marcie, how many times do I have to tell you that you can't scare those stupid birds with the shotgun?" said a tall man wearing a straw hat so old it was hard to make out exactly what its original shape might have been.

"Liam, I am tired of our guests being run out of the pool by the vultures."

"Tired of...you mean, this has happened before?" Winter asked, turning to Frances. "I was right when I said we were staying at the barn-and-breakfast. I think I'll skip laying out by the pool. I am not going to be cast in an Alfred Hitchcock *Birds* remake."

Another loud bang echoed through the area, followed by a strange howl-like laughter.

"Jesus H. Christ in the mountains, what in the H-E-double hockey sticks was that noise?" Dana asked. "It made me spill my wine."

"Damn it, Marcie. I wanted to shoot the cannon," Liam said as he came running out of the bar.

"Cannon? What kind of place is this?" Winter asked.

"Time to go and learn some Italian cooking," Dana said, gulping down the last of her wine.

"We are two hours early," Cheryl said.

"I think I've had enough of the booming gun and cannons. Let's go," Winter said.

They all piled into the truck and left an arguing couple in the parking lot.

"The vultures are still there," Cheryl said, watching the action as Frances drove down the curved road.

The modern pueblo-style home with stucco stained in soft oranges, red, and desert sand colors blended into the surrounding hillside, making one believe that it was part of the scenery. Frances pulled her giant F-250 diesel truck, affectionately named Snow White, up to a spot between a Mercedes AMG SL 63 and a Range Rover. The license plate on the SL made Frances pause: *SamIAm*.

"Hey, that sleek convertible has a fun vanity plate. Must be a Dr. Seuss fan," Cheryl said.

"Or their name is Sam." Dana hooked her arm into Frances's and started guiding the group up to the front door.

Frances had an odd feeling about arriving so early. She had barely taken a sip from her pint of Guinness when somehow the collective decided to leave the winery. She stopped at the edge of the driveway and turned to the group. One thing that would have pissed her off was a group of people arriving two hours early to a place that was substituted at the last minute.

"Dana, when did you get the email that we weren't to go to the winery for the class?" Frances asked.

"About fifteen minutes ago. They sent a text too. I'm waiting for the phone call."

"Why was it changed to their private home?" Winter asked. "I'm with Frances, I think we are on the rude side of early. But we should have brought our suitcases and moved in because this place is awesome."

"I'll read the message again. *Urgent: Change of venue for our kick-off to the Taste of Italia cooking weekend. Please arrive at the address given on the attachment. The Winery had an issue with its stove and oven. Our home is a beautiful teaching kitchen. The winery will be delivering the wines that were originally paired with each meal course. Look forward to seeing you all.*"

"We are so early. They just moved the event from one venue to this one. Do you think they would be ready for us? Maybe we should go tour the area or go to the Big Little Kitchen store," Frances pleaded, considering running back to the truck and waiting until the arrival time. "Dana, you've got one strong grip." Frances was not going to escape Dana's hand on her arm. She was stuck.

"The better to keep you, my dear."

The crew collected in front of the beautiful wooden double doors that added even more charm to the place out in the middle of Northern California gold country. Dana put her ear to the door before knocking. "I hear people inside talking and laughing—this mission is a go."

Frances could see the excitement in Dana's eyes, and she caved into her excitement. She loved cooking and couldn't wait to learn something fun and new. Mud pies were Frances's first foray into learning how food pleased people. While other kids used dirt, Frances used only the best ingredients—a combination of Snack Pack puddings and crushed Oreos purchased with her allowance money. Word got out in the neighborhood that Frances made pudding mud pies. Soon she had her own shop set up out of the garage. Agatha and Edna would sell the mud pies—one scoop in a Dixie cup for thirty cents. They paid her a dime for every fifteen cups sold. Man, she was stupid then.

"Earth to Frances. Are you going to come in or continue impersonating a lawn jockey?" Winter asked. "Take note, a real chef must live here—did you see the door knocker? It's one big-ass iron ladle."

A deep breath and Frances brushed away the mud pie memories to notice the very cool iron door knocker. Before she took a step forward, it was her turn to be encircled in the arms of a stranger.

"*Benvenuto nella nostra casa,*" Sherri said. She jumped from Frances to Dana and then Winter and Cheryl in lightning hug speed. "Giovanni is so excited you are all here. Glad you got the change of venue. And this must be the *Festeggiata*."

Dana was lost in the arms and cheek kisses of one very friendly hostess. Frances placed her hand under Dana's elbow as she seemed a little dazed from the welcome. The group walked into the front entrance that opened into a great hall of a room on the right side, while to the left was a long hall with a very inviting-looking room at the end of it. A large bed covered in a fluffy white comforter was unmade, and sheer curtains were softly blowing in the early afternoon breeze.

"A glass of wine before we get started?" Giovanni approached with short glasses filled with a light-colored wine on an oval wooden tray. "Welcome to a weekend of taste sensations. I am Giovanni, and you met my wife, Sherri. We are going to be your tour guides this weekend."

"You all get the award for being super punctual."

"I blame that on being overly excited," Dana said.

"I blame it on those darn vultures trying to eat the guests."

"Classic. I love the pool at Fitzpatrick's—you really must go try it while you are there," Sherri said. "The vultures don't seem to learn."

"It looks like a prison," Winter said.

"True. But it is a really nice pool, and it is shielded from the wind," Sherri said. "Just keep splashing, and the vultures will leave you alone."

"This wine is really good," Frances said, taking another sip. Each sip revealed another note of flavor—at first she thought she tasted vanilla, followed by crisp citrus. A motion out on the patio caught Frances's eye. A woman with long dark hair had stood up from an overly comfy-looking outdoor couch. There was something familiar about the woman. She walked back toward the entrance to look at a most unusual wooden statute of a laughing Buddha holding his hands above his head. The woman who Frances had seen stared at her for a moment before she closed the door to the bedroom at the end of the hall.

"Can you believe this place?" Winter caught up with Frances.

CHAPTER TWENTY-THREE

"Is something wrong?" Sherri asked, placing a hand on Frances's shoulder.

"I thought I saw…this is crazy…there is no way. Dana, get over here," Frances demanded.

"What's going on? I was getting a tour of the most amazing kitchen I've ever seen. They have their own wood-burning oven. That is the fabulous wood smoke smell that is in the air. We can make wood-fired flatbread and pizza."

"Dana, did you invite anyone else to your little Italian cooking weekend?" Frances looked straight into Dana's face with an intensity she had forgotten she had.

"No. Why?"

"I thought I saw a woman we both know. First out on the patio and now at the room at the end of this hallway." Frances pointed to the closed door.

"That woman you saw is my closest friend, Samantha Iverson," Sherri said.

The sound that escaped Frances's mouth was not quite identifiable. Instead of her usual flashes of red, Frances felt herself losing her hearing and a tunnel vision take over her line of sight. She had to tell herself to keep breathing. It explained the vanity plate on the very expensive car in the driveway. What the heck? This can't be happening. Why here? Why now?

"Frances, why don't you take a seat on the couch. You don't look too great. Maybe you shouldn't be mixing Guinness with wine," Dana said.

Frances looked at the closed door and fought her immediate desire to run to Sam. Frances followed Sherri into the great room and took a seat that allowed her to view the kitchen and most of the hallway.

"I'll be back in a moment," Sherri said as she walked down the hall and knocked on the door. Frances rose again and walked to view the full expanse of the hallway. The door opened, and Sherri blocked the face of the woman she was talking to. Dana had come over and stood by Frances.

"Shit. Cheryl, Winter, and people in the kitchen, remove any sharp objects." Dana put her hands on Frances's shoulders. "I swear on my grandmother's grave that I did not invite Sam to this weekend."

"She didn't. As I told you, I invited my friend for the weekend," Sherri said, walking down the hallway. "Oh my god...you're the runaway date."

"Great," Frances said and threw her hands up in the air.

"This is perfect. I can see what she..." Sherri burst into laughter.

Frances turned around and couldn't decide what to do. She was trapped in this house. Sam was here for the whole weekend? How could this be?

"Hey, did you guys see the menu for our afternoon lunch?" Cheryl asked, coming around the corner. "What'd I miss?"

"Samantha is here," Dana said.

"No way. This weekend is FOK'd," Cheryl said. "Dana, you are totally making that up."

"When did my initials become the word for screwed up?"

"The moment you entered the world," Winter said, laughing.

"Did Dana invite her?" Cheryl asked.

"No. I'm going to go get cooking. This is something bigger than all of us."

"I smell bread baking. This has got to be close to heaven," Winter said and was off in search of the bread.

"In all the Italian chef homes in all the world, we find ourselves face-to-face," Sam said, approaching Frances. In attempting not to pass out, Frances had missed Sam's entrance into the great room.

"Crazy. I . . ." Frances bit her lip. She looked at Sherri, who was trying to silence her laughter, and Dana, who looked amused and concerned.

"How about you two go out to the front garden and I will bring you . . . let's start with some Italian lemonade," Sherri said and waved Sam and Frances toward the front door. She then turned to the rest of the crowd.

"Come, everyone. Grab a place somewhere along the island. You are going to help with the pre-prep, and we will be good to go in no time." Giovanni started showing them how to chop the various vegetables laid out in front of them.

Back in the hallway, Samantha said, "Frances, I'll join you in a moment. I need to grab something out of my room, and I'll bring the drinks out with me."

"No worries." Frances managed to choke the words out. She walked out to the front yard, which resembled a rather elaborate rock garden. What was going on right now? Immediately, Frances's mind went to Molly. What were the odds of this happening? Dana had looked as shocked as she felt when she fully realized it was Sam. Frances turned and walked toward the driveway. Somehow, she had known that SL convertible was Sam's.

This was crazy. Why now, when so much was up in the air, and Frances felt herself finally figuring out how to fight for Molly, a woman she had chemistry with and admired. Frances touched her lips with her fingertips. That kiss from Sam. She had never forgotten it. There was more than a spark between her and Sam. She had felt her in this place before she actually saw her. Was this the universe finally tiring of Frances letting Sam slip away through her own stupidity?

Frances walked over to a Zen sand garden, picking up a rake and smoothing the surface of the sand. She watched two cars as they made their way slowly down the serpentine two-lane road that went by the bottom of the hill. Her head was starting to throb, and she sat down on a large rock that separated the front cactus bed from the driveway. *Why? Why? Why?* Frances yelled inside her head, looking around because she was not completely sure she had kept that yelling contained inside her head.

She reached down and picked up a handful of pebbles and started aiming at a rock down the driveway from her. She only pinged it twice after several tries and, disgusted with her poor aim, let the rest of the pebbles fall from her hand. The sun was hot, and she felt the trickle of sweat slide down the center of her back. She looked across to the distant hilltops and saw something move by the edge of the driveway. She searched and squinted as the rock she had been throwing pebbles at moved again.

"Great Scott! That rock is alive. What the—?" Frances stood and started to slowly approach what she had originally mistaken for a rock. "Rocks don't have heads."

"No. No, they don't. That is Rocky the speedy tortoise."

"Oh no! I was stoning a tortoise? I'm so sorry. I didn't know."

"Relax. You woke him up. He's looking for another place to nap," Samantha said.

Frances turned to face Samantha, who was standing at the edge of the path leading to the front door holding two cobalt blue glasses with ice and something that might be lemonade.

"You know, you really are adorable as your skin passes through more hues of red. I didn't know a human could turn so many shades," Samantha said and held out a glass toward Frances.

Frances touched her face with her hands and felt the grit of the sandy dirt. She kept repeating the phrase *don't run, don't run, don't run... run... no... no, don't run...* in her head.

"You look as if you're getting ready to run," Sam said.

"No."

"Really? I can see it broadcasting through your brain."

"How? How are you here? Of all the places . . ."

"And all the gin joints in the world . . ."

"I like old movies too. Play it again, Sam."

"I guess that line would be better if I actually played an instrument," Sam said. "Thought you might like to try the Italian lemonade. It's an acquired taste. I've grown to love it."

Frances walked up to Samantha and let the smile grow on her face. The woman standing in front of her was truly amazing, and Frances felt that deep in her soul. This feeling was so different than what she felt with Olivia and even Molly. It was a feeling she could only quantify as a messy, beautiful, passionate pulse coming from deep inside her soul. Sam looked so incredibly relaxed, comfortable, and sexy standing in the sun.

"What makes it Italian lemonade? Garlic?" Frances asked.

She reached out to receive the cold glass and misjudged the length of her arm. Time slowed as she dove toward the ground, trying to keep the glass from shattering on the flagstone pathway. Darkness passed over her for a moment as she caught the glass but felt a sharp pain travel from her kneecap up through her spine and into her head. When she opened her eyes, she was face down on the hard rock, an empty glass intact in her clenched hand, and a searing pain shooting through her right knee. Frances closed her eyes again and wanted a redo on the whole situation. Why was she such a klutz? Seconds passed, and she felt a cool hand touch the back of her neck. She was still face down in the dirt.

"I want to see if you can carefully turn yourself over. You hit the ground really hard."

"Sam, I'm fine. Truly. Would you mind giving me a little space?" Frances tried not to grimace as she turned over onto her back, scared to look at her knee. "I think I might have broken my kneecap."

"Slowly. Go slowly."

She let go of the glass as she took Sam's hand and watched as it fell to the ground and bounced. "It was plastic? I truly am an idiot. Plastic. I saved a plastic glass from shattering."

Frances exhaled and felt completely deflated as she got to her feet with Sam's help. This continued the long line of bizarre encounters with Samantha. Maybe this was not such a good idea. She looked at Samantha and gasped.

"What's wrong?" Sam asked.

"I'm not going to say."

"You must now. What is it?"

"I'm a complete klutz, and you are completely surrounded in Robert Redford lighting."

"Robert Redford lighting? What the heck is that?"

"You know, in all his films he was always in the gold sunlight glow."

"And who are you?" Sam asked.

"Let me think about who I match…I could be a hero of plastic glasses everywhere."

Frances, with the help of Samantha, hobbled over to a wooden bench and eased herself to a seated position, unable to bend her knee. She noticed the sunlight dripping through the oak leaves and into Samantha's long wavy hair. A large smile on Samantha's face filled her entire field of vision. No sooner was she getting lost in her face when Sam's lips were gently pressing on her lips, and Frances yielded to the kiss. Electric pulses shot through her body and overrode the pain from her knee.

Frances let herself go into the layers of anticipation and curiosity as the kiss progressed. Sam was now sitting next to her on the bench, and they were frozen in time as Frances gently tucked Sam's hair out of her face. The soft caress of Sam wiping some dirt off Frances's cheek sent anther shock wave through her body. There was a simple honesty in the way Sam pulled Frances toward her and kissed her a second time.

"You taste like honey and lemons," Frances whispered.

"Are you okay?" Sam asked as she looked down at Frances's knee. "You're bleeding."

"I wondered what happened to you two," Dana said, walking up to the bench. "Cut the duck with a chainsaw, what happened? Frances, you have blood soaking through your jeans."

"Well . . ." Frances tried to casually pull herself away from Sam, but her bracelet got caught in Sam's hair.

"Let me help you with that. Don't move, Frances, we don't want to scalp Samantha." Dana leaned into the fray and worked Frances's hand out of the bracelet and then freed Sam's hair.

"Dana, I think I might have busted my kneecap."

"Frances, you are truly FOK'd. We need to take you directly to the closest emergency room. I'll go ask them where that is—"

"Dana, I know where to go. If you can grab my keys and wallet, which are on the dresser in the room at the end of the hall, I'll get this plastic glass hero into my car."

Frances watched Dana take off like a shot and took Sam's hand to stand. "You think you'll be able to get me out of your car? Wait, I don't want to stain your car with my blood."

"No worries. I've got a beach towel in the trunk."

Sam opened the trunk of her car, revealing a small folded beach chair, a couple of towels, and a small picnic basket.

"Planning on a picnic?"

"Always have my beach kit ready. I drove up from my place on the coast a couple weeks ago. I miss the ocean."

"I do too."

"Here you go." Dana handed Sam her keys and wallet.

Frances watched in awe as the retractable roof opened up to the sky. This was going to be one heck of a ride to an ER room. Her last ride to a hospital, in the back of an ambulance after having fainted from Ethan's takeover of her loft, was rather blurry. But she was going to take this one and put it into her permanent memory bank.

"Wait, I've got some ice for Frances," called Sherri, walking up with a bag of ice wrapped in a dish towel. Sam gently placed it on Frances's knee.

"I feel so silly," Frances said. She noticed that Samantha smelled of fresh linen, sandalwood, and licorice. The smell was intoxicating. Dana came out with a pillow wrapped in a plastic garbage bag.

"Prop this under your knee so you don't wear yourself out trying to hold it still."

"Good idea, Dana. You're like a Girl Scout," Sherri said.

"Nope. A very experienced retired high school teacher. Those teenagers came up with the most interesting first-aid problems."

Frances looked down at her dirt-covered clothing. "I'm so dirty, and now my dirt is in this amazing car."

"That's what vacuums are for—not to worry. Time to go. I'll have her back as soon as I can," Samantha said.

CHAPTER TWENTY-FOUR
LOBSTERS ON THE RUN

J oshua walked down the street, energized over the three dinner seatings selling out for the evening. He had decided to offer a special surf-and-turf night to simplify his grand opening. The soft opening for Joshua's Otter Place was such a huge success, he wanted to focus the menu to top all expectations. It had taken some wrangling to convince his executive chef, Megan Bailey, but once she was on board, she researched the most environmentally friendly lobsters for the surf part of the specials.

When he walked through the doors of his restaurant, his waitstaff was already well into the table prep. He used to think that his favorite sound was the ocean waves he could hear from his bedroom window. Now he loved the sounds of his restaurant being prepared for diners. He practically skipped through the dining room, he was so giddy. Word of mouth through social media had spread through the whole area and into San Francisco. They were booking tables three months from now. He had hired two people to answer the phones from eight in the morning. They helped guests with other reservations too. It was an idea he had read about and liked. If there was no room in his restaurant for the night they wanted, his reservationists had suggestions for other places in the area.

He stopped and listened. He could hear Megan barking orders to the sous chef and line cooks. She was a pistol from Chicago and demanded almost complete control of the kitchen. With the exception of the grand opening tonight, he gave it to her. When he heard music start blasting from the kitchen, Joshua knew it was safe for him to enter. He hovered in the kitchen by the white board that listed today's menu. The aroma of food being prepped was starting to fill the air. They had more than two hundred guests coming in for dinner tonight. Those friends who had warned him that opening a restaurant was like experiencing a shipwreck were so wrong.

Joshua walked back out into the dining room to make sure the table settings were correct for the 5:30 seating. He stopped and looked up at Frances's painting. With the sunlight streaming in through the windows, he could see the depths of the brush strokes in the dark hues of blue. The water appeared to be moving to the tune of the Danish rock music coming from the kitchen. Joshua placed his left hand over his heart and thought about the woman who painted this art. Just as suddenly, his mind went to her smart-mouthed sister, Theresa. Joshua shook his head.

"Josh! I need you in the kitchen. Now!" said a short, stout woman wearing a pink chef's jacket with her name embroidered on the left sleeve.

"I'll be there in a minute, Meg."

"Chop chop, Mister Rogers, there's a riot in the neighborhood," Megan said, walking back through the swinging door into the kitchen.

Joshua took a deep breath and turned to count the tables. His back was to the kitchen, so he didn't see the Tasmanian Devil come spinning out toward him. Meg grabbed him by his belt and hauled him into the kitchen. Through the swinging doors, Joshua ran head first into a server carrying a tray of empty dinner plates to be placed on the shelves for service. The ear-piercing sound of ceramic crashing to the ground stopped all conversations among the workers. Joshua righted himself with the aid of the server he had run into. Meg raised both arms and created silence with one word, "Opa!"

Nervous laughter and light conversation resumed as a flurry of people went back to their tasks. Joshua locked his eyes on Meg's. He could not read the expression on her face. With a couple of deep breaths, he felt his heart rate come down as he walked into the office he shared with Meg.

"What's up?" Joshua asked as calmly as he could. With the manhandling by Meg, he knew this was not going to be a tour down the lane of niceness.

"Serious problem number one. We are missing half the line staff."

"Where are they? Did they understand we were starting three hours earlier?"

"I called them myself and told them that if they weren't here in twenty minutes, they'd be fired."

"Not again. Let me guess. That was twenty-one minutes ago."

"Yup."

"Can you get through tonight with the ones still standing out there?"

"Possibly. I have them working hard. I think we can do it. I'm pitching in on a lot of the prep too. It will be done right."

"Problem number two?" Joshua asked as he walked to the open door of his office and looked out into the kitchen. Everyone appeared to be working extremely hard. No limbs were missing, and they all appeared to have their fingers intact. He had hoped things with the line staff had been ironed out through the soft opening. The fact that everyone from the first line staff quit could have been an omen. Instead, Joshua used it to open a door for a group that ordinarily would have a hard time getting hired. It was a risk opening up to people fresh out of prison, but as long as they passed the California Food Handlers requirements and met Meg's even tougher standards, it was a gift. The crew currently busting their asses right now appeared to be working well together. Meg was raising their skill level daily.

"I can't believe you didn't notice our second problem," Meg said crossing her arms. "What the fuck? Did you not see the tank? You convinced me that we needed to limit the menu tonight to surf-and-turf, and we have no fucking surf to balance the turf."

Joshua turned toward the tank. "The tank? It has water in it."

Meg walked over to the large saltwater fish tank and acted like she was showing off a potential prize on *The Price is Right*. Joshua giggled as he noticed how short Meg really was, seeing that her outstretched arm didn't clear the top of the tank.

And then he saw the problem. "Oh, shit. Where are the lobsters?" Joshua said.

"Ding ding! Get this man a prize or a pair of fucking glasses," Meg said.

"Where are all the lobsters? They were delivered here this morning at seven. I was here—"

"It appears they swam away. I have no clue where they are because I never saw them."

"What?"

"I saw the tag on the stack of deliveries today. I was thinking I could get the appetizer lobster dish ready. When I sent the kid to the tank to fish out ten lobsters, he came back with nothing."

Joshua walked back to his swivel office chair and sat down, his face drained of color. "I had overpriced humanely harvested live lobsters flown in overnight, and they are missing?" Numbers ran through his head as he had spent a small fortune to do this and find lobsters that would rival anything from Maine. "Is this a joke? You're punking me."

"No sir, I am not joking. No punk pulled."

Joshua walked through the kitchen and out the back door into the empty alley, not sure what he thought he would see. A line of lobsters escaping toward the ocean? It was clear they were gone. He wanted to hit something, anything, or anyone. His mind was working a million miles an hour. Joshua walked around in tight circles, focusing on his scuffed black leather shoes. "I needed to polish my shoes."

"What does polishing shoes have to do with missing lobsters? Focus," Meg said.

His circles were becoming lines as he paced back and forth in the alley. Who steals lobsters? Had he locked the kitchen door? What about the staff? Who was the next person in this morning after himself? "Who opened the place?"

"I did. You said you had it, so I did my own work."

"Get on the phone to any fishmongers you know in the area and see what we can wrestle up."

"What are you going to do?"

"I had security cameras installed. I'm going to see if they recorded anything and call the cops." Joshua pulled out his wallet. "Here's my credit card. Whatever you can find that qualifies as surf, you buy it and get it here."

Before he did anything else, he rifled through his top desk drawer looking for his migraine medication. When he shut his eyes, the telltale pinpoints of light warned him that a nauseating head vice was going to grip him soon and hold him hostage. The head pain used to make him question whether life was trying to torture him for his choices. Where was that prescription? It cost him a fortune, and he knew he had three of the six pills left. His neurologist had told him to keep the medicine with him always because it had a very small window in which to work.

A knock on his office door stopped his frantic search. He turned. "Enter," was all he could muster.

"We have crab on its way from Redwood City. Don't ask any questions. I'm already reworking the menu. You need to figure out what you want to do about the cost issues."

"Thanks, Meg." Joshua went back to looking through his desk. He saw his jacket hanging on the door and sprang to it like a cat after prey. "Gotcha." He pulled out a small blue box and fought through shrink wrap to free the little orange pill, swallowing it without water. He hoped it was in time. Freed from an impending migraine, he turned on the computer screen and found the feed from his security camera system, installed to protect the art he had purchased and to satisfy the insurance company. Now he was glad he had it. He knew he would have the identity of the pied piper of lobsters soon.

Black-and-white images filled the screen with amazing clarity. He watched as a small open-bed Chevy truck drove up the alley and stopped right under the camera focused on the door from the alley into the kitchen. Out jumped a short-statured person wearing a long raincoat, rubber boots, and an oversized mariner's rain hat. Joshua blinked hard a couple of times as he watched the person try several keys until they had the one that opened the door.

As the video continued, Joshua dialed the Monterey Police Department. He knew most of the officers, who were regulars at his coffee place. He never charged them for their coffee and hoped they would be quick to help him locate the missing lobsters.

"Police, how may I direct your call?"

"Hi. This is Joshua over at my Otter Place. The restaurant."

"Hey, Josh. This is Erica. What's doin'?"

"I need to report a robbery, or maybe this is a kidnapping."

"I'll connect you to 9-1-1."

"Wait, Erica, aren't you at the police department?"

"Yes."

"Can I talk to Randy?"

"But if this is a robbery happening now, I need to connect you to 9-1-1."

"It already happened. No danger. Someone—and I think I might know who that someone is—took about one hundred and eighty live lobsters from my kitchen."

"What are you doing with one hundred and eighty live lobsters?" Erica asked.

"Erica, is Randy available?" Joshua asked.

"Hold on just a sec. Let me check," Erica said.

The conversation was testing his ability to control his patience. He watched the film clip over and over and knew exactly who had taken the lobsters. Should he hang up and go to her directly?

Erica came back on the line. "I talked with Randy and told him you have one hundred and eighty missing lobsters. Randy wants to know if you can make him a burger. He hasn't had anything to eat, and it's almost lunch."

"Does that mean he's coming over here?"

"I'll check. Hang on a moment."

"What the hell?" Joshua banged the phone receiver against his head.

"Randy said he'll come over to get the burger. You don't have to deliver it." Erica hung up.

This really cannot be my life, Joshua thought. Is this a joke? Am I being filmed right now? They are getting me back for the April Fool's Day coffee joke.

He placed the phone back on its cradle and stared at the computer screen. The picture of the lobster thief frozen on the screen had him wondering if Alice had done this because he had refused to respond to her flirting. He knew what it was like to be in love with someone who did not feel the same way, and he had been careful not to mislead her in any way. He was getting his life to the place he wanted, and it was not the time to be romantically involved with anyone. It was too messy.

Joshua rubbed his temples. The migraine was held back, but he could feel the tentacles of the head crusher reaching through the medicine and gnashing its teeth at the fringes of his consciousness. How was he going to proceed with this little situation? He knew he could not tell Meg. She would have no issue butchering Alice over it. If he pressed charges, would her job at the Aquarium be over? Or would they throw her a party? The fact she used five-gallon buckets stamped with the Monterey Bay Aquarium logo on the side was rather amazing.

He turned a couple of rotations in his swivel chair, lifting his feet off the ground—not the smartest thing to do when on the verge of a headache from hell; however, there was something freeing in the action. A knock on the office door made his heart sink. What else could happen today? Maybe he shouldn't even invite that question into his mind.

"Enter."

Meg opened the door and leaned against the doorjamb; the look on her face was not a happy one.

"What now? Someone walk away with the potatoes?" Joshua asked.

"Funny. Did you tell Officer Dumbshit that I'd make a burger for him?" Meg asked.

"His name is Randy, and I did. Is he here already? I didn't say specifically you. I said the kitchen could make him a burger."

"No, he called in and asked for his burger to be medium rare with blue cheese. Sounds good, doesn't it? Here's the thing, Joshua—we have no ground beef, and I don't do burger special requests."

"Can't you get one of those guys out there to grind up one of the steaks? I'm sorry."

"Just call me Ronald and put some golden arches up, and we're good."

Joshua pulled out his phone and looked at a picture he had snapped of Frances and Theresa when they delivered the painting. He needed something else to focus on in the moment. It had been so long since he had seen Frances. She didn't flinch when she saw him. His world had changed drastically, and she picked up like no time had passed. This time when the knock came on his door, Joshua jumped up and opened it. He was ready to yell down the next problem.

"Whoa, settle down there, tiger," Randy said, pushing past Joshua. "I am still trying to wrap my head around this one. Why would anyone come in here and take your lobsters? I'd understand a couple. Fry 'em up. But you can't sell them, can you? I don't know if this is in my wheelhouse—might want to call animal control. I got their number in my phone somewhere."

"Randy, it is theft. Someone took my very expensive food without paying for it. I'm out several thousand, not to mention all the disappointed people expecting a lobster dinner tonight."

"Settle down. Meg said you've got a video or something showing the theft?"

"Yup. I'll pull it up for you to watch."

"It smells amazing in here. Josh, you continue to surprise me. I thought you were just a caffeine jockey. Who knew we were getting another fine dining place."

"I think that's a compliment. Hey, your burger is here. You can have a seat at my desk."

"Perfect. Man, this is the best-looking burger. Play me what you got." Randy sat down, putting his plate on the desk. "Damn, this is delicious. Those convicts sure can cook."

"Don't call them convicts. Now, that is one nice burger because they ground up a rib-eye steak to make it."

"Let me finish this, and then we can look at your lobster thief."

Joshua pushed play and watched as it took Alice less time than he would have thought to snag the lobsters out of the tank.

"Think she took those lobsters to the Aquarium?"

"What the fuck? I think she's probably already got them first-class tickets on a flight back to the Pacific Northwest. Can't you go find her and arrest her or make her bring the lobsters back?"

"Well, I could, but maybe you should call and ask her where they are. You might be a smart guy—or at least that's what most of the women in this town seem to think—but you are seriously stupid. Everyone knows Alice has a crush on you. Did you do something to her that she wants to get even with you?"

"Joshua's a complete idiot when it comes to women. He failed to ask her to the opening of his restaurant," Meg said. "I knew it was Alice."

"How's the change to tonight's menu coming, Meg?"

"I'll give Alice a call," Randy said. "I got her number in this cell phone somewhere."

"This is classic. You know you're in a fucking small town when Barney Fife has the lobster burglar's number on his cell phone." Meg laughed as she walked back to the kitchen prep.

"Hey, Alice. Randy here. Yup. Kids all fine. Melissa and I would love to bring them over to the Aquarium again—they loved feeding the fish...Yup."

"Randy," Joshua said.

"Hey, Alice, I'm here at Joshua's Otter Place...I agree, rather strange name. Well, I watched some video of you toting some lobsters out of the place. Where would those lobsters be right now?"

"Does she still have them? Can I get them back?"

"Well, I didn't think about it that way...no...I didn't know that lobsters screamed. Really? They're the cockroaches of the ocean. Gross. I'll tell my wife that one the next time she wants to go out to Red Lobster. Okay, you know what you did was stealing, right? You can come on down to the station sometime today. I need to book you in on this one. Say hey to your parents when you see them."

"Where are the lobsters?"

"They are on the road. Guess she's getting them back to the waters they came from."

"Holy shit. Does she fucking know what's she's done?"

"Now Josh, I know she does. She's going to turn herself in, and you can press charges for the stolen property. Get me an invoice showing what you paid for them."

"Shit. Anything else I can do for you, Randy?"

"Wouldn't mind a piece of that cheesecake I saw out there."

"Help yourself." Joshua held his office door open and stepped aside as Randy walked out and chuckled, taking a slice of cheesecake.

CHAPTER TWENTY-FIVE
A FAMILY DISJOINTED

Theresa walked through the loft and studied the paintings that Frances had leaning against her window wall. They were subtle compared to some of her other work. The colors were muted and quiet. Kelly had cleared out of the loft before she and Russell had returned from their morning of shopping. No note. The silence in the loft was welcoming.

"Hello?" Theresa answered her phone halfway through the first ring.

"Hey, lil' sis. I got your text. Are you okay?" Agatha asked.

"Yeah. It's all so crazy. She's gone."

"What's Frances doing right now?"

"No worries—we can talk. She's away with her friends for the weekend."

"Edna thinks we need to talk with Frances."

"No, you really shouldn't. She's been so upset and crazy since Dad came out to her opening."

"I wanted to come out to see it too. Are you sure she's going to come back to the fold? She can play straight. You're doing it."

"We need some time. Hey, where are you guys with Bernard?"

"He's still as scary as ever. Brice called him a little Hitler yesterday."

"I'm sure that went over well. Has his DNA ever been checked? He is so much shorter than the rest of us."

"He has the Kavanagh red hair. No dice on him not being related."

"True."

"Hang on, I'm going to put you on speaker phone."

"Hey, T.," Edna said. "Have you told Frances you're going back to Notre Dame?"

"Haven't had a chance. Kelly and I broke up."

"That's probably for the best. You said yourself that she wasn't very supportive of wanting a family."

"I've got a question for you two. What's the real reason Bernard jumped all over Frances for being a lesbian? Why did they take her out of the will and not me?"

"Shit, Theresa. Why have you not—"

Edna interrupted Agatha. "Theresa, it is a long story, and I don't want to go into it right now. What I can tell you is that Bernard is wrong. But you need to have your own talk with Frances. We stopped talking with her because—"

"There is no good reason. Your silence has only hammered home that she is no longer part of the family. Dad was really weird when he came out here."

"Listen, you need to convince Frances to come back here for the picnic. I think we need to get everyone together," Agatha said.

"Theresa, let Frances know that we support her."

"Who is we, Edna?"

"Brice, Agatha, and myself…well, and you."

"I'll try, but she's pretty mad. Heard you guys had a tornado scare the other day."

"It was crazy. Did Mom tell you?"

"Yeah. She said you and Agatha were in Brice's minivan, and they were afraid it was going to take off with you guys in it."

"Hate the weather in St. Louis," Edna said.

"Why do you live there then?"

"Family."

They all laughed, and Theresa thought about how to get Frances to follow her into the closet and then back to St. Louis. She would have to let Frances think it was her idea. Then she broached the question she had been thinking about.

"What do you think would happen if I started dating a man?" Theresa asked.

"You'd have a parade thrown in your honor. What'd you think would happen? All would be forgotten. But what about what you told me? This isn't a choice, being with a woman. It is part of you like your eye color and breathing."

"A girl can change her mind. I hate the fact that Mom is so uncomfortable."

"Theresa, you can't keep changing based upon what other people think," Agatha said.

"But you and Edna compromise all the time. You didn't stop the letter or the change in the will. Did either of you come out here to support Frances? Mom told me that she accepted this is who I am but asked me to not be with anyone."

"What?" Edna asked. "Get thee to a nunnery."

"I don't know."

"Don't make any decisions right now. You are so fresh out of your 'closeted' relationship, it hasn't started to stink yet. It will. Don't try to Febreeze your way out of the smell either."

"Agatha is right—if you try to stuff that stinky pain down, it will keep you from moving forward in ways you can't even imagine."

"Okay, wise old ladies. I promise I won't do anything right now."

"Except be honest with Frances."

"I'll talk with her. You two promise you'll let me do the talking with Frances?"

"Yes," Agatha said. "Frances is the black sheep of the family not because of anything in particular but because she is the strongest one out of all of us. Her spirit was seen from the moment she was born. Dad said she had *question authority* stamped across her butt at birth."

Theresa hung up the phone and walked over to a painting that was flat on the floor. The pieces of shattered glass bottles, a tea cup, a saucer, and some wine glasses yelled of violence and destruction. She stood over the painting and wanted to pick it up and smash it into the dumpster. This was so different from Frances's other paintings. As

Theresa's eyes bounced from the sharp shards of ceramic and glass, she felt like Frances was cutting at her skin.

A pain in the back of Theresa's hand pulled her back to the moment, and she stepped back from the painting as she saw she had dug her fingernails into the back of her hand so deeply, she had broken her skin. Theresa sucked the small amount of blood into her mouth and tried to calm herself down. Everything was going to be okay, and she was going to be fine. Frances, on the other hand, was the unknown that could make Theresa's life unravel in ways she couldn't even see. She had to direct both the family and Frances into some kind of truce.

CHAPTER TWENTY-SIX
A ROAD LESS TRAVELED AT 90 MPH

As the sleek car took the curves and dips of the two-lane country road, Frances let her head rest against the creamy soft leather of the passenger seat and float through the world. The throbbing in her knee was being numbed away, leaving Frances with the unusual feelings of warmth and peace. It was so unexpected, she had to quiet her mind, telling herself it was okay. They passed a corner fruit stand where a couple of young curly-haired kids were playing. They brought an image of Theresa at that age to Frances's mind. What was going on with the fractures in the Kavanagh family? Frances had tried calling her father a couple of times since he had shown up in San Francisco, but he never answered.

Frances glanced over at Sam, who looked so comfortable behind the wheel of this Mercedes with an engine so powerful, it purred the faster she went. Frances touched her lips, and the electricity from the kisses on the bench was still there. A deep sigh escaped from her lips as she realized that she could not follow Theresa's suggestion to live in the closet to appease her parents. Bernard and the family were wrong. How could she even have entertained such an idea? Why couldn't she be allowed to fall in love with the person—male or female—that her soul found?

"My sister had told me about helping some street kids in New York who had been kicked out of their homes for being gay. They were young."

"That's a non-sequitur conversation starter." Sam slowed the car to under Mach one, quieting the wind noise. "What are you thinking about, Irish?"

"Irish? Interesting nickname. I suppose I fit that one. I was thinking about my sister Theresa. I know she is young, but I don't understand how she thinks going back into the closet is fine."

"This is a tough topic. In my own world, I am not in the closet, but I am not out in the front lines either."

"Our family is having a…It's complicated. Theresa wanting me to go back into the closet, after she was the one who pushed me out—it would make her life easier. Why does there have to be a closet at all?"

"You are in a purgatory of sorts. Let me guess—you are single and firming up your desire to be with a woman."

"Sam, you are so insightful."

"It was the way you kissed. You were more than invested in feeling our kiss. The kiss we shared. Honestly, I had not felt a kiss like yours since. We don't need to get into the history. Just know that it took me by such surprise that my own brain short-circuited. I really did not know that a kiss was capable of sending such electricity through my body again. Not that I want to share, but I've kissed quite a few women, and nothing has come close to what I felt in our kiss. It did raise some painful memories too."

Frances smiled and went back to watching the rolling hillsides pass. Choices were life and what kept it interesting. She had always said that whatever was happening—good or bad—as long as she could still make a choice and act on it, she had a chance to survive. She knew in her soul that the choice to open up her truth and fall in love with a woman would change her life in ways she could not even account for yet. A rush pulsed through her body as she knew this was a risk she was going to take. The jumble of contradictions that ran through her body did not come close to registering the guilt, shame, or regret her family wanted her to feel for being who she was understanding herself to be in this moment.

"Does your family accept your...I don't want to call it a *lifestyle* . . ." Frances said.

"It is my life. Not a 'style.' They are okay with it. It wasn't exactly smooth sailing; however, we all respect one another, and that is important."

Amador County grape vines were quickly taking over the hillsides. Traffic was increasing, and Frances guessed they were approaching the emergency medical center for this rural area.

Hours later, Frances limped out of the emergency room with a pair of newly cut jean shorts. The ER nurse had cut one leg off, and Frances borrowed her scissors to even out the look.

"I'm so glad it isn't broken or chipped. It hurt like nothing I had ever felt before." Frances allowed Sam to help lower her back into the convertible.

"Sorry you missed the cooking lesson this afternoon. Who knew that a rural ER would be so busy? But we've got time before they are going to serve dinner. Want to see a cool place on the river?" Samantha pushed the starter button, and the car purred back to life.

"An adventure? I'm game." Frances wanted more time alone with Sam. She hadn't noticed the wait as they spent the time talking and exploring the hospital perched on the side of a small mountain in the historic gold country.

Sitting inches above the pavement in this car gave her a rush as Samantha opened the car up on the straightaway portions of the quiet country roads. Pink came on the radio, and Samantha turned up the volume. Frances noticed the elegance of each of her movements, from the way her hand rested on the steering wheel, to how she tucked her hair behind her ear. With each action, Frances felt her heart pound in symphonic rhythm with "Just Give Me a Reason." Had their long history of crazy meetings been scripted before they even met? Was this all a cosmic plan or a happy happenstance? Frances shook her head and let her hair completely hide the smile on her face as the car sped toward the place Sam wanted to share with her.

A downshift in the convertible seemed to be questioned by the car's engine as it bucked a little. Frances turned to look at Samantha as she turned off the paved road onto a very uneven dirt trail.

"Sorry about the downshift." Samantha smiled as she brought the car to an abrupt halt at the very edge of a river bank.

"For a minute, I thought you had a much newer version of Chitty Chitty Bang Bang, and we were going for a boat ride."

"Loved that movie. Still do, actually. I had a huge crush on Truly Scrumptious."

"Who didn't?" Frances tried to tame her wild curly hair, feeling a little like the two Potts children when they first ran Truly and her car off the road. Her unraveling jean shorts were covered in dirt, and her T-shirt looked like she was fresh from playing in the dirt. Sam had hopped out of the car and was over opening the door to help Frances get out.

"Looks like I might need some oil in the joints. Feels like they are locked in place."

"Don't push it. Let me help you move your leg out of the car first. Pivot your hips, and I'll handle your leg." Samantha's hands gently held Frances's thigh and ankle as she helped her swing her leg clear of the car. The touch made her melt. In an instant, Frances was now standing face-to-face with Sam, looking into the most beautiful, soft, light-brown eyes she had ever seen. They kissed gently, and the softness continued.

"Let me show you why I brought you to this spot." Samantha softly touched Frances's cheek and attempted to tuck a stray curly lock behind Frances's ear. It put up a good fight and sprang back into place.

Frances took Samantha's hand into hers and gently kissed it. "Trying to tame my hair is a lost cause. Show me the treasure of this place."

They slowly made their way along a narrow path through long sweet grasses and around the boughs of willow trees gently sloping toward the ground. The two women stood on the edge of the middle fork of the American River and watched the water flow past. Frances was struck by the beauty of the rock bed seen beneath the clear waters of the river. Further upstream, the water turned a dark green as it slowed through a massive set of boulders that changed the channel of the river.

"Frances, your eyes are the color of my favorite swimming hole."

"Can we swim?"

"This water is from the snow melt. Might be a little cold right now."

"I can't believe how beautiful this place is. It is so peaceful. How'd you find this place?"

"I grew up in these hills. This was a piece of property that I always wanted to own, and when it came up for sale, my wife and I bought it."

"You were married?"

"I was. Eliza and I had plans to build our little sanctuary up here. A place where we could raise our horses, dogs, and . . ." Sam went very quiet and walked a few steps away from Frances.

"What happened? You still have the property?" Frances asked.

"It's okay. I'm not sure you will understand this, but I think Eliza likes you." Samantha started to walk toward a fallen tree and sat down.

Frances knew that she needed to follow and listen. There was a new breath of life coming into her soul, and she suspected it was something that she needed to nurture carefully. It was clear that Sam was attempting to hold it together and share a very difficult time in her life. Frances kept herself from speculating and slowly made her way over to Sam. "I can do this," Frances said as she tried to lower herself down to the log. Gravity took hold, and Frances was on the other side of the log, flat on her back, looking up at the deep blue sky of the late afternoon.

"Oh, Frances, I hope you are okay. I'm sorry...I can't stop laughing."

Frances started laughing too. "I'll take a hand when you find a break in your laughter."

Sam sat down on the log and swung her legs over to give her some leverage to help Frances sit on the long beside her. Frances snuggled into Sam's shoulder and let herself be completely in the moment. Sweet smells of grass, pine, and the warm sun filled the air around them. Frances felt nature wrap itself around her and Samantha, encouraging them to stay in this moment. Frances whispered into Sam's ear, "Take your time. I am here."

Sam stood and grabbed a flat stone and, in one fluid motion, skipped the stone across the twenty feet of river surface and onto the opposite river bank.

"Impressive, Ms. Iverson."

"I used to compete with my brothers and dad. Kind of like riding a bike. Once you learn the magic of the skipping stone, you never forget."

"How large is your family?"

"Two brothers and myself. My parents wanted more kids, but finances and time got tight for them. Then when they built their businesses, they decided they were over training kids. I have four nephews. They are awesome."

"Do you mind if I take you back to your wife?"

"Eliza was an amazing woman, and I fell deeply, madly in love with her."

"Where is she now?"

"In my heart. She's here at the base of the willow tree. Don't look so worried. Eliza died too young. She battled ovarian cancer."

"My heart, I . . ." Tears formed in Frances's eyes as she saw tears also forming in Samantha's.

"She died three years ago. People tell me that it gets easier with time. I don't know what they mean by *easier*. It really doesn't."

Frances put her arm around Samantha and held her. She watched the river gurgle past them and bees dance around the wild flowers. The music she had played on the piano in the small lobby of the hospital was a prelude to this moment, and the melodies of the composer Ennio Morricone played through her soul.

"Eliza played the piano too," Samantha said, as if reading Frances's thoughts. "You, today, when you sat down at the piano...There is a quality that I can't explain about you. But..." Samantha's voice broke, and she coughed, fighting to hang onto it. "But why did you play those two songs?"

"Those are my favorites. I don't normally play them out in public. Something inside brought up "Gabriel's Oboe," and that led into the *Cinema Paradiso* theme song. Those melodies are the essence of music. I feel something so deep in my soul when those melodies play."

"They were beautiful. Both of them." Samantha stood and wiped her eyes and put her sunglasses on, looking toward the car. "I probably need to get you back before they send a search party out for us."

"Playing the piano gives me the energy needed at the time. Today it was both calming and exciting."

"Your energy definitely changed as you played, and it was beautifully brilliant."

Silence settled between them as the water meandered past and the breeze whispered the peaceful melodies, a dragonfly with iridescent blue and silver wings dancing and skimming along the tops of the tall grasses. Samantha walked the couple of steps back to Frances and, intertwining their fingers, helped her up. Frances leaned into the strong body of Samantha and fell into her arms, resting her head on her shoulder. The spark that had been placed in her heart from the very first kiss was well lit, and Frances raised her lips to Samantha's and fed the spark more fuel.

"We really need to go," Sam said. "I have a confession I'll share with you on the way."

"I didn't know you were raised Catholic?"

"I wasn't. It's a turn of phrase. You know that day I saw you in Specialty's? You were dressed as a walking billboard for the University of Washington."

"I can't forget. It was almost death by cinnamon roll." Frances's face flushed hot.

"I saw you from outside and stood there for several minutes watching you watch the world around you. You have no clue how beautiful you really are, do you?"

"I'm not sure I know how to take this confession?"

"I wanted to ask you on a date that moment."

"Great. You mean we could've been enjoying kisses like this afternoon so much earlier? You had me so freaked out at dinner."

"Because I kissed you?"

"No. Because the kiss registered so deep in my soul. It was something I had never, ever felt before."

The car accelerated as Frances knew that she and Sam were finally at the right place and the right time to explore whatever this was between them. Her phone buzzed in her pocket, and Frances pulled it out to see Theresa's silly mug shot fill up her phone screen.

"Hey? What's up?" Frances tried to plug her other ear and felt Samantha slow the car to give her the chance to handle the phone call. "Theresa, slow down. You're breaking up—I'm only getting every fourth word. Sorry—I don't have the best reception." Frances looked at Samantha, who had completely pulled the car to a stop on the side of the road. "Say again? Jimmy's in a well and we don't have a collie to get the rescuers to the right place? I'll try calling you back. Love you."

"Who was that?"

"I think it was my sister. I couldn't catch what she was saying. Forward to the feast. Do you think they'll let us eat with them tonight?"

"I know they will. Sherri is horrified by my attraction to you."

"What did you tell her?"

"Enough to know you are a wonderful challenge."

"I do resemble that comment." Frances took her hand back and tried to hold her hair away from her face as Sam drove them over the winding roads, back to the land of food, wine, and friends. In the side mirror, Frances caught the beauty of the setting sun and thanked the gods of love for letting her have these silly, messy moments with Samantha.

CHAPTER TWENTY-SEVEN
A TWISTED PUZZLE

Molly hesitated before walking into the meeting room. Through the open door, she saw that Lieutenant Brian Corrigan was just taking a seat along the wall. He had made it very clear to her that he did not believe that any woman should be a detective, let alone in charge of a special team. The importance of going public was well established. The police chief and the mayor had won that argument, overruling the FBI and her own concerns. There were so many unknowns, and by going public, she felt the killer or killers would gain insights into the investigation. But in the media landscape, she knew that the stories were already circulating, and it was time for the police department to become the main news source. This meeting was to discuss how much of the information to release and what message they wanted to project. Molly felt a wave of nausea pass over her as she thought about this information and the impact on the public. The news agencies would start digging, and threats not even contemplated might come out about how they dealt with the information. Todd had cautioned her about the ability to shield her Uncle Henry. It was highly possible that someone else would pick up on the threads and weave together the parallels, or the conspiracy masterminds would start to see what she and her team were piecing together.

"Molly, you ready?" Todd asked.

"I don't really think we have any other choice." Molly walked into the captain's office and took a seat in the closest chair to the desk. Todd placed a hand on her shoulder. She knew he would follow her lead.

"Woods and Gruggs, glad you both are here. This grim business is making me lose what little hair I have left."

"Captain, you look distinguished," Woods said as she flipped through her notebook.

"I am going to introduce you two as the main SFPD detectives on this case. We will be putting a spokesperson in place, and they are only to talk to you and me. No one else has the authority to release any information. Clear?"

Molly and Todd looked at one another and both nodded that they understood. "Captain, are you going to suggest that we might have a copycat killer?" Woods asked.

"I read your report, and I don't quite see the copycat. This killer is doing a whole lot more than placing the victim on a beach towel or blanket."

"Captain, did you have a chance to look at the map overlay? The body placement is not random."

"It might be too early to make that call. Woods, can you give the group here a rundown of what you and Gruggs discovered?"

Molly cleared her throat and opened the file folder that Lucy had put together for her and Todd. She scanned the bullet points, took a deep breath, and caught Todd's expression. "Right. With the four killings that have happened over the course of the past several weeks, the team has been following every lead and going over the evidence collected. A disturbing pattern has emerged." Molly stood and walked to the front of the group to the enlarged poster board wall map of the city. "The red push-pins represent the latest locations the victims have been discovered. The green push-pins show where the victims of the series of murders attributed to the Beach Blanket serial killer were found."

"Detective Woods, you have four crime scenes that overlap, but I know for a fact that over the years, other bodies have been dumped in those locations. I think you are making a connection that won't hold up," the mayor said.

"I appreciate that we only have four crime scenes and that it's hard to see the pattern, but one is there. Call it instinct, but we have reason to believe that this killer is following or continuing unfinished business," Woods said.

Molly watched the room as this caused some commotion among the mayor's team.

"Mayor, what Detective Woods has seen is a possible link, but we are still fully investigating these crimes and have not yet linked them to one person or group. Our goal is to stop the killings and not see the whole star pattern with the bear repeated."

"Captain, I really don't care if they are linked or not. You need to catch this killer. Control the news on this—I can't afford to have panic over this," the mayor said, walking toward the door. "The police department needs to be out in front of this, and don't you dare tell people this is a serial killer."

"Sir, we are going to handle this, and my team is working harder than I can quantify to find the person responsible."

Molly walked over and shut the door after the Mayor and his entourage left.

"Captain, I know that we are not at a true copycat, but like those other killings, these bodies are being prepped. The killings happened at one location, and the killer or killers placed the victims at very specific locations. With each victim discovered, the scenes have become more elaborate. The positions were the same points used by the Beach Blanket killer. That killer, for those of you not familiar, had left his victims on a beach towel in a pattern that matched the SFPD shield."

"A star? How did—that seems so strange, no cops were killed by that killer. I read the confession given, and he said that he liked stars."

"I think we might need to do some more research." Molly looked at her notes. "That killer left small 'gifts' for the police at each scene and then the 'gifts' started showing up at crime scenes not related to the original killings. Many of you worked the Ethan Charna case last year. A package was left in the parking lot of an active and controlled crime scene."

"Why is this the first we are hearing of this?" A young FBI agent perked up at hearing this information.

"Calm down. I instructed Woods and Gruggs to keep the evidence under wraps. We worked with our internal investigations unit because we did not know what we were dealing with until the Charna case answers started to emerge. Continue, Woods," the captain said.

"We are passing around a map of the city that shows where the victims of the Beach Blanket were left—those are in blue. The newest scenes are represented by red dots."

"Holy shit. I had no clue there were so many killed by that—"

"We traced forty-two killings to that string. The dots in green are unsolved murders that the FBI suspected might have been part of the Beach Blanket killings. If those had been linked, you see there is no mistaking the shape."

"Molly, don't forget to show them the pictures of the two scenes," Gruggs said.

"Yes. I'm passing around a photograph of a murder scene from 1981 and the most recent one. Todd, take over from here," Molly said as she passed around the copies of the two murder scenes.

"Anyone notice anything between the two scenes?" Todd asked. "Molly was the first one to spot the similarities. When we saw the pattern repeating in the body placement, we went into the old case files. Our concern was that we were dealing with a copycat killer who had inside knowledge. That meant someone either helped the killer, who is in prison, or was part of the first killings."

"Like an apprentice? Did that killer have any family? You don't think a cop is doing this?"

"Don't know. These serial killers have groupies. They went to the prison to check the visitor logs of the Beach Blanket killer," the captain said.

"He had a few news interviews, but no one had visited this guy more than twice, other than the legal team handling his appeals, and we were able to clear all those people," Molly added.

"Anyone see anything in those photos?" Gruggs asked again.

"Other than the bodies are rather waxy in appearance? The crime scenes we are dealing with are so much more detailed. Just tell us."

"The teacup and saucer," Molly said. "It is strange that these very ornate teacups are in both scenes."

"In our crime scenes, the cups are filled with blood. What we found out was the DNA is a match to DNA in the package left at the Ethan Charna crime scene," Gruggs said.

"This keeps getting more bizarre," the captain said.

"I am trying to find out what was in the teacups in the Beach Blanket crime scenes." Molly said.

"What was the link between the victims back then? Is there a link with the current victims?" asked an officer who had been taking notes during the meeting.

"We are still working on that with the help of the FBI, but we have not found a link between the victims. They vary in age, gender, and background. That part of this macabre puzzle appears to be random," Gruggs said.

"We need to be careful about how we message this out to the media," the captain said as he sat down behind his desk. "If it wasn't for the mayor, we would not be going to the media now. He is right though on one prong. Because the word is out, and I want to control the news on this. The City needs to know this is going on, and we need help. We are anticipating another scene in a few days if the killer stays on the schedule started. Undercover cops are stationed at the points that appear to be corresponding to the earlier murders," the captain said.

"Gruggs and I have not been able to trace the pattern on the teacups. We don't know if the cups are related. We are working on trying to find out where they were made."

"What about the evidence from the Beach Blanket case?"

"No luck. If the teacup had been collected, it is no longer in the files that were kept on the case. We could not find anything in the notes."

"Molly, wasn't your uncle one of the cops that broke that case? Have you talked with him?"

Molly looked directly at the lieutenant, and her skin crawled. "Yes, my Uncle Henry has already been in to speak with the team and the captain concerning what he remembered about that case."

"We are giving you all the major details, but I do not want anyone to discuss the teacups. If you are questioned by the media, or anyone for that matter, you can say that we are on the trail of this serial killer. If anyone brings up the Beach Blanket killings, you can agree with them that some parallels exist. And remind them that the killer responsible for those killings is in prison on death row." The captain looked around the silent room. "We are crafting the statement with the press office. I will be there and answer basic questions. Your job is to give whatever support you can to Woods and Gruggs as we try to stop this killer before he kills again."

"How do we know that he hasn't already killed the victims?" Lieutenant Corrigan asked.

"We don't. We are still waiting for the medical examiner's report from the last scene. Thanks, Woods and Gruggs. You can get back to it."

Molly stood and collected the photographs and walked out of the room. Her heart was racing, and she could not shake the growing darkness in her mind. There was something they were missing. The clues were starting to add up with the connections between the teacups, body location, and the significance of the last scene. Gruggs was right behind her, and Molly decided to wait until they were back in their command center.

"Todd what did you think of Lieutenant Donkey Balls?"

"Now that is a good one. He does look like a Donkey. Although Brian might take the 'donkey balls' as a compliment. That guy is sore over you getting the lead on this case. Ignore him."

"I wonder if he knows something about Uncle Henry and that investigation."

"Wouldn't surprise me. You nipped that in the bud when we went to the captain and Uncle Henry basically told him the truth."

"The captain has us. I trust him. What we need to do is figure out who this killer is and why they are doing this."

"It would help if we knew who the real Beach Blanket killer was and why those murders stopped. There is a different kind of sophistication that has entered into these killings."

"It is a different world today," Todd said. "Women can vote and carry a gun."

"What? Todd, sometimes I do not follow your fragmented thoughts," Molly said.

"Sorry. I was going back to Donkey Balls."

"There is something that keeps bugging me about that package that was left at the Ethan Charna crime scene. Why? I don't see the link? Ethan was at a whole different level. He was a voyeur and had a very particular business. He was hired to kill. Most serial killers act out of their own motivation. When you reached out to Emily after Frances told you she recognized the teacups, she said the family had sold them years ago."

"There is so much we don't know. But I keep worrying about Frances and Emily."

"Relax. Ethan is dead, and they are safe," Todd said. "I'm going to go grab some food—can I pick anything up for you?"

"No thanks. I think those teacups are going to lead us to the killer," Molly said as she watched Todd leave the room. There was no rest for her as Lucy came bouncing into the command center.

"That was fast," Lucy said.

"What?"

"The announcement that the captain is making with the mayor. They are doing it right now. I thought you were going to be there?"

"Thank god I'm not. We've got work to do. The reporters are going to go crazy over this. What are you doing here? You were to take some much needed time off. Don't make me order you."

"Listen to you, Miss Boss Pants. I got an all-hands-required-to-work email. I'm here. Is there anything you want me to get for you?"

"You know you don't have to come in on your vacation days," Molly said.

"No sweat. I was at home literally watching paint dry. I think HGTV needs to be banned. My sweetie thinks all house projects take thirty minutes to complete. Right now, my bathroom is a series of duct-taped tarps and exposed floor joists. Thought we would do a complete bathroom overhaul in an hour."

"That's rough. I find myself hooked on that tiny house show. I really don't get it."

"Imagine how much easier your life would be," Lucy said.

"How?"

"You could bag the whole house and put it in the evidence locker. A self-contained crime scene."

"Sick." Molly thought about it and finally laughed out loud as she walked to her desk and tried to think through the next steps. Molly pressed her hands into her tired eyes. It was getting harder and harder for her to focus.

She had spent several hours going through the real files and evidence of the case her uncle had worked so many years ago. Molly knew that she would have to wrestle with some of the lies her uncle and his partner supported in order to make that case look closed. What would she do? The arguments and justifications were written into their notes. It was almost as if they had both hoped they would be found out. Newspaper clippings from that time showed a public that was hysterical with fear. In these days of social media, what was going to happen? The gamble was to get some real leads that would stop this killer.

Molly stood and walked to the command center boards they had been trying to utilize to help find the pieces that would lead them to the person responsible for the killing. She looked through her notebook and added the name and age of the latest victim. "Lucy, would you mind trying to find us a picture of this victim. As recent as possible."

"I'm on it." Lucy started typing faster than Molly thought humanly possible. She knew there would be a printed picture of Erica Johnson, approximate age twenty-two. A medical bracelet had identified her as being allergic to penicillin. The killer was not taking much time between his acts, putting more pressure on Molly and her team to crack the key and find this killer.

"Detective Woods, any thoughts?"

"Hey, Gruggs. Thought you were going to get some food. I'm in the dark. The meeting told me that the rest of the people working these murders are also scrambling. You might consider bringing in a couple changes of clothes and pass that along."

"I know we'll get this sicko, but it is going to require our around-the-clock attention."

"Time to start sharing some of those thoughts you've been keeping in that computer brain of yours," Gruggs said.

"My hunch is telling me they are all connected. The killer is using different methods and trying to make us think that it is different people doing the killing."

"What if it is?" Lucy asked. "I read this book about a killing cult. Creeped me out."

"We will be getting the DNA analysis back, but on the first three, the same unidentified DNA has been isolated." Molly walked to the coffee maker and poured herself a cup of tepid coffee and wished she had not taken a sip. "This is revolting."

"Think it was made yesterday afternoon," Lucy said. "Don't look at me—it isn't in my job description. Oh, all right, I'll go to Blue Bottle and get you a real coffee. Any other takers?"

"Thanks, Luce."

"That's *Lucy* to you, sir."

Molly laughed and walked to her desk. She needed to grab a few hours of sleep. Until that miracle happened, she pulled up the latest files that the FBI shared with them this morning, looking at possible suspects. Was this a rabbit hole that was going to take them further away from the answer?

"Hey Todd, would you mind coming over her for a sec?"

"What's up, Molly?"

"Do you remember the night we were in the loft during the Ethan investigation—the guy that pushed through the police line? Turned out it was Ethan's brother," Molly said.

"When did he say he had arrived on the scene to see his brother?"

"I don't remember. I'd need to go into the notes. I was the first one to interview him. He asked so many questions, I felt I was being cross-examined. It was strange. Emily did give a positive ID. Neither Winter or Frances said they noticed him, but he was in the still shots taken from the security cameras. Ethan had to know his brother was there." Molly turned to her computer and searched for her crime scene report.

"When Lucy comes back, have her pull any crowd shots that we collected from the news media and our own police body cams."

"The guy was a creeper. It must have run in the family. One of the things he told me when I was interviewing him was the most bizarre fact about how a corpse can sit up because the muscles in the back contort. Why would anyone know that?" Todd sat down and sighed deeply.

"Let me know when you've had a chance to review the crowd shots. I want you to look at this picture taken last night after the news media arrived at the murder scene." Molly hit the magnify on her computer screen and isolated a clear photograph of Gabriel standing in the small crowd. "Gruggs, one of the things I've been going over in my head is why Ethan's brother, Gabriel, is in the crowd at our latest murder scene?"

"It was a very public place. There were a couple thousand people there going to movies, bowling, you name it. That place has got it. Molly? You don't think this is our crazed serial killer, do you?" Todd asked.

"I don't know. You know what they say about those that are seeking recognition and think they are smarter than the rest of us?"

"I got chills running down my spine. But didn't the captain say we are done interviewing him? The kid had some fancy lawyer hit the department with a harassment lawsuit," Todd said.

"There has to be another way. Let me think about that and find out if he shows up at any of the other scenes where we have video or photographs."

Molly dialed up her uncle's phone and hung up after the fourth ring. There was something in the newspaper clippings that had her thinking. She walked back to the board and read the names of the victims and looked at their pictures. There was nothing on the surface linking these people in any way. "Gruggs, do you remember the picture in the newspaper that showed a group of school children watching the police tape off a Beach Blanket murder scene?"

"We looked at so many clippings. That is not ringing a bell. Why?"

"One of the scenes was across the street from a Jewish Community Center. I wonder if we can identify who those kids were."

"I know where you are going, but Gabriel wasn't born yet. Good try though."

"Oh my god! That is too funny," Lucy said as she distributed coffees from her special run to the Coffee Bar.

"I sure hope that is a non-sequitur, Lucy. Otherwise, your humor is more twisted than mine. I could use some funny," Molly said.

"Silly. I just saw your latest Instagram post when I was waiting for the coffee. Not sure why I missed it, but who is the purple grape playing paintball?"

"Frances. She is crazy about purple."

"Has she seen this picture?"

"She's linked to my Instagram account, so if she's on it, she'll have seen it."

"This is the artist? The one I called and canceled on for you? She's rather cute."

"Lucy, this is not appropriate office banter. Not to mention, you were using your work time to check your Instagram account?"

"Busted you, young whippersnapper," Todd said.

Molly wished she had not said that as Lucy stood up ramrod straight and saluted Molly, making a military precision turn and marching back to her desk.

"Point taken. Sorry."

"Why don't you ask this woman out? You two look pretty close in this picture?"

"She had won the game for us because the opposing team underestimated Captain Purple Pants. They thought she had been blasted with paint and was wandering around the playing field."

"Do you need me this afternoon?"

"Is that a trick question? You are scheduled to be on vacation right now."

"Gruggs has asked me to help go through the hours of video and stills looking for that creeper."

"I'll know where to find you."

Molly pulled out her phone and called Frances. Before it clicked over into voicemail, Molly remembered that she was away for Dana's birthday weekend. Simon and Russell had suggested dinner, but she was too busy to think straight. The day of paintball was going to be her last bit of fun until they stopped the serial killer.

CHAPTER TWENTY-EIGHT
CAUGHT RED-HANDED

Theresa hated the fact that she was alone. She wanted Frances home now, but it was only Saturday afternoon, and her sister was going to be gone through Monday morning. Theresa sat looking at a bill for six thousand dollars for some wood, power tools, and paint she had taken from the theatre. Her friend and fellow stagehand had come by to drop it off, along with her personal items and the news that she was fired. The manager at the theatre had never liked her anyway. She had taken the wood and paint but was told they were going to throw it away anyway. She walked over to the tools, arranged neatly on a shelf, and muttered, "I wasn't going to keep the tools. I had every intention of returning them—now I think I will just keep them. Fuck."

This was not the first time she had been caught helping herself to items at work. When she was working in the library at Notre Dame, she had been able to kiss her way out of the stolen paper. She had become the paper source on her dorm floor. Reams of paper vanished from the stock room of the library six weeks into her starting her work study. The head librarian was a closeted lesbian, and Theresa had no problem giving her sexual favors to keep her quiet. She branched out and stole paper from other departments when she delivered or picked up the library books loaned to them.

Fired. This was not exactly a shock, but she had always talked her way out of trouble before. Were they going to call the cops? Would Molly help her? *I can't tell Molly about this,* Theresa thought. She sat down on the sofa and thought about calling Frances again but knew that was not going to work. Who could she call for the money? This had to go away. Theresa called Bernard.

"Hello. I don't have a lot of time. Did you do what I asked?"

"Bernard, I have been over this loft with a fine-toothed comb. Not to mention the police have also swept this place. I have found nothing. I think you think Frances has something she really doesn't have. She has never done drugs, and I don't know why you feel you need that to hold over her too."

"Are you going to be able to get back here for the picnic?"

"I don't know. I need your help. I got myself into a little hiccup."

"What'd you do now?" Bernard asked.

"I kind of borrowed some tools and stuff from the theatre group I was working for, and they gave me a bill for 6K."

"What do you want me to do about it?"

"I don't want to go to jail. I promise it was a misunderstanding. Can you wire me the money?"

"When I paid for your abortion, you promised that was the last time you would ask for money."

"That was different, and I really appreciate your help. Please. I am getting my life back together and going to go back to Notre Dame."

"I don't want you running to Mom about this, so I am going to bail you out this last time, but I am taking it out of your portion of the inheritance that Dad is leaving you."

"Fine. I'll text you my account number."

"Don't text it, you idiot. Tell me what it is, and I'll write it down. You'll have the money by this afternoon."

Theresa hung up. She had gotten what she wanted. Now she had some nice tools too. Theresa did not respect Bernard, but she knew how to use him to get what she wanted. When she had slept with the director of the play she was working on in New York and had gotten pregnant, Bernard had helped her get the abortion. She was shocked because Bernard was so Catholic. To him, the sin of out-of-wedlock pregnancy was the worst. That director had charmed her. Was it because she had so disliked him that she found him attractive? He had conquered her, and there was something that excited her about that. As her mind went back to the crazy wild sex she had with him, Joshua popped into her mind.

Joshua held some similarities to the director. He was definitely sure of himself. Was that because of his money? Why had Frances been so strange about him? He had the most amazing eyes she had seen on anyone. Theresa had always known she was attracted to men, but she had hidden that part of herself in order to be with Kelly, who was so into the whole never-being-with-men thing. Kelly was gorgeous, and Theresa wanted her at that time.

A picture of Frances and Joshua came up on her phone as she was thumbing through her photo albums. Theresa was captivated by Joshua's look. There was something so attractive about him. She didn't have to go to work tonight. The boys said she could borrow their Mini Cooper anytime. This was the time. Theresa threw a couple of shirts, a bra, some underwear, and a toothbrush into her backpack and went to borrow the car. She was going to go have some fun in Monterey.

CHAPTER TWENTY-NINE
LEMON FLOWERS ARE SWEET

F rances followed Samantha in through the front door of Giovanni and Sherri's home. Laughter and aromas of food cooking wafted from the kitchen. They walked into the great room to see a beautifully set table out on the darkening patio with glass lanterns providing a soft glow of light.

"Wonderful—you're back, and you have both your legs," Dana said and clapped her flour-covered hands together.

"Sorry we are so late. The ER was on a very different time schedule," Frances said, hoping that her face was not betraying her desire to be alone with Samantha.

"You are in time to catch the tail end of the demonstration for the final touches on dinner and dessert for tonight," Sherri said. Frances noticed that Sherri was studying Samantha with intensity. How well did they know one another? There appeared to be a familiarity between them that suggested they knew one another extremely well.

Frances hobbled over and took a seat opposite the action at the kitchen island and picked up a stapled packet of papers that held the night's recipes and instructions. Giovanni returned to instructing the group on how to fold the liquid into the dry ingredients to make the batter, which would coat the squash blossoms before frying them. Several dishes were being plated by his kitchen elves, and Frances felt the rumbling in her stomach. She had missed Samantha leaving the crowd. A glass of wine was placed in front of her, and she decided that she could handle a glass on top of the Advil they had given her at the hospital.

Small plates that displayed the culinary delights of the afternoon—from spiced potatoes and garlic to perfectly done carrot, beet, and tomato fritters—had been set out on the far end of the kitchen island, away from the plating and cooking action of the crew. Frances breathed a sigh of relief not to be late. She looked out to the large patio and saw Winter curled up under a blanket on a chaise lounge. That was perfect. Sleep was probably much needed.

Frances jumped slightly when Sherri hooked her arm into Frances's, not giving her a chance to get away. "We are going out to get some Meyer lemons off our tree. You can lean on me. It might do your leg some good to get blood pumping."

"Okay." Frances furrowed her brow at Cheryl, who was busy helping herself to the cured meats, and then followed Sherri out to the garden.

"I wanted to get you out of the fray. You can slow down. Samantha shared that she took you to her property this afternoon."

"It really is a beautiful place."

Sherri plucked a couple of lemons from the tree and placed them in Frances's hands. She struggled not to drop them as Sherri went back for more. Frances pulled out the bottom of her shirt to hold the large yellow fruit. Surrounding the lemon tree, which looked like it had hundreds of lemons, were planters bursting with herbs and vegetables. At the opposite end of the twenty-foot-long path stood two avocado trees, each one bearing so many avocados that the branches were being pulled toward the ground from the weight.

"What did Samantha say about that land?"

"I'm not sure what you're asking? She told me she had purchased it with her wife, and they had planned to build a sanctuary."

"She said that?"

"Yes."

"Really? She told you about Eliza?"

"Why are you so surprised?"

"I guess I underestimated her interest in you. She...Sam is a very special person, and I don't want to see her hurt."

"What is your relationship with Sam?"

Frances let Sherri deposit five more lemons into her makeshift shirt tote, trying to read the expression on her face. How would she know if this woman would tell her the truth? She didn't.

"Do you know what it means to truly miss someone?" Sherri asked.

"I do. Not that it is really part of this conversation, but yes, there is someone in my life I thought I knew so well that I could anticipate her every move. The reality is that I don't know her, or the rest of the people in my family. I am missing them more than I could ever explain. I know it isn't the same as what Sam has gone through with her wife. But I know loss and pain, if that is what you're asking."

"Are you capable of falling in love with a woman and not running at the first sign life is going to hit you so hard in the face that it breaks your nose?"

"Sherri, I'm already there. I don't know what the future holds or even if I will be on this earth tomorrow. What I am sure of is my ability to love. Sam and I did have quite the introduction, and I must appear to you to be less than deserving of someone like her...but you don't know me. The best way to deal with your fears is to gain knowledge. I would like to get to know you too."

Frances started to gingerly walk back toward the kitchen and felt her heart do a triple somersault when she saw Sam walking out toward her. The night air was warm, and Sam had removed her cotton shirt to expose a close-fitting, sleeveless white T-shirt. Frances wanted to drop her shirt full of lemons and run into her arms. She wasn't sure if Sherri was behind her or not.

"What's in your shirt?" Sam asked.

"Sherri volunteered me to help her bring some lemons in for something Giovanni decided to add to the dessert menu."

"Did you survive? She is not so subtle sometimes."

"I need to know...did you and Sherri ever—"

"No. We are sisters from other mothers. She is my dearest and closest friend. I'm afraid she can be overprotective."

"Because someone has to look out for you. You might be a brilliant woman, but your—"

"Thanks, Sherri," Sam said, waiting until her friend had walked past them and into the house.

"She was going to say you have horrid taste in women, wasn't she?"

"Possibly."

"She's worried that I'm experimenting with you and will move on and discard you," Frances said.

"That could happen—after all, I'm a professional lesbian," Sam said and slipped her arm around Frances's waist, guiding her toward the light of the kitchen. "I'm willing to take the risk."

Once the lemons were handed over to Giovanni, Frances hobbled back out to Sam on the patio and took her in her arms. "I know this is all rather new to me. I want you to know I am following my heart, and my heart is screaming that the running away is over."

"Unless there's a fire, or we're on a beach and a giant wave is coming in...or what about a stampede? Would you do the running of the bulls?"

"Sam, I have the strongest feelings I've ever felt for anyone before with you."

Frances gently kissed Sam before taking her hand and leading her toward the table to join the feast and their friends.

CHAPTER THIRTY
FINDING A WAY INTO A CALCULATED WORLD WITH MAN CURRENCY

Theresa turned her phone navigation instructions off when she turned right onto David Avenue in Monterey. The drive took her longer than she had anticipated, and she arrived to catch the last of the sun dipping below the horizon of the Pacific Ocean. This was not her plan. She had wanted to arrive in the afternoon and steal Joshua away from his work. Her knuckles went white as she gripped the steering wheel, anticipating how he would look at her when she showed up. Joshua had extended the invitation to come back to Monterey to both her and Frances. He actually had made a point to make sure she had heard him suggest they come back to eat at his restaurant. The traffic was inching along Cannery Row when a parking spot opened up a few doors down from Joshua's little coffee bar.

The street lights were on, and the foot traffic was starting to increase. Theresa turned south and squinted. The Aquarium must have been closing soon as a steady stream of people appeared to be exiting. Her heart was beating faster and faster the closer she came to Find Your Porpoise Fine Coffee and Teas. What was Joshua thinking when he came up with that mess of a name? It did make her laugh. She had not forgotten it, and it played into the name for his new bistro.

Joshua was busy taking apart his espresso machine. Theresa stopped and watched him carefully clean each piece of the machine and then put the pieces back into their place. She was relieved that no one else was in the coffee closet. An image of her kissing Joshua flashed through her mind.

It was getting harder and harder to stand and watch him as she was caught in his undertow—the way the light caught the stubble on his cheek, and the flexing of his arms as he worked through the different parts of the machine. His motions were as fluid as they were the first day they met. There was a measured strength in each one of his actions. When they had helped Joshua hang the painting he purchased from Frances's show, she had gotten tangled up in his arms as he tried to make the chalk marks on the wall for the wall hangers. She wanted to get lost in his body—to explore every inch of him. Any thoughts about women were being pushed out of her mind.

"The place is closed. If you want coffee, you need to go to the 7-Eleven. It's two blocks away," a short woman sporting a chef's jacket said as she walked past Theresa and stepped inside the little coffee store. Joshua looked up and noticed Theresa standing on the sidewalk. Her heart skipped so many beats, Theresa thought she might have to give herself chest compressions.

"Hey Meg, hold on a second," Joshua said as he vaulted over the counter and walked toward her. "Theresa, what a brilliant surprise! Is Frances with you?" Joshua asked.

"Uh…I…what?"

"Is Frances with you? Are you two here to enjoy the restaurant? You might have to sit in the kitchen, thanks to Meg. Meg, come out and meet the baby sister of the artist, Frances."

"You know your stalker? So, baby sister, do you have a name?"

"Theresa. I wasn't stalking—"

"Come on in and you can keep me company while I get Fiona back together."

"You named your espresso machine Fiona?"

"Oh, he has names for everything in the kitchen at the restaurant. I think if I allowed him to, he would rename me," Meg said as she snapped her gum. "Hey Joshua, it's your lucky night. Don't look now, but here comes your lobster thief."

"Meg, don't call her that. We worked it out. I want the okay to serve the halibut cheeks as the main special tonight."

"You're the boss. We are serving the cheeks tonight. No thanks to the idiots you saddled me with. I had to teach fish butchery 101. They ruined the first batch."

"Have you ever tasted halibut cheeks?"

"No. I had no clue fish have cheeks. Does not sound that appetizing," Theresa said.

"I can make you a PB and J if that is more your style," Meg said.

"Excuse Meg—she can be a little harsh. Where's Frances?" Joshua asked, ducking into the back room and leaving Theresa alone with Meg. Theresa turned her back toward Meg when a woman walked in wringing her hands so much that Theresa wondered if her hands were going to fall off.

"Frances is off in the hills panning for gold or cooking. It was her girls' getaway to celebrate a birthday." Theresa walked to the counter directly in front of the open door to the back. When Meg moved her hand, the other woman appeared to flinch. What was Joshua doing? It was taking him forever. Theresa glanced at the woman wringing her hands. "My name's Theresa."

"Alice."

Theresa turned to Meg. "How long have you been working in a kitchen?"

"I don't work in a kitchen. I own the kitchen."

"Meg is the executive chef at my restaurant," Joshua said as he came out of the back, carrying a banker's box of papers that he set on the counter. "Alice, I want you to have this done in four days. Does that work for you?"

Alice nodded her head, reached up to take the box of papers off the counter, and walked out of the shop without a word.

"What's that about? You are having her file your garbage?" Meg asked. "She should be in jail."

"No, she is working her mistake off. I'm having her sort all the recipes I collected over the years I spent traveling through Southeast Asia."

"That's classic. You're having a—"

"Meg, you need to watch your language. Did you have any other questions about dinner service tonight?"

"What time are you coming in?"

"I'll be there as soon as I get Fiona back up to snuff."

"So, I won't be seeing you then."

"Funny."

"Theresa, did you say that Frances was away this weekend?"

Theresa watched as Meg took another long look at her, snapped her gum, and left. It was a strange interaction, and Theresa wasn't sure she quite understood what was going on. Joshua had quite the characters in his life. Why did he keep asking her about Frances? Maybe this was a huge mistake.

"Can you drink coffee at night?" Joshua asked. Before she could answer, he was busy grinding coffee beans and steaming milk. In less time than it took for her to be completely annoyed by Meg, Joshua placed a latte in front of Theresa. "How's it taste?"

Theresa picked the cup with both hands and tried to hide the fact that she was nervous. She took a deep sip and let the creamy liquid rest on her tongue before she swallowed. "Divine."

"Great. Now I'll show Meg that I can fix it and be at the restaurant for service tonight. Life is busy when Fiona gets jealous of the restaurant."

"What was that all about? The woman who walked out with your box of shredded paper?"

"Alice felt the need to adopt some lobsters. We are working it out."

"Oh."

"Come—you can take your cup with you. Stroll with me to the restaurant. What brings you to Monterey?"

Theresa felt Joshua's eyes focused on her. She took a moment to collect herself so she could walk and hold a cup of coffee. Her heart was banging around her chest trying to break free. What was going on? Her plans were to go back to school. Not get involved with anyone.

"You. Isn't it obvious?" Theresa said as she walked and carefully sipped the latte. Joshua was not making this easy as his beautiful eyes stayed fixed upon her. Theresa could not stop glancing at him. She took another sip from the latte. So far, so good—she had this down. What Theresa failed to notice was the uneven sidewalk, and as she took a step, her foot landed at an odd angle, causing her to spill coffee down the front of her T-shirt. "Great. Now I look like a Jackson Pollack wannabe."

"You can try to clean the T-shirt at the restaurant. We have a washer and dryer in the basement. I wonder if I have any of the T-shirts left from my coffee store opening. You'd look so cute with an otter holding a cup of coffee."

Theresa pulled the sweatshirt from around her waist. "I'm fine. I don't want to be a bother. I know you are getting ready for dinner service." Theresa tried to hide the fact she was not wearing a bra at the moment. Could Joshua see that she was letting her girls hang free when the coffee covered the front of her T-shirt? If Joshua was a woman, would she have declined the offer so quickly?

"If you get tired of being in a wet, coffee-dyed T-shirt, let me know and we can wash and dry it."

The process would ensure her hanging around longer. They were about five steps away from his restaurant, and Theresa could not contain herself. "I lost my job today."

Joshua stopped walking and turned to look at Theresa. His focused attention made her breath disappear. "I'm so sorry. Are you okay? Was this the job at the theatre company?"

"Yes." She wanted to hide her face and tell him the truth, but what would he think?

Theresa fought back tears when Joshua gently took her hand. "Tell you what...why don't you plan on having dinner here with me tonight? You can talk about it or not. Be my guest. I need to go before Meg tans my hide and serves me up for dinner."

"Is she a fan of *Sweeney Todd*? You don't serve meat pies, do you?"

"Never liked that musical. Gross. Remind me to run if I ever see a meat pie appear on the menu." Joshua smiled as he opened the door.

As they walked into the restaurant, the sound of laughter was coming from the kitchen, and the first few diners were in quiet conversations. Theresa liked the warmth of the place. Frances's painting really did look stunning on the wall above the fireplace. Joshua had asked her several times about her sister. Frances had not shared much about what had transpired between them. She didn't know if she should follow him into the kitchen, and so she went and took a seat at the bar.

"There you are. Come on back here. You might be more comfortable in my office," Joshua said.

She wasn't sure why, but when he gently touched her back, giant tears welled up in her eyes and spilled down her face. This time she didn't try to hide them.

"What's wrong?"

"I feel like fodder for a country song. I lost my job, and my relationship with Kelly is over."

"Let me get you a drink. What's your cure?"

"Don't you mean poison?" Theresa asked.

"I like to think of my predilection for scotch as more like a cure—it has helped me through more heartbreaks than I care to count."

"I like Long Island Iced Teas."

"I'll get you one of those. A great choice. I think it has the whole catalogue of hard stuff." Joshua was gone in a flash.

Theresa wiped her face with the back of her shirt sleeve and took a couple of deep breaths to try and stop the stupid tears. Joshua's office was comfortable and had a most unique mess of melted candle wax on a table in the corner. She walked over to it and realized it was a working sculpture.

Returning, Joshua handed her a tall glass with a cherry floating in the drink. "That was started when I first opened my coffee cart. People kept adding on to it with their own candles. It got too big for the Porpoise, so I had it at home. Then I thought it would bring me some luck here."

"Fire hazard didn't cross your mind?" Theresa asked.

"It did. I only allow it to be lit when I'm in here and not running around. Now, we can talk about the pros and cons of a candle mountain, or you can tell me what's going on with you." He sat down in his office chair and pointed to the comfy-looking love seat against the wall.

Her brain was yelling at her to be honest. There was something she wanted from him, and she did not understand her attraction to him. What would this do to Frances if she pursued him? Theresa was used to getting what she wanted. This was a runaway train, and she didn't know how to stop it. She took a sip of the drink, and it went down a little too easily.

Setting the drink down, she walked over to Joshua and took the glass of water out of his hand. He didn't stop her. This encouraged her to bend down and kiss him. His lips were dry and chapped and tasted of coffee. The whiskers from his three o'clock shadow tickled her face as she pressed into him with an increasing urgency. Joshua put his hands on Theresa's waist and met her kiss with his own probing frenzy. His tongue parted her lips, sending shock waves through her body and raising a wild wanting.

As quickly as the kiss started, Joshua firmly pushed Theresa back away from him and stood up. She blinked hard, confused by the sudden reversal. The noise that was coming from the kitchen had stopped, and Theresa glanced over her shoulder to see Meg standing in the doorway with her arms crossed.

"I'll come back," Meg said.

Joshua pushed past Theresa to catch up with Meg. Was there something going on between them? Theresa cursed her light complexion as she felt her face flush hot. Before she could collect herself, Joshua was back in the office and had made sure the door was left open.

"Theresa, I'm sorry. I can't do this. Not now and not with you."

"You...didn't it feel good? I know you felt it."

"I am so sorry—there is so much you don't know. I used to fantasize about your sister. This is complicated. I know this is going to sound lame, but it has to do with me and not you."

"Try me. I think I can handle complicated."

"I was in love with your sister, and I basically ran away from her with no explanations. I hurt your sister in ways that I do not fully understand. When I saw her at the gallery, my heart was opened again."

"You know she isn't into men? She's kind of dating this detective woman."

"She is? She told me she wasn't seeing anyone right now."

"She's a full-blown lesbian. That's part of the reason the family has kicked her out."

"What? But aren't you in a relationship with a woman?"

"I told you I ended that, and I am here because I know there is something between us."

"I think you need to understand that...Look, I'm not the guy you think I am, and I—"

"Joshua, they need you out front. There's an issue with a bottle of wine that was opened." Meg stood in the doorway, looking at Theresa the whole time she spoke. Joshua walked out to handle the latest issue.

"Listen, baby sister, I don't know what you think you're doing here, but Joshua needs to focus. Hands off."

"Are you his keeper?"

"I'm invested in this place, and I'm not going to have some young pup come in and disrupt a good thing."

"You're interested in him."

"God, you really are dense. I play for the opposite team. Trust me when I tell you Joshua and I have a lot in common. You are not his type."

A large crash in the kitchen pulled Meg's attention away, and Theresa took a breath again. That woman was scary. She watched as the kitchen rats scurried to aid the dishwasher, who had dropped a whole bin of glasses. Theresa couldn't help it as her eyes lit up when Joshua walked back into the office.

"Theresa, please don't say anything to Frances about this—I don't want to hurt her."

Theresa picked up the Long Island Iced Tea and sucked the whole drink down. She set the glass down and walked out. "Don't worry, you won't see me again." She had hoped he would follow her, but when she was halfway down the street to the Mini Cooper, she knew he wasn't behind her.

Joshua turned his Jeep Wrangler onto Del Monte Avenue. He had spotted Theresa getting into a black Mini Cooper with a Union Jack on the roof. She couldn't be that far in front of him, and he knew the roads well. Because she came from the City, she was most likely headed north on Highway 1 toward Santa Cruz. The traffic lights seemed to be exceedingly long tonight. The evening tourist traffic was not helping as the side roads appeared to be bottlenecked too. He wished he had paid more attention and gotten her phone number. His hands gripped the custom leather steering wheel he had put in his Jeep. His phone rang, and he looked down to see Meg's hand holding a cleaver appear on his smartphone. He had objected to the picture, but she insisted that when she called, it meant business.

"What's up, Meg?"

"Joshua, I know this is your business, but you can't let your groin run your life. What am I supposed to do when Alice comes in here tonight? I don't have time for your woman drama. I'm trying to get this place a quality reputation."

"You are correct. This is none of your business."

"It becomes my business when it interferes with this business. You are the face of the place. People ask for you and want that special touch. I can't be in the kitchen and grand standing in the dining room."

"You love your public. Stop bluffing...is there something else eating you?"

"Interesting choice of words. I know you enjoyed yourself as much as I did."

"This call is almost sounding like a jealous witch sort of call."

"I'm not a witch, I'm your work wife...with benefits. Does that little drama queen even know about your—"

"I don't think so, but her sister does so maybe she does. Listen, I think I see her car. I'll be back before the first seating service is over."

"That is in an hour. Clock's ticking."

Joshua threw his phone into the passenger seat and sped past a few cars as he approached Sand City on Del Monte. His nerves were on edge, but he smiled as he thought about how he had convinced Meg to finally take the job. It wasn't the money he offered—it was the no-strings-attached sex. He shook his head because he knew there was no such thing as *no strings* when he fooled around with women. Meg was different though. She was tough, sexy, and as much a womanizer as he was—and that was part of the attraction. The sex was primal and intoxicating.

Theresa was now only two cars in front of him. Most people made the mistake of staying on Del Monte instead of getting on Highway 1. He knew he could catch her long before Santa Cruz. What was he going to say? How would he get her to pull over? His mind was racing. He had never chased anyone down with a car before. A stoplight gave him his opportunity. He raced his Jeep around to the left of Theresa in the through lane. Joshua hopped out of the Jeep, ran to the front of the Mini Cooper, and placed his hands on the hood. It really was a toy car.

"I'm sorry. We need to talk!" he yelled. Joshua hoped she would give in without too much groveling. Theresa laid both hands on the car horn. Thank god it was a Mini, as the horn reminded him of something off a bicycle. It was so cute he actually started laughing. He knew he could shout over the horn. He started waving cars around them. He noticed a woman two cars back had whipped her phone out and was most likely recording the incident. *Let's make this good,* Joshua thought to himself and lay down in front of the car.

He knew that she would either back up and drive around him, or she was going to get out. When he heard the engine turn off and the car door open, he knew he was now in the driver's seat.

"What are you doing?"

"I am lying in front of your car until you agree to come back and have dinner with me."

"Why would I do that?"

"Give the guy a break," a motorist watching the scene yelled from his car. "Say yes. You'll marry him."

"Not what he's asking," Theresa yelled and turned back to look at Joshua, who was still lying in front of the car. "You need to stand up. This is dangerous for both of us."

"Not until you say you'll have dinner with me. I wasn't fair to you. I want to explain some things, and we can see after that."

"See what?"

"Theresa, call me stupid. I realized that when you walked out the door that all I wanted was to kiss you."

"Dinner. But not at your restaurant."

"I've got to work."

"Meet me at In-N-Out Burger back by that park."

"I will." Joshua stood up and walked to Theresa. "Are you hungry now?"

"What about work?"

"I will be fine. I know the boss, and he's a pretty cool guy."

Joshua held her car door open and smiled as she started the engine and did a quick U-turn. He scrambled and hopped into his Jeep and followed her U-turn with his own, adding screeching tires on top of it. Joshua raised his eyebrow as Theresa pulled into the drive-through at the In-N-Out. He drove right behind her.

He was not surprised when he pulled up to the window and was told he was paying for her order. The girl could eat. She had ordered two cheeseburgers animal-style, with an order of fries, a chocolate shake, and a Coke. Joshua found himself suddenly craving a burger and fries and knew this one slip in his normal routine would be okay. When he got his order, he drove through the parking lot until he found the Mini Cooper and the spunky redhead chomping down on a burger while leaning against the hood of the car.

"I was wondering if we would be eating together?"

"Prime seating. Come join me. Thanks for the food. I realized I didn't have any cash. Couldn't believe they let me slide through giving you the bill. I'll have to do that more often."

"Theresa, you wouldn't."

"Maybe."

"Listen—the reason I kept bringing up Frances isn't because I like her. I do... This is not sounding right."

"Joshua, have a bite of your burger and relax. I am feeling so much better with some food."

"Did Frances tell you anything about me?"

"She really did not talk about you. When you say you like her? Is that why you—"

Joshua cut Theresa off by kissing her. Her lips tasted of burger and salt. Joshua pressed himself into her and spread her legs apart on the car. He knew he needed to stop and give some thought as to what he was doing. But he wanted this woman. She was captivating and she wanted him.

"Frances didn't share much except that you basically disappeared. One day you were in classes and the next you were gone."

"Can you please spit out whatever it is you are so afraid to say? Did you and Frances hook up?"

"No. I wanted to, but she and I were on opposite teams then. That doesn't make sense. She wasn't into women, and I was a woman in college."

Joshua watched as Theresa took her hands off his neck and scooted back on the car hood. This was not the reaction he wanted, but he was used to it. When they found out he was transgender, they all of a sudden rejected everything that had attracted them to him. He studied Theresa's eyes and saw that she was looking as intensely back at him.

"Slow down. I need a second for my brain to process this information. I felt your groin. You are hard."

"It is firm. I'm packing."

"I got it." Theresa pointed to the car that pulled up and had about sixteen kids under the age of ten piling out of it. "Do you want to sit in the Coop or the Wrangler?"

"Better idea. Lock your car and let's go to the beach."

Joshua smiled as Theresa climbed into the Jeep. He felt a surge of excitement race through his body as he pulled onto the road and headed south toward one of his favorite spots on the bay. He was relieved that the place was empty, and he pulled the Jeep to a stop. The waves were beautiful as they crashed against the rocks. Lights were coming on in the houses on the bluff behind them. They could talk without fear of upsetting delicate ears.

"You can ask me anything," Joshua said.

"Are you attracted to me?"

"You want me to kiss you again?"

"Yes. But how long have you been a man?"

"I knew I was a man when I was about three years old. Everyone kept telling me that I was a girl, and I knew it wasn't right. I told my mom she had made a mistake. I know you were asking about the surgery and all the rest of it. When I came into my trust fund, I went to Thailand. I had been living as a man for two years before that, binding my breasts and taking hormones. It was a bizarre time. I had facial hair and boobs. My voice deepened."

"Joshua, you feel like a man, and that is confusing me. I was telling everyone that I'm a gold-star lesbian. But that isn't true. I know that I could be with a man."

"I tell you what—I want to get to know you, but I also know you are freshly out of your relationship and a job. I know you didn't think I was listening, but I heard every word."

"Honestly, I have never had such a strong attraction to anyone before. When I first met you, I wanted to hate you. I saw how you looked at Frances, and I wanted you to look at me that way."

"Stay with me tonight. I promise I will respect whatever it is you want, but don't drive home tonight. You need to sleep and be safe. Here are the keys to my place. Give me your phone number, and I'll text you the address. Let yourself in and make yourself at home. I need to get back to the restaurant. Alice is coming in to work off some of her debt, and I really don't want Meg to quarter her up and serve her to the guests."

Joshua started the Jeep and drove back to the parking lot at In-N-Out and made sure Theresa had directions to his place. He found himself smiling all the way back to his Otter Place. He would worry about the fallout later. There was something about Theresa that made him want to surrender into her arms.

CHAPTER THIRTY-ONE

DISTRACTED

"**O**ur birthday warriors have made it safely back to base camp." Russell patted the empty chair next to him. "Frances, have a seat next to me—we have something to discuss."

"That sounds ominous," Theresa said, taking a seat opposite Frances at the round table closest to the Buena Vista's bathroom. "Winter, you are looking kind of green. Does anyone else notice Winter looks green?"

"I'm fine. When I get some sugar in my system, I'll be fine."

"Winter, you are marinating that child in sugar. I heard that for the ride home from Sacramento, you made them stop at every Krispy Kreme shop you passed," Russell said.

"Okay. My body and what I put into it are none of your concern. Take it up with the US Supreme Court."

"How was the birthday weekend?" Simon asked.

"I think Frances had the most fun. Notice hop-a-long there...she had to practically break her kneecap to eke out time alone with Sam."

"What?" Simon perked up. Frances noticed the look that passed between him and Russell.

"Is there something you two are cooking up? I saw the look. That look means trouble."

"We might have encouraged something that we might need to call off. Are you talking about Sam, as in the woman in that million-dollar suit that you ran out on after she planted one on you? The one y'all set our little Franny up with on that ambush of a date?"

"The very same one," Winter said. "It was like the universe finally whacked those two over the head and put them out in the middle of nowhere with no options to escape."

"Tell us everything," Russell said.

"Good morning," Sam said as she walked up to the table. Frances stood and kissed Sam.

"Everyone, I know I don't need to introduce you again. This is Samantha Iverson. Sam," Frances said and kissed Sam again on the cheek.

"Now we really need to do something," Russell said, leaning over to Simon. "You go intercept her before she gets here."

"Hi," Molly said, appearing at the table. "Looks like I'm a little late."

"You can say that again," Winter said.

"Let me grab another chair. Looks like our family is growing." Russell hopped up and offered his chair to Sam. "It is so nice to formally meet you. I know there was a moment sometime last year. I'm Russell, and this is my husband, Simon."

"I don't know if you two have met. Molly Woods, this is Samantha Iverson," Simon said.

The two women smiled at one another and quickly took a seat at the table. "Molly is the police detective who handled the whole Ethan thing," Frances said, taking Sam's hand.

"Your world must be filled with some rather frightening things," Sam said.

"When I'm off the clock, I don't do shop talk," Molly answered.

"Ice anyone?" Winter said.

"What was that, Winter?" Frances asked.

"I need more ice in my Sprite."

"This is going to be interesting. It's been a while since I've seen two lionesses circling," Simon whispered to Cheryl.

"What are you talking about?"

"Anyone care to fill the table in about the vultures that almost ate the sunbathers?" Frances said, trying to diffuse a rather tense situation. "Theresa, you left early this morning?"

"I wanted to go for a walk along the bay before the coffees."

"I haven't seen you much. They must be working you to the bone," Frances said.

"Theresa, you didn't tell me you got your job back?" Russell said.

"Who wants an Irish coffee? I'll go to the bar and get the order. Russell, you can help." Theresa stood and started counting the raised hands at the table.

Frances noticed that Molly was wearing mascara, and her hair had some new highlights. She was wearing a crisp, blue shirt and had a light purple sweater draped over her shoulders. Molly had dressed up for the Buena Vista Irish Coffee Club. Simon was nervously twisting the napkin in his hands, and Frances went back to Molly. She looked strikingly beautiful. She could tell that something was up between Molly and the boys, but she couldn't quite put her finger on it.

"Sam, what do you do?" Molly asked.

"I'm in change management and promotions."

"That sounds important. How do you know Frances?"

"Her friends set us up on a date."

"You're the one?" Molly looked at Frances, who was blushing. "I can't believe you ran out on that."

"I'll take that as a compliment," Sam said as she helped free Theresa's hands of one of the Irish coffees.

"I've got a topic I need some help with, and you all must pitch in on this one," Theresa said as she took her seat.

"Theresa, if I told you once, I've told you a thousand times...I am not going to marry the pig who got me pregnant for a little sausage," Winter said.

"Not going there, Winter. This is actually rather serious. Frances has told me that she is not going to travel to St. Louis due to some things that have happened with our family."

"She told us about the letter and the will, Theresa. Rotten. The whole family is filled with—"

"It isn't that easy, Simon. I agree they have no concept of what it means to be gay."

CHAPTER THIRTY-ONE

"Theresa, really? Can we not rehash this family drama? I'm over it."

"Frances, I need the help of your chosen family. After Dad came out to your opening, I called Agatha and Edna to find out what was really going on with the family. Bernard is an idiot. They don't support what has happened, and they want us all to get together and talk in person."

"Theresa, not one of them has called, emailed, or included me in any way...the silence is the loudest message that I've been cast out of the family." Frances felt her anger rising, and she could tell Theresa was not going to let this go.

"Because they are silent is no reason to turn down their invitation. Maybe they are worried they would say something wrong. Please, Frances, come back to St. Louis with me."

The table got very quiet as Frances played with the collar of cream on the top of her Irish coffee.

"When do we leave for St. Louis?" Frances asked.

"I'll handle all the tickets. Where would you like to stay?" Theresa asked.

"Would—"

"I think we might want our own space and not stay with anyone in the family," Theresa said.

"I've got points with Ritz. I'll book the Ritz Carlton in Clayton. It puts us close to Agatha and Edna and not too far from Mom and Dad in Webster Groves," Frances whispered, already sorry she had agreed.

"Sounds like a plan," Theresa said.

Frances stood and walked away from the table. She knew that Sam would follow and continued to walk out the door of the Buena Vista. She walked across the street and navigated through the line of people waiting for the next cable car. Seagulls were soaking up the sun and looking for food in the park.

"Do you want to be alone?" Sam asked and reached for Frances's hand.

"No. I'm glad you're here. Thanks for walking out with me. That is not what I wanted to introduce you to. Usually we are laughing so hard, you wouldn't need to work your abs out for a week."

"I know this is all very new—do you want to slow things down? I understand."

"Not with you. With the family, I do. Theresa and I need to go face the family together. I'm not sure exactly what she's up to though…I know she's been in contact with the family. Only I've been written out of the will."

"Can I help?"

Frances turned to Sam and smiled. Her look of concern brought comfort to Frances in a way that gave her peace. "Keep your phone line open. I know you have some big deals coming through. I'll be fine. It is going to hurt and I really . . ."

They walked along the edge of the bay in silence.

"Sam."

"Yes?"

"Would you mind taking me home?"

"To my place?" Sam asked.

"Not today. I need to go to my home, but I don't want to be alone."

CHAPTER THIRTY-TWO

BREAKING BAD WITH BROCCOLI

"Who put speed bumps in the sky?" Theresa asked, her hands squeezing the armrests so tightly they were completely white.

"I don't think it is an omen. Maybe this will make talking with the family a piece of cake," Frances said. "I hate flying into the Midwest. It is always bumpy."

The plane jumped up and then dipped, giving Frances the feeling of zero gravity for the slightest second before it pitched to the right, flinging her into the stranger next to her, who had been attempting to sleep.

"Sorry," Frances said, pulling herself back toward Theresa.

Frances looked at Theresa and noticed she was an odd shade of light green. She decided to commit fully to supporting Theresa and to stop questioning her every step of the way while they were in a metal tube being bounced around like rag dolls. Fear was fear, and Theresa was scared. Frances had flown so many miles that she never really noticed much. This time though, the turbulence was intense. Not to mention, being so upset with Theresa was exhausting. Sam had come into her life. Frances knew she had sold another four paintings after the gallery show and picked up three commissioned works. It was time to declare a truce with Theresa.

Her instincts kicked in, and she started to check the seat pockets in front of her for a barf sack. There was nothing. What is wrong with airlines? People still get airsick—probably now more than ever with how squished they pack everyone into cattle call airplanes.

"Hang on, Theresa. We will be landing soon."

"Folks, this is your captain speaking. It looks like we are not going to be able to land on time as there are reported wind shear problems ahead of us. We are diverting to another airport and will let you know our destination as soon as we know."

"Maybe they'll send us to St. Louis, and we won't have to take another flight," Frances said. She placed her hand over Theresa's. Theresa let go of the armrest and clamped down on Frances's hand so hard, Frances was worried she might not be able to ever straighten out her fingers. The roller coaster flight continued to bounce them around. It was a flight like this one that had convinced her to get off the consulting rodeo circuit. To be tossed around like a helpless crash-test dummy thirty thousand feet above the ground in a flying tube did not keep the allure of travel for her. Babies were crying, and people were now calling on Lord Jesus and his old man, God, to let them live.

Frances glanced across the aisle, noticing that pretty much everyone was white knuckling it through this flight. A kid a couple of rows behind them screamed that the plane was crashing when it dropped suddenly. Frances forced her stomach back down, telling herself she was not going to throw up. Theresa's grip increased, and Frances was sure she was suffering broken bones now.

"This must be what a cowboy feels like riding a bull," the guy sitting next to Frances said. Or at least that is what she thought she heard.

"Frances, I'm going to throw up," Theresa said.

The pilot came back on. "You folks are going to be happy about this—we are on our final approach into Kanas City. There will be a few more slight bumps. Please make sure your seat backs are up, and hang on. Thanks for flying with us."

"This is crazy. When this plane gets on the ground, I'm not getting back in one. We can rent a car and drive the five hours to St. Louis."

"Theresa, think about how bad the weather must be on the ground to give us this kind of flight. We're talking softball-size hail probably. If it is too dangerous, they won't let the planes take off." Frances tried to move her fingers, but Theresa's grip was so tight, she had no room to move. The pain in her hand was keeping her mind focused there.

Frances hated the middle seat. The guy next to her in the aisle seat was so rigid, she wondered if he was still alive. He had the same look of terror on his face she saw on Theresa's, and the few moments she cared to look in his direction, she didn't think his eyes blinked. His hands were clamped down on the armrest and had not moved. The plane continued to stay airborne even as it pitched and dropped. It reminded her of the Tower of Terror ride at Disney's California Adventure. It used to be her favorite ride. She glanced back at Theresa, who had gone from a light pale green to matching the deep green color of Kermit the Frog.

"Hang in there, Theresa."

"Ouch! What the hell, Frances? That really hurt. Why did you pinch my leg like that?"

"You're no longer green. Now you are a red color."

"I'm not a fan of your form of distraction therapy."

The landing gear could be felt opening under the plane, and Frances felt a sense of relief. It felt like the wheels touched the ground for less than a second when they were airborne again, followed by a wallop of a thud as the plane's wheels hit the runway a second time. The plane hopped forward and pitched to the right as if the pilots were wrestling with an invisible monster trying to flip the plane.

"I think we've fallen out of the sky and on a house. If someone starts singing 'Defying Gravity,' I'm going to punch them," Theresa said.

The plane hopped up again and slammed back down on the ground before rolling forward. "Whew! I think we might finally be on the ground," Frances said.

A chorus of "praise Jesus" ran through a number of the passengers.

A flight attendant came on again. "Ladies and gentlemen, thank you for joining Captain Kangaroo and his hopping plane. What a ride. It is my pleasure to welcome you to Kansas City."

"Did we kill the witch?" someone yelled.

"No witch killing. Please stay seated, with your seatbelt fastened. We have not made it to the gate yet, and those crosswinds are fierce."

The plane finally rolled to a stop, and after the briefest of seconds, the passengers started applauding the end of the flight.

"Frances, I really don't want to get back up in that air."

"I'm with you. But let's see what the rest of the day looks like. Let's get something to eat to help settle our stomachs."

"I can't eat anything right now. Please, Frances—"

"Attention. If you are continuing on to St. Louis, we are doing a quick turnaround to beat the incoming storm system. Please limit your terminal time to ten minutes."

Frances seriously thought about renting a car, but maybe it was better to get right back on the horse you fear you'd never ride again. The turnaround was going to be so quick, it would put them in St. Louis ahead of schedule.

"I need to get off this plane. Now," Theresa said.

"Hang on, Sis, no one is moving at the moment. Relax."

"Not helping."

"Look, we can get up now. Don't take your suitcase out of the overhead because I had to shoehorn that thing in. I really don't think it is an approved carry-on. Let's go use the cement-and-mortar bathrooms and get something cold to drink. You'll feel better." Frances raced up the aisle before Theresa could say a word in protest. When they walked into the terminal, Theresa dropped in dramatic fashion to the floor and kissed it. "Thank you, Jesus!"

"Amen, sister," said a woman waiting to board the plane.

"Come on, Meryl Streep, there is a bathroom stall waiting for your autograph."

"You go. I think I sweated out all available bodily fluids." Theresa scrunched up her nose. "And I smell like it."

"Fine. I will pick up something to drink for us. Any requests?"

"Long Island Iced Tea?"

"How about a Coke?" Frances did her impersonation of an Olympic speed walker to the women's restroom. On her way, she noticed that the only available food in the Kansas City airport appeared to be fried or from the pizza food group. It was another indicator she was no longer in California. The fact that she grew up thinking a salad consisted only of iceberg lettuce, a tomato, and some sort of white dressing encapsulated her Midwestern upbringing. Frances thought about the layered salad that had been a frequent side dish at family meals when she was growing up. The first layer was iceberg lettuce, followed by layers of Miracle Whip, shredded cheese, and peas (if they were being fancy), repeated until the top of the dish. The thought of that salad made her more nauseous than the air turbulence that played ping-pong with her stomach.

Frances walked down the concourse, checking for something that would give her some nutrition. The food choices were about as appetizing as her Aunt Janice's idea of a Jell-O dish. Who shreds carrots and cabbage and then puts them into green Jell-O? It was as if the people of St. Louis got together and played a mean joke on the taste buds of their children. Aunt Janice made hers extra special by making a Miracle Whip and bacon bit dressing that she poured over the top of the molded Jell-O tower. Even the various dogs who lived with the Kavanaghs through the years wouldn't touch the stuff. One Christmas dinner, they had tried to get their cocker spaniel, Possum, to eat it. She would eat pretty much anything from shoes to worms. Possum took the bite of Jell-O, held it in her mouth, walked to the kitty litter, and deposited the bite. She took a piece of kitty-made Almond Roca out of the cat litter and chomped on that instead.

"Bingo," Frances said as she spied a refrigerated case selling quick grab-and-go cups of cut vegetables and fruits for the health-conscious traveler. Frances grabbed a cup of broccoli and one of carrots, with a couple packets of ranch dressing.

"That was fast," Theresa said, reaching for the cup of broccoli florets. "Frances, that's our flight they are getting ready to board. I was hoping it would be canceled and we could drive."

"It's such a short flight. Come on—we have our plastic reboarding passes, so let's go before the herd is let loose. They are trying to beat the huge tornado-producing storm that we flew through to get here."

"They wouldn't fly into a tornado, would they? Why did you say that? Are you teasing me?"

Frances took hold of Theresa by her shirt sleeve and pulled her down the walkway onto the Boeing 737.

"Maybe this flight won't be as full and we can keep the middle seat empty," Theresa said as she peeled the plastic wrap off the top of the cup-o-broccoli.

"What's that smell?" Frances started to gag.

"I don't know...I think it might be the broccoli. It looks okay, but something is very—" Theresa raised a piece of broccoli to her nose. "Oh, this smells worse than shit."

Frances stood and took the piece of broccoli and threw it back into the cup and ran down the plane to the restroom. She threw the cup away in the restroom and shut the door. The odor was so strong the whole back end of the plane smelled like a dirty diaper.

"Theresa, get up. We are moving." Frances worked their bags out of the overhead. "They are getting ready to board the next set of passengers." The smell seemed to be getting stronger. Frances gagged again as she handed Theresa her oversized carry-on bag. A woman with a baby in the last row of seats kept wiping her nose; Frances noticed she was looking around. "Keep going forward, Theresa. The smell seems to be following us."

Finally, Frances was able to take a breath free of the soiled air, and they were up to row six. Theresa threw her bag in the overhead and slid into the window seat. Frances followed and saw that the mother with the baby was now busy changing the little nipple-biter's diaper. A faint whiff of the broccoli had made its way to row six. A flight attendant came through and hesitated around row ten. She turned toward the front and studied the seated passengers. Frances tried to look cool and act like she was reading the in-flight magazine. A couple of other passengers behind them started to poke their heads up and cough. The flight attendant asked another attendant about the smell, and they both stood, almost visibly gagging.

"Frances, they're going to figure out we terrorized the plane's air with broccoli gone bad," Theresa whispered loudly, leaning over the center seat.

"Shut it. They have no clue. Keep it cool. You usually are the one snowing everyone. What's wrong with you?"

"Excuse me, do any of you smell a rather offensive odor?" the flight attendant asked.

"It smells like a baby diaper in here," Frances said. "Maybe somebody left it on the plane." On cue, the baby at the back of the plane started crying.

"You know, you are so right. She's right." Both flight attendants hurried back to the poor woman with the baby.

"Frances, you should be ashamed of yourself. You're going to blame an innocent baby?"

Frances leaned out into the aisle and watched as the flight attendants, holding their noses, took the offending bag out of the restroom and opened the rear door of the plane to get some fresh air into the plane. Frances tried not to giggle as the pilot, who came back to see who had opened a door, visibly gagged. The rush of fresh air pushed the smell of baby poo broccoli forward, and then it was gone. Frances winked at Theresa, and the case of the broccoli odor bomb was closed.

CHAPTER THIRTY-THREE
FIRST STOPCROWN CANDY KITCHEN

T he air was still as they walked out of the St. Louis International Airport and boarded the Avis shuttle bus. Clouds were coming in from the west, and Frances was relieved to be on the ground. She looked at the business travelers who were on the shuttle bus. No one looked happy, and the pallor of the faces around her showed that all the flights must have hit the edge of the weather front moving across the area. There was a comfort in seeing the Drury Inn by the St. Louis airport. Frances shifted in the bus seat and found herself ready to spring out the moment the driver opened the door. Her mind went to Sam and the wonderfully sweet and long kiss good-bye. Sam did not press her for any explanations about this trip, and for that Frances was grateful.

"What about a stop at Crown Candy to share a shake?" Theresa asked.

"That, and a BLT? Sounds like a perfect plan. No one knows we're here yet." Frances noticed that Theresa looked away at this mention of their surprise arrival.

"It's close to two. I think it should still be open," Theresa said.

"I thought you were going to say it would still be safe to go at this time of day. You know we were always told not to go to that part of the city."

"Frances, I can't believe you said that."

"I remember the first time Agatha drove all us kids over there in the barf wagon."

"You're the one who made it the barf wagon. I was just a baby."

"You have no clue the tortures I endured. Mom was so angry when we all got back, I thought her head was going to explode. I had no clue that it was in a bad area of the city. We were focused on the milkshakes."

"Remember Dad teaching us all how to safely run a red light in North St. Louis? Man, we were little racist Webster Groves brats," Theresa said.

The shuttle bus stopped, and Frances and Theresa gathered their bags and headed to the kiosk. In ten minutes, they were driving east toward St. Louis and the unknown. "Do you remember if I take the St. Louis Avenue exit off I-70?" Frances asked.

"Thank god for phones and instant mapping. Slow down or you'll be to the Arch before this thing populates."

"We are in Missouri, where people will stop and back up to take the exit they missed."

"Frances, don't remind me. Yes, take the St. Louis Avenue exit and then take a right."

The saints of excellent parking were riding with Frances as she pulled the Chrysler 300 into a street parking spot directly even with the front door of Crown Candy Kitchen.

Frances stepped out of the car and smiled at the familiar and well-weathered green-and-white striped awning running the length of the restaurant front. Theresa was right about the car—it looked like a pimp mobile with its chrome tire rims and smoke-colored windows. How this made it into a rental car parking lot was beyond her.

"Can't get much closer than this. I take it as sign we are to enjoy the shakes, and the calories don't count."

"I think you should do the milkshake challenge," Theresa said as they walked into the front door and stepped through a wormhole back in time. The white walls, white booths, and white pressed-tin ceiling were exactly as she remembered them.

"We hit this place at the right time—there is no line," Theresa said, walking to the last booth against the wall. The ice cream flavors were up on the board on the opposite wall over the old soda fountain counter. A waitress came over to take their order. "I can't wait to have real ice cream. San Francisco thinks they have good ice cream—none of those shops hold a candle to this place."

"Or Ted Drewes Frozen Custard," Frances added.

"What can I get ya?" the waitress asked, standing about five feet away from the table. Theresa and Frances looked at one another, not quite sure she was talking to them, even though their table was the only one without food. "Any time, you two gingers." The waitress started laughing and walked over. "You should see your faces."

"Holy shit, it's Charlie," Frances said. "When did you start working here?"

"Well, my life has changed quite a bit. My husband—you remember Jackson? Well, he and I started flipping houses in North St. Louis and down in the state streets. The crash happened, and we lost everything. I work here and at Tony's. I couldn't believe it when I saw you walk in. When was the last time we saw one another?"

"I think it was the ten-year high school reunion," Frances said.

"Now which sister is this?" Charlie asked.

"Sorry. Theresa, this is Charlie. We had the same classes all through high school."

"Yeah. Would you believe it, I even graduated from Wash U, and here I am taking orders at Crown Candy Kitchen."

"Frances just had her first full gallery show in San Francisco," Theresa said.

"Wow. You're an artist? I thought you were working in your dad's firm?"

"I did, but I left that a few years ago." Frances was starting to get nervous because she didn't know if Charlie had seen the news stories about what had happened in San Francisco. "So do your parents still go to the same church?"

"You didn't hear? Why would you—we are in different worlds now. Both my folks passed. Mom about three years ago and Dad last year. It was rough. He had dementia."

"I'm sorry. How are your kids?"

"Wild. They take after Jackson. How long you in town?"

"We're here for the week."

"You're in town for the Kavanagh picnic and Fourth of July party, I bet. Of course, your family threw the best parties. What can I get you two?"

"I'll do my usual—a chocolate malt and a BLT," Frances said.

"I thought we were sharing?" Theresa asked.

"Get your own."

"Hey, your shakes are my treat. It's so good to see you. Man, Frances, you were always so creative."

"Well, since you're buying, I'll do the black cherry shake and a Reuben."

"Excellent choices—can't go wrong there."

Charlie walked back to the kitchen, and Frances turned to Theresa. "I don't think she saw the news stories."

"Or she has no memory. You heard her say her dad had dementia."

"She remembered me. I didn't recognize her."

Less than five minutes had passed when Charlie delivered the large silver shake mixing containers, two tall glasses, and two long spoons. Frances savored her first sip of the thick chocolate malt, rolling the smooth, soft ice cream across her tongue. She didn't want the feeling and flavor to end. The BLT was plopped in front of her in lightning speed. The bacon was piled so high, Frances seriously questioned her ability to get her mouth wide enough to take a bite. Theresa was busy smashing down her Rueben to get a bite of the warm sandwich on marbled rye.

"This is a food memory I will be able to enjoy as long as I live," Theresa said. "Do you think this tastes better because it is our home or because the food really is that much better than what they make on the coasts?"

"Both. Do you want to taste the best chocolate malt ever?"

"Sure. This is pretty awesome. On the count of three. One…two…three…switch." Theresa and Frances slid the silver grails of malt and shake across the table and delved into the other's tasty treat.

"Do you think Merb's is still open?" Frances asked.

"The chocolate-covered strawberries! Those are the best. Where do you think they get those huge strawberries?"

"Grow them in a nuclear waste dump outside of Earth City," Charlie said as she set down two cups of water.

"Not true. Is Merb's still in business?"

"Yup. Not that I'm sending you to a competitor. Bissinger's is still open too."

"Thanks for the temptations. I'm going to be rolling back to San Francisco," Frances said as Charlie walked away to take orders from another table.

"Should we go check into the hotel next?" Frances asked.

"I can't believe we are staying in a hotel. This is the city where our family lives. We grew up here. This is our home."

"Theresa, you know how people like to gossip here. Please keep your voice down and don't talk about our issues in public. No one else needs to hear our business. Can you wait until we are back in the car before you start freaking out? Yes, let's go check in. I don't think I can finish this."

"Frances, you are sounding like Dad. No one is paying attention."

"Seriously. This is St. Louis—the walls not only have ears, they have mouths and repeat everything."

Frances went to the candy counter and paid the check. She purchased a couple of items and surprised Theresa with the chocolate truffles. Theresa looked in the bag with some delight. Frances was not sure if she should confront her sister over how much she really knew. Theresa was a much better actress than Frances gave her credit for. She had to have known their father was coming out to San Francisco because she had let his hotel slip out before he had given that information to Frances.

"I don't know that I am feeling this is my home anymore."

"Frances, this is hard enough without you pulling one of your question-everything freak outs."

Frances slammed the car door. "I'm not pulling anything. We were not given an invitation to come here. Or at least, I wasn't. You saying that our siblings wanted me here is suspect. I have a feeling they are going to be happy to see you."

"Let's not fight. I am your sister, and you are not alone. You know that, right?"

It took all Frances had not to lash out at Theresa. She focused on driving the car without getting lost in the streets that she used to know like the back of her hand.

"Maybe we can blow off a little steam and go dancing at Novak's? I always wanted to go there, and now I'm legal."

"What about The Complex?"

"Oh, I went there. That place was so easy to get into."

Frances shook her head and imagined that, chances were, she and Theresa could very well have been dancing with all the gay boys at The Complex at the same time. "Do you think those clubs are still open, or have they been shut down by vice?"

"Or Saint Louis University. That school was buying up all the best places around their campus. St. Louis was a lot more fun when you were coming of age."

"It might seem that way. But you were given so much more leeway. The rest of us broke Mom and Dad in for you."

"Nah, I think they were exhausted when I was a teenager, and they figured that if the rest of you lived, I'd be fine."

Frances thought about running into Charlie at Crown Candy and how time really did seem to stop. St. Louis was a shell of its old glory. It always amazed her how places like Crown Candy continued to thrive in what were virtually empty neighborhoods. St. Louis wasn't a ghost town, but it did have its ghost neighborhoods. Buildings with ornate brick and iron were vacant and home to the ever-encroaching trees and shrubs that moved in as the buildings slowly fell away.

CHAPTER THIRTY-FOUR
TO JUMP OR NOT TO JUMP

Frances got onto westbound I-65 and smiled as she passed the exits for Forest Park and the St. Louis Zoo. The world had changed drastically as new buildings pushed the skyline up in the Central West End. She would have to come back and explore this area. She wondered if the Chase still had the elegance it did when she was younger. St. Louis was a beautiful city with tree-lined streets and colorful flowers. One thing the Midwest did well was their lawns. The smells and colors were amazing, as were the storms. To watch a thunderstorm in the Midwest was hypnotic and sometimes downright scary. She didn't miss the tornado warnings, but she did miss the beauty of the thunderstorms.

In the fall, this stretch of freeway was always so beautiful when the autumn colors arrived on the trees. Compared to San Francisco and the gray that settled in through the late winter months, St. Louis had four distinct seasons. There was not always snow at Christmas, but there was a better chance of it than in San Francisco. Christmas lights on palm trees was not the same as viewing Christmas lights on houses in St. Louis with snow on the ground.

"Do you think Mom will be happy to see us?" Theresa asked.

"She'll be happy to see you. I don't know that happy is what she'll feel when she sees me."

"Frances, you need to stop playing like Mom hates you. You know she doesn't."

"You speak for Mom now?"

"No. Dad told us that they both love us very much."

"Theresa, do you hear yourself? They wrote me out of their will. No one stopped Bernard from sending that stupid letter. What the fuck?"

"Relax. I'm sorry I brought it up. After we get checked in, I'm going to call Agatha and Edna."

"Why?"

"I told you that I talked to them, and they want to see us. Maybe we can all meet at Uncle Bill's Pancake House."

"You thought you told me. I would remember that. How 'bout a truce."

"I wish we could all get along. It could happen."

"Yeah, and pigs could fly."

"See? That is what I'm talking about. You are so cynical about the family and life."

Frances drove the car up to the valet and bellman station at the Ritz-Carlton and ended the conversation by hopping out of the car without answering Theresa. She handed the keys to the young man wearing a white coat trimmed in gold. The lobby was virtually empty as she walked in, and she hoped that meant this would be the quickest check-in ever. She wanted to take a shower and reset herself. Maybe Theresa was right. She was expecting the worst, and that might not be fair. It put stress on her, and the energy would jump to the family. Frances found staying in a really nice hotel always helped her adjust her outlook on life. It was something she started doing when she went to work for her family. Her first workcation was at the Chase Hotel in the Central West End. It was an escape hatch in her life. There were times she needed space to get the work done without anyone pulling her in a thousand different directions.

Frances gathered the room keys and walked to the center of the lobby where she waited for Theresa to come in and find her. She considered going out to get her, but she needed more space so as not to yell at her sister. Time was ticking away, and Frances finally walked out the front doors and tapped Theresa on the shoulder. "Here's our room key. I'm going up to take a shower and get the layer of travel yuck off."

"I think I still smell the broccoli," Theresa said.

"I only smell bacon. Crown Candy Kitchen was perfect. You don't have to worry about our bags. They'll bring them up. Consider yourself in your own little world of *Downton Abbey*," Frances said and gently punched Theresa's arm.

"A downstairs staff? A dream of mine. I hope the rumors are true about them making a *Downton Abbey* movie. I was so addicted."

They walked back into the lobby and made it up to their room in record time. Their bags were magically set out on benches upholstered in silver fabric at the end of each one of the queen beds. Frances walked to the window and glanced out. They had a view toward Washington University. The room looked like it had been updated.

"Is it me, or is this what it would feel like to be inside a Jiffy Pop?"

"Exactly! I don't think I've ever seen so many hues of silver in my life—from the drapes to the bed comforters to the carpet. Maybe it is platinum."

"It is a little cold." Frances shivered and walked over to the thermostat.

A knock at the door caused them both to freeze. Their bags were already delivered. Frances walked to the door and was surprised to see the valet who had taken her keys.

"I thought you would want this. Dangerous to leave a bag of Crown Candy in the car."

"Dangerous? Why?" Theresa asked.

"Settle down. He means they would eat it." Frances tipped the kid a twenty, and he looked shocked.

She shut the door and turned to Theresa, handing her the bag with three chocolates left.

"When did you become such a big tipper? I can't believe you tipped him a twenty for a six-dollar bag of candy."

"Oh shit—that was a twenty? I need to pay attention. I think I'm tired—don't let me ever tip that much again."

"Actually, I thought you were showing off. Maybe hanging out with Olivia—"

CHAPTER THIRTY-FOUR

"Don't you ever mention that woman to me again. You understand?"

"Okay. Don't bite my head off. Different topic…You want to shower first?"

"Go ahead. I'm going to see if I can turn down the air conditioner in here. And I promised Sam I would give her a call when we got settled."

Theresa grabbed herself some clean clothing out of her suitcase and waltzed into the bathroom, shutting the door. When Frances heard the shower running, she flopped back on the bed, enjoying the luxurious way it folded in around her body. She hit Sam's number and held her breath as the call went through. Her smile flattened as the familiar voicemail prompt answered the call. "We are in St. Louis. The storm clouds are forming over the city, and that is the way I feel about this trip. Hope you are having a strong day."

She hung up and smacked herself in the forehead with her open palm. What the heck is *a strong day*? That was what she needed. Could she catch a plane back to San Francisco tonight? She really did not want to deal with the family. Frances stretched and pulled a silver throw that was folded on an angle across the bed across her upper body. Even the ceiling was painted silver. She looked to her left and thought the other bed looked like it was wrapped in aluminum foil. A thought crossed her mind, and her smile grew wide. She flipped her shoes off and got herself up on her feet. The last time she had done something like this, she was quite a bit shorter.

What was it about two beds so close together that triggered her jumping switch? The shower was still running in the bathroom, and Frances warmed up with a couple of baby bounces on the bed. She took her jacket off and tossed it toward the silver-and-white striped reading chair in the corner. She saw the image in her mind and knew she could do it. She bent her knees and judged the distance to the center of the other bed to be about five feet. Easy. She could do it. She jumped up and ducked, worried she was going to hit her head on the ceiling. She got separation between her feet and the bed. Yup. This was a go. The ceiling was higher than she first judged it to be, and so she took a second test jump. Her hair flew up around her and her pulse was revving up. She looked down at her stocking feet, and with a couple more spring-loaded bounces, Frances looked toward the hallway and the bathroom door. It was still shut, and now she could see steam escaping from underneath. On her return to the bed, she bent her knees deeply and told herself this was like riding a bike. Frances let herself be free and took the launch jump that would allow her to fly across the canyon between the beds. Misjudging her angles, she hit the mattress so hard it shifted out from underneath her, and Frances found herself yelling, "Abort! Abort!" It was too late, as her left shoulder hit the wall first and then her head. Her body fell between the bed and the wall.

Frances didn't feel any pain at first. She started to take damage reports in her brain from her legs and arms. Of course, her right knee, which still sported stitches from her fall in Somerset, was cursing up a storm. Every other major body part reported minimal damage. She was still intact. The shower water had turned off shortly after her crash into the wall. The door opened, and then Theresa was standing at the foot of her bed, dripping wet with a towel hastily wrapped around her body.

"Holy shit, Frances. What the heck did you do? This room looks like a fight happened in here."

The phone in the room rang, which made Frances break out into laughter. "I'm fine and very stuck. Answer the phone and then please help."

"Hello?" Theresa answered the phone with the highest voice she had ever heard come out of her mouth. Theresa covered the mouthpiece on the phone. "Frances, stop laughing. They are asking us if everything is all right. Someone called, saying they heard a loud crash." Theresa cleared her throat and dropped her voice down an octave. "No, we're fine. It was just a suitcase that fell off the bed. So sorry if we caused anyone to worry. Thanks."

Frances was laughing so hard, she had wedged herself even more, with her hands and feet above her head. "Get me out of here," Frances pleaded through her laughter. "You dropped your towel."

"Oh, shut up. I thought someone or something had fallen through the ceiling. You aren't ten anymore. What made you think you could jump on the beds? You are crazy."

Frances tried to pull herself up with Theresa's help but failed. Theresa finally freed Frances by pushing the bed over next to the other bed. Frances fell to the floor, laughing and crying as the pain started to seep into her not-ten-year-old body.

"Are you okay?"

Frances rolled over onto her stomach and pushed herself up. Her whole body hurt from the failed jump, the laughter, and being folded like a taco in the landing. The room looked like a couple of rock stars had gone wild. Frances helped Theresa reposition the beds and straighten the covers. Her normal breathing patterns were returning. Theresa went back into the bathroom and came out wearing one of the fluffy white towel robes. She crossed her arms and tried to look cross at Frances. But Theresa's mouth showed the slightest twitch, and Frances started to laugh again. That was it—the first giggle escaped. Theresa tried to stamp the laughter down. It was too late. Frances caught the giggle and raised it to a full belly laugh. The two of them flopped into bed, laughing.

"You know if we continue like this tonight, I think I'm going have to wear Depends; otherwise, I'm going to pee my pants," Frances said.

"Not helping," Theresa gasped.

A knock at the door caused them both to sit up and go silent.

"Leave it to the fear of getting kicked out to send the laughter into silence," Frances said. She stood and timidly walked to the door. "Who is it?" she asked.

"Ms. Kavanagh, is everything all right? I am Richard, the manager tonight."

"Yes. Everything is just fine."

"Would you mind opening the door? I'll hold up my ID badge. Can you read it?"

"Well, I can read that, and I believe you are the manager. My sister is in the shower."

"I won't be but a minute. You can close the bathroom door."

"Frances, I'm wearing a robe. Let the man see we are alive and fine so he can go back to playing solitaire on his computer."

Frances opened the door and stood aside, allowing Richard to walk into the room. "Is there anything I can bring you this evening?"

"No, not that I can think of right now. Theresa?"

"We are perfectly good," said Theresa from the bathroom.

"Perhaps a trampoline?" Richard asked.

Frances and Theresa both burst into laughter. They had been caught trying to cover up the scene of the crime. Damn, when did hotel mangers get so smart?

"I promise. You won't hear any noise from our room tonight. I've been grounded."

"I won't ask. But please don't let me revisit you tonight over a concerned call from another guest."

Frances walked the manager to the door and made sure to put the extra door lock on after she shut it. The experience would be one that she was going to have to share at the Buena Vista.

"That was a trip. I felt like I was in grade school again back in Sister Rosemary's library," Frances said.

"He was sort of nun-ish, wasn't he?"

"Although he could be a police detective. 'Perhaps a trampoline?'" Frances mimicked his stance by placing her two hands behind her back and turning her nose up slightly. They laughed but made sure to quell the sound. As the laughter faded, Frances's thoughts returned to the fresh wounds cut into her heart by the letter and silence of her family. Frances had tried to capture in words for Sam the hole of loneliness that was growing bigger inside her over the loss of her family. This was harder than accepting the death of a loved one. She had experienced that finality with the loss of her Grangran and grandfathers on both sides. This was different. Her parents and siblings were alive and chose to not talk to or include her in anything anymore. The foundation of the family had been ripped out from her spine, and she tried to stand but failed.

"Do you think we should go see Mom and Dad now?" Theresa asked.

"We could, but I thought you said we could see Agatha and Edna. They might be able to bridge the distance between me and Mom and Dad."

"Frances, there is distance with them and me too."

"Theresa, you have never had to earn anything. Everything you've ever wanted has been given to you. Mom has her favorites, starting with Bernard."

"Don't give me that horse shit. It is easier for you to say that Mom and Dad never loved you than face up to the fact that you are a difficult person. When we see sunshine and smile, you are off crying and saying it's raining. Get a grip, Frances. The family is fucking scared of you. It isn't about your sexuality. They don't like you because you are one heck of a fucking downer. Everyone always tiptoed around you because we never knew when you were going to explode."

"I need a shower." Frances turned and went into the bathroom. She stripped off her clothes as hot tears filled her eyes. The burning in her eyes reminded her how dry they were from the air in the plane. Was Theresa right? Part of Frances knew what she was saying was true. As the hot water pelted her back and shoulders, Frances cried, feeling so far from herself and everyone else. How did her life get to this point? Would Agatha and Edna confirm what Theresa was saying? Frances remembered all the laughter. Those memories fell away, and she shivered under the heat. She wanted to start all over. How could she start all over and not make the mistakes she had made?

"You can't go back—you can only go forward." Frances heard Dana's voice in her head as she turned off the shower. This was where she was right now, and she had to trust herself not to crumble. When she saw her dad at the gallery show, she had reverted back to being a little girl again, complete with the feeling that she was never going to be mature enough to take care of herself. He disarmed her and dismissed her work. Frances stood still in the steam. The white marble with silver-gray streaks made her feel like she was showering inside a mausoleum. A morbid thought. Death's curtain was so final in this world, and Frances felt something similar and maybe worse than death fluttering around the Kavanagh clan. Banished from the family was a torture that was real and one Frances knew was here. Frances wanted to pull the curtain down and clear the way for life.

CHAPTER THIRTY-FIVE

I WILL FIND YOU

"Hey, Uncle Henry. Auntie said you were out here working in your garden." Molly took a seat on the grass next to the flower bed he was weeding. "I know I was supposed to meet with you last weekend, but the murderer has struck again."

"Take a few moments and enjoy the fresh air. I am out here meditating with the flowers. Doc said I needed to be kind to my heart."

"Is it working?"

Her uncle ignored the question. "How's the case? I saw the news. How many murders does that make now?"

"Well, we are up to nine scenes and seventeen bodies."

"That is faster than what we were working with. Any luck on discovering the source of that china?"

"No. It's like it was never made. I am so frustrated. We have undercover cops all around the expected locations, and the killer has been able to get in and set up the elaborate scenes and get out without detection."

"You need to take some time off."

"I can't. You see the news. Each hour that passes, the pressure on us increases tenfold."

"Oh Molly, you can't let this pressure take you over. Do not let it control your life. The killer is counting on you being overworked, tired, and irrational."

"I think we are dealing with killers. This last scene was so disturbing and so intricate, I have no clue how one person could move the bodies without detection."

"Step back. Start at the beginning. Go back to your earliest notes. Try to look at the case with new eyes."

"Easier said than done."

"How's the other case with the snuff films? Have you guys identified any more of the victims?"

Molly walked over to a patch of garden and started to pull up some weeds. There was something relaxing about clearing away a small part of the garden. The sun felt good on her back, and she took a deep breath, pulling in the smells of grass, dirt, and fresh air. She sat back on the ground and turned to her uncle.

"Don't stop. You're doing a good job. Have you thought about putting a garden in your backyard? I could help you."

"I have, and I lay down to let the feeling pass."

"Molly, I am concerned about you. You need to do something to handle the stress."

"Stop the killers and put an end to this deadly game. That would take some stress away."

"Game?"

"Each murder scene—well, *murder scene* is not correct because the victims are not being killed at these locations, but the medical examiner says the bodies are only hours into death when they are placed. We are dealing with a killing machine. I am so scared. There is this growing fear that—"

"Stop. You need to stop that line of thinking right now. You need to get into the mind of the killer, the person who is planning this, and don't let him or her control your mind."

"Her?" Molly asked. "Why do you think it's a woman?"

"I don't. Did I say her? Maybe it was a slip."

Molly stood up. "I've got to go."

"You can't stay for lunch? I know Auntie would love it. Stay and we can work through more of your puzzle."

"Okay. I do need to eat. But we need this to be a quick lunch."

"Molly, you have got to relax. Trust me. Give your brain a break, and that could be the way you crack open the case. Now you can continue pulling weeds, if you'd like."

Molly laughed and lay down on her back. It was an unusually warm day, and it felt good to be outside. "So, this is what a yard can look like if you take the time to work on it. You're an inspiration."

"Okay, smart girl, I'll let you lounge in the sun, but tell me something about you. Not the case. I'm getting to be an old man, and I need to know you are creating a rich life for yourself. I feel like we never talk anymore. I'll never forget the time you talked to me about asking a girl to prom."

"You took it all in stride. I was lucky."

"Have you asked out that woman you were talking about? The artist?"

"Nope. She's seeing someone else. The case is still open. I remembered your caution to never date anyone on the force or a victim."

"Is it serious?"

"What do you mean, 'Is it serious?' I won't go there based on your advice about not dating a victim. I don't know. She looked pretty cozy and happy."

"Shoot. You weren't supposed to listen to me. Molly, I am going to level with you. How do you think I met your Auntie?"

"Uncle—"

"Hear me out. I love my wife more than I love myself, and that kept me going and alive on the job. I am worried about you. How are you going to pull out that extra support you need when everything has been squeezed out of you? You need someone special to help recharge your soul. That summary you gave me concerning what you and the team are up against worries me. This is a war, and right now it looks like you are losing the battles. Each time this killer strikes, it eats away at you. What if I had done X? Or talked to Y? Don't kid yourself, Molly, this killer is after the SFPD and your team. Back to your Auntie. Her house was robbed when she was in college. I was the first officer to respond. There was no looking back. She hooked me from the start."

"What was that story about the soda fountain? I thought that was where you met?"

CHAPTER THIRTY-FIVE

"That was our first date."

"Why did you tell me never to date a victim?"

"Because you want to rescue and save everyone. I wanted you to find an equal. A person who could rescue you when you need it."

"Uncle, you are so sweet."

"Now that we are being totally honest, your Auntie and I are glad you are out of that relationship with what's-her-name. She was no good for you."

"Why didn't you say anything to me before? We were together for five years."

"Molly, we love you, and do you think you would've listened? What we saw was a passive-aggressive, rhymes-with-witch of a woman using you for your money. If I had to listen to one more lecture about 'the man' or 'feminist superiority,' I was going to puke."

"Ouch."

"Tell me you weren't sick of her?" Uncle Henry asked.

"You're right. I didn't think anyone else would love me."

"Now that is bullshit. That girl did a number on your self-esteem. Those passive-aggressive emotional abusers are the worst."

"Have you been taking psychology courses on the side?"

"Sorry. I know that I have never seen your face light up the way it does when you talk about that artist."

Molly closed her eyes and sifted through her uncle's words. She knew she needed to follow through on her own instincts. She had never felt at ease discussing her attraction to women with her uncle, but he had never said a cruel word to her about it and welcomed her different partners through the years into the family.

"I know you're going to do it your way, Molly. It is who you are, but think about what I said."

"Shall we go and enjoy a heart-healthy lunch?" Molly asked.

Molly got to her feet and helped collect the pile of weeds that had been pulled from the garden. Uncle Henry was slower and had a stiffness she hadn't noticed before. She suspected it had to do with his buddies getting nervous about why she was doing so much digging in the past. There was something going on here, but she decided not to confront him about it yet.

CHAPTER THIRTY-SIX
PAPER DOLLS AND PANCAKES

F rances sat on the edge of the bed she had launched herself off of hours before, thinking about how Agatha had given her all her paper doll books when Frances was so sad after their pet turtle, Mr. Toad, had died. The reality was that Mr. Toad had been dead for several days, but the girls had thought he was hibernating like a bear. It wasn't until the cat jumped into his turtle tank and started to play with the dead body that they realized the turtle was no longer alive. Frances had cried all night over Mr. Toad. Agatha had come into the room Frances shared with Brice, Beatrice, and baby Theresa with the paper doll book and a pair of scissors. She didn't say a word. They sat on the floor and cut the dolls out and then the different outfits. Agatha let Frances dress the paper dolls any way she wanted. When Agatha had to leave to go babysit the Armstrong's kids down the block, she told Frances to take care of the dolls for her.

Memories like this flooded into Frances's mind. She was cried out at the moment. Theresa was telling her that when everyone saw one another, the distance would be bridged and no one was getting kicked out of anything. Frances scrolled through her Instagram account, looking at the smiling faces of her nieces and nephews. It was the one form of communication that continued for Frances. She figured they had forgotten she followed their accounts. She gently wrapped her arms around herself and dropped her chin to her chest. *Lonely*. That was all she could summon up in the current state she was in as she waited for Theresa to finish applying her make-up.

Russell and Simon had tried to help soften the reality of the situation, but now that she was here in person, her whole being hurt. Frances stood and walked to the window. Agatha had asked for the meet-up at Uncle Bill's to be postponed for a couple of hours. She was helping clean up after the high school production of *Oliver!*. Frances had wanted to go see her nephew in the role of the Artful Dodger, but Theresa talked her out of it, knowing the rest of the family was going to be there.

"Time to go. Are you ready?"

"All set. Do you remember how to get to Uncle Bill's?" Theresa asked.

"Does the Pope wear a funny hat? Of course I do. I think that place is a rite of passage for angst-ridden teenagers in St. Louis."

"What do kids do who don't have Uncle Bill's?" Theresa asked.

"Denny's, I guess."

Frances walked out to the rental car. She loved the ease of having a valet service. It was like magic. The roads were quiet in Clayton at this time of night. The bars were coming to the bewitching hour in St. Louis and the surrounding counties. This caused most of the night traffic to head east across the Mississippi over to the all-night strip clubs in Illinois. More memories that Frances would rather not admit to involved her and her friends exploring the nightlife their parents had forbidden them to see. Those were some crazy times. She remembered her friend Becca pulling her up on a table in a strip club and getting her to dance. There was something addictive about the feeling.

"What do you think Becca would say?"

"Where'd that come from? When was the last time you talked to Becca?" Theresa asked.

"It's been a couple of years."

"That girl was wonderfully wild. I wanted to be just like you two when I was a teenager."

"Really? You wanted to be like us? Theresa, she wasn't wild. She was so much faster than everyone else, she—"

"She was wild. That girl was afraid of nothing, and she threw the best parties. I remember when Mom and Dad came home early from their trip, and Becca and Agatha had rigged that zip line from the roof of the house to the neighbor's garage."

"I need to give her a call while we're here. I miss her."

Frances took a right turn onto South Kingshighway Boulevard and was surprised at how quickly they arrived at Uncle Bill's. She was glad the parking lot still had spaces available. "Do you think they still have that porcelain toilet seat clock?" Frances asked.

"I see Edna's Prius. That means they are all probably here," Theresa said. "That toilet seat clock has to be there—it is a part of the St. Louis identity. Kind of like the Arch. Generations have paid homage and wondered about that ugly toilet seat clock. Care to take a wager?"

"It depends. If I can take the side that the clock is in the same spot, I'll do it."

They walked through the dark brown door and down the long hallway that led to the glass case where the toilet clock was proudly displayed. A part of Frances settled down, seeing that part of her history still in place. They had added some butterflies and gnomes to the case, but the world was okay because Uncle Bill's was basically unchanged.

"Time for a pancake sundae with extra chocolate syrup," Theresa said. "Look—I see them in the middle wall booth."

Frances clenched her hands into fists and forced herself to walk toward their table. No one was smiling. Agatha and Edna looked rather stern. Brice was busy reading the menu. Agatha got out of the booth and pulled Theresa into a hug. Edna and Brice stayed seated.

"Frances, get over here." Agatha started to cry as she pulled Frances into her body. Frances wrapped her hands around Agatha and let her tears fall. She gripped Agatha's shirt and never wanted to let go. All of sudden, she felt like she was a little girl running from the monster under her bed. "Agatha . . ."

"Shhh . . . Frances, I am so sorry."

"Let me get in on this." Edna hugged Frances and Agatha at the same time. Theresa slid into the booth next to Brice.

"You're going to be okay, lil' F.," Agatha said, stepping back.

Frances let her grip go and followed Agatha into the booth. She did not know how much pain she had shoved down until she saw her older sisters. Her life came roaring back in flashes and still images. These were her people. They knew her history and shared a common bond. Frances did not appreciate how terrified she was of losing them until she saw them and Agatha touched her. It brought all this madness front and center.

"I hope you don't mind. We ordered a couple items for the table," Edna said.

"Please tell me you ordered a pancake sundae."

"Two. Why else does one come to Uncle Bill's in the middle of the night?"

"To sober up." Brice smiled as he reached for the brown water they passed off as coffee. "Good to see you both."

"Thanks, Brice. I appreciate you are not crying like a hydrant," Frances said and took his outstretched hand.

"Tell us, Frances, how did your show go?" Agatha asked.

"I...did you know Dad came out?"

"Theresa filled us in, and that was not the question. How did your first large solo gallery show go?"

"Several of the paintings have sold."

"All of the paintings have sold. Frances, you know they all sold by the end of the first week," Theresa said.

"Wow. High five, lil' F."

Frances used to object to Agatha calling her lil' F. It was short for what it sounded like. But Frances had learned to embrace the power in having initials that could be pronounced like the word *fuck*. The elephant was sitting on the table, and Frances couldn't handle the idle chitchat anymore.

"What are the chances that Mom and Dad would reconsider...how do I put this—"

"Frances, Mom is really hurt. She's trying to figure out what she did wrong with you."

"Edna, seriously? What she did wrong? She's hurt? You have kids. What would you do if one of them told you they were gay?"

Frances watched as Agatha and Edna exchanged glances. "Mom is from a different generation. You can't compare what we would do to what she's feeling. You need to step into her shoes."

"Are you seriously going to continue with the 'I don't care about anyone else' line of bullshit? I do care, and that is why it hurts so much. I did so much to help and went out of my way to help Mom and Dad. Did you see the letter Bernard sent on your behalf? Were you in on any of the conversations they reference with the priest or bishop or whatever the fuck the pedophile church of America calls him?"

"Back to why we are here tonight. We are trying to figure out how to get you and Theresa in to talk with Mom and Dad. First things first, you need to convince me that you are straight or back in the closet, so act straight. Keep your sex lives hidden," Edna said.

"My sex life? I don't have a sex life. What do you think the definition of lesbian is s-e-x? Are you being serious right now? It is like me saying that when you talk about your husband mowing the lawn, you are rubbing my face in your 'straight' s-e-x life." Frances crossed her arms and stared at her sisters.

"Frances, you are so off. Edna and her husband haven't had sex in years," Agatha said, laughing. "That is why they don't have any more kids."

A waitress brought a large tray and set it down on an empty table close to the booth. She delivered the pancake sundaes with extra chocolate and ice cream, a plate of onion rings, a plate of fries, a grilled cheese sandwich, and a huge order of biscuits and gravy.

"Heart attack and diabetic coma. That is all I see on this table," Brice said as he reached for the plate of biscuits and gravy.

"Frances, I am not talking about your sex life anymore. You don't have to tell people that you're a lesbian. People hide it all the time."

"This conversation needs to change. I know we have troubles that suck, but would someone please hand me one of the pancake sundaes?" Theresa had her spoon ready.

The food gave Frances a gag reflex. Maybe it was the reality of her pain being tapped by seeing her oldest sisters and knowing that this was a futile journey. Brice held the truth of what was going to happen on his face. He was somber, and his eyes were sad.

"Why don't you and Theresa plan on coming over the day of the picnic. Mom and Dad will be in a good mood. Everyone will be there, and we will help," Agatha said.

Frances's heart was faint as she tried to find the answers she needed to know that she was okay, that she was not a monster or freak of nature. Sam. Frances shut her eyes and saw Sam's beautiful smile and light-brown eyes reflecting the American River. Frances had transported herself to the river bank and was dancing with Sam.

"Geeze, Frances, stop daydreaming," Theresa said as she snapped her fingers next to Frances's ear. "What do you want to do tomorrow? We have a free day."

"I thought we could go check out the Central West End. Catch a movie?"

"You checked out of the conversation. I wish I could fly to the moon as often as you do," Edna said.

"Maybe I'll look up Becca."

"Now there's a name I haven't heard in a while," Brice said as he cracked his first smile.

"Brice, do you know what's she's up to?" Frances asked.

"Nope. We dated in high school. In other words, I have no clue and don't really care to know."

"Edna, do you need help with any food prep?" Theresa asked.

"Sure. Theresa, you can come over in the afternoon. Becca married Andrew's little brother, Nate. I think she has two kids now. Last I heard, they had a house over in Dogtown."

Frances thought about tagging along, but no one suggested it, so she was going to keep her day clear tomorrow. It was a free day in her hometown. Maybe she would take in a movie. A free day. She sighed as she realized she wished that Sam was with her.

"Or…maybe I need to stay with Frances. We could be tourists in our own city," Theresa said.

"That could be fun. I'm kind of tired. Do you think we could wrap up this little after-dinner *Bridge of Spies coup d'état*?"

"I'm with Frances. Time to go home and go to bed."

Frances was the first out of the booth when Brice had seconded the request to leave. Agatha placed her large hand on Frances's back. Frances leaned back into it and wanted to turn and hug her sister again but stopped herself. This world had changed, and Frances was going to have to find her own way through it. She no longer knew the language or the currency. She was a stranger in her own family.

CHAPTER THIRTY-SEVEN
DOORS CLOSE, AND ALL WINDOWS ARE BOARDED UP

E arly morning used to be a favorite time of day for Frances. This morning, the early morning light was gray and muted as a layer of clouds hung over the St. Louis metropolitan area. Frances sighed heavily as she turned onto Agatha's street in Webster Groves. Agatha had stayed the closest to the family home. She once said that it had something to do with gaining power for the family energy. The Kavanagh parents still held court in the big, white, corner house on Oakwood Avenue. Their late-night meeting at Uncle Bill's had killed any hope Frances had concerning changing her family's collective mind. She had not talked with Sam and was feeling rather distant from everyone at the moment.

Frances jumped as the silence in the car was shattered by the sound of Minions saying "Bananas." She picked up her phone. "Hello?"

"Where are you?" Theresa asked.

"I'm over at Agatha's house. I didn't want to wake you. We were up late last night."

"Are you going to see Mom and Dad?"

"I don't know yet. I was stalking Agatha this morning. It was good to see her last night." Frances bit her cheek to get control over her wavering voice.

"Would you come back and get me?"

"Yes. I'll be there as soon as I get there."

Frances drove toward the end of the street and took a left to get herself heading south back toward Clayton and the Ritz. She was wondering about some of the comments about Mom being hurt over Frances and Theresa living their truths. She could not get Theresa to explain to her how their *lifestyle* was any different than that of Agatha, Edna, Beatrice, Brice, or Bridget, all of whom were married to people of the opposite sex. Yes, they were all out-of-the-closet heterosexuals. When they talked about their spouses, no one went screaming into the other room complaining that they were giving graphic details about their sex lives.

Theresa was waiting outside the main doors of the Ritz when Frances pulled up.

"Why do people think I'm talking about sex if I mention a woman's name?" Frances asked.

"Let me see if I can follow the origin of this question. If you tell someone that you are dating a woman and then mention her name, their tiny little brains translate g-a-y as s-e-x. They will only think about how you have sex with another woman. Even if you are talking about the most tragic thing ever."

"People aren't that stupid."

"Frances, you know they are, and Agatha said don't come back to the house. Bernard and Mom are coming over this morning to help with some prep for the family picnic."

"She saw me? I was there for less than five minutes."

"Guess you are not a good stalker."

"Can we not talk about being a stalker?"

"Sorry."

"I don't agree with Edna, who said this choice defines who I am. First of all, I don't see it as a choice. Second, I am not going to apologize for being who I am. They don't."

"Preaching to the choir, sister. Settle down," Theresa said.

"Why did we come here? Agatha is too scared to have us show up because Mom and Bernard are coming over? What was that hug last night then? All her big talk. Why am I here in St. Louis?"

"Frances, I'm tired. When I think about family, I think about the summer nights when we used to watch the fireflies under the big plantation fans lightly turning with Grangran telling us stories about being a little girl in St. Louis."

"Our family has always been loud and crazy. I remember the yelling over bathroom time and you having to wander around looking for a place to sleep once I grew out of the dresser drawer." Frances started to smile, but the tears broke through.

"Don't cry, Frances. Let's go over to Edna's. We know Mom won't be over there, and it would be good to see the kids."

"I think we are failing miserably."

"What?" Theresa asked.

"Mom, Dad, Bernard—all of us are getting this wrong. Instead of being open and filled with love, we—or at least I—am being met with rules and judgement."

"Why do you keep pushing me away? I don't understand. I am here sitting beside you."

"But why are you here, Theresa? When your foundation of who you thought you were and where you thought you came from is shaken to your core, it isn't true."

"What's not true?" Theresa asked.

"The family is not our salvation in this situation. Instead, the family is causing the pain."

"We are the ones who changed. Not them. They were living their lives, and then we drop a fucking bomb on the family."

"I'm hoping for an end to this situation, and I don't think it's going to be the happy ending you are thinking you can pull out of all your bluffing."

"Is this because I didn't tell you that I was thinking about going back to Notre Dame?"

"No...Notre Dame?" Frances looked at her sister, and her mind started adding up the pieces. "Theresa, you've never been out of the family fold. What did you tell them? Did you tell them that you were faking being a lesbian to get close to me?"

"Do you hear yourself? You are crazy. Let's go to Edna's and talk this out. I want to finish my degree. Notre Dame was the right place for me, and Mom and Dad pleaded with me—"

"They pleaded with you? Get real, Theresa. You don't want to be without your share of the silver spoon."

Frances looked straight out the window and made sure she watched her speed as she drove into Town and Country. This small little hamlet west of St. Louis housed a different level of home owner. Edna had moved to this neighborhood of rolling green lawns and sprawling estate homes less than six months ago. Her husband had sold his security software company, and they leapt over several tax brackets to become members of the top one percent.

"This is intense."

"Frances, I think we should have called first. They have a gate across their driveway. Who has a gate across their driveway?"

"People who don't want bad news to arrive unannounced." Frances pulled the car over to the side of the road and parked on a patch of dirt that had been cleared by the construction crew who built the gate. "Holy shit. I had no clue they had bounced so high."

They both shut their car doors as quietly as possible. No one was around, and they were far enough away from the houses to not disturb anyone parked out on the road. Frances's legs moved so slowly, she started to wonder if the pull of gravity had changed for the rich. She steadied herself with her hand on the trunk of the car. What she was looking for was a way into Edna's place. The light stone-colored house was barely visible from the road. The place looked completely dark in the early morning hours. When others would be up getting ready for work, this place looked as quiet as an abandoned castle.

"Why don't we just call her? Or push the gate intercom," Theresa said.

"We're talking Edna. Maybe we should scrap this and go get some gooey butter cake."

"Coward." Theresa hit the intercom button and heard a buzz and then nothing.

"Why not pepper them with ding-buzz, ding-buzz…that is what it sounds like to me." Theresa kept pushing the button. "Ding-buzz, the wicked witch is dead."

"It is ding-dong, and Edna is going to be madder than the wicked witch if you keep holding that button down. I don't know why I came over here."

"I do. You have hope."

Frances was screaming inside her head to leave and abort this whole attempt to save her place in the family. Why? Because they were the people who gave her life? They were the people who said they loved her? Who was she trying to kid. Her world was very different from Theresa's, and it wasn't her role to point that out.

"Hello?" A disembodied, garbled voice came through the intercom.

"Hi, Brian. Is Edna home?"

"Who is this? Rather early to be coming—"

"Your sisters-in-law, Theresa and Frances."

"Oh. Maybe you should come back in a few hours when everyone is awake."

Frances found the lump in her throat growing, and she started to walk back toward the car. They were not going to see the voice behind the family this early.

"Come on in. I'll buzz you through the gate."

Theresa and Frances looked at one another as the large gate magically started to open. Frances scrambled to get into the car and didn't wait for Theresa to get in before she backed up onto the road and was through the gate. She slowed enough to let Theresa get in the car as she realized the driveway was longer than it appeared. It curved around a park-like setting with a manicured lawn and flower beds around the base of the trees. This was not the same as the house off Edgar Road in Webster.

The whole front of the house was now awake and bathed in light. Brian, Edna's husband, stood in the open door dressed in a red robe and slippers. His hair reminded Frances of that of a little kid whose mother tried to paste it down by licking her fingers, only to have it pop back up.

"You could have called to warn us. This is remarkably early," Brian said.

"I like the element of surprise. Wow, this place is impressive," Theresa said, walking into the front entryway.

A giant double stairway led to an open loft area upstairs and what looked like a hallway. Frances turned and saw a photograph of the family hanging on the wall. The image took her a moment to register. She had known all the family portraits because they stopped after Gall was killed. The wedding photographs of the family were different. There was no one in a wedding dress in this picture. It was a new one. She walked over to it and was trying to place the time. Mom and Dad were holding a handmade sign between them. They were seated on hay bales, and all of their family was around them—all of Frances's brothers and sisters, their spouses, and children. Frances and Gall were the only two not in the photograph. Tucked next to Mom and in front of Bernard was Theresa. She was smiling wide. Theresa was there.

Frances squinted to read the sign that her parents were holding. Her heart stopped thumping and went silent. The reason this was an unknown picture was because it was taken this year. It captured the family celebrating their parents' anniversary. The party that Theresa had said she was not invited to either and so had spent the week in New York instead.

The light at the end of the tunnel had gone out. Frances didn't hear what was being said. She heard the voices, but the words all jumbled together. She walked out the front door, got into the car, and didn't look back as she drove away. Her tears were gone. Frances noticed the morning sun was starting to peek through the trees, but she felt this world wasn't made for her or who she was. The doors in St. Louis were closing, and Frances felt her dreams and all of the things she believed in were no longer on life support. The plugs were ripped out of her heart, and silence filled the car.

CHAPTER THIRTY-EIGHT
HAIL MARY FULL OF GRACE

F rances drove around St. Louis for the next hour with no destination or place in mind. The Arch was in view as she drove east on Market Street, past the fountains and the old courthouse. She considered heading west on I-70 and going to the airport. The only person she wanted to see at this moment was Sam. Frances drove down to the latest version of Busch Stadium. She had loved going to Cardinals games in the heat of summer. She looked at herself in the rearview mirror and didn't recognize the lack of light in her eyes. Frances looked hollow. Headed east past the stadium, she decided to escape the road and got herself over to south 18th Street. She headed toward Lafayette Square and the comforting coffee haven of Park Avenue.

When she pulled into a parking spot down the street from Park Avenue Coffee, she pushed down the hiccupping cries that were trying to fight their way out. These troubles were not going to surface right now. Frances got out of the car and looked across the street to the Wireworks Lofts. The years had been good to this part of the city. Frances had an idea spark inside her, and she was willing to surrender that once she was part of the Kavanagh family.

Right now, her plan was to get coffee and as much gooey butter cake as she felt like eating. Frances walked into Park Avenue Coffee and smiled at a couple who were already enjoying their morning coffee. The smell of freshly ground espresso mixed with baking gooey butter cake took Frances to a better place. It was a refuge in the midst of her emotional awakening. She glanced at the menu board but knew what she was going to order and stepped up to the counter. Unable to decide on any one flavor of gooey butter cake, Frances ordered one traditional, one chocolate, and one blueberry. The three pieces were boxed up for her, and a hot cup of dark brewed coffee topped off her order.

Frances took her vibrating phone out of her pocket and saw she had missed several calls from Theresa. There were no messages. She turned her phone off, gathered her goodies, and walked out. The sun had lit the rest of the sky, and morning was swallowing the start of another day. Frances got into the car and decided that Forest Park would be her next stop. She had to get out of the car and stop running over memories that were begging her to leave—to leave all of this and go home to San Francisco.

"I love them. I love them. I love them!" Frances screamed in the car.

Forest Park was quiet, with a few joggers running past as Frances slowly made her way up to the empty parking lot on the side of the Saint Louis Art Museum. This gave her a view of the beautiful lake that she had helped raise money for to bring back to its former glory. The city had built the park for the 1904 World's Fair. Over the years, it had fallen into a mess, and a group of people formed the Friends of Forest Park. Her parents got all of them involved in saving this jewel of the city. The lake sparkled in the morning sun. It was quiet right now, but later today it would be filled with people in canoes and paddle boats. Some Canadian geese were busy feeding on the cool morning grass. Frances got out of the car with her coffee and the gooey butter cake and walked across the path to the base of the King Louis IX statue that presided over this section of the park. She was glad they kept the long sloping grass hill that spread out below King Louis. She walked to the stone wall that separated his space from the hill and sat down.

Her first bite of the traditional gooey butter cake instantly settled her mind for the moment with pure memory joy. She wished she was sharing this part of her St. Louis world with Sam, but maybe not under these circumstances. The sky was clear, with the exception of a few light-pink, cotton-puff clouds dotting the sky. The trees that lined the ridge of the hill had matured and were beautiful in the morning light, the green standing out against the light blue of the sky. This was the place she would come with her friends, and they would double dog dare each other to race down the hill and play chicken with the lake. Even though the lake had been cleaned up, Frances was still afraid of what might lurk in that dark water. A couple more sips of coffee, and Frances found herself back in time. She kicked off her shoes and watched them roll partway down the hill. Not completely stupid, she threw her legs back over the side of the concrete wall and walked over to King Louis. She smiled and bowed to the King.

Like a gun had gone off at a starting line—or, as her friends would say, "This is St. Louis...was that a gun shot or a fire cracker?"—Frances took off running. She cleared the stone patio that framed the King's world and was on the grass in seconds. She stopped to pull off her socks and then resumed her run down the hill toward the lake of her teenage double dares. The speed of her run surprised her as she reached mid-hill. Frances slowed her steps to turn and take in the view of King Louis and the majestic art museum behind him when she tripped over her foot. Frances tumbled backward and tried to morph her body into a backward somersault. Her arms flailing, she was airborne and going to hit hard. Her body turned in the air, and then she hit the ground. She tumbled several feet before her body rolled to a stop. Frances, face up, did not move for several seconds. She was breathing and felt a slight pain in her side with each breath. Had anyone seen her?

"Are you okay?" a man with a bike helmet asked her. He was in her line of sight now. She could no longer see the sky.

"I think so." Frances stayed still as she tried to get a handle on if she could feel the rest of her body.

"Do you want me to call someone or an ambulance?" he asked.

"No, I think I'm fine. I just need a minute."

Now a person jogging in place and a woman walking a dog were asking the man with the helmet if she was okay. Frances ignored them all and sat herself up. She tried to brush some of the grass and dirt off her purple University of Washington sweatpants. Thank god she was wearing a black sweater and not the matching purple sweatshirt. She really needed to rethink her wardrobe.

"That was quite the fall. Are you sure you should be sitting up? Did you hit your head?" asked the woman with the dog, who was ready to be anywhere but standing still at the end of the leash.

"I'm fine."

"You don't look fine," helmet-head said.

Frances let out a giggle because the guy had no idea how correct he was about her. No, no, and nope—she was not fine, and she didn't know if she was ever going to be fine again. She pulled her legs under her and pushed herself up without assistance. "See? I'm fine. Thanks for stopping."

The fall had to have been rather spectacular, she thought as she started her slow and somewhat awkward barefoot walk back up the hill. She located her shoes and socks and charted her course of recovery. The small band of three who had stopped to check on her were back on their way. Frances found herself reciting the prayers of the rosary as she collected her shoes. Over and over again, "Hail Mary, full of grace. Our Lord is with thee. Blessed art thou among women…Holy Mary, Mother of God, pray for us sinners, now and at the hour of our death."

CHAPTER THIRTY-NINE

LEFT

F rances sat in the car and breathed in the silence. The family house had a steady stream of people walking in and out as the picnic set-up was well underway. After her challenged run down the hill, Frances had returned to the Ritz to shower and saw the bruises starting to appear on her body. She had walloped herself pretty well. In the steam of the shower, she had made the choice to stop the insanity of trying to claw her way back into the family. She had realized when she saw the photograph hanging in Edna's mansion that she needed to move on and stop her futile attempts. There was no god for her to pray to today. The warnings that this was her journey were written across her memories. She took a deep breath and got out of the car.

Theresa was on the front porch and stood up when she saw Frances, who looked down at the ground and wondered how long Theresa had been here. Edna and Agatha were now standing next to Theresa. They were never wrong. Frances knew this was not her day to win. Would she keep her temper? Would she swallow their denial of hate? Whatever happened today, she knew she was going to be okay. It hurt, but she was going to be okay. She didn't have to worry about Theresa anymore. Theresa was in with the family. Frances had to stop asking why. Her heart had already walked away. So when she felt the pain rip through her chest, she stopped and wondered if she was having a panic attack or, worse, a heart attack. She took another step toward the stairs that led up to the porch and front door. The pain had stabbed her and was gone.

"I'm here to face the 'collective' family judgement," Frances said.

"Frances, we aren't judging you. We don't know who you are anymore. I don't understand why you have to be so vocal about your sexuality. Get yourself some help. Theresa is working on herself and has mentioned that she is interested in a man. You can change too. You were married to a man. This is not who you were raised to be by Mom and Dad. I don't know how to explain it. You make everyone so uncomfortable. You always have, but this is way beyond anything you've done before," Edna said.

Frances pushed past them and walked into the house. Why did she deserve this treatment? Did they wish she would leave and not come back? Who taught them all how to hate so much? Who taught her how to be so angry and to stuff it down and not honor it? She told herself she wasn't going to cry. Her family was busy getting ready for the giant family picnic. Her nieces and nephews, as well as kids she didn't know, were running around excitedly. This was the day of fireworks, grilled hot dogs, and ice-cold watermelon. Each step deeper into the family house took more and more strength. The wood floors had been refinished and the interior of the house painted several shades lighter than she remembered.

"Hey, Frances," Brice said, carrying a bucket of ice out to the Igloo that was set up on the front porch. "I wondered when you were arriving. Don't make a scene. Not today."

"I'm not the one who broke the family apart."

Frances walked into the family room and saw their mother sitting in her chair, working on a needlepoint pattern. She did not look up. The chill in the room was growing. Theresa, Agatha, and Edna had followed Frances into the room.

"Hi, Mom," Frances said.

"Frances, why don't you come with me," Agatha said.

Frances watched as her sister Beatrice put down the knife she was using to cut carrots and grabbed a hand towel. The expression on Beatrice's face told Frances that her sister was still going to support whatever Bernard had told her to do. This reunion was not going to be friend-ly.

"I'm here to talk with Mom and Dad. That is the only reason I am here."

"Now? Your hand grenade style timing shows you really don't give a damn about anyone else," Beatrice said and turned back into the kitchen. "I thought Bernard made it clear we don't want you here. I helped him with that letter. I'm not sure what part of it you didn't understand."

"I'll round everyone up," Brice offered.

"Thanks," Frances said.

Beatrice came back into the family room, wiping her hands on a paper towel. Agatha, Bridget, and Edna all took a seat on the long couch pushed against the wall. No one would make eye contact with Frances.

"Where's Dad?" Frances asked.

"In the kitchen. He said he was busy at the moment," Brice answered.

Frances noticed that Bernard was trying to stand as tall as he could behind Mom's chair. His arms were folded, and he had a smirk on his face. Theresa came up to Frances and touched her shoulder. Frances didn't move.

"You were told not to come back," Bernard said. "I know you can read. Explain to me why you are here interrupting a family function you are not invited to attend?"

The question echoed in Frances's head as she was pushing down all the anger that was rising in her core. With each stitch her mother pulled through the stretched linen fabric, Frances felt a sharp stabbing sensation in her soul. Her mother was silent and never stopped her needlepoint. Theresa's hand on her shoulder was starting to burn.

"Mom, I am here to apologize, but not for what you or anyone else thinks. I'm sorry I wasn't honest with you sooner about who I am."

"Frances, stop. You have no clue what you have done to Mom, to Dad, and to this family. You have never thought about anyone else. You are only about yourself," Bernard said and came around to stand less than a foot away Frances.

She was not going to back away from him. Frances held her ground.

"This isn't about being selfish. You're the one who doesn't understand. Do you hear the irony in what you said to me? If you stopped thinking about yourself, you would not be treating me this way. I did not ask for this. I didn't ask for any of it. Theresa shot her mouth off and announced something that I wasn't sure of myself. Now I am. I am going to live my life the way it happens. I'm sorry you don't approve of it, Bernard. Don't tell me what to do or not do. I love Mom and Dad and this family. I will never respect you, Bernard, but you are still my brother."

"Frances, you need to leave now." Bernard pointed toward the door. His face was bright red.

"Is that it? Is anyone going to say anything?"

Frances turned to her siblings and looked at each one of them directly. She removed Theresa's hand and actually gave it a squeeze. "Theresa, I don't know what deal you made, but you might be working with the devil."

"Shut up, Frances. The only evil in this room is you," Bernard said as he tried to place himself between Frances and their mother.

Frances watched as their mother carefully tied a knot in the thread, stabbed her needle into a tomato pin cushion, and took off her reading glasses. "Enough. Bernard, stop it. Frances, do you want to know why I am so upset?" Bridgette asked.

Frances tried to step to the side of Bernard so she could see her mother's face.

"Mom, you—" Bernard tried to take over the conversation as he stepped back into Frances.

"Silence. Bernard, don't interrupt me when I'm talking."

Frances watched as her mother never took her eyes off her needlepoint sitting in her lap. Her mother's Irish brogue was thick. Her words came out carefully as she spoke.

"You hurt me in ways that no child should ever hurt a parent. Your father and I have agreed with Bernard that, to preserve this family, we have to practice tough love and withdraw any support to you."

Frances crumpled to the floor. She knew this was going to be the outcome, but what she did not plan on was the complete silence from their father, her sisters and from Brice. Frances realized that the complete absence of her father in the room meant that the fractured ties with the family would be the way going forward. Frances looked up to the couch but did not see any details through her blurred vision.

"Frances, get yourself off the floor," her mother said. She had put down her needlepoint and was looking directly at her.

Frances tried to stand, but she wasn't strong enough. No one moved in the room. It was clear Frances was going to have to stand on her own.

"Mom?" Frances whispered through her tears. "I don't understand."

"I don't understand either, Frances. Out of all the children I have had and the miscarriages"—her mother was so angry, she was spitting—"why couldn't Gall have lived and let you be the one hit by the drunk driver? He deserved to live. Not you."

Frances cried out in pain from her mother's words. She pushed herself up to her feet. Bernard stepped between Frances and their mother, throwing Frances off balance. Frances rolled her right ankle and fell into the fireplace hearth. A sharp pain drilled into the center of her head, and she reached up to the side of her face and felt the wetness. When she turned to look at her hand, she saw the bright red of her blood and felt it dripping down her cheek. Echoing through her head were her mother's words: *He deserved to live. Not you.*

Frances watched as Bernard walked away. No one else moved, and her mother did not look at her.

"What's going on in here?" Patrick Kavanagh entered the room. "Bridgette, I heard what you said to Frances. This is an unfortunate situation. Frances, I love your mother and my family very deeply. I think you should leave."

"Dad, why did you come to San Francisco? I am part of this family too. Why did you ask me to work with you again? I am here because you came out and told me you loved me, that I don't understand *my family*. I'm your daughter."

"Frances, stop. You need to leave." Patrick turned and walked toward the kitchen.

"Dad? Did you go to San Francisco?" Bernard called after him.

"I don't know what she's talking about."

Frances turned toward Theresa, who was silent. This was over. "Is there anything else you want to say? When I leave, you won't see me ever. Theresa, I don't know what to do about you. Anyone?" Frances was looking directly at her mother.

Her mother stood, quietly and slowly putting down her needlepoint. Frances's heart leapt as she thought maybe her mother would help her stand.

"Frances, I am at peace with my god. I do not care to see you ever again. If I had my choice and had known what you would become, I would have aborted."

The room was silent, and Frances closed her eyes, trapped in the pain. Her head was throbbing. Her heart dropped to the bottom of her soul. She saw Gall, and he was smiling at her. Frances got to her knees and used her hands on the fireplace to pull herself up. Aware that no one was coming to her aid, she touched the side of her head and turned and walked out of the family room, through the front door, and continued walking down the street. What was going to happen now?

"Frances! Wait." Theresa ran out after her.

Frances kept her arms at her sides when Theresa hugged her. "Please, Frances. Don't leave. I love you. This is not right. I am here for you. I don't know what to say. Say something?"

"It is time for me to go. I think you need to think about finding another place to live."

"Frances, I love you. You are an amazing woman, and I am here with you."

"Theresa, you don't have to do this. You need to go back to Notre Dame and figure out your own life. I am figuring mine out. My Christmas shopping list got a whole lot shorter without the family and all the nieces and nephews."

"What are you talking about?"

"It was a bad joke."

"Don't push me away."

"I didn't do the pushing."

Frances walked down the street past the rental car. She pulled her phone out and called a yellow cab. Frances knew that Theresa had gone back into the house. As she walked away from the family home, lines from a play by August Wilson popped into her head: "I had been with strangers all day, and they treated me like family. I come in here to family, and you treat me like a stranger."

The lights of the ER increased the pounding in her head. Frances welcomed the physical pain as it helped mask the pain that was working through her soul at that moment. Bonds, foundations, and understanding were being ripped apart inside, and Frances was in shock.

"Frances?" A short blonde woman wearing dark blue scrubs stood at the door between the waiting room and the ER intake at Mirror Baptist Hospital. Frances stood, making sure to hold the napkin the taxi driver had given her to try and stop the bleeding from the side of her forehead. "Oh my god! Frances! I can't believe it's you. When did you get into town? Nate and I were talking about you this past weekend."

Frances recognized the voice, and it took her a moment to focus on the smiling face.

When it registered that this was her friend Becca, she wanted to collapse. Tears started to fall, and she walked forward and gave Becca a strong hug.

"Let me get you back to a room and see what's going on . . . were you out partying on the East Side without me?" Becca said and directed Frances to a gurney behind a curtain. "Care to share what happened?"

"Well, I'm a lesbian, and my family has excommunicated me," Frances said.

"Okay. How did you get this rather nasty bleeder on the side of your face?" Becca asked as she applied some sterile gauze.

"The universe felt I needed to learn the lesson both emotionally and physically. I hit my head against the fireplace in the family room."

"Ouch. Are you sure you aren't protecting someone with the 'I fell down the stairs' excuse?"

"Bernard did make me lose my balance, but it all happened so quickly."

"Do you want me to go get anyone out of the waiting room? It is going to be a little while before the doc gets in here."

"Nope. I'm alone."

CHAPTER THIRTY-NINE

"Really? Not one of the red-haired Kavanagh army is invading our waiting room?"

"As I said—I'm no longer a member of the family."

"Holy shit. They didn't kick you out when you and I got arrested for speeding through East St. Louis after a night out at the strip clubs when we were under twenty-one, or the time you wrote the paper on the Catholic Church being a cult. I figured you were golden."

"Well, they have an eject button, and for me it was coming out as gay."

"Holy shit."

"How's life with Nate?" Frances asked, taking over the holding of the gauze.

"He's good. We have two kids now."

"Two? I knew about Charlie. Man, time is flying. I am so sorry I have not been in touch."

"No worries. Charlie is great, and he has a little sister. You'd better sit down."

"I am."

"We named her Frances! We call her Frankie. She is wild like you, and I love her dearly."

"You didn't name her after me. But thank you for saying that."

"Oh yes we did. You forget how much you meant to me. I don't care if we don't chat for years. You will always be my friend. I want to hear more about this wild world of yours, you lesbian. But I need to go do work. Are you fine? Someone will come in and check on you. I'll be back as soon as I can. The moon is full, and that makes for some fun times in the ER. I always knew you would be into the pink taco."

Frances closed her eyes and felt a smile over Becca's crude jokes. She missed her friend and was grateful to have the life raft of Becca thrown in her direction. Frances thought about calling Sam but decided to try and just be in the moment. Her tears had stopped, and she was counting the thumps in her head. What more would this day bring?

CHAPTER FORTY
IRISH COFFEE CLUB WHISPERS BRING SOUL HEALING

F rances had taken the red-eye out of St. Louis. Sleep was non-existent on the flight as she kept seeing the image of the family photograph taken at their parents' anniversary party. *Choices.* The word *choices* kept going through her mind. That was what defined her life. Were her choices worth the banishment? Were her choices any worse than the ones her parents and siblings were currently making? Frances felt the weight of all her choices but breathed deeply, knowing she was being true to her own life.

Exhausted but unable to sleep, Frances looked around her loft and deposited her suitcase and shoulder bag near her front door. The Buena Vista Irish Coffee Club was exactly what she needed. Thank god the club had grown in its own strength to meet when she was not around. She ordered a Lyft driver to get her to the Buena Vista café this morning. The sun was up early and shining brightly as the sky was unusually clear of clouds. As the Lyft driver easily navigated the empty city streets, Frances texted Winter because she wanted to keep her surprises to a minimum. They weren't expecting her back until Monday. And she did not want to cause an early delivery of Winter's baby.

Frances stood on the sidewalk in front of the café and looked through the windows. The warmth cast from the light bouncing off the warm woods that made up much of the Buena Vista interior worked like a soothing balm on her aching heart. She reached up with her hand and gently touched the stitches through the bandage on the side of her head. Her choice was to live and to love. Choosing to seek out the people who chose to love her and with the sands of sadness collecting around her feet, Frances stepped up toward the front door of the Buena Vista and friendship.

A group of four walked around her to enter the Buena Vista. The young guy who had ushered his party through the door smiled at her. Frances let being cut off go and returned his smile. She didn't hesitate another second and walked into the warmth of the Buena Vista. This was her home.

"Howdy, Frances. You're early this morning. Would you like an Irish coffee?"

Frances walked over and gave Mary a hug. "Thank you. Mary, you know me too well. Yes. I love the wonderful energy of this place." Frances walked to the third table in the row of six round tables and took a seat, staking a claim. Her coat off, she let her eyes wander to the view outside the window. She was aware of the growing number of people in the Buena Vista. Her mind wormholed her back to her cab ride to the ER in Saint Louis. It was cheaper than taking an ambulance. The world worked in such strange ways. The Buena Vista was melting the ice-cold aloneness that had encased her during the cab ride and the solo walk through the doors of the ER. She touched the bandage again and wondered how a family could collectively say *we don't love you anymore.*

She knew she wasn't in a dream as a couple asked if they could share her table. Mary came to the rescue and pointed them toward the back counter. Frances watched the commotion and felt the levels of ice breaking away from her. It had started—the melting of the cold—when her physician's assistant turn out to be Becca. After the doctor had stitched up the side of her head, Frances and Becca had laughed so hard, Frances almost passed out. Promises were made to see one another. Becca had texted her about fifty pictures of her kids. Frances put her hand over her heart and knew she would always have connections to Saint Louis. Life was taking unexpected turns, and she raised her head high and knew she was strong enough to meet them.

As the warmth of the Buena Vista surrounded Frances, she felt herself start to relax. It could have been the Irish coffee doing its magic, but she knew it was deeper than the whiskey. She spied Mary carrying another one to her.

"Thanks, Mary."

"Where's the rest of the crew?" Mary asked.

"On their way. It feels good to be home."

Frances texted the crew, minus Theresa, that she had secured a table. She had hoped that Dana would join them this morning, but she wouldn't hold out hope. Dana had been so sweet on the phone last night. She helped Frances use her courage to take the plane home. Dana had stayed on the phone until the plane doors were shut. They talked of many things, but mostly they talked about the choices made in one's life.

"Would you like me to go get you a coffee chaser for the one you're nursing while we wait for the rest of the stragglers?" Dana asked.

"Dana! Jesus H. Christ in the mountains, you came. You are better than any coffee," Frances said, hopping up and hugging Dana.

"Theresa?" Dana asked.

"I have not called her. And she has not called me. I haven't talked to anyone from the family since I walked out of the house."

"Frances, I know you, and you need to stop waiting on a miracle or magical thinking."

"Dana, this is a different world. I trusted in the family."

"You did. That was your birth and your foundation. But look at you. Today. You are the miracle you are waiting for, and I don't want you to lose your power."

Frances chocked back the tears and took Dana's outstretched hand, squeezing it tightly.

"I'm here, and I'm ready for an Irish coffee. You stay and guard the table from the tourist vultures. Use the bandage to scare them away."

"Thanks, Dana. The bandage is huge. Is it that hideous?"

"If I wasn't a biologist and used to gross stuff, I would be sick." Dana laughed herself up to the bar. Frances tried to hide her bandage with her hand but knew that was a futile gesture. She was thankful that the bartenders were in rare form and turning out the Irish coffees in record speed. Dana was back at the table before Frances sunk into a pit of self-conscious despair.

"What does *black Irish* mean? Am I missing something? That guy up there said that he was black Irish," Dana asked and pointed to a white man with dark, curly hair.

"There is a myth about the true black Irish coming from the sea faerie that shape-shifts from a beautiful seal into human form and back. They bred with the Irish, creating the beautiful, dark, curly-haired Irish. The sea was always their true home, and when able, they often returned."

"I am still not tracking. Very interesting story—"

"Morning all," Molly said. "This place is popular today."

"Could you whip your badge out and scare some folks?" Dana asked.

"If only that would work. You know I'm a cop and not a wizard."

"Oh, but you are—I've witnessed you part the traffic seas on 101 with that magic little light on top of your car," Dana said.

"You weren't supposed to tell anyone about that…shhhh," Molly said.

The dark circles under Frances's eyes spoke volumes about the pain and exhaustion she was processing. Frances hoped that she didn't look too horrid. With the laughter and smiles at the table, Frances found herself leaving the exhaustion behind, and she pulled her chair in closer to the table and reached for a menu. Food was definitely needed, and she was ready to order the whole menu.

"That's quite the bandage. What happened?" Molly asked.

"Ha. The universe taught me a physical lesson. Those pesky life-lesson teachers figured I wasn't getting the lesson quickly enough. To drive it home that I can survive without my family, I found illumination. I literally cracked my head open on the fireplace in my family's house. It happened right at the point the family basically kicked me out."

Her words brought all conversation at the table to an end. Silence hung between them. Dana fought back her tears and was relieved when Molly reached out to Frances and pulled her close. Frances closed her eyes as Molly gently kissed her on her forehead and tightened her arms around her.

"Group hugs. I want in," Russell said and joined the hug fest.

"Looks like a scrum to me," Simon said and kissed Dana on the cheek. "How you doing?" he asked Frances.

"I'm here. I realized that getting kicked out of an Irish family and then coming to an Irish bar—it has some poetic beauty," Frances said and took her seat. She was feeling a little woozy from all of it.

"Frances, it's perfect. Where else can one get a solid Irish coffee and great music? We should have a wake for the old family," Russell said. "Too soon?"

"Where might the double-wide Winter be at this hour?" Simon asked.

"She texted that she wasn't coming this morning. She was not feeling up to it," Molly said.

"Really? I had texted her to let her know I was going to be here. She said she was coming."

"Frances, that woman is more unpredictable than a bear lost in a sweets shop." Simon squeezed Frances's hand and smiled.

"How are we supposed to settle on a name if she keeps missing me?" Russell asked.

"Molly is going to work after this—what are you boys doing today?" Frances asked.

"Molly, is it true? Is the Beach Blanket serial killer back?" Simon asked.

"Where'd you hear that rumor?" Molly asked.

"The *Chronicle* this morning. Front page." Russell started to look for a paper.

"I remember those murders. There is some guy rotting in the big house over those," Dana chimed in as she waved Mary over.

"Dana would know—she lives next door to San Quentin. Do they give you a list of every criminal in the place?" Simon asked.

"No. But I remember my little Isabel being scared to go to the beach and use a beach towel. Bath time was no picnic either as she would only dry herself off with a washrag. She was in third grade at the time those murders happened in the City. Did they not get the right person?" Dana shook her head. "I could not imagine being locked up for forty years taking the fall for crimes not committed. Although I distinctly remember the trial being really short when the guy changed his plea to guilty."

"In the *Chronicle*, the story reported he got life instead of the death penalty for pleading guilty to all the murders," Russell said. "It makes my skin crawl and the hair on the back of my neck stand up."

Frances watched Molly pounce on a newspaper folded on the bar. Mary came over and took orders from everyone at the table. Molly stayed at the bar and read the story on the front page. Soon, Dana, Russell, and Simon joined Frances's gaze, and they all watched Molly as she read the paper. Frances noticed Molly had lost the glow in her cheeks as she walked back toward them.

"Any comments, Detective Woods? Is the story right?" Simon asked.

"What I can tell you is the killer today is not the same person who did those Beach Blanket killings."

"How do you know? Do you guys know who is doing this?" Dana asked.

"We have some strong leads, and I can predict that due to that story, I will be working non-stop. My social life is over until we end this rash of serial killings."

"Molly, are we in danger?" Russell asked.

"Honestly? You live in a city. I can't tell you that you are safe."

"That is comforting. Not," Frances said.

"Has anyone seen Cheryl?" Dana asked. "Hurry up—figure out what you want so we can get our order in and hopefully get served before nightfall. I really don't want to talk about serial killers unless someone gets me a bowl of cereal."

"I need to know what you did, girlfriend, to get that giant bandage on the side of your head," Russell asked.

"For the last time. I hit my head on the fireplace in my parents' house and had to get stitches."

"Frances, I think we need to address the elephant sitting on the table." Simon produced a small gray needle-felted wool elephant.

"Edith, you look wonderful," Frances said. "I remember when I made Edith the Elephant. She was my first attempt at felting an elephant. It makes me so happy to see you are getting her out and about."

"Seriously, I don't want you to lock your heart away. Just because your family is acting this way right now doesn't mean they will always be that way. When Russell came out to his parents, they kicked him out. Now they are head of their PFLAG chapter. Is it still PFLAG, or is it something else? Anyway—you, our dear Frances, are pure love, and your family does not comprehend as a whole what they have done."

"All due respect, Simon, this was pretty final. I was shocked when I hit my head on the fireplace. No one moved. Not one of my siblings. My dad said nothing to Bernard and denied coming out to San Francisco. He called me a liar. I know everyone will say it was my klutzy balance, but he helped gravity. I don't know if I was angrier at Bernard or the rest of them for standing and not doing anything." Frances covered her face with her hands, fighting back her tears. She had no energy to deal with any more crying. This was her life now.

Dana put an arm around Frances. "Frances, I have come to love you as one of my dearest friends. This group of people you have around you right now is so very special, and there is so much love here. It won't stop the pain. And it won't replace your family because that is not possible."

"Dana, I love you too. Thank you," Frances said.

"Frances is in tears with what looks like a pillow taped to the side of her head. What did I miss? There was a huge traffic jam around Hayes and Steiner streets. I think it had to with all the police cars all over that area," Cheryl said, picking up Dana's Irish coffee and helping herself to a sip.

"Why were you over by the Painted Ladies this morning?" Russell asked.

"I am late this morning because I tried to fit in a boot camp workout before I came and ate thousands of calories. We were meeting at Alamo Square."

"Not the morning to be late," Simon said.

Cheryl turned to Frances. "Frances? You are not supposed to be back yet."

Mary deposited a couple plates of food to the table.

"Frances was kicked out of her family for being a lesbian and flew back last night. They whacked her head on the fireplace, and we are talking about the Beach Blanket serial killer being back in the City," Russell said.

Cheryl picked up a forkful of food, took a bite, and with a full mouth said, "You know, my family pushed me out for dating a black man. They didn't speak to me for four years. Then they found out I had broken up with him, and they came flocking back like everything was hunky dorky."

"Cheryl, why haven't you ever said anything about this before?" Frances asked.

"I didn't want to remember it because it sucked. I am so sorry you are going through this, Frances. I say let's all have another Irish coffee and the day will seem hunky dorky." Cheryl gave her a hug.

"You mean *hunky dory*?" Dana said.

"Nope. *Hunky dorky*. It's a term I use when all I want to do is break things apart and scream at the world and everyone in it. When I refer to family, I am a dork. My family are all dorks. It works, and no one must understand my language. The other thing I do is to go hit a bucket of golf balls or practice my tennis returns with the ball machine turned up to superfast. It helps. You can join me anytime." Cheryl reached for Frances's Irish coffee.

"Right now, I am deep in a mass of contradictions. There are so many things I know I did wrong."

"Do you hear yourself? Frances, you haven't done anything wrong. Who cares that you love women. That does not make you evil. You love women. Love is love. What is evil is your support for that Green Bay Packers football team. Now that is criminal," Cheryl said.

"Cheryl is correct. You might not be the model daughter, and you are quite frankly crazy, but you don't deserve to have love withheld because you are being exactly who you are," Dana said.

"I am rethinking my definition of compliments." Frances smiled. "There are so many things I am replaying in my head. At one point along this path, my mother said that I had purposely done this to embarrass her. The one that keeps ripping me apart is her telling me that I should have died, not my brother Gall. My mind doesn't even comprehend that statement and so many others that were thrown out."

The table fell silent again with Frances's words. Frances wished she was home wrapping herself in her feather comforter as she figured out how she was going to move forward.

"There is no easy way through the pain. We won't let you fall any further than you have. This pit feels deep, but we have you, and you are going to climb out of this. Life is about loss. It is how we work through our losses and changes that creates who we are, and you, Frances, are amazing." Dana took Frances's hands in hers.

"This is going to pass. As Dana said, lean on us and don't be afraid to pick up the phone and call," Molly said.

"Ditto. We are right next door and have our gay merit badges for helping fellow queers navigate the PFA world," Russell added.

"PFA?" Cheryl asked.

"Post family apocalypse," Simon said.

"I remember when the family was full of love and laughter, and it was amazing," Frances said. "What do I do now?"

"I know you, and you are going to be stronger than ever as you walk through this pain. Keep your heart open and know that we are here to love you, cry with you, and especially laugh with you, my friend," Dana said.

Frances rested her head on Dana's shoulder, and the tears came. Molly, Simon, and Russell surrounded Frances with hugs. Someone in the crowded restaurant started singing, and Frances heard Molly's voice through the rest. It was beautiful, clear, and strong as she sang *Drinking Whiskey on a Sunday.*

The party was broken up when Molly's cell phone took her attention away from the music. Frances watched as Molly read her text and noticed her face go from soft to hard.

"Sorry, folks. I've got to run." Molly threw out forty dollars and was gone before anyone could object to the amount.

"Looks like she's bought your breakfast, Frances," Simon said.

"I bet she's on her way to Alamo Square," Cheryl said.

"Let's follow her," Russell added.

"I'll take a pass. The murder scenes described in the article sound absolutely horrid," Simon said.

"Another round?" Frances asked.

"Already on its way," Mary said as she whisked by with her arms full of several plates of food.

Frances sat back and let the music, the food, and her little band of friends cradle her battered heart. She wished Sam was next to her but was unsure how all this heaviness would mix into their budding relationship. Dana had pointed out that life was change. This change was so jarring that Frances knew she was never going to be the same.

CHAPTER FORTY-ONE
NATHAN TESTS HIS POWER

F inally rested and her world not rocking like a little boat on hurricane seas, Frances felt strong enough to deal with parts of her life she had been putting off. After the love and support shared by everyone at the Buena Vista, Frances had gone home and let herself sleep until she woke up on her own. No alarm clock. Oddly, it was one of the best sleeps she could remember in quite a while.

Frances was using her newfound energy to go through her long-neglected email. She scrolled through the mishmash of spam mail and email that looked official. She finally opened an email sent from Nathan over a month ago. He had verbally told her about the invitation to come and have a chat, but she had never addressed the invitation directly. She kept putting him off—maybe because she knew what he wanted to cover. He was feeling his own guilt and wanted to make himself feel better.

"My life is change. I guess I'm a little curious." Frances shivered as she realized that Nathan was a common denominator between her ex-husband, Olivia, and Ethan—three people who had similarities that pointed to an ability to manipulate. Frances typed out an acceptance and hesitated before finally pressing the send button.

In her note to Nathan, she had listed a couple of times she could make work, and he took the first one. Still hurting from her stitches, Frances had decided to take a Lyft to Nathan's house in Marin and not fight with the parking situation in that area. She was not completely sure of where his place was, but she had attended a party one time in Mill Valley and ended up parking her truck so far from the house, she barely made it to the party by hiking into the area.

She was glad she had let someone else do the driving as the road narrowed to one lane through the redwoods in this part of Mill Valley. Houses appeared to be built in a random pattern as the driver slowed to handle the obstacle course of parked cars that took most of the single lane. Frances marveled at how this part of the world could be in such high demand. She wanted to leave, to be out at the beach or in a park where she felt like she had space to stretch out. The City felt more open than this place. Not normally claustrophobic, Frances was borrowing breaths from another source as it felt like her oxygen supply was being used by the closeness of everything in this neighborhood.

"I believe it is the house up that brick stairway," the driver said.

"What house?" Frances asked.

"You probably can't see it from that side of the car. When you get out, you'll see it."

"Do you think another driver will be able to find this place?" Frances asked.

"Sure. It's on Google Maps. You'll be fine. There's only one way in and one way out of this part of Mill Valley though. Hope there's no earthquake or fire."

"Thanks. Thanks a lot," Frances said and hit her phone app for three stars instead of four for this driver's ability to scare her to death.

Frances didn't wait to watch the driver figure out how to turn his giant black SUV around in a space made for a kid's pedal car. She put on her sweatshirt as the temperatures were cool in the shade of the trees. The house, which was situated on a flat area, looked nice enough. White trim popped against the deep blue-gray of the painted shingles. Frances started to count the steps up to the front door after the second landing. How does visiting a friend turn into a cardio workout? The third landing and turn to the last set of ten steps revealed the massive-ness of the house that was set above and apart from the other homes in this overstuffed valley.

"Frances, come join me in the sun over here."

Frances heard the familiar voice but did not see Nathan yet. She tried to control her heavy breathing and was relieved to hear the familiar music of Patricia Kaas coming from hidden outdoor speakers. Frances took the last three stairs without hesitation and turned in time to see Nathan rushing toward her with a huge smile and outstretched arms. It felt like years had passed since she had seen him at the gallery for her opening.

"Welcome, welcome to our humble escape from the City," Nathan said, kissing Frances on each cheek.

"This is so—"

"Frances, you don't have to be shy. We finished the remodel last month. This has been a work in progress for two years."

The patio was decked out in dark gray wicker furniture with overstuffed forest-green cushions. Planter boxes filled with bright-pink geraniums outlined the perimeter of the deck. In the center was a gas fire pit built of stone, adding to the overall suggestion that this outdoor space was designed to be used. Against the wall of the house was an outdoor kitchen area with a fridge, a sink, and two beer pulls. The deck extended out into the woods behind the house. An empty hammock rocked slightly in the breeze that was filtering through the trees. A stone dining table with eight chairs took up a good portion of a platform that was raised above the rest of the deck.

"What can I say but *wow*? When did you and Felipe have time to do this project and open the gallery?"

"When it pours, it rains— or something like that. Oh, my precious Frances, we need to celebrate with some champagne."

A young man appeared out of the open French doors that led into the main kitchen area of the home with an ice bucket, an open bottle of Dom, and two champagne glasses. Without a word, the sparkling elixir was poured and a glass handed to Frances.

"Sweetie, you can close your mouth. Meet Michael—he helps us out on occasion," Nathan said. "Now we must have a toast to your most amazing success. You sold the show out."

They touched their glasses and both drank a long sip of the champagne. Nathan directed Frances to take a seat. It was at this point that Frances finally noticed how round Nathan's face appeared. Lost were the angles of his cheekbones and chin. He reminded her of cupid. Also gone were his curls. He lacked any hair at all. No eyebrows, no facial hair, no arm hair—and the color of his skin was not quite right. Frances quickly took another sip of the bubbles and closed her eyes. She was looking for a memory. A photograph of what Nathan looked like before this moment. He must have been wearing a really good wig at the gallery.

"I know my appearance is somewhat shocking when I'm not ready for public consumption. Don't worry. I know I look worse than I did at your opening. Things are going to be fine."

"Felipe said that you had some medical issues and that was the real reason for your abrupt disappearance. Is it AIDS?"

"Frances, my dear girl. When you are a gay man, still alive in my generation, the answer to the questions in your mind are most usually yes. In my case, what caused this wonderful look was treatment for lung cancer. I finally stopped smoking. I need to get something out about the elephant that follows us around. First, an apology about Ethan and how I failed you. I knew he attacked you that night at his gallery show. I am so sorry I didn't do what I needed to do."

Frances had no control over her body as she started to shake when Nathan brought up that horrible night. She was shaking so much, the plate sitting on her lap crashed to the ground and shattered. The world felt like it was spinning out of control, and Frances forced herself to take a breath.

"Frances. Please, Frances, calm down. I didn't mean to upset you more. I am so sorry. There were so many things I should have done. I investigated and found some things out about Ethan that scared me. He was not as he presented at all. He killed women for hire."

"Nathan, Ethan wanted to kill me." Frances pulled her knees up to her chest and hid her face.

"Frances, I don't know if there is anything I can do to make amends to you. You are going through so much. Can you forgive me?"

Frances raised her tear-stained face and looked at Nathan. She wanted the world to disappear and leave her alone. Every time she thought she was past the horror that Ethan had unleashed, it was brought crashing back into her life, causing the color to leave. Ethan stood in front of her, painting everything black, draining the life from her heart.

"I was so angry with you."

"I am angry with myself too. I didn't do anything when he attacked you at the gallery. I am the worst."

"Honestly, that is part of the reason I have had a hard time seeing you."

"Can you forgive me? I need you to forgive me for my failing to protect you."

"Nathan, you're scaring me. I was angry, but life goes on and I am here. I can't talk about Ethan."

"Frances, when I heard what happened with Ethan, and then you went off to Hawaii and Olivia, I knew I had failed you. Ethan was dangerous, and I knew that and didn't warn you. Worse, I stood by and let him get away with attacking you. Then, I failed you—"

"This—"

"Please, let me get this out. I knew all about Olivia's proclivities for seducing women. I should have warned you not to go down that road. She can be charming like a snake. Trust me, she is probably the closest thing to working with the devil that I have experienced in my life."

"Okay, you failed. You got cancer, thought you were going to die, and now you are here making amends. Is your conscience feeling lighter? I don't hate you, Nathan. You helped stick it to my dickhead ex-husband, after all. You have brought me my success in the world of art. I'm angry, but I don't hate you."

Frances carefully stood on her tip-toes to try and avoid the broken plate. She picked up her shoes and slowly walked over to a shard-free zone and started to put her shoes on without looking at Nathan.

"Are you leaving?"

"I am going to clean up the plate I broke."

"Leave it for now. I need to know that we are okay."

She walked over to the love seat and sat down next to Nathan. Frances threw her arms around him and placed her head on his shoulder. No words passed between them for several minutes. "La Vie en Rose" was playing through the speakers, and Frances let the deep throaty voice of Patricia Kaas wash through her soul as she held her friend.

"Why do you always play Patricia Kaas when I'm around?" Frances asked.

"I play Patricia Kaas because she is so dramatic and she transports me to another time."

"Nathan, are you better?"

"Better? Well, I am managed. That is what the doctors say. My beautiful round face is a result of all the steroids I take so my body can function with the cancer treatments."

"Do you have a date?"

"Felipe and I were planning on a night out downtown next week."

"Not what I meant. Do you have a stage for your cancer?"

"Cancer on stage? Oh, that could be…no, I think that might be too depressing, and no one would buy tickets."

"Nathan, stop teasing me."

"Well, my sweet woman, you need to work on your communication."

"Are you going to die? Wait. No, you are going to say that we all are going to die sometime."

"Frances, I will let you off the hook. It wasn't really classified because the cancer had spread. They think it started in the lung. Felipe did not want to watch me wither away and die. He had gone through that with his previous lover and did not want to do it again. I understood, having lost my own soul mate to the dreadful AIDS. We found a place in Mexico that claimed to have healed cases like mine. If not, it was going to be a nice place to die. Beautiful blue water, white sands, and the most perfect climate one could imagine. I watched the whales and the dolphins play from the window of my little death home. When the clinic doctor said that they could do nothing more for me and that the cancer continued to ravage my body, he asked if I wanted to live. I had to think about it. The pain was unlike anything I had ever felt before. You know, all the clichés, like 'I've had a great life,' passed through my mind. Then the anger set in, and I wanted to live. Death was not going to come and take me yet. I love Felipe. I love you. I love this life too much to leave it."

Frances sat up and faced Nathan. Her eyes were filled with tears. She reached up and wiped the tears away from Nathan's cheeks with her gentle fingers. Nathan took her hands in his and got her to sit back with him in the love seat.

"Frances, there are some things you need to know from me. I want you to promise me that you will listen and not react right away."

"Nathan?"

"Listen. Please promise me that you will override that temper that makes you so wonderfully full of crazy."

"Was that a compliment?"

"Let me get the champagne."

Nathan stood and retrieved Frances's glass and refilled it to the top. He did not refill his, and Frances noticed.

"Should you be drinking if you are getting treatment?"

"Shh. I am not going to keel over from a couple sips of champagne. You are young and can enjoy the nectar of the French. Where was I?"

"On your deathbed in some undisclosed location in Mexico with dolphins and unicorns."

"Right. The dolphins and whales were true. It was part of what made me take the leap of faith into a drug trial not approved in the US."

"That doesn't surprise me."

"We will come back to your cynical outlook on life. I hope you are prepared to stay overnight because you are not leaving until we are done."

"Spontaneous sleepover. I love it. Will Felipe be joining us?"

A Steller's jay flew and landed on the gas fire pit less than three feet away from Nathan and Frances. Its bright blue feathers popped as the bird tilted its black feathered head from left to right. Frances and Nathan froze as the bird took a couple of hops toward them. It was now in a ray of sunlight that had made it through the thick canopy of trees that sheltered the patio. The stocky, long-tailed bird bobbed its black head a couple more times. The sun brought out the iridescent beauty of the blue feathers on the wings of the bird. The spiky crest of his black feathers on top of his head reminded Frances of a punk rocker.

"He's here for the peanuts. Felipe had a bag of peanuts he left out here, and this little guy has fallen in love. We watched him carry away peanut after peanut. I figure he was stashing them somewhere. Felipe went and got another bag and started leaving them for him. We call him Arthur."

"You are pulling my leg. That sounds like a squirrel."

"Maybe he was a squirrel in a previous life."

Michael came out carrying a tray with delicate sandwiches and lace-like cookies. The door opening caused Arthur to fly up to the gutter of the house and scold Michael loudly with a scratchy, loud chortle of notes that he repeated several times.

"Go away, Arthur. You've cleaned them out. No more peanuts," Michael said.

"Do I detect an accent?" Frances asked Michael as he set down the tray with the goodies.

"You do. Can you guess in what country I was born and raised?"

"Will you tell me your last name?"

"That would give it away," Nathan said.

"Nathan, you can say my last name."

"French. You are a Frenchman."

"Correct. My last name is Rousseau, like the philosopher Jean-Jacques Rousseau."

"You're right. You can't help it when you say your name."

"I will leave you both now. I am going to shop for dinner. Would you like some tea before I go?"

"I am perfect with the champagne," Frances said.

"Maybe some cold water, no ice. Thanks, Michael," Nathan said.

Frances put a couple of the small, cut sandwiches and a cookie onto a plate and sat back into the love seat. The food was a welcome surprise. She watched Nathan closely as he took one small, triangle sandwich and a cookie. His Panama hat sat a little askew on top of his round bald head. The shirt he wore hung on him in a way that spoke of a time when he carried more bulk in his chest and shoulders. Now the sleeves hung below the cap of his shoulder, causing the short sleeves of the shirt to reach mid-forearm. The sun had worked its way around the fire pit and was now casting its light on Nathan. His skin looked waxy and pale. Frances wondered if she should move them inside and out of the sun. But when Nathan turned his face to the sun and smiled deeply, closing his eyes, she decided to relax. She kicked off her shoes and curled her feet under her.

"Now with a little nosh, we can settle in for some soul sharing. Where were we?" Nathan asked.

"You were explaining your Mexican drug connection. Is there going to be a movie, like *Dallas Buyers Club*? I want Jennifer Garner to play me."

"I think we need a true red-haired beauty to play you. How about Bryce Dallas Howard or that young woman who killed Tom Cruise over and over again in that—"

"Emily Blunt?"

"Yes. Emily Blunt. She would be a perfect Frances."

"I don't know that she would agree. Are you looking at the same person? The one I see in the mirror has me wondering if Elmo, the red monster Muppet, wouldn't be more appropriate with a few more pounds added."

"Stop it. When are you going to stop cutting yourself to shreds?"

"Different issue, and we are off topic again. Now focus."

"I believe my name should have been Longfellow, given the length of this story. I went on a drug trial where they took some of my cancer cells and some of my healthy lung cells and did some Frankenstein science in the lab and shot all that back into me. The pain was horrific. At one point, I asked them to end my life because I couldn't handle the pain. It felt like my body was on fire from the inside. I cried. I pleaded. I made deals with god to take me. Then, a couple weeks after going through four injections over the course of twenty-seven days, I woke up and there was no more pain. I stood up on my own and used the toilet without any assistance."

Nathan went silent. Frances reached out and touched his hand. She could tell that he was on the verge of crying. Unsure of what to say, Frances held Nathan's hand and waited in his silence. The breeze had died down, and the air temperature was warming with the sun. She let her focus change from Nathan to the beauty of the trees that created a natural barrier around the back of the house. The deep-red bark added a touch of mystery to the moment she was experiencing with someone she had come to think of as a mentor and more. The music playing through the speakers had changed to a voice Frances did not recognize.

"Who is this singing? Her voice is so beautiful and hypnotic."

"Anne Marie Almedal—she is from Norway, I believe. Felipe turned me onto her music. He was watching some show, and I couldn't stop listening to the opening credits because it was her voice."

"Do you listen to anything with English lyrics?"

"We are off topic again. I'm bored with my story. Basically, I am okay. The cancer is not gone, but it is a lot smaller, and it isn't growing or spreading. Knock on wood," Nathan said and tapped his own head.

"That is wonderful news, right?"

"Yes, Frances, it is wonderful news, and I still get to enjoy celebrating life and showing love to those people I adore. We have to chat about your opening. You sold your show out. Felipe has told me you have orders and commissions coming in weekly. Do you know what this means?"

"I made money?"

"Yes, and?"

"I don't know."

"You are going to do a show in New York. Get painting, woman. Felipe and I are arranging it with a gallery I adore in New York. You have shot for the moon and hit it directly."

Frances sat back and thought about why she was not jumping around like an idiot who got everything she wanted.

"Why the quiet? Did you not hear what I said?" Nathan asked.

"Theresa and I went back to St. Louis. It was brutal. Let's end this for now. I don't really want to talk about it."

"Sometimes you need to take an old man at his word. Trust me. I'm an old man who has made many mistakes and have been given some time to try and rectify them." Nathan patted Frances's hand. "You need to give your family time. I have no doubt that you will be united with your family again."

"I don't think so."

"Frances, you can't place expectations on your father or family that aren't real. No one can live up to what we wish or make up."

"You might be right. There is something I am trying to convey but am not doing so very well. I need to use the restroom."

"Oh yes, through the door, through the kitchen to the front hall, and it will be the second door on the right."

Frances walked into the house in search of the bathroom. The kitchen was spotless, and the white concrete countertops stole her focus. She had never seen anything like them. A butcher-block center island had a couple of large bowls with lemons, apples, and strawberries. She walked over to a pocket door and figured this might be a good spot for a bathroom. She opened the door to see three of her paintings from the gallery sitting in the room. Frances did not know what to do. Why were these paintings here? She had been in the gallery earlier and hadn't noticed they were no longer hanging.

"Let me explain," Nathan said.

She had not heard him come into the house, and the deepness of his voice scared her and made her jump.

"What the hell, Nathan? Why are these paintings in your pantry? And who has a pantry large enough to fit three giant paintings?"

Nathan chuckled. "Frances, you truly are special. I bought those paintings. Felipe wanted to get them out of the gallery—"

"Why? I saw the sales sheet. Your name wasn't next to those paintings. Some name I don't remember, but it wasn't yours."

"Let's sit down."

"No. You tell me, and you tell me now."

"I need to sit down. This has been more energy than I have expended since your opening."

"I bought those paintings through a straw man for some art collectors who did not want to be named. Well, two of those paintings are for other people. I bought *Big Trouble* for my own collection."

"You did? You bought *Big Trouble* for your own collection? Why not tell me that and put your name on the sales list?"

"Would you have sold it to me for the listed price?" Nathan asked.

"I would have given it to you."

"Exactly. Frances, that is why I put it under another name. You deserve money for your art. Your talent is not to be squandered. Don't give yourself away. This is how you are going to feed yourself and buy more paint. It doesn't help the sale price of your work if you keep giving it away because someone you know likes your painting."

"I am not going to apologize. I am tired of saying sorry for things that break when I am not responsible. I don't think I can stay. I'm exhausted," Frances said.

"I understand. Why don't you take a Jacuzzi? It is out back and the perfect place to completely unplug. Michael is going to make us an amazing dinner. If you still feel like going after that, then I will have Michael drive you home. Please. Let me spoil you."

"Turn the music up a little. I don't have a swimsuit."

"No suit required, and I will make sure no one goes back there. It is very private."

Frances walked through a very comfortable and well-appointed great room. A stone fireplace anchored the north wall of the room. She walked through a screened door into a very private screened porch and a hot tub that looked like it had been made out of a redwood wine barrel. A rack with fluffy white towels was next to a hall tree that had four fluffy white robes hanging from it. Frances looked up and saw the crowns of the redwood trees that made up the natural border to the back of the property. She turned once again to the house and decided to let herself relax. Frances quickly slipped out of her clothing and folded it on a chair next to the Jacuzzi.

The warm water felt amazing as she leaned back and looked up to the blue sky. At this moment, she started counting her breaths and stopping all other thoughts. An image of Ethan was on the fringe of exploding into her memory when Frances dunked herself under the water. It felt good, and she chased the images of Ethan, her father, Nathan's stories, and the world away. She let the gurgling sounds of the water block everything else out. Frances wanted to hold onto herself and the promise that her life was going to get better. She wrapped her arms around herself and squeezed as tightly as she could. The world above the water was going to come crashing back in, but for the moment, she had made it under water without breathing for forty-two seconds. *Hold on, Frances, you could break your own record*, she told herself.

There was something about the way Nathan put all the detail into his stories that caused Frances to question his honesty. What was the real reason those paintings were in his house? He dealt in art but never truly expressed that he cared much for any of it. A good cigar and a bottle of wine were his loves, not to mention beautiful men. Nathan was not a collector of art because he liked the pieces.

The warm water soothed Frances as she leaned back into the jets on her back. Was she safe? Had she found herself in another twisted world? Frances held her breath and plunged herself back under water. She opened her eyes and thought about how the water made the redwood trees look like they were part of the liquid world.

CHAPTER FORTY-TWO
DISTRACTED

S amantha sat at her desk with her thoughts wandering back to how her friends kept telling her how she could not possibly be in love. Sherri and the crew claimed that there is no way people fall in love with one glance. She could understand their fear. After all, she had slowed them all down after they started setting her up with some very wonderful single women. But none of them stuck, so to speak. Sure, she did have some fun.

She sighed as she reread the email from Frances explaining in full detail what had happened on her trip home. Sam wanted to be with her now but respected Frances's request for both space and time. Her heart told her to do more than send her a stuffed redwood tree she had found online. Frances called as soon as it had arrived. There were so many thoughts running through her mind, and she wanted to take Frances's pain and hold it with her. Sam shifted in her chair and looked at the picture she had snapped of Frances when she wasn't looking. Frances's beauty shined through in the photo. Sam had caught her right before she burst into laughter over something at the Dana birthday weekend.

Sherri had gotten after her and said her lust was still kicking in with Frances. This was not a forever relationship, and she should play, have fun, and move on to a real relationship. No U-Haul trailers until she got herself out there and dated some real contenders. That meant women who her friends gave their stamp of approval. Sam replayed the conversation that placed her back to feeling like a kid being lectured about safe sex. It was not right to date someone who didn't even know she understood what it meant to be a woman in love with a woman. At the first sign that the world was going to send a backlash for being gay, they were the first to run back into the arms of a man. Life is so much easier when you are 'traditional.' Sam smiled to herself as her friends always emphasized their point of view like they were the experts of her heart.

What she needed was more time with Frances—time away for the two of them to talk, laugh, and get to know one another. She wanted to wine and dine Frances, to introduce her to her favorite places and share what she liked. Even more than showing Frances her idea of San Francisco and the Northern California coast, she wanted to learn what made Frances smile—what she liked, what her favorite music was. It was time for a real date. One without any friends in tow from either camp.

Sam went back to her computer and reread the email that Frances had sent to her explaining what had happened in St. Louis. Sam's heart ached, and she identified the ache as frustration over not being able to hold Frances, to kiss her, and to let her know that she thought Frances was an exceptional person. Each minute felt like an hour to Sam as her work day progressed. She knew that they would see each other soon, and when they were together again…Sam smiled to herself as she knew exactly where she wanted to take her.

She stood and paced around her office. This distraction was coming at a rough time with work. The final push for her largest project was kicking into high gear. Of course, the goddess was having fun sending cupid's arrow into her heart. The dating record had not been good. She had dated a few different women, but each romance had ended with her feeling like maybe she was only given one great love in this life. Sam flopped back into her chair and rocked back, putting her feet up on her desk. It felt good, and she wanted to be crawling into bed for a good sleep—the type of sleep that is so deep that she would feel like a new person when she woke up. But that type of sleep was going to be days away. In front of her were the results of the field-study testing her team had put together for a company attempting to save its chain of stores from declining sales.

"Sam, there's a call for you on line two," James, her assistant, said.

"James, did you catch who is holding on line two?"

"I think it is one of your friends. She said her name was Ford Perfect. Is that a real name?"

"Yes, James, that is a real name, only it's not that person's name. Thanks. Will you please confirm everything for the meeting at four today? Make sure Allen has his computer up and running in the next hour."

"The meeting is four hours from now. I don't even know where Allen is."

"You have my permission to put GPS tracking on Allen. Get him here, please."

Sam hit her speakerphone, thinking about the meeting and the last computer fiasco that had happened when this client had come in; it did not provide the image Sam wanted the client to have of them.

"Hey, Ford, what planet are you calling from today?" Sam asked.

"Sherri called and told me you are going to take that redhead to the coast. I know you're crazy. This is not the type of woman Eliza would want you to be with; you are not here to rescue everyone."

"Suzanne, I didn't know you and Sherri were on speaking terms. Before I forget, please stop teasing James."

"I knew you would take the call."

"You know, there is something special about this woman. I feel tingly all over."

"That's a rash. Get yourself some ointment. That woman is special all right. Do I need to remind you about…Hey, open your office door—I can't handle both coffees and the door handle."

"Shit," Sam said as she sprang from her desk and let Suzanne King into her office.

"You know, this is my work. I need to concentrate."

"I checked with James and know you don't have a meeting until this afternoon. He is so much easier to get through than that other gal you had for a few months. She was like that door keeper of munchkin land. 'You don't get to see the Samantha, no way, no how.' James is so easy.

For example, I know you are headed out for three weeks. He makes it so much easier to stalk you. Seriously though, I am here to talk some sense into you before you are back at my place refusing to let go of Thad."

"Thad loves me."

"He does. But even Thad has his limits. He told me the next time he sees you, it had better be for a walk at the beach and a steak."

"A steak? Okay, Thad is upping his game. The latest picture you texted looks like he is posing for *Playgirl*."

"I know. That is his favorite position, on his back with all four paws up in the air, showing off his family jewels."

"Thank god, he's a furry little guy, and those jewels are well hidden. Isn't he neutered?"

"Yes. And we are not here to talk about the fathering capabilities of my dog. Or the lack thereof, for that matter. I am here out of concern."

"Would you raise your grand-puppies? If Thad knocked up that poodle down the street? He's sweet on her, you know."

"Are you running a reality TV show? What kind of question is that? And, no, you are not getting me off topic. Although those would be adorable little...What would they be? A cardigan corgi and a poodle...a corgidoodle or, no, a coodle!" Suzanne leaned back and sipped her coffee.

"They would be darn cute puppies and accessories. Before you knew it, they would have their own Instagram and blogs. I need to settle a score with you. Last month at dinner, y'all were ganging up on me to put myself out there and to stop with the 'girl-in-every-city.' You made me sound like a guy. My dating life is fine."

"You call those one night stands you pick up on the road a dating life? I've been out in the jungle with you. There are so many wonderful, single, geographically available women right here in this city who know who they are and who aren't experimenting with women or divorced from a man."

"What, are we only dating exclusively gold-star lesbians now? And when has geography ever come into the equation? I travel all the time."

"Don't know about gold-star whatever, but I do remember you in college, and you took some turns with the other team, just like me—"

"You slept with women in college? You are breaking my heart."

"Knock it off—we would've never worked and you know it. Although, I do know you were the cause of many a man's morning woody on our dorm floor when the rumors went around that you were a carpet eater."

"Do you have to be so crass? Your husband kisses you with that mouth. Wait, don't answer—I do not need to hear any more about your amazing sex life after...how many years of marriage?"

"Again, not here to discuss my life. I'm here to get under your skin and make sure you don't make a big mistake. Marriage is legal for you people now. You get to pay the huge divorce bills like the rest of us. I think the only people truly wanting marriage for anyone to anything are the divorce lawyers. More business."

"Cynical much? Honestly, Suzanne, you can talk to me. How's your marriage?"

"Love story is still going strong. I think the main reason is the lack of two-legged children. We are a team without those little manipulators plotting against us."

"We are friends because?" Sam asked.

"Because we survived crew together. Do you remember those stadium stairs? If it weren't for you, I'd still be lying on those steps."

"Are you sure you didn't study drama? Back to topic. What did Sherri say about Frances?" Sam asked.

"Said she threw rocks at Tuffy the tortoise. Who throws rocks at a reptile? You love animals."

Sam couldn't help but laugh. Her friend was staring at her over the top of her reading glasses. Sam got up and walked to the window. Her view looked down on Bush Street and directly across to the Mills Building. She liked the Romanesque design elements on the Mills Building, which was built when people still put carved stone work on buildings. She thought about the times she had caught glimpses of Frances at the Specialty's over on Pine.

It wasn't until after the fateful date at Meadows Bistro that Sam talked to her. The whole slew of Frances memories had her laughing out loud.

"If you are losing your mind, I know this great place—you check in and it's like a spa. Maybe you need to do that for yourself?" Suzanne said.

"What I need is to follow my heart. Eliza would like Frances. Did Sherri say anything nice about her?"

"She said she's attractive and younger than you. She loved her friends Dana and Cheryl. Maybe Cheryl is available."

"Cheryl is married but not. She's been seeing some guy she met online ten years ago. I am not a tennis girl. I think Cheryl is a complete tennis nut and into the stick and ball thing."

Sam walked around behind Suzanne and placed her hands on her shoulders. "I appreciate your concern, but you helped me realize that this woman makes me laugh and keeps me on my toes."

"She sounds like an accident waiting to happen. I don't want you to get hurt—you are too special. When we watched what happened through Eliza's illness...You are the most loving, caring person I know," Suzanne said, taking Sam's hand and kissing the back of it.

Sam walked to the chair next to Suzanne and sat down. Her heart was breaking as memories of Eliza came flooding back into full view. A picture of her and Eliza was on the credenza behind her desk.

"Do you remember when you took that picture of us?" Sam said, pointing to the silver frame holding the photograph of her and her Eliza frozen and in black and white.

"That was quite the day. She had decided to surprise you with kayak lessons. You were so excited, you knocked the cake off the counter and directly into the dog's dinner bowl. He was so happy. That picture is one of my favorites. You look great in buttercream."

"The doctor called thirty minutes after you took that picture. I thought it was the worst birthday ever. I was wrong. The worst birthday ever was the first one without her. She made me promise I would collect as many birthdays as I could because there are so many things that I want to do in this life."

"Damn it, Sam. You're making me cry."

"Frances makes me laugh. Do you remember when I first met Eliza, you told me to run away? I'm seeing a pattern here."

"I didn't tell you to run. What I said was you need to start working out because she was going to run you over."

"Not what I remember. What I do remember are all the talks Liza and I had when she knew that the chemo wasn't working. I miss her so much," Sam said and let her face fall into her hands. "When is it not going to hurt so much?"

"I don't know. You two loved so much, it put the rest of us to shame."

"Sherri is wrong. I think Eliza might be helping me out here."

"Now you're making things up."

"She plays the piano."

"Lots of people play the piano," Suzanne said.

"Yeah? Well, I had never talked to her about music. I drove her to the ER to get her knee looked at—"

"I heard you two disappeared for six hours."

"It was an ER in Placerville—I'm shocked we aren't still there. We were hunting for something to drink, and there was a piano in the front lobby. She played. Do you know what two songs she pulled out of that brain of hers?"

"Not going to guess. With that lead-up, it was clearly a song you…Wait, two songs? Oh no, that is—"

"First, she played 'Gabriel's Oboe' and then merged into the love theme from *Cinema Paradiso*."

"You had to have said something to her about Eliza and your wedding. Someone had to have said something. That is not random. Maybe she knows someone who was at your wedding."

"There were six of us at the wedding, eight counting Eliza and myself. None of you have met Frances. We didn't broadcast the ceremony, and there are no videos—although now I wish there were."

"What did you do when she started playing?"

"I sat down and listened—a little in disbelief."

"Have you told her?"

"No. Talk about freaking a person out. Hey, did you know you played the two songs my dead wife played to me all the time?"

"Did you ask her why she played those two songs? This is wild."

"I did. She said she loved the composer. She said she always started her piano sessions with 'Gabriel's Oboe' because it was so amazing. Then she went to a Morricone film night put on by the UW School of Music and cried through the music for *Cinema Paradiso*. She said she hardly ever plays those songs in public because she feels they are a prayer to the music gods that blessed her with the ability to play. She plays beautifully."

Sam watched as Suzanne stood up and walked over to the framed picture of Eliza. She picked it up and traced her sister's face. "She loved you so much. I remember when you two first met—it scared me. I was worried I had lost my best friend. You had come home with me for Thanksgiving that year. My mom thought you and I were going to come out to her as a couple."

"We did finish each other's sentences."

"Eliza couldn't take her eyes off of you. I had no clue my sister was gay."

"You didn't talk to me for almost three months after we started dating."

"Trust me, I remember. I took heat from everyone over it. I was jealous."

"You weren't a lesbian. And you are my best friend."

"Exactly. Then Eliza became your lover and best friend. I don't want to lose you again."

Sam stood and hugged Suzanne. "You aren't going to lose me. I haven't told anyone about Frances playing the piano. I need some time with her away from everyone. I'm going to take her on a real date and ask her if she would like go to the coast. We need space, and she needs some time to recover. The past year has been a hard one. The two of us need to work this out. She doesn't know any of the details about Eliza. She knows that I was married, to a woman, and that woman died. Sherri and her big mouth."

"Does she know you are rolling in cash?"

"Oh my god! She's not a gold digger. She makes her own money."

"Sherri said she's an artist. That is code for 'I want someone else to pay my way.'"

"She had a one-woman gallery show and sold every one of her paintings. Are you sure you aren't my mother from a different life reincarnated?"

"Weird. I am scared. Sherri called me out of the blue and told me to get my butt over here."

"Let me explore this with Frances. Trust me. You are always going to be in my life. I couldn't live without Ford Perfect. Did I mention she is a huge Douglas Adams fan?"

"Well, tell her 'so long, and thanks for the fish.'"

"Are you calling me a dolphin?"

"No, I want you to be happy, and I don't want you with a spastic ginger."

"Rude."

"I can't change your mind?" Suzanne asked.

"Nope. I'm going to jump into this with both feet."

CHAPTER FORTY-THREE
THE FOG LIFTS

Frances was up early and did not want to disturb Sam, who was still in a deep sleep. She quietly rose and walked out to the early morning light-indigo sky. Frances had marveled at the beauty of the deep canyon when Sam turned off Pacific Coast Highway 1 onto a narrow road that led to this almost floating house perched on the edge. When they had arrived yesterday afternoon, it was a beautiful day, and the house on the side of the canyon wall looked straight down the canyon to the ocean. It took Frances's breath away to be in a place where the redwoods reach out and practically touch the ocean.

Her mind danced through the images of yesterday as she quietly poured herself a glass of orange juice and walked to the wall of windows to look where the ocean had been yesterday. The dense valley overnight had transformed itself with a low-lying, thick, gray cover of clouds. The house was above the fog layer, and Frances loved counting the tips of coastal redwoods that poked through the top of the cotton candy fluffy clouds. "I need to capture this contrast of the dark green from the trees to the pale pink and blue dawning sky on canvas," she said, wrapping a Chief Joseph Pendleton wool blanket around herself as armor against the cool morning air. Frances tiptoed out the French doors that led to a porch. The fog extended out so far, it hid the coastline and the ocean from view. Had she not seen the water when they arrived yesterday afternoon, she would have not believed this house thirty minutes up a coastal mountain canyon could have such a spectacular ocean view.

Sam's house went beyond any expectation Frances had. The redwood beams that created the vaulted ceiling were kept natural and rough. A wall of picture windows surrounding French doors let the outside in, and it was spectacular. The gourmet kitchen was well stocked with any kitchen tool one might need and set on the canyon side of the home. When Frances had stood at the sink washing the pans from dinner last night, she felt like a kid in a tree house as the forest of the canyon fell away from the window.

A fireplace artfully positioned in the back corner of the main room created orange warmth that filled the home without blocking the views. Sam had given Frances a tour of the art that was hung throughout the three-bedroom home. Most of the art consisted of framed black-and-white photographic prints that Eliza had taken on their travels. Eliza had an eye for capturing the beauty of people. A picture of a woman in a hill town in Northern Italy was so full of energy that Frances couldn't help but smile. The smile and laughter in the eyes of the woman was infectious. Frances sat down on a carved wood bench that was remarkably comfortable and pulled the blanket tightly around herself. She replayed the conversation that led her to playing a piece of music she had not played since her beloved Grangran had died, whose funeral she didn't attend.

"What an amazing piano," Frances had said. She realized there were many emotions in Sam tied to the piano because Sam walked to the windows and had such a distant energy as she looked past the horizon.

"Eliza found that beast of an upright in an estate sale. It was full of spider webs and had missing keys. She paid the guy twenty bucks for it. I had no clue what she saw in that thing."

"You don't see such large uprights anymore. I agree it is a beast, but an exquisite one."

Sam walked over to the piano and touched the side panel. "This piano was a labor of love for Eliza. It took her eight months to fully restore. When we decided to move it here, it took five guys and a jerry-rigged bobcat to maneuver it down the ten steps to get into the house. She was a nervous wreck during that move."

An early morning bird call brought her out of her replay of last night, causing Frances to open her eyes as the tears were forming. She was calm and blinked back the tears with a smile as she recalled how Sam invited her to play the piano last night. Sam had taken her hand and said, "I keep it tuned. I assume the piano tuner plays it, but I have not heard the piano since Eliza played about six months before she died. Please let the music out."

Frances took a seat on the smooth, wood piano bench. With two hands, she had gently opened the cover exposing the black and white keys. A thin layer of dust had coated them, and Frances felt her heart beat with an intention to honor Eliza. In those silent seconds, the melody of the music came to her from Chopin.

This music, a prelude, represented a penetrating and beautiful story of love and loss. Frances played Prelude in E Minor, Op. 28 No. 4. With each note that came from the piano, the beauty of the melody created by this work brought the emotions forward. Frances wept as she played.

She did not look at Sam and closed her eyes as the notes built the peak of emotion. A short piece, it awakened the love that was growing through the connections with people that Frances had made in her life. When Frances played the last notes of the piece, her hand stayed on the keys. She wept with a clarity that spoke to the losses she had faced. Sam had come to Frances and taken her hand; they walked onto the porch and watched the night sky in silence. There were no words to share in that moment because the music held them together in ways that told them they were survivors and alive. This was their time to live and learn from one another and from their growing love.

Frances had turned to Sam and knew that her eyes reflected the beauty and shine that Sam's eyes showed her. It was a moment that Frances wanted to hold onto forever, and she knew that music would help her do so.

"The music made my heart and soul feel so full, so complete," Sam whispered. "Thank you."

"I understand. When I played Eliza's piano, I felt her hugging me. An upright piano is an intimate instrument because the music and sound falls over you. I love my grand, but the music goes away from you. It is different."

Frances touched her lips as she lived through the gentle passionate kiss Sam gave her last night. Frances had pulled Sam into her with her arms around her waist, and they danced to the music of the canyon. There were no words. Frances let the fullness of the music linger around them as they turned and watched the sun set over the Pacific Ocean.

"Good morning, beautiful," Sam said, handing Frances a fresh cup of coffee. "Can I join you under the blanket?"

Frances handed back the coffee and opened the blanket wide, exposing her naked body to the cool morning air. "Hurry. This morning air is cold," Frances said, folding the blanket around Samantha as she snuggled up next to her.

"Words are lost to me," Sam said.

"Over this amazing view? I've never seen anything quite like this before. You said I would understand why you have this place, and I think I do. Did you know that our dinner date at Picco would lead to this weekend away? I had heard lesbians do marathon dates. Now I completely understand and approve."

"Not the view, silly—you. My words are lost because all I can think about is how it feels to be with you under this blanket. I had a pretty strong hunch that you would say yes. It was the way you kissed me hello."

"That makes two of us. Dana told me this was going to happen. But I must say—she looked like she saw a ghost when the universe finally threw us together again. I still see Dana's face when you walked down the hall at Sherri's house. She was serious when she wanted all knives put out of reach."

"I wanted to know you even more when you ran out of that restaurant. If your friends had not come over, I was ready to chase after you.

The universe played with us though. What can I say but that my heart was harpooned, and you didn't even know."

"Did you?" Frances asked.

"Yes. I couldn't explain it, but I didn't want to leave you in Specialty's. You were such—"

"A jerk. I was so embarrassed. There you were in your million-dollar suit, with your million-dollar people, and I looked like a walking grape."

"A unique artist."

"Don't lie. I looked like a woman who had escaped from an asylum."

"You looked like someone who listened to techno metal, loved the University of Washington, and was addicted to cinnamon rolls."

Frances cuddled into Sam and pulled her feet up beside her on the oversized bench that was carved out of what had to have been a massive redwood burl. "I never knew how wonderful it would feel to do absolutely nothing with you," Frances said.

Warm under the blanket, Frances let Sam take the coffee cup out of her hands and met her lips with a softness that suggested that she was falling deeply into the beginnings of something she didn't want to define. Her heartbeat was steady as her lips parted, and the kiss confirmed for Frances that she was letting herself feel.

"Sam?"

"Hmm? You taste wonderful this morning," Sam said as she caressed Frances's neck.

"I need you to look at me."

Frances held Sam's face between her hands and looked deep into her light-brown eyes. She saw more than she could have ever imagined. The tenderness made her choke back tears. Sam placed her hands over Frances's and met her gaze. With a touch that sent electricity running throughout Frances's body, Samantha leaned into her and kissed her forehead, placing kisses down the bridge of her nose and softly hesitating over her parted lips. Frances could feel the warmth of Sam's breath and the touch of her hands as Sam pulled Frances into her and the world fell away. The kiss led them into the love of the morning.

Their hands found the secrets of one another, and Sam gently laid Frances back on the blanket. Frances felt her heart open completely as she gave herself to the moment, to the touch, to the warmth of this woman who was showing her how to explore and let go.

Time stood still as Frances found herself pulling Sam up to kiss her lips.

"I'm simply falling into you in ways that I had never imagined," Frances said.

"Are we moving too fast?"

"Let us fall at the rate we are going to and not question this, because I feel this deeper than I know how to explain," Frances said.

Frances pulled the blanket over them as Sam lay beside her on the bench. *Now you know what it means to feel the love of someone who is special,* Frances thought to herself, the fingers of her right hand gently spelling out the word desire on Sam's arm. The quiet of the morning was giving way to the songs of birds. A distant rush of water gave away the location of a creek rushing toward the ocean.

"Have you thought any more about what I shared with you last night? I know it was a lot, but I wanted you to know the whole story about what happened with Eliza," Sam said.

"I am still processing our conversation. Why do you think you are here now? Ready to risk your heart?" Frances asked.

"It is you. You have this energy that envelopes me. When you look at me, I feel you. I know this is really new, and we do have quite the odd history of introductions. Through it all, you have been wonderfully you. You share yourself so freely. There are no masks with you."

"One reason I can never play poker. People really can read me like an open book."

"Friends had introduced me to possible lovers after they felt I had been single long enough. A few of those women were wonderful, but they all made me miss Liza even more. I compared them all to her. You are so unique and beautiful. I appreciate my love with Eliza, and I am here with you."

"You two were together for ten years."

"I think one reason I know this is right is because I don't hide her from you. When you played the Prelude by Chopin yesterday, I felt the loss of her but also the knowledge that she is free, and I would like to think she wants me to love again."

Frances raised herself up, resting on her elbow so she could look down into Sam's face. She traced Sam's eyebrows, nose, and lips. There were so many words running through her mind that she wanted to let things settle down. This woman told her about a great love she shared with another woman—one that was no longer here due to the horrors of disease.

"I don't want you to hide her away. She is part of who you are today. Let Eliza be alive with you and honor her the way that is right for you and her family without apology."

"You are so peculiar and wonderful. I know it is weird, but I wish Eliza could know you," Sam said.

"Are you trying to tell me she's a ghost?"

"Do you believe in ghosts?"

"Sometimes. I think my brother Gall visited me a couple years after his death. Then there was Grangran, who did visit me. I was on my honeymoon when she passed. My family did not tell me because they didn't want to 'ruin' my honeymoon. But I knew she had passed. She appeared in my hotel room. That was the last time I played that piece of music. She helped me know I was going to be okay after I realized my marriage was over."

"I went to this psychic medium shortly after Liza died. I so wanted to talk with her again. I wanted to believe that there is more after this," Samantha said. "I hungered for her voice and her touch, and then one day I was out walking on a beach in Hilton Head. The water was so warm, and I saw the strangest thing—it was a horseshoe crab."

"They are really weird looking. Are you saying your Eliza looked like a horseshoe crab? You better hope she isn't listening to this conversation. If I see an object suddenly take flight toward your head, I'm going to say she did not appreciate being called a horseshoe crab."

"Nope. I didn't say she was the crab, but the crab had been walking through the sand, and it was sitting on this cardboard box. The box lid only had the letters L-I-Z-A. I got this brilliant jolt through my heart. Then I started laughing because the crab scuttled away toward the water, and there were three perfect sand dollars lying in the sand. Liza and I always had a game about finding sand dollars when we walked on beaches. She won."

"I got chills down my arm. Do you want to go hunting for sand dollars today?"

"I don't need to because you are letting me talk about her, and I feel no pains of jealously from you."

"Sam, I am a lot of things. Jealous is not one them. You must promise me that as we go down this road, you respect us enough to end this relationship before you start another one. After Richard and Olivia, I am well aware of the pain that comes from such lies."

"It comes down to trust."

"My friends really do not want me dating you. It is an uphill fight with them," Sam said.

"Understood. My family doesn't want me at all, and you heard the story. Theresa and I are not talking much either."

"I am not looking for perfection, Frances. I am looking for another who will work and fight for the us that grows."

"Are we really dating?"

"Why? Did you rent the U-Haul truck already?"

"What is it with lesbians and U-Hauls? I might have to invest in a lesbian-to-English translation app," Frances said.

"Do they have those?" Sam asked.

"You know, Russell and Simon had me believing there was a gaydar app for my phone that would let you know if someone was gay."

"That is both scary and funny. Are you sure you are okay with my travel schedule?"

Frances sat up and stretched. She let the blanket fall off her and let her skin soak up the sun. It felt amazing to be sitting so free and relaxed with Sam. Inside she felt a passionate simmer smoldering for more. She wanted and needed this person in a way she never thought possible. The thought of not seeing her for a few weeks was both freeing and scary. Sam was looking at her and waiting for an answer. Frances, feeling bold, stood and walked to the railing of the porch. The fog was still covering the majority of the valley, and Frances felt completely open in the privacy of this home floating above the clouds.

"You have your world of work, and I have mine. I hope you are okay when I lose concept of night and day. I go through periods of creative optimization where nothing else matters, not even sleep."

"A creative and a logical pragmatist meet and fall in love…"

"Are you falling in love?" Frances asked.

"Already fell off that cliff, and I am soaring."

CHAPTER FORTY-FOUR

BABY CAKE

T raffic was at a standstill over the Golden Gate Bridge, and Frances had to talk herself down with only forty minutes to get back to the loft before the baby shower was to start. This was not the way the day was supposed to go. Russell and Theresa were with Winter, keeping her occupied shopping for a baby crib. The last text had been an hour ago, and Theresa said that Frances owed her big-time for dealing with a cranky pregnant munchkin. Winter was short, but the term munchkin totally worked.

"Can you believe Jason really did walk out on Winter?" Dana asked.

"I actually thought they were going to make it when Winter finally said yes to his fourth proposal," Frances said.

"One thing she can't stop is that baby. She's so looking like she's ready to have that baby. If she were wrapped in tinfoil, there'd be popcorn all over."

"What?"

"Jiffy Pop. Winter looks like Jiffy Pop," Dana said.

"People think I have strange associations. That one takes the cake, and don't you dare repeat it to Winter. Theresa texted that if Winter asked her if she looked fat one more time, she was going to tell her she looks like a beach ball with feet."

"Glad I picked the party-planning side of this baby shower. How are you and Theresa getting along?"

"Okay. We decided to forge forward with our relationship and not talk about the family. She's going back to Notre Dame. I have no clue if she will talk to me once she gets back into her own life."

With each passing minute, Frances gripped the steering wheel a little tighter, effectively shutting off all blood flow to her fingers. The traffic wasn't moving, and she was trapped. Any other day, being stuck on the bridge would be a welcome sight-seeing interlude. With thirty people showing up to the loft for Winter's baby shower two days after Jason had finally moved out of Winter's condo, Frances wanted the superpower gift of flight. Or at least a flying truck.

"You know, this is probably exactly what Winter needed to move her focus onto the new paths she is being forced to take by the universe. A baby is bigger than anything I can truly think of to explode a world wide open," Dana said.

"Do you think she's going to be okay?" Frances asked.

"What is okay? Winter has had a crazy road. No question, you two are an interesting pair. That type of question is wandering into the existence of life and why are we here...what is life, anyway? Winter is going to be a mother. We are going to be here to help her. We're all stumbling through life, and soon we'll be going to the 99-cent shit store and thinking that is completely normal."

"You lost me," Frances said.

"My grandsons love the 99-cent shit store because everything in there is under a dollar. They feel like they are rich because they can buy a whole bag full of crap with their allowance money."

"How much do they make? I didn't know kids still got allowance."

"They get twenty dollars a week."

"I want to go live with your daughter. I think I made twenty dollars in ten years of doing chores."

"Frances, you knucklehead, Winter thought working for that hoity-toity law firm was arriving in life. My grandsons think the 99-cent shit store is the place to go. All of them are being fooled by a bunch of shit."

"Language! Thank god, it looks like traffic is finally moving again."

"Winter is going to be fine, and so are you. I am so proud of you."

"Dana you've already—"

"Frances, you did a brave thing and something that most people only dream about doing. You need to know that creating art and putting yourself out there is really important."

"Not like teaching kids or finding the cure to cancer. It's just paintings."

"If this truck weren't so huge, I'd smack you upside the head. Don't discount your accomplishments. You may have been trained to discount yourself, but stop it. You are a creator, and you are doing it."

"You know, the boys gave me a lecture about being an artist a while ago. They told me that the moment I picked up a brush, I was an artist. And that I shouldn't let money change how I view that and to know that this ability to create is in my soul."

"They are right."

"Does that mean being a biology teacher was your soul connection?"

"I loved it. I hated it too. Oh my god, some of the parents I had to deal with were…Oh hell, I can't wait to see how Winter deals with her kid's teachers."

Frances and Dana laughed as the traffic finally opened up. Snow White pulled into the loft parking lot with three minutes to spare.

"Thank god, Russell's car is not in its parking spot. We have time. Now get the lead out," Frances said.

The loft was filled with people Frances did not know, and she was a little taken aback by the ice sculpture of what was supposed to be a pregnant woman but looked more like a giant beach ball with feet. Frances was glad to see the catering crew was all set up without direction. The best thing she did was call Felipe for help in pulling the party together. She had waited until the last minute to get her list of items done.

"Frances, it's about time," Simon said. "Dana, you look fab."

"Have you heard from Russell?" Frances asked.

"They are a little delayed because Winter wanted to stop for a piece of focaccia at Liguria's."

"That place sells out by noon. I bet they are closed, and I really don't want to deal with a disappointed Winter," Frances said.

"Maybe we should start sending some of the food around. These strangers are looking restless. I had no clue Winter had so many friends," Dana said.

"Who picked the music? I am not feeling the Propeller song," Cheryl said.

"Everybody loves the Wiggles," Frances said.

"The baby is still at least two weeks away, and even then, this torture can wait until the baby blob is walking and talking," Dana said. "Someone cut the music."

Frances changed the music to keep the surprise baby shower victims happy. The food was slowly being passed out as Cheryl and Simon finished off the different baby shower games they were going to force people to play.

"Simply disgusting," Simon said.

"What are you making that is so disgusting?" Dana asked.

"That diaper looks like real poo! Who put that together?" Frances asked.

Dana pointed to a woman eating the rest of the chocolate. "She said she was a mother and knew what a poo diaper looked like, and I agree—that looks like real poop. Promise me you won't faint if you participate in the game."

"Not going to do that one. I like the decorate-the-diaper derby game myself."

The loft was full of so much pink, Frances knew what it felt like to be on the inside of a cotton candy ball. Who knew they had so many shades of pink crepe paper? The pink baby diaper balloons were a new one. "God, I hope she's really having a girl," Frances said. She sat down next to the cake, which was surrounded by fifty cupcakes with chocolate pacifiers.

"That's quite the cake. Looks almost lifelike. Do you think it was a good idea to have a baby cake made to look like a baby?" Cheryl asked.

"It's all the rage. The catering company ordered the cake. I think I'll let someone else cut the baby cake. When I first told Felipe I wanted a baby cake, he thought I actually wanted the cake made out of babies," Frances said and snagged one of the cupcakes.

"Oh, that looks yummy. I need a chocolate fix too," Cheryl said, grabbing a cupcake and taking a bite. "This is some good cake. I don't normally like cupcakes. All about the frosting for me. Still can't believe that is a cake. Creepy baby cake."

"Don't let anyone else eat a cupcake. It might upset the whole layout." Frances tried to hide the fact that two cupcakes had been heisted. "When is Winter going to arrive? We are now post thirty minutes. Theresa and Russell get an epic fail."

"Places, everyone. They are on their way up," Simon said.

"Why is it when someone does a surprise, the loudest moments are everyone trying to be quiet?" Dana said. "Not like we can hide—this is a loft."

The door opened and in walked Theresa and Russell, both making a sign that no one quite caught as the crowd yelled *surprise!* Winter was not with them.

"Where is Winter?" a collective question came from the group.

"She couldn't make it any longer, and we took her home. She was in a mood and wanted to be left alone," Theresa said.

"Are you serious?"

Winter jumped from around the corner. "Gotcha!"

Frances hugged her friend and brought her into the fold of the guests waiting to coo over the pregnant woman. The mini-heart attack on the reverse surprise would not be forgotten. Frances saw that Winter pulling a fast one made her all smiles, and the party was now in full force. Someone had started the kids' music, and the crazy thing was, a couple of the adults were bouncing to the beat of "The Shimmy Shake."

The people twisting and shimmying in the loft gave Frances a peek into the future of parties. She walked around and made sure people were having fun. She wasn't sure who had thought white liquid cocktails were a good thing, but people seemed to be enjoying them. Was it wrong to serve? Nope.

"Explain to me who found the boob squirt guns?" Dana asked.

"They were at the 99-cent shit store," Frances said.

The games were beginning, and Guess the Number of Jelly Belly's in the Diaper Bucket was getting a lot of attention. Winter looked happy as the Guess the Stain game was being passed around. A woman who must have been a friend from Winter's law school was starting to herd the party goers toward the mountain of gifts. She assigned a note taker and put Theresa on collecting trash. Frances liked this person. A knock at the door took her attention away.

Frances opened the door to two women dressed in red and green skirts and white puffy shirts, with accordions strapped to their chests. They burst into the party playing a rousing and very loud polka.

"Everybody ready to polka?" one of the women asked.

"What the heck? I think you have the wrong party," Frances said.

"Come on in, ladies. I told you I could take care of it," Dana said and escorted the accordion players into the center of the loft.

No one moved or said a word as the women turned and stood back-to-back and started playing something they called "Accordion a Go-Go." Frances cocked her head and looked at Dana, who was bouncing and clapping her hands.

"Frances, what's with the accordion players?" Cheryl asked.

"I think I know. Come with me."

Frances made her way over to Dana and tapped her on the shoulder.

"Dana, who told you to get accordion players?" Frances asked.

"I thought it was strange, but I know not to question a request for a pregnant lady. I taught with Annie, and I knew she and her sister played the accordion. They were so excited when I called them about this party. They haven't played a party in years."

"Would not have guessed they haven't played a party in years. They are so happening," Cheryl said.

"Dana, you volunteered to do the aquarium. Winter wanted an aquarium because she heard something about how they help calm a person down," Frances said.

"Aquarium? I specifically heard accordion. I think I need to have my hearing checked. How come no one said anything?"

"Dana, you're an AP biology teacher with a background in marine biology—there wasn't anything we could add when you said you were on top of it."

The polka sisters continued playing to the shocked crowd. Soon the Midwestern folks showed their true colors, and someone requested the "Chicken Dance." Who knew that people had a hidden polka request library?

"Ladies, time to focus. Thank you, polka people."

Frances let the woman who had taken control of the party continue marching them through the pile of gifts. This party was going to go into tomorrow at this rate. Winter looked surprisingly relaxed as she was the center of attention. The girl did love gifts, and right now, the party was giving her some very needed items.

"Who wants some cake?" the drill sergeant of the shower asked as Winter was finally reaching the bottom of the wrapped pile of gifts.

"Winter, you stay where you are—the cake will be brought to you," Frances said.

Theresa and Simon very carefully maneuvered through the obstacle course of boxes, discarded wrapping paper, and people to set the lifelike baby cake in front of Winter on the coffee table that had been hidden under a pink wave of crepe paper and tulle. Frances realized that she would leave all her party setup to the gay boys. The pink tulle worked so well, and the loft really had been transformed into a baby shower extravaganza. The accordion sisters took the silence as an invitation to start playing again. No one stopped them.

"Wow, that is…I have to cut this baby?" Winter asked.

Dana walked over to Annie and got her to cut the polka music for the moment. Phones had been whipped out to take pictures of the baby cake.

"Look, they even got drool coming out of her mouth," someone said, pointing.

"How come everyone thinks I'm going to have a blonde-haired, blue-eyed baby? Do I look like a walking recessive gene?" Winter asked as she held the knife first over the feet and then by the middle of the baby. "This is just cake."

Winter decided to cut into the middle of the baby. The knife penetrated into the molding chocolate that made the skin look so lifelike and into the red velvet cake with raspberry filling. The gasp from the crowd was loud enough to cause Winston to bark next door.

"He doesn't bark with all the polka music, but a horrific gasp, and he goes nuts," Russell said. "That is truly disgusting."

Winter started crying, and Frances climbed over the sofa trying to get to the cake. No one knew quite what to do. The drill sergeant of the shower looked green. A couple more gasps were heard.

"Frances, you need a round of applause," Simon said.

"Everyone, please know that Winter's favorite cake is red velvet, and the fresh raspberry cream filling might not have been the best choice for this style of cake. I had no clue. There are chocolate cupcakes on the counter. Please help yourselves," Frances said. "Winter, I am so sorry. Honestly, this was not meant to upset you."

Winter hugged Frances and tried to stop her crying. She started laughing. "Where's Molly? This looks like a murder scene."

"Molly apologized, but she was called into work. I'm sure she'll get a kick out of the video replay of this little 'what not to serve at a baby shower' moment."

CHAPTER FORTY-FIVE

A NEW FAMILY EXPANDS

When Frances pulled up into the circle drive to the Betty Irene Moore Women's Hospital, her heart skipped a beat at the sight of Molly Woods standing outside talking on the phone.

"She's like a TV detective," Theresa said.

"What do you mean?" Frances asked.

"Molly is hot. I don't know anyone else who can rock slacks and a simple white button-down shirt like that."

"Keep your pants on and know that is not open for discussion. We are here for Winter and to find out why Winter was with Molly," Frances said.

Frances watched as Theresa hopped out of the truck before she had it in park. In less time than it took Frances to check her teeth in her rearview mirror, Molly was climbing into the passenger side of Frances's truck.

"I think you might have this confused with a Lyft," Frances said.

"No confusion. I am going to help you get the truck parked. I sent Theresa into the lobby and put her in charge of getting everyone signed in with security when they arrive. Winter is fine. I wanted a few moments to talk with you, alone."

"That sounds foreboding. Do I need to call an attorney?" Frances asked. "I'm kidding—Winter knows she got herself involved in that mess. She doesn't hold you responsible. I think Winter sees you as her saving angel. Although she was sounding uncertain about her future when she was disbarred."

"That was rough. We asked for a suspension. Guess the attorneys in charge of lawyer ethics felt she could not redeem herself. That's rough. I don't know what I would do if I were told I couldn't work as a detective. How are you?" Molly asked.

Frances reached up and self-consciously pulled her hair forward, trying to cover the stitches on the side of her head. Her hands gripped the bottom of her steering wheel. She wanted to fall into Molly's arms. This was not going to happen. Frances took a deep breath and exhaled.

"A lot is going on, but I can't talk about it right now. What happened that would put Winter into labor? She's two weeks early, and I don't think anyone won the baby pool."

"Winter is one stressed-out woman. The whole issue with losing her law practice and Jason—personally, I think she worked herself into labor," Molly said.

"Sometimes I question my friendship with her, but I love her at the same time. Hard to explain."

"I will tell you that if it was not for her, we would not have discovered the crime and arrested the people responsible. Do not hate the messenger. I believe that when she found out, she started to collect the information that would put those people away for good. Without her, we wouldn't have a case," Molly said.

"Is Jason here?"

"No. He told Winter he would have nothing to do with her."

"What about the baby? It takes two," Frances said.

"Right now, we need to focus on helping Winter through the delivery of her baby," Molly said and hopped out of the truck.

Frances followed and caught up to Molly as she walked across the parking lot. Theresa came out and handed Frances a white visitor's sticker with her name on it.

"Frances, you can go up to the triage. I think that is on the fourth floor. They are assessing how far along Winter is and what the next steps are," Theresa said.

"Do you think there will be any blood?"

"There's no blood. You'll be fine," Molly said. "I'll take you up there. Theresa, can you wait here and direct the rest of the crew to the waiting room when they check in with security?"

"Yes, ma'am," Theresa said, making a salute.

"Excuse my lil' sis. She's taken with you, and that makes her act a little crazy."

"No harm. Frances, I am here if you need to talk," Molly said.

"Not ready. I am going to be processing what has happened for quite some time. What happened when you came out to your family?" Frances asked.

"It was a different situation, and no blood was shed. But it wasn't easy," Molly said, reaching out and placing a hand on Frances's shoulder.

Frances hit the button to call an elevator. She felt her skin flash red with heat. She placed her hand over Molly's and wanted to turn and fall into her arms. The ding of the elevator doors conditioned her to walk forward away from Molly. She could not even allow herself to imagine. Molly was off limits. It didn't matter that the woman had the ability to hypnotize her.

"Do you think Winter is going to have a name ready?" Frances asked.

"Frances, I'm sorry."

"You know I am seeing Sam."

"Yup. We're friends, right?" Molly asked.

"Friends."

The elevator doors opened, and Frances hesitated as she saw the word *triage* over the entrance. She closed her eyes and tried not to notice the smell of hospital antiseptic that was usually enough to make her go a whiter shade of pale than a ghost. People in brightly colored scrubs were walking quickly in and out of different rooms.

"You can do this. Focus on Winter. The boys will be here soon, and then you can exit to the waiting room because they won't want all of you in the way."

"They can step over me when I faint," Frances said.

"Let me go find out exactly where she is. I want you to stand here against this wall and don't move," Molly said.

"I think I might take a seat." Frances let herself slip down the wall. There were aspects of herself that she really hated. This propensity to faint with the thought of blood was one of those things she wished she could change about herself. She sat on the floor in the hall with her back and head resting against the wall.

"You are off the hook. Winter is in labor, and you are not on the list. Russell and Simon will be allowed in when they get here. Let me walk you to the waiting room."

"Is she going to be okay? This is so not going the way she described it at her baby shower."

"Frances, take a deep breath. And another. Winter is in great hands here, and they are going to deliver her baby soon," Molly said.

When Frances and Molly walked around the corner and into the waiting room, Dana and Theresa came running up to them. Theresa took Frances and guided her to a chair.

"No offense, but you look like the wreck of the Hesperus," Dana said. "Here—have some M&M's. These are my go-to food when I'm nervous."

"Winter is having this baby. Do you know where Russell is? Winter is alone," Frances said.

"Here comes Simon. My guess is Russell is helping Winter with the birthing coach part," Theresa said.

"This is quite the surprise. Wow," Simon said.

The crew took over a corner of the waiting room and settled into the unknowns of birth time.

"Should someone call Jason and let him know his baby is being born?" Frances asked.

"Frances, Jason had a check paying her back for the gym. It was delivered to Winter with a letter stating that he would sign any parental rights over concerning the baby."

"What? That was quite a big sum," Simon said.

"He sold the gym. Jason has left town. Said he was taking a flight home to see his folks in Ohio. Winter gave me the rundown as my partner and I drove her to the hospital. We were with her when her labor started," Molly said.

"Good riddance. That guy was not right for Winter. She was trying to make it work," Simon said.

"Simon, don't be unkind right now. Let's focus on Winter and the new little bundle of life she is bringing into the world."

Tired of standing, Frances sat next to Simon. They had talked about plans should Winter be alone when she had this baby. They had created a roster of who was going to do the shopping and who would be staying at the hospital.

"Looks like we need to access the plan. Molly shared how truly freaked out Winter is about having this baby," Frances said.

"When did things have to get so complicated?" Dana asked. "Winter has got to know she isn't going to get rid of us."

"Ready to meet Autumn Catherine Keller?" Russell asked. He was immediately mobbed by the group that was waiting to learn about the newest addition to the crew. Russell was still wearing a blue gown and shower cap over his clothes. His smile broadcast the miracle and excitement of the baby.

"How's Winter?" Dana and Frances asked at the same time.

"Mom and Autumn Catherine are doing great. They are getting Winter set up in her room now. We'll be able to see her soon. It was amazing. I got to cut her umbilical cord. She is perfect. She has a full head of dark hair. Winter looks radiant," Russell said.

"Autumn Catherine... I wonder what the story is behind that name? I don't think that came up on the list," Frances said.

"Makes sense to me. Winter... Autumn ... " Cheryl said. "She stayed in the seasonal naming genre."

"Why not Summer or Spring?" Simon asked. "Themes—people really need to stop this naming theme business."

"Everyone is a critic," Frances said. "Autumn is a beautiful name."

"How big is the baby?" Molly asked.

"She's a big little girl at seven pounds six ounces and twenty inches long. The doctor said that she's not the normal premature baby. Had she baked for another two weeks, she would have come out walking,"

Russell said. "Before you go in to meet Autumn, there is something else you need to know about the baby."

"What? Is she okay? Is she missing fingers, toes?" Theresa asked.

"Without being a scientist, I can tell you that Jason is not the father. Unless there is a serious recessive gene in his family for very dark skin."

"Really? When you said she had dark hair, did you mean really curly hair?" Dana asked.

"Bingo. Hair so curly the girl won't ever need to get a perm."

"Did Winter respond?" Dana asked.

"She was crying and cooing at the same time. They placed Autumn on her as soon as they could. I can safely say she doesn't care, and as soon as she held her in her arms, she told Autumn how extraordinary she is and that she loves her more than anything in the world," Russell said.

"Winter didn't say anything else?" Cheryl asked.

"She did say something about thanking the gods that Jason wasn't the father."

"That sounds like Winter. Now I wonder if she knows who the baby daddy would be?"

"There are some striking features on this little one that might give her a couple of clues," Russell said.

Frances, Molly, and Dana all melted into a hug when they heard Russell recount Winter meeting her daughter. The boys hugged and kissed. Simon got out chocolate candy cigars and handed them out to everyone in the waiting room. A nurse passing through the waiting room rushed in, and Simon popped one into her open mouth.

"No one is smoking. We are not crazy. These are chocolate," Simon said.

The waiting room erupted into congratulations over the news as they all started talking at once about what needed to be done. They had done a baby proofing of Winter's condo. The guest room was set up for the rotation of people to stay and help her with the baby. Winter had protested, but when Dana said she and Russell were going to be the first to stay with her, Winter quieted down her protests.

"Frances, don't forget the flowers. Theresa, you grab the stuffed animals. I have the balloons. Let's go meet Autumn," Cheryl said.

"I can wait out here."

"Detective Molly Woods, you are not waiting out here. Whether you like it or not, you are part of this group."

"I think Molly is worried she'll upset Winter," Frances said.

"We are going to overwhelm the woman. Molly, come with us—it is all about Winter and Autumn," Dana said.

Frances hung back and watched the crew on its way to welcome Autumn into the family. The smile on her face grew from such a deep, warm place inside that Frances felt a grounding from her friends. In this life, she knew that the loss of her family would continue to cause her pain, but with each step she took down the sterile hospital birthing center hall, Frances was walking into the love of her chosen family.

When Frances followed the train of friends into the suite that was Winter's room for the next couple of days, she lost herself in the happiness of the occasion. Dana and Russell were right next to Winter, who was holding Autumn, now a tightly swaddled baby burrito with a pink knit hat covering her head.

"She's so beautiful," Theresa said. "Her face is so perfect—not smooshed at all."

"The advantage of not being shoved through the birthing canal," Simon added.

"How are you doing, Winter?" Frances asked.

"I'm in love for the first time ever. Can you believe I have a baby that is so dark, people will not believe she's mine?"

"Tell people you are the nanny."

"I have a question," Simon said.

"Relax, Simon, no one needs to know—"

"I don't know who the father is, Simon. There was more than one, and you know what? I really don't want to know. This baby has all of you," Winter said.

"Winter, her name is beautiful," Dana said.

"Autumn is my favorite time of year, and I added Catherine because I always admired Catherine the Great."

"I thought it was because of Bill the Cat always saying 'Ack!,'" Frances said.

"Who's Bill the Cat?" Molly asked.

"An orange cat from Bloom County whose sentiments about the world were 'Ack!' and 'Thppt!'. Exactly what I am thinking about in today's political climate. We need Bloom County to come back," Russell said. "Frances, not nice."

"What? It is...I have the inside scoop on what it's like to grow up with F.O.K. as initials."

"You are quite the expletive, aren't you?" Simon said as he gave Frances a hug.

"This moment is amazing. Winter has a daughter," Dana said. "A whole new world is opening up for you."

"Autumn, this is your family," Winter said and kissed her daughter on the nose.

"She looks like an angel sleeping in your arms," Frances said.

"Wonder how long that's going to last?" Russell asked.

"Okay, troops, we ask that you limit your group size to four at the most," a nurse said, coming into the room to check on Winter. "That means...thin your ranks, or I'll do it for you."

Good-byes were said, and Simon, Theresa, and Molly left the room with promises to go get the group some food. No one wanted to leave. Dana took a seat in the rocking chair, and Russell sat on the foot of the bed. Frances walked over and kissed the baby and then Winter.

"I am so excited for you. This is going to be amazing, and I am so honored to be part of your family."

"Frances, she has long fingers. Do you think she'll play the piano?"

"She'll be able to try it out at my place. I can't wait to break out the finger paints." Frances came over and kissed Winter gently on the top of her head.

"She's amazing, but she is basically in human 1.0 mode, meaning...she's going to eat, sleep, and poop. I will be lucky if she even knows who I am," Winter said.

"She knows who you are, Mama," the nurse said. "The pediatric nurse will be in next, and then I'll come back and help you try and feed her again."

"Have you tried to feed her yet?" Frances asked.

"Yes. This girl might play for your team as she latched on right away. They gave her to me within the first hour. I was stable. Strange though because they were still stitching up my abdomen putting me back together...and I'm feeding this little one."

Frances felt herself losing her hearing. The tunnel vision started and she tried to sit down. "No. I can't be fainting over this." Frances sat down on the floor and tried to hang onto her consciousness. Who faints when meeting a baby? Winter wasn't showing her the blood.

Two nurses and a resident came running in to attend to Frances on the floor. She was out cold. Dana was standing by, trying not to be too concerned. It took two rounds of smelling salts to bring Frances back to life.

"That was fun," Frances said.

She sat up and leaned against the male nurse who finally got her to wake up again.

"Sorry," Frances said.

"Did anyone see if she hit her head?" a nurse asked.

"Well, when she hit the ground I think she hit her head," Dana said.

"I think we need to take you to get checked out," the nurse said. "We are going to get a wheelchair and take you to see a doctor."

"I'm fine. Honestly, I faint in hospitals. This is not unusual," Frances said.

"She's right. We even had a pool going for not *if* but *when* Frances faints," Winter said.

"I think once you get checked out, you need to go home," Russell said.

"I'll go get Molly. Simon and Molly can take Frances home," Cheryl said.

"They went out to get us food. Let me take her home. It isn't that far from here, and I'll Lyft it. Be back in a flash," Dana said.

CHAPTER FORTY-SIX

PRIMAL PAIN

D ana opened the car door for Frances, who felt her head and heart pounding in unison as she stepped into the street and the late afternoon sunlight. The doctor felt she was fine, and no one said they saw her bounce her head when she dropped. He seemed more concerned about the redness of the skin around her stitches and ordered an antibiotic for her. Frances fumbled with her keys looking for the key to let them into the lobby of her building. The happiness about Winter's baby was being replaced by the dark clouds of Frances's loss of her own family. She was headed back into her own home where she had tried to erase her previous life, but her memories were not that easy to erase.

She continued to fumble for her keys as she remembered the celebrations of her various nieces and nephews being born. What she thought was love and family—a solid in her life—was now gone. Frances kept turning the keys in her hand over and over, never finding the right one to open the lobby door.

"Let me," Dana said.

"It's the bronze key. Usually I can find it without issue because it is twice the size of the other keys. The birth of Autumn has my emotions running amuck. I remember when the first nephew was born. It hurts to be told you're not loved anymore."

"My dear Frances, you need to cut yourself some slack."

Frances walked through the open door and directly to the elevator where, luck would have it, the freight elevator opened. She was tired and ready for a nap. This was turning into the never-ending day. Frances noticed that Dana took her own key ring out and slid her key into the loft door.

"Did I give you a key to my place?" Frances asked.

"No, I had one made."

"Do I have a key to your house?"

"If you were me, would you give you a key?" Dana asked.

"You did that on purpose. Would you like something to drink? A coffee?"

Frances walked to her kitchen and turned back. That was when she remembered what she and Theresa had been doing when they got the call about Winter being in labor. She clasped her hands together and leaned onto the counter. In front of her was the partially painted wall. Theresa had managed to get most of the pictures boxed up, but a small pile of about fifteen pictures was on the floor. The happiness of Autumn was pushed aside with the barren reality that Frances's family had cast her out.

"What's going on here? A new idea?" Dana asked.

"It hurts more than I can express. Our parents, the family—"

"Oh, sweet Frances, it is going to hurt and hurt for a while," Dana said.

She swept Frances into her arms, and Frances collapsed into the sorrow and let Dana hold her. The pain of the loss shot through Frances's body. Her sobs felt like they would never end as she gasped for a deep breath, trying to slow down the hurt. Dana continued to hold her and didn't let go. Frances's arms wrapped around Dana's body, and she held on to keep herself from falling into the bottomless hurt that was pulling her down.

"Frances, you are going to shine. Hang onto me. Hold tight, because I have you," Dana said.

The sky went from blue to dusk outside, and Dana stood holding Frances. Stiff from the act of standing in one spot for so long, Frances slowly let go of Dana.

"Are you okay?" Frances asked.

"A chair would be good about now. Thank god I am still doing yoga."

"Sorry."

"No. You do not apologize to me or anyone. You are exactly who you are, and you are hurting. You were made with the most beautiful, full heart. Shame on your family. Frances, you are one of the few people I know who truly smiles in the rain and rejoices in the sun."

"I keep playing over and over the conversation. Where people were sitting. My mom was doing needlepoint and not talking. The sisters I thought...our father . . ."

"Frances, you will process the hurt. Remember you are made of the sun. You are so bright. Don't let the hate and the smallness of what happened dampen you."

"When I was little, I saw a picture of the ocean. It was a white-sand beach with perfect blue waves. It was probably some island somewhere, but I said I was going to live by the ocean when I grew up."

"Now you are."

"Not exactly, but I am close. I love the ocean. Something I didn't understand exactly was lost...I felt like I was underwater when my mom started talking. I was back in the womb, and the umbilical cord wasn't connected. I wasn't able to breathe. Then, the next thing I felt was this pain on the side of my head. Sharp pain. I no longer heard anything, but blood was on my hand and on my face. Everything in the world changed at that moment."

"The question for you is, how are you responding to the change?"

"When will this hurt stop? Winter with Autumn was beautiful, but it made the pain of what was said and not said that much worse."

"Frances, there are no wounds like the wounds family can inflict. My mother has been gone for several years now. I loved her, but she hurt me more than I can ever quantify. I'm afraid that I may have passed that along to my own daughter. I hope I haven't, but in some respects, I think it is inherent."

"I asked my mother what I could do," Frances said.

"Could do about what?"

"How I could make things better—fix things or something like that. But I don't think I communicated that to her. Instead, I think I demanded a response from her and set off an explosion."

"Sit back and look at the dynamics of your family. You have so many kids in your family. All families are tenuous social systems. If someone tells you they have a perfect family, they are lying."

"I get your point. There is no one way to exist, and I am not going to judge because I have been judged, and it hurts. I think I was trying to find fault to ease my pain, but that doesn't work either."

"Judgement and jealously are two human idiocies. They have the power to burn your insides out, leaving nothing but a charred shell of a person," Dana said.

Frances wanted to lay down and wake up, carried away from the hurt and the pain of her current situation. Wave after wave of hurt pummeled her, and her exhaustion was beyond anything she could ever remember. She was moved so far away from the core of her foundation that she wondered if this is what people talked about when they spoke of life devoid of living. She glanced back at the tree she had started painting on the wall. The trunk of the tree was a shadow of pencil strokes on the white wall. The bright colors that she had started with stood out in stark contrast to the muted grays that filled her mind and her heart.

Dana had gone over to Frances's bed and pulled the covers down and climbed onto the bed.

"Come, Frances. Let me hold you as you drift off to sleep," Dana said.

The sun was gone, and night was here. Frances wanted to sleep. She shed her shoes and took off her jeans. Her sheets were soft, and the comforter was a warm world that Dana tucked in around her.

"Will you stay? I don't want to wake up alone," Frances said.

"Little fish, go to sleep and know that I will be here when you wake up. But if this big fish is sleeping when you awake, let me sleep!" Dana said and hugged Frances.

— 🍷 —

Frances woke to the smell of bacon and coffee. A hint of cinnamon was also in the air. She sat up in bed and saw Theresa and Dana cooking together in her kitchen.

"What happened? Did I go through a wormhole in the universe?" Frances asked.

"Howdy, morning glory. You were sawing some serious logs in your sleep," Dana said. "Look who the cat drug in with the morning paper."

"Hi. May I bring you a cup of coffee?" Theresa asked.

"Give me a minute. I'll be right over." Frances dashed into the restroom and splashed some water on her face.

When Frances emerged from the bathroom, she was pulling on her favorite fluffy purple robe and her shark slippers.

"What the heck? Who's screaming?" Dana asked as she flipped the bacon in the pan.

"My shark slippers. They have a speaker, and like every tenth step, you hear the theme from *Jaws* followed by the screams. Aren't they awesome?"

"They are not awesome. Don't wear those around the baby. Here's some breakfast. Coffee cake is baking in the oven. It still has about twenty minutes. I promised Russell I would take Winston out for a walk. See you two in a while." Dana kissed Frances and hugged Theresa before she left.

"That wasn't subtle."

"Frances, we need to talk."

"About what? You know where I am, and I am not going back in the closet. Theresa, I don't know that I can trust you."

"I understand. I am not going to abandon you. I love you and will always love you."

"Does the family know you are here?"

"Yes. I know this is going take time to repair. I was stupid. I was scared and made some wrong choices."

"What's this?" Frances reached out for the baby-blue box that Theresa had placed in front of her on the kitchen counter.

CHAPTER FORTY-SIX

"Open it."

Frances took off the white ribbon and opened the box to reveal half of a silver heart on a silver bracelet. "It's beautiful, but what does it mean?"

"I have one too. You are the other half of my heart." Theresa held up her wrist and showed Frances her broken heart.

"These are expensive. You spent your money on these?"

"I'm going to tell you how I got the money to buy these. Bernard and Mom had been sending me money to see a therapist who reprograms people to end their 'gay ways' and I pocketed the money instead."

"Theresa!"

"What? I wasn't making enough to cover my expenses with that stupid stagehand job. Bernard is an ass. They have the money, and besides, this is a much better use of it."

"Thank you." Frances shook her head and smiled. She was not going to judge her sister. She didn't understand Theresa, but she was learning that it was important to meet people who were trying at least part of the way. She put the bracelet on and stood to hug her sister. "I love you, little bird. Please know that you can trust me."

CHAPTER FORTY-SEVEN
BUENA VISTA CELEBRATING WINTER'S AUTUMN

"We have a new little human to corrupt," Dana said. "I am still so excited I feel like I could burst."

"Hear, hear! To Winter and Autumn," Cheryl said, holding up her Irish coffee.

"See? That is exactly why Simon was right about the whole theme-naming thing. It sounds like you are toasting the seasons and not people," Dana added as she took a sip of her Irish coffee.

"Did you invite Molly?" Theresa asked. "And what about Sam?"

"Sam is still out of town. And I know Molly got the email invite," Frances said.

"I think I like Sam. I need more time with her to get to know her. Arrange that, Frances," Cheryl said.

"I know what you are hinting at, and Molly is a friend. She is on the email list. You and Dana need to stop your speculation of this common disaster that would be Molly and me hooking up. She is working some really gross murder case right now anyway."

"Morning glory, what's the story?" Simon said as he gave Frances and Theresa a big hug and kiss.

"This is a surprise," Frances said.

"Russell wants me to smuggle him home an Irish coffee. I told him I would buy the kit and make them all one. I think Winter needs one. Have you seen her?" Simon asked.

"I'm the one who drove her home. It was the longest cross-city drive I've ever done. Talk about being protective. Once we got the approval from the car seat police, I thought it would be smooth sailing. Winter was a nervous wreck."

"Frances, you can't blame her. You do have a tendency to drive like you're jockeying for position in Rome. And those are the scariest drivers ever," Simon said.

"You did great, Frances. You didn't go over five miles per hour. Thank god Molly gave you an escort home."

"That was sweet of her. Is she coming this morning? Look—a table. Quick!" Simon said and plowed through the crowd, snaking the table from another group that tried to angle to the table from the bar.

"Whew. Time to get this breakfast party started," Theresa said. "There might be an additional person at breakfast this morning."

"Theresa, you are blushing. Where'd you meet her?" Frances asked. "Morning, Mary, can we get a round of the usual to get us started?"

"Mary, Winter had her baby four days ago. Autumn Catherine Keller is beautiful," Simon said. "Geez, Frances, sometimes I wonder if the drinking gene in you isn't a little too focused."

"Ouch."

Mary walked over and gave hugs all around. "This first round is on me. You let Winter know how happy we are for her," Mary said and was gone into the crowded Buena Vista.

Frances froze when she saw Joshua's smiling face coming toward them. Her head cocked to the left and then the right.

"Frances, are you channeling Winston?" Simon asked.

"Joshua?"

"Surprise! I hope it's all right. Theresa thought this might be as good a place—"

"What? Good place to—"

"There is something that I...Frances, I wanted to wait to tell you, but with what happened at home and then Winter's baby, it hadn't seemed like a good time. I know you are dating Sam, and the two of you need your privacy. Life is...well . . ."

"What Theresa is trying to tell you is that she is going to come live with me in Monterey," Joshua said.

"What have I missed? Why are you two holding hands?" Simon asked. "Joshua, you know that she's a lesbian, right?"

The Irish coffee arrived in time for Frances to avoid what was being presented to her. She picked up her glass cup with the white foam, held it up to the table, and took a long drink. She ignored the hot temperature of the coffee and let the heat burn her throat on the way down. Frances looked from Theresa to Joshua and back to Theresa. What was she to do? Did she have anything to say? Did Theresa know about Joshua?

"Frances, I know what you are thinking because your face betrays your thoughts. Theresa knows," Joshua said.

"I don't care about that and figured she would. What about the age difference? A job? School?"

"You are sounding like—"

"Don't you say it because Mom would fucking flip. Although, you could pull it off."

"Okay, someone throw me a line. I have a sinking feeling that I really don't know what is going on here," Simon said.

"Joshua, do you mind?" Theresa asked.

"Simon, I am transgender. I went to college with Frances, and I crushed hard on her for years," Joshua said.

"I am so glad I came to breakfast this morning. Damn good idea."

"What's a damn good idea?" Molly asked as she sat down at the table.

Frances crossed her arms and couldn't imagine this morning being any stranger. Mary was at the table with another round of Irish coffees, including the coffee for Joshua and Molly.

"Time to celebrate," Mary said.

"Celebrate?" Molly asked.

"Winter and Autumn," Theresa said.

"Hey, Frances, you need to see the woman standing in the front, to the right of the bar," Molly said. "She is wearing a really nice suit."

Frances knew she had to be going crazy. Sam was not in town. She had told her she was going to be gone for the next four weeks. But before she turned to look through the crowd, Frances felt her heart beat faster and her breathing accelerate. She wiped her hands on her jeans as they were suddenly clammy. Her ears betrayed her first. The heat turned them bright red. Thank god she wore her hair down today—mostly to cover the side of her face with the stitches. Frances rose and turned right into the arms of Samantha.

"I figured I would find you here this morning," Sam said. "Dana called me. I caught the next flight out I could."

Frances reached up and pulled Samantha into a kiss that said it all. She was sinking, and Sam arrived to throw her a line in a way that she didn't even realize she needed. The kiss stopped only when Sam put her hand on Frances's chin and looked into her teary green eyes.

"I'm here," Sam said.

"Hi, Sam. Let me re-introduce you to Molly and to Joshua. This is Sam," Simon said.

"Detective Woods?" Sam asked and held out her hand.

"You can call me Molly. Nice suit."

"Joshua."

"Pleasure to meet you, Sam."

The table sat down, and Frances could not believe Sam was sitting next to her. There was so much she wanted to tell her. Mary kept the table filled with food and drink. Theresa and Joshua took over the conversation. It did not surprise Frances that Molly was silent. She stole a couple of glances toward Molly and found herself wondering what she could say. Molly laughed at some of the conversation and the retelling of Frances fainting after meeting the baby.

"Sam, where are you coming back from?" Molly asked.

"London. We are working on the redesign for a group of clothing stores that wants to reach a younger audience based in London."

"Welcome back to the fog. Should feel right at home."

"Well, yes. How's the baby? Does anyone have any new pictures?" Sam asked.

Simon pulled out his phone and started clicking through. He finally handed it over, with instructions to scroll through them. "Russell and I are worse than anyone. I think I snapped a diaper change."

"She has quite the head of hair, this little giant baby. Are you sure she was two weeks early?" Sam asked.

"There is some question about that and who the father might be—we think that Winter might have not quite accurately remembered when she had her last period," Theresa said.

"That's an understatement. She and Jason had called it quits right after he had proposed to her the first time, and it looks like Winter went out and had some fun," Simon said.

"Sam, what about the rollout? You can't be here," Frances asked.

"It's okay. I know how to delegate—that's why I get paid the big bucks. Don't worry, and you need to trust me."

Frances was watching her friends at the table and felt herself feel the love. It was truly amazing to be with this group of people. The Irish coffee mixed with the noise of the Buena Vista Café to help wipe away a little more of her pain.

"I don't know where I was, but I don't think we met," Cheryl said as she turned to Joshua.

"Cheryl, this is Joshua. Frances went to school with him, and he lives in Monterey," Theresa said. "He and I are moving in together."

"You bought the painting. I know you. Frances talked about your coffee place and restaurant. But what a crazy world."

"Thought you were playing a tournament today?" Frances asked.

"Turns out that I've been replaced. I did this tennis thing for fun, but somewhere along the way, they decided they wanted to win. I've been benched. This is so much more fun anyway. I get to eat, drink, and laugh. Hey, let's introduce the newbies to our Darwin game."

"I'm game," Simon said, picking up a spoon and directing the attention toward Joshua.

"No. Not anyone at the table. Off limits," Frances said.

"Testy. Frances, you need to get some sleep. I was going to explain it using all the spoons at the table."

"Sorry, folks. I need to step away. Police work never stops. Thanks to my team, I think we are on a real lead and closer to stopping the current rash of murders," Molly said.

"At least you didn't say *duty calls*."

"Frances, get your mind out of that eight-year-old kid," Theresa said.

"You all laughed. I might have the humor of a kid, but you all laughed."

CHAPTER FORTY-SEVEN

"She's right. Duty does call," Molly said and exited the table.

"Sam, it's nice to see you again," Cheryl said.

"I see you survived the Italian cooking weekend," Sam said.

"Was that the last time we saw you? Why do I feel like—"

Frances was trying desperately to kick Cheryl under the table but missed and got Joshua.

"What Frances is trying to do is stop me from saying I feel like you've been around because you are almost the only topic of conversation. Hey, I thought you and Theresa were on rotation at Winter's?"

"When you arrive so late to the Buena Vista, you do not get to force everyone into rehashing the morning's conversation. CliffsNotes: Winter really only wants Russell and Dana. Theresa is moving to Monterey to live with Joshua. He knows that she is a lesbian. She knows he is transgender. Sam came back because Dana called and told her I was having a breakdown."

"Not a breakdown. I heard you were heartbroken, and I am here because I couldn't be so far away wishing I could hold you."

"Wow. Not only does she dress well but she speaks well too," Joshua said.

"I'm curious, and I'm going to put my foot in my mouth. How did Molly react to meeting Sam? Have they met before?" Cheryl asked. "I don't remember."

"Molly left," Theresa said.

"The plot thickens at the Buena Vista," Sam said.

"I'm exhausted. Do you think we can head out?" asked Frances.

"Frances, I came with you, and I'm not ready to leave yet," said Theresa.

"Theresa, dare to think outside the box—wait...you already are, and I'm sure Joshua will be happy to give you a lift," Frances said.

"I am so lost. Someone please fill me in, and I don't want to be left here alone eating breakfast. I can only handle being benched from one group at a time," Cheryl said.

"We aren't going anywhere. Mary, another round for the four of us long timers. Let Frances go kissy face with Samantha. I remember—I think I do anyway—what it was like to be in the first stages of love," Simon said.

"That is our out." Sam stood and reached for Frances's hand.

Frances stood and held tightly to Sam's hand. She walked through the crowd of people in the Buena Vista and out into the world with the only person she wanted to spend time with at the moment. Unsure of her future and everything that meant, she was sure about the hand that held hers so warmly.

CHAPTER FORTY-EIGHT
GREEN EGGS AND SAM

F rances walked over to her piano and sat down. It took her a few
moments to find her center as she played with the bracelet on her
wrist. Frances quietly placed her hands on the ivory keys. Her heart
beat out a soft rhythm inside her chest; when Frances felt she had the
tempo captured, she let her right hand strike the first notes. With each
key, her finger touched the piano as the music gained its voice and gently pushed the silence of the loft away.

In this morning, Frances realized that she was in the presence of a
new love. The notes were fresh and sprang from the piano, giving voice
to the visions playing out the history of Samantha and her. Each single note quickly melted into another, and then another, creating a music landscape with harmonies that lifted Frances's soul into a dancing
lightness. The music she played started out so gentle, almost hesitant
at first, but the longer Frances explored the improvisational song, the
stronger it grew. She was diving and twirling into the sounds and knew
her desires were bubbling up through her soul.

Sam walked up behind Frances and gently wrapped her arms
around her, resting her head into the crook of Frances's neck. Frances
continued to play and leaned back into Sam, who had started kissing

her slowly and gently on her neck. Frances turned to meet Sam's lips, and the sweet kisses cradled them in the early morning light.

"I didn't mean to stop the music. What were you playing? It's tender and beautiful," Sam said.

"I think I'll call it 'Illumination.' Sometimes music comes to me, and I am barely able to get the music out quickly enough." Frances turned back to the piano and let her fingers attempt to find the music again. "It is a patchwork of images of our meeting."

"That explains why part of it placed an image of a rabbit hopping quickly out of a vegan restaurant," Sam said.

Frances stumbled as she stood, her laughter causing her to fall into Sam's open arms. She let herself fall, and the two ended up on the floor, giggling and kissing. Frances's heart was alive and pumping blood faster, causing her to feel a surge of energy. She cradled Sam's head with her hand and slowly kissed the tip of her nose and her lips, opening the fluffy robe Sam had borrowed, exposing her beautiful smooth skin to the coolness of the air. Frances laid her head down on Sam's chest and melted into the touch of Sam's hand gently stroking her hair.

"I really think the bed would be a much more comfortable place to continue this little jaunt."

It did not take Frances more than an instant to hop up and hold her hands out to pull Sam to a standing position. The women embraced and fell into a long, passionate kiss. Frances felt the warmth of Sam's passion ripple through her body, causing her to desire the woman who was sharing herself so privately with her. They stumbled toward the bed, and Frances was able to work the robe off Sam, at the same time letting the blanket she had used to cover herself fall to the floor.

Frances took Sam's hand, and their fingers intertwined. For a moment, she felt so completely alive and free. It was a feeling she had not remembered having, and she laid her body next to Sam's, knowing this was a special sharing with another person. She looked at Sam, who was smiling at her, and reached to tuck her crazy, long, red hair behind her ear. The electricity buzzing between them was recharging Frances's soul, and she wondered if Sam was feeling the same.

"Can I make you something to eat? Then maybe I can inspire you some more?" Sam asked gently, kissing Frances's lips.

"I'm in the mood for green eggs and ham," Frances said.

She rested her head in the crook of Sam's arm and let her fingers trance the gentle curves of Sam's body.

"I am Sam. Sam-I-am. No tickling before breakfast, said Sam-I-am," Sam said, trying to wiggle away from the tickling.

"But I do very much like Sam-I-am. I would like her here or there. I would in a box. I would with sox," Frances said, and then the giggles started, allowing Sam to escape and wrap the robe back around herself.

"I'm borrowing your slippers. This concrete floor is cold. Now...I am going to start with some coffee. After last night, I need to rehydrate," Sam said. "Funny. I don't think that is exactly how that children's story was written."

"You don't?"

"I am wondering how one's mind goes from romance to Dr. Seuss?"

"You're the one with the vanity plate referring to the Dr. Seuss winner. How could I not go there? We've got to go as green eggs and ham for Halloween," Frances said.

"You are a confident one. Halloween is still months away."

"I'm an optimist about us. Do you really need to leave this afternoon?"

"Do you really need to paint?" Sam asked.

"Touché. Do you want help with breakfast?"

"Nope. Believe it or not, before I met you, I did cook my own food. I also can drive a car. Green eggs and ham okay with you?"

"Totally! What are you saying? I like to drive. Snow White is an awesome tuck."

"How do you think I got around before we met?"

"I figured you stood on a corner with your thumb out. Kidding . . . you used Uber."

"Who has the fast convertible sports car?" Sam asked.

Frances climbed out of the cloud of comforter and threw on a T-shirt and pair of flannel pj bottoms. Her slippers were being used, so she grabbed some socks out of the drawer. Sounds of chopping, singing, and pans clanging were coming from her kitchen. The loft filled with the savory smells of sautéed onions and garlic. Frances walked over to Sam in the kitchen and hugged the woman busy cooking breakfast. It struck Frances that Sam could sing. *Note to self not to sing.* She smiled as she remembered how her nephew, Spencer, at age two told her "no sing, Aunt, no sing" when she was singing "Twinkle Twinkle Little Star." It was mortifying, but he had covered his ears with his little hands as he said that, and she was crushed. Frances walked over and placed her arms around Sam. She hugged her close and laid her head on Sam's back. She realized that the pain was subsiding, and Sam had helped her reclaim her love of the piano and her own good memories of her family.

"It smells so amazing in here. What did you forage out of the fridge?" Frances asked.

Frances grabbed Sam mid-step to the stove and kissed her. Sam pulled Frances into her, and the two spoke through the touch of their lips. Frances opened her eyes and stepped back, looking at what she thought was the most beautiful person—man or woman—she had ever known.

"What?" Sam asked. She turned to stir the onions and add some eggs into the mix.

"I know that the woman I see before me is truly special."

Frances walked around the kitchen island and took a seat, watching the ease at which Sam took over her kitchen. The world was kept at bay as Sam cooked, and Frances took in each moment, cherishing each second for the tapestry that was being woven by the two of them. They were strangers not long ago, and now Frances knew she trusted this woman with her heart, her fears, and her world.

"You are so quiet," Sam said. "I love the flannel pj's."

"I'm addicted to flannel. As a kid, I hated it. But there is something to wearing flannel in a loft with concrete floors. The key is to never layer flannel," Frances said.

Frances took a sip of the Nespresso that Sam brought over. She pulled Sam into her and buried her head in the fluffy robe. Sam's arms wrapped around her. Frances looked up into Sam's eyes.

"Where are the places we will go?" Frances asked.

"I don't know what to say? Except that you had me when you asked me if I was a professional."

Frances stood and waltzed with Sam around the loft and stopped when they reached her bed.

"Whatever happens, I am willing to take the risk," Frances said.

Sam took Frances's face in her hands and gently kissed her lips. Frances followed Sam as she led her over to the piano and gently directed her to sit at the keys.

"What music comes?" Sam asked.

Frances let her mind go blank and waited. She raised her hands to the ivory keys. In a moment, her hands were guided to the notes, playing the first few notes of Leonard Cohen's "Dance Me to the End of Love." Frances moved into Sam's hand that was resting on her shoulder as Sam's voice sang, *"Dance me to your beauty."*

I appreciate you joining Frances and her chosen gang of friends. This story had some serious peaks and valleys handling the difficulties of differences. Love and laughter continue to heal and in some ways, builds a bridge between some. As Frances finds her voice and her strength life continues to move forward. The characters are back in book three with more humor, drama, and love. Please join them for an Irish Coffee at the Buena Vista.

Watch for announcements on my author website:
www.sheilamsullivan.com

SHORT QUESTIONS & ANSWERS
WITH THE AUTHOR

Q: Are you Frances?

A: Nope. Frances is her own woman. I enjoy the time I get to spend with her and she does surprise me. She has a very unique set of qualities and I am excited to see what she reveals next.

Q: What inspired you to write this story?

A: The story evolved through the characters and what was happening. I know people think that the author plots out the story. I listen to the characters and the plot takes care of itself. This story came about through hearing the stories of an individual forced out of their family due to one issue or another. In my own life, I do have friends that lived their truth and were cast out of their families. While this story focused upon Frances's falling in love with a woman and exploring the fluidity of her own life; I have a friend that married a person from a different religious background and went through a similar banishment. The difficulties in being human are what these characters are exploring. How do you live true to yourself? What are the costs both personally and professionally?

Q: Did you grow up in Saint Louis, Missouri?

A: I grew up behind the Redwood curtain otherwise known as Humboldt County in Northern California. However, I did live in Saint Louis for a couple of years and fell in love with the people I met there. It really has the most amazing food and art scene. When I lived in St. Louis a I found my way into a very creative and wonderful group of people. We would meet most Saturday mornings for breakfast. It was a wonderful time and they inspired the Buena Vista Café group for Frances and her friends in San Francisco.

Q: Do you have a favorite character?

A: No. I am sure that is not the answer you are looking for and I can explain it this way. My work as an author is to write the stories of these characters. I do not judge nor do I really direct them. You can stop shaking your head. Honestly, when I write I really do not know where the story is going and let the characters guide the way. My editor could tell you that it is a messy way to write. My wife shakes her head because more often than I care to disclose she will hear me objecting out loud. I myself thought that Frances and Molly would have been a great couple. Readers seem to agree but the story took a different route.

Q: Fine. Do you have a most hated character?

A: Interesting and I like how you are attempting to box me in to find out how I feel about this cast. They all have parts I admire. I would say though that Ethan really creeped me out. His voice was dark.

Q: What is next for Frances and the Buena Vista Café?

A: I hope Frances finds some happiness as she and Sam learn more about one another. There are a couple interesting twists that are coming up in book 3.

Q: Will you share any of the story from book 3?

A: Olivia, the woman who bought Frances's first painting in book 1 and whisked her off to Hawaii, she is back in book 3.

Q: That is all you are going to share?

A: I promise there will still be laughter in book 3.

ABOUT THE AUTHOR

Sheila M. Sullivan grew up in Northern California enjoying adventures with her siblings deep in the heart of the redwoods. The love of books was instilled by both her parents who enjoyed a lifetime of reading and book collecting.

Today Sheila spends her time traveling with her wife, writing daily, and playing with their adorable Cardigan Welsh Corgi.

Drop me a note at: info@sheilamsullivan.com

Also by Sheila M. Sullivan
Spectrum, Book 1 of the F.O.K. Series

Made in the USA
Middletown, DE
07 August 2018